Sullivan

THOMAS MAXWELL
KISS ME ONCE

THE MYSTERIOUS PRESS • New York

Permission to quote from the following is gratefully acknowledged:

"The Nearness of You" by Ned Washington and Hoagy Carmichael. Copyright © 1937 and 1940 by Famous Music Corporation. Copyright renewed 1964 and 1967 by Famous Music Corporation.

"You'd Be So Nice To Come Home To" by Cole Porter. Copyright © 1942 by Chappell & Co., Inc. Copyright renewed. International Copyright Secured. ALL RIGHTS RESERVED. Used by permission.

"It's Been A Long, Long Time" by Sammy Cahn and Jule Styne. © 1945 Morley Music Co. © Renewed 1973 Morley Music Co. International Copyright Secured. All Rights Reserved. Used by permission.

The Mysterious Press, 129 West 56th Street, New York, N.Y. 10019

Printed in the United States of America
First Printing: October 1986
10 9 8 7 6 5 4 3 2 1

Library of Congress Cataloging-in-Publication Data

Maxwell, Thomas.
  Kiss me once.

  1. World War, 1939–1945—Fiction. I. Title.
PS3563.A926K5 1986   813'.54   86-47542
ISBN 0-89296-163-5

For Elizabeth

KISS ME ONCE, as you will soon notice, casts a long look at and owes a real debt to all those creatures of film noir whose legacy it respectfully represents, all those who might have gathered on the RKO lot to make the picture.

Dana Andrews	**Lew Cassidy**
Dan Duryea	**Terry Leary**
Lizabeth Scott	**Cindy Squires**
Morris Carnovsky	**Max Bauman**
William Bendix	**Bennie the Brute**
Walter Slezak	**Harry Madrid**
Laird Cregar	**Markie Cookson**
Elisha Cook, Jr.	**Bert Reagan**
Sonny Tufts	**Bryce Huntoon**

and

Alida Valli .... *as* ...... **Karin**

Listen to me, Al.
The river is deep and cement is cheap.
Call me if you need me.

—Max Bauman to Alfred E. Smith,
Democratic presidential candidate, 1928,
over dinner at Locke-Ober in Boston.

Author's Note

Readers with a keen sense of historical detail may occasionally find themselves confronted with what seems to be historical error. You may be right, so rest easy. The responsibility is mine, whether I was playing with things a bit to make a point or was simply mistaken.

There are, however, a couple of details which I can explicate at the moment. There was a National Football League game played at the Polo Grounds on the date in question. The visiting team was the Brooklyn Dodgers, a moderately hapless franchise which endured through fifteen seasons, from 1930 through 1944. The home team was, of course, the New York Giants. Not surprisingly, the Giants dominated the rivalry, winning twenty-two times, tying three, losing but four. Oddly enough, on the date in question, the real-life Brooklyn Dodgers prevailed, 21–7.

One might also inquire as to how, at 1:05 P.M. in New York, it could be 7:35 A.M. in Hawaii. The answer is simple. In those days, time zones were divided into half-hour slices once you got out there in the Pacific.

In the course of creating a group of characters bearing some resemblance to their counterparts inhabiting all of our lives, an author risks cutting too close to the bone. However, it is usually a bone or two of his own, which is doubtless for the best. In any case, should you find any specific resemblance to any specific individuals, then I've done a pretty fair job. But of course the resemblance is basically coincidental.

And, finally, a word about the title. I had been considering the idea of telling Lewis Cassidy's story for some time when I was following my normal custom one Sunday morning, listening to the world's best disc jockey *cum* raconteur *cum* cabaret singer, Jonathan Schwartz. And following his normal custom, he wasn't just playing a record: he was making a prefatory observation or two about it. The recording—Louis Armstrong's, I believe— was *It's Been a Long, Long Time* which, I suspect, most people think of as *Kiss Me Once*. He was making the point that, contrary to the bouncy rendition the song usually gets, it carried a very potent, powerful message that long ago summer of 1945 when it was the country's big hit. It was a song about the war and coming home from the war to a world that would never be the same again, to a life— as well as the loves in your life—that had changed forever. A whole lot had happened to everyone during those years. It had been a long, long time. And maybe the most you could really count on was a kiss and a prayer. That was what the story of Lew Cassidy was all about. Mr. Schwartz had given me the title. Herewith, my thanks.

—**Thomas Maxwell**
New York, May 1986

PROLOGUE

Cassidy was ready to start killing people.

It occurred to him as he crouched in the cold and the darkness, aware only faintly of her excited breathing somewhere behind him, that if you pushed a man hard enough, if you backed him into a corner, if you killed his pal—well, then you either broke him or turned him into a nasty, scary piece of work. He hadn't been quite sure which way it would go with him until now, and now he knew. There was still one person left alive he cared for and that was what tilted the balance. Made him realize just who and what he was at the core, what he must always have been. Waiting in the darkness of a very cold four o'clock, he smiled to himself. It was a smile of recognition.

He waited, kneeling on the floor he couldn't see, resting the barrel of the Purdey over-and-under on the back of the couch, pointed directly at the doorway. The pale moonlight, forcing its way through the clouds, reflected off the deep crusty snow and he knew they were out there, deciding how best to get inside and do the job. The wind

1

whacked angrily at the windows, rattling them in their frames.

Then he heard the first creak of footsteps on the porch. The snow squeaked as someone came slowly toward the door. Slowly. Cassidy knew he had one advantage. They didn't know they'd been spotted. They weren't being quite careful enough. He had one advantage and it wasn't going to last long but the first guy through the door was going to pay a hell of a price.

The footsteps stopped.

The storm door was pulled back, wheezing on its hinges. The doorknob began to turn, rattling ever so slightly. The door was easing open, inch by inch by inch . . .

Cassidy heard the footfalls in the darkness, one, two steps into the room, the shape black on black, too hard for him to center the barrels on. Snow blew noisily along the porch.

Now, now, he willed her to do it . . .

She hit the wall switch and all the lamps in the room came on in a blinding flash.

The man stopped dead, threw an arm across his eyes.

Just as suddenly the darkness engulfed them again, like the hood dropped over a parrot's cage, but the after-image of the man hung suspended before him as he adjusted the barrels.

The man with the long pistol in one hand, wearing a black-and-red-plaid parka, a matching hat with the ear-flaps turned down . . .

Cassidy centered on the memory of the man imprinted on his eyeballs and squeezed off both barrels and took the kick.

The shell casings ejected onto the floor and he slid two more into the chambers while the man was being sprayed back out into the night. Wood splintered, glass exploded, and he heard the corpse smack heavily onto the porch, slide across the slippery snow dusting, and crash off the edge, through the thick crust. The door had been blown off the hinges. It banged noisily, clattered off a wooden pillar, and pitched off into the snow. A blast of cold air poured in

2

and the sound of the blast echoed and slammed off the walls and then after a while it was silent again.

She came and knelt beside him.

"They've got to come inside to get us," he said. "It'll be a war. We've got to dig in."

They pushed the couch over to the stairwell and got in behind it, hunkered down in the nook below the stairs. They sat with their backs to the wall and she shivered against him. He kissed her hair and wondered if he'd ever see her face again.

The tommy gun began its unmistakable burping and the room was full of slugs and flying glass. It made a hell of a racket. Bullets chewing at the wall, slivers of wood and chunks of plaster spraying everywhere, splintering the knotty pine. He saw the flash of muzzle fire, like live electricity darting out, tongues of flame in the darkness beyond the holes in the walls where the windows had been only seconds before. Slugs thudded into the couch. He pulled her down onto the floor. Slugs were ricocheting off the stone fireplace. It sounded like a Panzer division rolling through the farmhouse . . .

He tried to pull the world in over their heads. She was grabbing at his hand, frantic, fingers icy cold. The guns just kept chattering and ripping.

Somewhere they were coming inside now, under cover of all the racket . . .

It was going to be over pretty soon and Cassidy held her tight, wondering what it all had meant, wondering if it had been worth it . . .

Behind the deafening din of the machine-gun fire he remembered how it had all begun, a Sunday afternoon a thousand lifetimes ago, a football game. It seemed like yesterday, watching the ball climb through the air and hang almost forever before it began to come down and the ground all around him started shaking and, hell, he'd been scared then, too . . .

CHAPTER ONE

Lew Cassidy was twenty-nine that year. An old twenty-nine because of a couple of things built into the core of his life. One was his occupation, the other was his wife, Karin. Together they'd put some years on Cassidy.

When he came jogging through the echoing tunnel from the locker room, the cleats chattering on the runway like a bad case of pregame nerves, and was funneled out onto the grass at the Polo Grounds, he felt as if he'd spent all twenty-nine years with a hangover. Which wasn't of course the objective truth. The hangover that Sunday was strictly the result of Saturday night with Terry Leary. And it was a beaut, big and dark and mean, like a Cuban girl Terry had introduced him to at a New Students Mixer before the Bucknell game in 1933. Alicia had been her name and for a while there she'd been a lot more fun than this hangover.

But that was all old news now and Alicia had become a memory by the time they'd played Harvard two weeks later. The funny thing was, though, Terry was still running

5

around with the prettiest girls in town and Lew Cassidy was still absorbing a weekly shit-kicking on the football field. One of the pretty girls was on Terry's arm right there in Max Bauman's box as Lew trotted past, lobbing a football to Frankie Sharansky, who actually caught it— something he'd never be able to do once the game started.

"Hey, Lew, howsa boy? Come on over here—hey, baby, how ya feeling? Howsa head?" That was Terry, standing at the box railing, beckoning with a pigskin-gloved hand. A flask bulged in the pocket of the soft caramel-colored polo coat with the belt like a bathrobe and a huge collar flopped up against the December wind. With his pencil-thin moustache and slicked-back black hair he looked like a cross between a movie star and the highest priced gigolo in New York. He was a cop. NYPD, working homicide. With his looks, his personal manner, and the hot cases he kept getting, Terry was a star of sorts, certainly in his own circle, as Lew was in his, and Terry loved living up to the role he'd created for himself.

"Lew, listen, I'd like you to meet Naomi. She's a big fan of yours, right, Naomi?"

Naomi was the kind of girl you never get to her last name. She was a redhead with too tight a permanent but Terry's hair was cut well enough for both of them. The rest of her, so far as Cassidy could tell, was okay, though one beauty mark would probably have been enough. He figured she was wearing a little gold ankle bracelet, too. Terry had a collection of them in his jewelry box, said they always came off in the heavy going.

"You're just swell, Mr. Cassidy." She batted her eyes and looked at Terry to see if she'd read the line right. "Terry's told me what pals you are—"

"Sign her program, will ya, Lew? Sign it, ah, 'Billy, I hope you're out of the hospital soon and back to football— Your friend, Lew Cassidy.' Kid's dying, some damn thing, it's her brother—"

"He's not dying, Terry. He's got polio . . ."

"Whatever's the matter with the kid, thatsa boy, Lew, Billy will love it."

6

Cassidy signed the front of the program. The crowd was getting noisier as game time approached. From nearby boxes people were craning their necks to see Lew Cassidy up close, without his leather helmet.

"Thanks so much," Naomi said. "Score a touchdown for me today, okay?" She batted her eyes and looked at him from behind a grillwork of thick lashes, heavy with mascara.

"Anything you say, Naomi."

Terry hugged her expansively, possessively, and puffed one of Max Bauman's enormous cigars. He leaned forward like a man plotting mischief and winked. "Not too many touchdowns, kid. I got five hundred bucks down says the Giants wipe the floor with you guys, twenty-one points or better."

Cassidy shrugged. "You never know," he said. Which was a barefaced lie since everybody in the Polo Grounds knew Terry's money was as safe as the crown jewels. They'd all come to see the Giants whip the Bulldogs but they'd also come to see Lew Cassidy score some touchdowns. He'd scored eight in the last three games, including three against the Bears, and was leading the league in both scoring and rushing. He'd had a helluva season, running from tailback like a Mack truck, providing the Bulldogs with enough offense to get the Giants' or anybody else's attention, but defensively the 'Dogs had crashed in flames long ago. Though Cassidy was undeniably a powerful, crushing runner, his play at defensive end when the ball went over was characterized more by energy and determination than by tackles. He had the defensive end's fatal flaw: He was too aggressive, too eager to get into the play, couldn't hold back and box the ball carrier in toward the clogged center of the field. Time and again he would overcommit, get taken out of the play by a blocking back while the runner cut up the turf going around him and heading off down the sidelines. In writing about Cassidy and the pitfalls of the end run, Grantland Rice had observed that Cassidy had "the heart and soul of

7

a born sucker and there's nothing on the Good Lord's green earth he or the Bulldogs can do about it." Cassidy felt it was always nice to be noticed. And Rice had also called him "the toughest runner and headbuster in the game once you're inside the twenty and heading for the end zone."

"You got any money down yourself?" Terry gave him an innocent, open-faced choirboy look. "You want me to put some down for—"

"Come on, you know I only bet us to win. Haunts you if you go the other way."

Terry nodded. Cassidy had a hundred each riding on the Redskins and Sammy Baugh down at little Griffith Stadium and on Sid Luckman and the Bears to beat the crosstown Cardinals for the championship of Chicago. He hadn't put a nickel on the game he was about to play.

"Hey, Cassidy, get your butt over here. You got some football to play!" Coach Horse Farraday was frowning at him over his spectacles. Nobody knew why they called him Horse because he was a small man who, with his long nose, tiny shining eyes, and weak chin, far more resembled a rat than, say, the mighty Seabiscuit.

The team in its black jerseys and pants with the red and white trim gathered around Farraday for a final inspirational word. The word was always the same. "All right, you assholes, go out there and wear 'em down. Be tougher, be meaner, be dirtier, just so's you don't get caught at it. Wear the bastards down, don't let 'em get their hands on the ball . . ." It went on and on in that vein and Cassidy had been hearing it for seven years, which was a hell of a long time for a guy who carried the ball thirty, forty times a game. Today wasn't going to be any different because Farraday was one of those wear-'em-down coaches who hadn't had a new idea since Amos Alonzo Stagg was a pup. For seven seasons he'd had Lew Cassidy to wear 'em down. Give the ball to Lew and let Lew run over 'em and wear the bastards down. When it came to the forward pass, Horse Farraday figured there were three things that could happen to the ball when you started throwing it around and two of them were bad. He used to say that when the going got tough, the tough got going, which Cassidy figured was all well enough, except it was hard to keep saying it when you'd only won the one game and Christmas was less than three weeks away.

While Farraday kept on extolling the virtues of rock-'em, sock-'em play, Cassidy looked back at the crowd and saw that Terry and Naomi had now been joined by Max Bauman, in his black chesterfield with the velvet collar and the soft homburg, and a blonde in a mink coat. Her name was Cindy and she belonged to Max. Cassidy had met her last night and she'd—no, he couldn't think about last night. Had to think about football. And anyway she was Max's. But just then she looked like the symbol of beauty and chastity for whom Saint George might have slain any number of dragons. Either that or a Vassar girl at the Yale Bowl in a cigarette ad, though maybe that was only another version of the same thing. You never knew when it came to symbols. It was tougher to see Max Bauman as Saint George, unless your idea of the dragon slayer was five five, Jewish, bald, easily induced to weep, and a big-time gangster. Max was all of those things and for all Cassidy knew the dragon hadn't been made that Max couldn't slay. Max saw Cassidy and gave the thumbs-up sign, which could have meant just about anything since Max was also the main owner of the Bulldogs though he didn't like it generally known. Maybe if they were winners but, as it was, he didn't think it was such a hot idea. A football fan, that was Max's weakness, and the Bulldogs were, each and every one of them, his toys. Thumbs-up could have meant Cassidy should go out there and show 'em how a real man played this game, wear 'em down and rock 'em and sock 'em. It could also mean get out there and go in the tank because my pal Luciano's bet half of Jersey on the Giants by twenty-one. You just couldn't tell.

Behind Max, like one of the newer skyscrapers, was his shadow, a full load called Bennie the Brute. Maybe that's how Max would deal with dragons and damsels and errant knights alike. Just wind Benny up and point him and wait awhile for the screaming to stop. Anyway, they made quite a picture. The cop and the gangster with their cigars, the pile of muscle standing guard behind them, the remote can't-take-your-eyes-off-her blonde on the gangster's arm, and Naomi, who was just passing through, asking for Mr. Touchdown's autograph, and moving on having added her ankle bracelet to Terry's collection.

"So, goddammit, you sorry piss ants," Farraday observed, concluding his final pregame remarks at the top of his lungs, "go out there and play some football so you can hold up your heads and look 'em in the eye when you collect your paychecks!"

He was such an emotional, inspirational leader. Cassidy could barely contain his enthusiasm. He was making six thousand dollars for the season, highest salary on the team, and Farraday was making four. Cassidy figured he earned his six and, if laughs counted, Horse was probably worth the four.

•   •   •

It was always the same, like standing at the bottom of a deep well of noise, waiting for it all to come crashing down on you.

A Sunday afternoon at the Polo Grounds, gray sky without any sun glare, not too cold, the grass mottled green and brown, spongy underfoot. He hadn't gotten all the clumps of mud and grass from where they'd wedged between his cleats during the warm-up and now it was too late. He was waiting now, just waiting for the kaleidoscope to shake, for the game to begin.

The crowd was standing and yelling behind a curtain of smoky haze. The radio station banner, the big white letters WHN on a navy-blue background, hung from the broadcast booth on the mezzanine level. He glanced over at the scoreboard where the other games were listed. There wasn't any word yet from Washington or Chicago but he knew he'd keep checking instinctively as his own game ground onward.

His helmet was pinching his ear, which was tender from last Sunday when somebody had knocked the helmet off in a plunge at the goal line and somebody else had kicked hell out of his head. His pads and jersey smelled like sweat from another century. By the end of the season they couldn't clean the smell away anymore. Maybe winners had more sets of uniforms. He couldn't believe the Giants smelled this crummy.

Cassidy was the lone return man. Art Hannaford had gone down with a broken leg just before Halloween leaving Cassidy as the only kick returner. Everybody on the team had congratulated Art, laughing at what Cassidy was in for. Art had gone back to his job at a bottling company in Hoboken.

Far away, on the horizon, beyond the drainage hump in the center of the field, the kicker moved up and the noise got louder, like the *Twentieth Century Limited* bashing through the bedroom wall, and he put his leg into the ball.

The ball climbed up the flat, leaden sky, end over end, like a fly moving up a gray wall. He waited for his depth perception to click in so he could get an idea where the hell it was going to intersect with planet Earth.

Kickoffs always scared him. Waiting, wondering what he was doing at twenty-nine, seven years out of Fordham, playing a kid's game, wondering what would happen when the ball came down . . .

The ground began to tremble. It was always the same but nobody who'd never been out there for the kickoff could quite believe it. It was like an earthquake he'd once sat through in a Los Angeles hotel. He'd been scared shitless then, too.

It was doing a trapeze act up there, twisting and spinning in the gusts of wind, and he seemed to stand at the five-yard line for an eternity, waiting for it to top out. The Giants came down the field snorting and puffing and blowing like the horses Karin used to ride out near Princeton . . .

There he was, waiting for the kickoff to come down, and the crowd was on its feet bellowing and the ground was

11

shaking and he had one hell of a hangover and even then he couldn't stop thinking about his wife.

It was always the same.

•　•　•

He met her at the Winter Olympic Games in 1936. His father, Paul Cassidy, had put him on the payroll for the trip, calling him a talent scout for the sake of his accountants and the tax people. The football season was over. It would be a perfect time for the two of them to pal around together, visit Paris, and meander down to Nice afterward, all the while scouting the talent.

The talent that stopped Lew in his size tens was a twenty-year-old ice skater and the story going around Garmisch-Partenkirchen, the swanky German resort town where the Games were held, was that Adolf Hitler himself had his eye on her. In 1936 Adolf Hitler's name didn't mean all that much to Lew except he was the guy running the whole damn country. The Germans seemed crazy about him and the posters of him on the walls were pretty striking. The Charlie Chaplin moustache didn't seem funny—just somehow Germanic and authoritative. He seemed to have the country and the people revved up and everybody was having a fine time in Garmisch. The Führer thought the young skater, Karin Richter, was the answer to the twenty-four-year-old Norwegian Sonja Henie, who had brought her ballet training to the sport and revolutionized it while winning gold medals at Saint Moritz in 1928 and at Lake Placid in '32.

The Germans were hopeful that winter of '36. But, as it turned out, Karin Richter skated well and looked exquisite, which wasn't enough to get a medal, let along dethrone Henie, who won again. Rumor had it that Hitler canceled a reception he'd been planning for her had she won, and maybe he had. She never found out for sure, not even when she got to know Dr. Josef Goebbels, who was busy by then arranging his own parties for her. But that came later. At the time, Cassidy turned on the charm and told her the Olympics hadn't been a complete loss for her.

She'd met him. She'd nodded patiently but didn't know what he was talking about when he told her he was the star tailback of the Bulldogs. Which only made him work on her all the harder.

Though he was the one who spotted her first, getting a good look at her early one morning when she was practicing at the rink just beyond the window of the hotel dining room where he was having breakfast, it was his father who approached her. Paul Cassidy was a movie producer back in Hollywood. He liked to insist that he was the first one with the idea of making Sonja Henie a movie star. Turned out he was a brick shy of a load in the money department but, then, that was the show business for you. If you were in the movie end of things, you didn't even think about giving up. Paul Cassidy thought maybe he'd lucked into something when Lew dragged him out to the rink to watch through the morning mist the gorgeous girl doing her figure eights.

She was certainly a good enough skater to build a lightweight movie career around and, to tell the truth, Paul had never seen her as doing Lady Macbeth. He was, however, looking past strictly ice-bound pictures, past her legs which were unusually long for a skater, past that cute little fanny where Lew's observations had stopped for some time to catch their breath and deliver a heartfelt sigh. Paul was looking at her face because, though he might not know about skating, he sure as the devil knew about movies. He knew it was the face that mattered. A woman could be badly underslung, flat-chested, bow-legged, and overweight, with all her springs badly sprung, but if she had the face—well, she had the face, and that was what it took to do the heavy work in the movies. Karin Richter had the face, all right. Classically high cheekbones, a nose just less than haughty length, which made her more approachable, level eyebrows over solemn, oddly pale brown eyes. Her upper lip was thin, the lower full, hinting at a kind of permanent pout, thankfully unlike her temperament. It was a face as likely to stick in the memory as any he'd ever seen.

13

Lew dropped like a stone into those bottomless brown eyes, the brown equivalent of the blue you sometimes saw in pure mountain lakes. He didn't come up for air until he'd followed her back to Cologne, met her austere scientist father and faintly dismayed mother, and convinced her to marry him. They came back to the States together, Lew and Karin and Paul. Almost before she knew it she had a husband and a producer and was getting ready for a screen test.

Herr Dokter Goebbels, who was Hitler's propaganda expert in Berlin, had to be consulted by Paul Cassidy regarding his plans for Karin's future on the silver screen. Goebbels made a big deal out of it, talking about the German film industry's vitality and the opportunity it afforded beautiful young German actresses, which was where Paul remarked that while that was undeniably true and he bowed to no one in his respect for the German cinema, it was also true that Karin was a skater, not an actress.

"Just for the sake of argument, Joe—you call me Paul, Joe," Paul said over the cognac late one night after dinner with Goebbels and his wife, "let's say the girl comes to Hollywood, does the test for me, and she's got something up there on the screen. That magic which not one of us can resist. But she's still a skater, see? So she learns her way around the camera in her first five, six pictures. We've taken the risks, we're stuck with the kid if she just sort of lays there. You never heard of her, see? But if she can act, if she connects, well, then we work out a deal. You want her to come back, do a picture or two every now and then, no problem. If we're lucky, hell, she's an international star. Whattaya say, Joe, why not let us take the risk for you?"

Goebbels just laughed and grinned crookedly. He was a swarthy, funny-looking little geek with a clubfoot and damned if he didn't wear his uniform to the dinner table. He limped across to where Cassidy sat uncomfortably on an austere chair, shook hands, said, "For our American friends, why not? How can I deny her the chance to go to Hollywood? I'd like to see it myself; perhaps someday it can be arranged. Who knows?"

Later Goebbels saw him to the front door where a venerable Daimler-Benz and driver waited to return the movie producer to the Adlon. "Now listen to me, my friend," Goebbels said, shaking a finger beneath his guest's nose, all in mock seriousness, "I know about your movie business. All furriers and junk men and moneylenders—Jews, all of them. You take good care of our little girl, she's your responsibility. Don't let the Jews get their hands on her! And you make her a great star!" They shook hands again and Goebbels said, "*Auf Wiedersehen*, Paul," and Cassidy went back to the hotel thinking about the impossibility of Goebbels's final instructions. She should be a star . . . but no Jews could be involved. He shook his head. A contradiction in terms. So Goebbels didn't know batshit about the movies, in Hollywood or Germany or anywhere else, apparently.

When Lew and Karin were married up at Lake Placid in 1938, the good doctor took time off from helping Hitler devour Europe and sent a lengthy Teutonic wire from the Reichschancellery congratulating them on their mutual good fortune, wishing them a long and happy life together, and hoping they would soon visit him in the bride's fatherland. He also sent about five hundred dollars' worth of roses, which cleaned out all the florists for miles around the little church where the ceremony took place. Karin blushed and frowned. "More proof, the Nazis have no taste, no sense of restraint," she said. She found them intolerably vulgar, from their manners to their uniforms to their torchlit rallies. "The only one I ever liked was Fat Hermann," she'd once told Lew, referring to Reichsmarshall Göring, the epic hero of the Great War. "He bounced me on his knee once when I won a children's skating competition. Pinned the little medal on my blouse." That was the only good thing he'd ever heard her say about the Nazis. Lew figured Fat Hermann was overly fond of little girls but had the sense to keep his mouth shut.

The warmth of Goebbels's words as well as the sheer number of roses led Lew to believe that the propaganda

15

minister had not seen the first Karin Richter picture which Paul Cassidy in his wisdom not only produced but wrote as well. It was called *Murder Goes Skating*. Lew never understood why stars like George Brent and James Gleason agreed to costar with Karin but apparently they both went back a long way with Paul. And they got a month in Sun Valley out of it. There had to be some reason. *Murder on Ice* followed a few months later, much the same kind of thing though Tom Tully signed on for the ride. Her third movie, *Bless Your Heart*, was a little Christmas number and she only had to skate in one scene where she was teaching kids at a orphanage with lots of nuns also taking to the ice. It was a marked improvement. Karin's career looked more than just promising. She was an American citizen by then. It was 1939.

•   •   •

While the German army was taking big bites out of the map of Europe, while Lew was playing his kid's game, while Karin was letting Paul Cassidy try to make her a movie star, Herr Professor Ernst Richter, Karin's father, was getting sick. The reports he sent were sketchy, reticent, and stoic but worrisome. It sounded serious: Nothing less would interfere with his government work and he admitted that it had. What it sounded like was cancer.

Karin decided she had to go back to see him, to be with him if he needed her, since her mother had died not long after she and Lew had gotten married. What could Lew say? A father was a father and wouldn't he have felt the same if it had been Paul? Europe was going to hell from the looks of things but everybody was saying it had gotten as bad as it was going to get. Hitler had the *Lebensraum* he'd been yelling about, and now it would all calm down. And, anyway, it was her father.

She sailed from Pier 42 on the Hudson, bound for Lisbon on the American Export Line. She'd then catch a Lufthansa flight from Lisbon, heading into the heart of the Third Reich. Berlin. Then on to the family home in Cologne.

There was only one big problem once she got there. They wouldn't let her come back.

No strong-arm Nazi stuff, just Dr. Goebbels feeling that a good German girl's place was with her dying father, as he was sure she would agree. And as long as she was back home, he felt that it was only logical that she make a movie or two. He invited her to tea in Berlin, then went to Cologne to continue making his case. The troops, he said, would worship her as they devoted themselves to the greater glory of the fatherland. They needed such exemplary models of German womanhood to keep their morale up. He told her that her father needed her by his side if he were to continue his work as long as he could. Goebbels told her of the special laboratories which had been built for him, one in Cologne, one in the mountains. He arranged interviews for her with her father's doctors, who were none other than the same men he, Himmler, Bormann, and—yes—even the Führer himself depended upon. He told her that all Germany needed her skill and beauty to fill the cinema screens. He wasn't kidding but a snow job from a Nazi was like a death threat from anybody else.

Lew decided it was time for the old football hero to make an end run and go rescue his wife.

But Karin wrote begging him not to do anything rash. She begged him to stay in New York. She said that there were old family friends who had become Nazi sympathizers: not monsters, she wrote, just friends of her parents' whom she'd known and trusted from her childhood. They assured her that there were no plans for a wider war, that it was all over, that peace in Europe was at hand. They told her that once Goebbels got a movie out of her she'd be welcome to come and go as she pleased and as her father's condition warranted. They told her that her father worshiped her, depended on her, would fall like a leaf in winter without her. Stay, they told her, until the vigil was over, if that was the will of God. Make the movie, *Liebchen*. And don't worry so much, you'll put lines on that lovely face.

The only thing she had to worry about, they told her,

was an impetuous American husband who didn't understand the way things stood in Germany. Keep him back home, her old family friends kept telling her, and the time will fly and you'll be together again. Like little lovebirds. But if he comes barging into Germany making a fuss, they couldn't be responsible for the consequences. To her father, to her, to her husband. They clucked and shook their heads and peered through their monocles. They were full of good advice.

So Lew didn't go.

He waited and played football and read the papers and watched the Nazis club Europe damn near to death. He watched the Blitzkrieg and Dunkirk and the Battle of Britain from afar and counted the letters that got through from Karin.

He never did find out if she made Goebbels's movie but he supposed the Reichsminister had a lot on his mind in those days and maybe he'd just never gotten around to it.

Paul said it probably wouldn't have been worth a shit anyway since all the good Kraut moviemakers had escaped to Hollywood.

• • •

Saturday night before the Giants game.

Cassidy's last letter from Karin had come through in September, posted by a friend passing through Lisbon. She told him not to worry, that her father's condition had stabilized—it had turned out to be leukemia—and she was well enough, more or less untouched by the war. She hoped he knew how fouled up the mail was, what with Europe, North Africa, and the Atlantic all mired in one aspect of the war or another.

He knew about the war, all right, probably a good deal more than she did. And he believed what she wrote about her present state of mind, how much she loved him, missed him, and thought about him. Yet, hearing from her so infrequently, he couldn't help feeling pointless, empty, a man going through increasingly senseless motions. He began drinking more than was good for him, had gotten in the habit of hanging around the nightclubs while trying to mask the emptiness, the worry, the loneliness.

The fact was, without Terry Leary he might not have made it through the season. He sure as hell wouldn't have had the best year of his career, not without Terry. Because it was always Terry there to rescue him from the black hound of depression, to listen while Lew opened the taps and poured out his troubles. Terry understood because he knew Karin, too, had been best man up at Lake Placid, struggling to control all those goddamn roses from Goebbels.

Whenever Cassidy got too far down, Terry would make it his business to do the cheering up. "Gotta get you out of yourself," he'd say, and nobody was better at that than Terry. He knew what was going on in New York: It was his style, his city. Another cop once told Cassidy: "That Terry, he's got eyes in the back of his head. Eyes that see around corners. He knows what's coming before it's coming. That Terry, you gotta get up before breakfast to get ahead of him."

On Saturday nights, with games looming the next afternoon, Terry took it upon himself to keep Cassidy out of trouble. Hell, there was always somebody who wanted to outpunch or outdrink a football hero and Cassidy was a big man, easy to spot, an easy target. But Terry could see around corners, and besides, he was a tough guy by profession and inclination. A cop.

Sometimes Terry's magic worked and sometimes it didn't.

That Saturday night they began as they usually did with drinks at the Taft Hotel, Seventh and 50th. They met in the lobby, all combed and brushed with clocks on their socks and shines on their shoes. Terry had come directly from his regular weekly appointment at the Terminal Barber Shop, which wasn't as ominous as it sounded. He was grinning, shooting the breeze with the cigarette girl and kidding the bellhops, wearing his smooth shit-eating Irish-malarkey grin, his ebony hair slicked straight back from his high square forehead. He was normally very pale but not since he'd discovered the Suntan Shave at Terminal where for half a buck you also got zapped by their new sunlamp. He'd developed of late a sort of pinkish-tan flesh tone, not quite Palm Beach but closer than any other cop gave a damn about getting. The tan went well with the belted camel's-hair polo coat.

Terry had made it to NYPD plainclothes faster than almost anyone ever had, or so the story went, and he'd had to face the resentment of some older, more traditional colleagues. Not only had he risen fast, he always had lots of money to go with the good-looking dames and the big cigars. It was obvious that he lived way beyond whatever his cop's salary was, and for a long time Cassidy fell for the line that he specialized in not only beautiful but also generous lady friends. In any case, Cassidy figured it was none of his business.

Terry had always been good at having plenty of money, even back in Fordham, where there'd been a story that he supplied very discreet, highly companionable young ladies for social evenings with some of the priests. He used to say that he wished he'd thought of that himself since there was bound to be money in it. Cassidy didn't really know where the money for the women and the Park Avenue apartment came from but he had some ideas. There were such things as gratuities from an appreciative public who enjoyed helping out a deserving cop, particularly a celebrity cop, which he'd become when he blew the Sylvester Aubrey Bean murder case wide open and then artfully put the lid back on. It was a masterful inside performance and every homo in New York owed him one.

Terry led the way into the Tap, said something to Charley Drew, who was working the piano for all it was worth, and settled in at the bar. He ordered a couple of Rob Roys and when they came he clicked his glass against Cassidy's, the ice tinkling.

"Absent friends, Lew," he said. "Any news?" The toast and the question composed their private ritual. Terry missed her almost as much as Lew did. He missed her *for*

20

Lew because underneath the polish and the jazz he was a sentimental mick, full of Irish heart and blarney.

"Dr. Goebbels says the German *Volk* must accept the idea of a long, hard war," Cassidy sighed. "I know it's true 'cause I read it in the *Times*. He says defeat will be worse than an inferno for the German people. So they have just begun to fight. I'm not encouraged."

Terry nodded. "Tell it to the Bolshies. It'll get worse before it gets better. Think of it, kid, she may be making a movie over there right now . . ." Terry was star-struck. Always had been. He always said the introduction of sound film was the most important event of his lifetime thus far. He loved to come up with funny litle bits of information that Cassidy never was sure he could believe. He said that Theda Bara's real name was Goodman, that "Theda Bara" was an anagram for "Arab Death" dreamed up by some studio genius. Even Paul Cassidy hadn't known that and he claimed to have come within a gnat's eyelash of screwing her in 1925 when she was thirty-five and her career was almost over.

Through the second Rob Roy, Terry kept the conversation going, told Lew way too much about the Bob Hope movie he'd seen the other night, *Caught in the Draft*. He could have gone on about movies all night but he switched gears and said he'd bought a mink coat at Russek's that afternoon for two grand. When Cassidy asked the name of the lucky lady, Terry just laughed, slid off the stool, waved good-bye to Charley Drew, who was playing "My Indiana Home" for a couple from Terre Haute celebrating their anniversary, and asked Cassidy if he was hungry.

They headed downtown in a cab. There was a heavy mist and the windshield wipers clapped raggedly. Times Square looked like a cheap, gaudy dream of Christmas. The marquees twinkled in the night. Lillian Hellman had a hit show, *Watch on the Rhine*. Cassidy looked away. Germany again. He couldn't get away from it.

He was a hero to the guys hanging around Keen's Chop House and it took a few minutes to get through the crowd wishing him luck against the Giants. Then a table was ready for the guy leading the league in touchdowns and they got down to a couple of serious steaks. Halfway through his, Terry put down his knife and fork, patted his mouth with the heavy linen, and lit a Dunhill Major, one of the new long cigarettes. "Listen, pal," he said, "I may be needing your help one day soon."

"Spare me the bad news," Cassidy replied, dunking a piece of steak the size of a hockey puck in the Lea & Perrins. "What's the matter?"

"I don't know exactly. That's the problem. Some people pass me the word, that's all. I'm on the wrong list, or so they say. Right at the top. Kinda news like that, hell, ruined my lunch. I was at the Harvard Club, too. Damn fine lunch. Max invites me to lunch and then I get this call. From a friend with his hankie over the mouthpiece. You know? Couldn't finish my rice pudding."

"What can I do? Want me to go out there and wear 'em down for you?"

He laughed and shook his head. "No, just stay my friend, Jocko." Terry called him that sometimes, an old Fordham nickname, mainly when he was thinking about the old days, wishing they were back in them. "Anyway, maybe it's a joke. Or a false alarm." He finished his cigarette and dug back into the two-inch-thick porterhouse.

"Max Bauman? He went to Harvard?"

"Where else?"

"I don't know. Not that many Harvard men wind up making license plates and twine up in Dannemora, that's all. Bootlegging, running girls, running guns, Havana casinos, funny money . . ."

Terry shook his head, amused at the recitation. "Misunderstandings. And all a long time ago. You know how it was during Prohibition. Hell, I used to deliver hooch for my uncle in Jersey City when I was just fourteen. Max, he's in trucking, scrap metal, he's got the club, he made the big mistake of buying the Bulldogs, he's putting some money into the movie business." He shrugged. He was wearing a gray suit with a white chalk stripe broad as the yard lines out on the field. There was a maroon silk in his breast pocket, suspenders to match, a pearl pin in his maroon swirled tie. Finchley's on Fifth at 46th, three hundred bucks for the works.

"Whatever you say," Cassidy nodded. "You're the cop."

"Max is aces with me, pal. Wouldn't hurt a fly."

They went on from Keen's to a couple more joints where sports types hung out. Two broadcasters who'd be doing the next day's game were good for another set of Rob Roys and then Terry said they ought to work their way back uptown. They came to rest in the Savoy Room listening to Hildegarde sing "The Last Time I Saw Paris." The last time Cassidy had seen Paris was the spring of '36 with Karin, and their hearts had definitely been young and gay. Hearing the song and seeing the chanteuse in the spotlight made him blue. So they went on to Heliotrope, which was just down West 52nd from the Onyx, where Count Basie was in residence. Cassidy didn't have to think very hard to know who'd be in residence at Heliotrope.

Max Bauman.

He was the first guy Cassidy saw when his eyes adjusted to the purple darkness and the indirect lighting that came from he knew not where. He was sitting at a corner table with Bennie the Brute, who had probably been a classmate at Harvard and a secret Jane Austen scholar.

Bauman waved to Terry and they drifted over, sat down. Max always wore a tuxedo at his club. So did Bennie the Brute, who was doing the impression of the world's largest penguin. Pretty soon they were all lapping Courvoisier from snifters the size of cowboy boots. Max passed out Havanas from his private stock at Dunhill. First they'd sniff the brandy. Then they'd sniff the cigars. Cassidy's nose hadn't seen so much action in years.

Max was somewhere in his fifties, a sports fan who'd never had the luxury of competing himself. He asked Cassidy lots of questions about the Giants and Cassidy pretended to give him complicated inside dope. It was just a kid's game but they were sitting around bullshitting over brandy and cigars so what the hell. Most of Cassidy's mind was still on Karin and the news from Europe. The Brits seemed to keep chasing Kraut battleships around the Atlantic. You had to give the limeys credit. They had pluck.

When Max got to talking about his son Irving, his eyes filled up. Nobody noticed but Cassidy. Irving had left Harvard during his sophomore year and joined the navy. "He's quite a kid, Lew," he said, his face full of a father's love. Cassidy saw the boy at his bar mitzvah, getting a gold watch and a fountain pen and pencil set and lots of checks. "Said he figured there was a war coming and he wanted to be in on it. You know what those bastards, those Nazi bastards, are doing to our people over there? Sure, you know, you're a bright boy, a college man. Hell, I'm too old to do much fighting but Irvie, he says he wants to get ready to fight when the chance comes . . . my mother and father, Poland, they lost everything and now they're just gone, poof, and my Irvie says fuck that, he joins the navy! Whattaya think of that, Lew? Hey?"

"Irvie's got guts, Max."

Bauman wiped the corner of one eye with a hairy knuckle, nodded. Nice manicure. "The *Yorktown*." He swallowed hard. "Irving Bauman, Lieutenant j.g., USN. Some kid, my Irvie." He waited, watched a girl singer go stand beside a white baby grand. Her silvery-blond pageboy swung forward and cloaked one eye. She gave their table a barely perceptible smile. "Communications officer."

"What?"

Bauman leaned over, his eyes darting from the girl to Cassidy. He smelled like the kind of cologne Cassidy could never find. "Irvie. My son. He's communications officer on the *Yorktown*."

"That's great, Max. You should be very proud."

But Max didn't hear him. He was transfixed watching the girl.

Bennie the Brute touched Cassidy's arm when the girl began singing in a low, almost hoarse voice. "Listen to her,

Lew. Quite a nice voice. A real stylist." He wore silver-rimmed spectacles with thick circular lenses. He had a nose like a zucchini. He always wore a polka-dot bow tie, even with his tux. He was big and friendly and gentle, like a large dog who when aroused might eat you in an excess of high spirits. "Delightful," he said.

"Delightful," Cassidy agreed. You'd have to have a hell of a good reason to disagree with Bennie. Besides, the girl could sing.

"Miss Squires," Bennie whispered. He wore nice cologne, too, but the effect was lessened by the fettuccini with garlic and oil he'd had for dinner. "Miss Cindy Squires," he said like a man repeating the answer to the only question that mattered. She sang "Chattanooga Choo Choo" and everybody clapped. Max Bauman looked very pleased. Bennie was whispering again. "Mr. Leary told us about her. Mr. Bauman hired her the first time he heard her sing. He called her a thrush. Mr. Bauman has a finely educated ear."

"Well, he is a Harvard man."

Bennie nodded. Speaking of ears, Cassidy had once seen Bennie the Brute bite a man's ear clean off during a late-evening dispute in Hell's Kitchen. No clam sauce, no oil and garlic, just an ear, *al dente*.

Moments before Cindy Squires sang "The White Cliffs of Dover" Bauman leaned across the table and tapped Terry's arm. The two profiles came together in the dim light and Max whispered, "You pick up the coat for me, Terry?" Terry nodded and Bauman patted his sleeve.

She was singing about the bluebirds over the white cliffs on some better, happier day when the world would be free. The crowd was eating it up. Everybody had seen the newsreels and read the papers and knew what *Collier's* and *The Saturday Evening Post* and H. V. Kaltenborn and Ed Murrow and Bill Shirer were saying. They knew all about Churchill and the brave fly-boys of the RAF and the Spitfires and the Hurricanes. Cindy Squires knew how to sell the song, conjuring up all those images by some kind of magic. Cassidy thought she was just about the classiest-looking girl he'd ever seen, well bred, with a fancy accent. Vera Lynn would have been proud of her. Everybody was proud of her. Everybody was proud but Terry Leary, who must have figured that finding her for Max had brought his account up to date. Terry looked bored. Still, he kept checking her out over the rim of his snifter. Terry didn't miss much.

After she'd finished the set Cassidy got up to head for the Gents. Max said, "We never own liquor, Lew. We only rent it." Terry yawned. "Through those doors, take a left." Max pointed the way. The corridor was painted a hot shade of heliotrope with dim lights in wall sconces shaped to look like jungle foliage. He was occupied in the Gents for two, maybe three minutes, thinking that it was time to get home before his head got any foggier. It was past midnight. Twelve hours away from his customary throwing up in the locker room.

He came back into the hallway, adjusting his eyes to the gloom after the bright lights on the shiny white tiles. He heard something from the end of the hall, shook the booze out of his perceptions. A woman's voice, angry, rushed, out of breath from behind a closed door. "Bloody bastard, you . . . bloody . . . bastard!" It was a loud whisper and there was no *r* in bastard; it came out sounding like *bah-stud*. Then he heard something slam against the wall, cutting her voice off in mid-curse.

The door wasn't locked and he saw a gold five-pointed star at eye level. He pushed it open.

Cindy Squires stood with her back to her dressing table mirror, perfect blond hair disheveled, clutching a silk dressing gown to her thin body. She was reaching for a vase of roses behind her. A large man stood between them, his back to Cassidy, one hand grabbing at the front of the flimsy robe. As Cassidy came through the door the man ripped her arm away and tore the robe open. Her tiny breasts, the fragile rib cage, registered in Cassidy's mind: He'd never seen such vulnerability. She clawed with one

26

hand at the man's face, her perfect heart-shaped face a mask of determination, unafraid. The man let out a yell of pain and Cassidy saw scratches on his cheek leaking blood. He turned back to her, looking from the blood smeared on his hand to her spitfire face, made a low growl, and lunged at her in a fury, knocking her backward, bending her against the mirror.

Cassidy took him by the collar of his tuxedo jacket, yanked him backward, twirled him around, and threw him at the wall hard enough to stick. Like spaghetti. The eyes were glassy with too much liquor and just enough confusion. Cassidy gave him a sour frown and hit him in the chest, right on the onyx stud below his sternum. The man coughed and went walleyed.

"Get out of the way, Miss Squires. He's gonna lose his dinner—"

"Jolly bad luck for him," she said. She was holding the vase of roses over him.

"Better not hit him with that. You could hurt him—"

"Good!" She flung the vase at him. He was sliding down the wall, eyes pointed in different directions, and the vase clunked off the wall. Drenched in water and smothered in roses, he reached the floor, closed his eyes, and tipped over.

"Services will be held at Mount Olivet Cemetery." Cassidy grinned.

Cindy Squires had closed her robe and cinched the belt tight. Her nipples seemed enormous, protruding beneath the silk from her boyish chest. "Flowers in his hair," she muttered. "Swine!" She bit her lip and looked up at Cassidy. "I suppose I owe you thanks—so, thank you." She looked back at Sleeping Beauty. "But I could have handled him, actually. I had him right where I wanted him. Still and all, thanks." Her solemn face hinted at a smile. Her voice was very soft and husky.

"This sort of thing happen often?"

"Never. Most people know about Max and the thrush, which is how I'm usually described among such . . . people." She made the final word an insult. "Maybe he's an out-of-towner." She took Cassidy's arm and hugged it spontaneously. "Who are you, anyway?"

"One of those people, I guess."

"Well, you're my Saint George. And you've more or less slain the dragon. A friend in need—" She leaned up and planted a quick kiss on his mouth. She took a hankie from the pocket of the robe and quickly wiped it away, destroying the evidence. "He seems to be coming around . . ."

The man lifted a leg experimentally, looked at it as if it were an unfamiliar piece of farm machinery. Then he figured the hell with it, let it flop loudly back onto the floor. "All wet," he observed with great dignity. His eyes closed and he sighed like a man who'd already had to put up with too much.

"What the devil's going on here?" Max Bauman stood in the doorway. He sounded curious, not angry. "You all right, my darling?" He went past Cassidy and put a protective arm around her shoulders, pulled her tight. Her face powder smudged the lapel of his dinner jacket.

"This drunken oaf was making a nuisance of himself," she said softly, matter-of-factly, her eyes turning toward Max, "and this nice chap came in and dealt with him." Cassidy smiled at that. *Dealt with him.* "I threw the vase at him. I'm sorry about the roses, Max—"

"I send her roses every night," he said to Cassidy, winked. "Plenty more where they came from." He held Cindy Squires at arm's length, looked her over. "You're all right?" She nodded, raked her hair into place with long nails. "Good girl. Lucky you were nearby, Lew. I won't forget it."

"It's nothing, Max. I enjoyed it."

"He enjoyed it," Max said, chuckling. "That's good, Lew."

Bennie the Brute cleared his throat in the doorway. "Can I be of any assistance, Mr. Bauman?" He needed a bigger doorway. He looked crowded into this one.

Max nodded at the man on the floor. "Take out the trash, Bennie."

Bennie whisked the limp body off the floor after brushing the roses away. He carried him like a man putting a child to bed. When he went out, they heard the sound of a door opening into the alley, then a crash as Bennie filled one of the trash cans.

Cassidy watched the girl. She smiled shyly and said she ought to get dressed. Some girl, he thought. Had him right where she wanted him . . .

"In a minute, baby," Max said. "Have you met young Lochinvar here?"

She shook her head, put out her hand. "I'm Cindy Squires . . ."

"Lew Cassidy, Miss Squires. It was a pleasure . . . dealing with our friend." He watched her eyes, looking at him frankly, one from behind the pale curtain of hair.

"Lew works for me," Max said. He slapped Cassidy on his broad shoulders, an owner's gesture. "He's got some business to take care of for me tomorrow. You'd better get some shut-eye." Cindy Squires nodded politely and pulled away from Max. She brushed at the powder she'd left on his jacket. "Thanks again, kid," Max said. Cassidy nodded and left them together. Cindy Squires had turned her back and was untying the belt on the robe.

They were finally leaving a little after one o'clock. The new closing-hours law was supposed to put the city on a more wartime footing should war come. No one seemed to know just exactly how, but then no one much cared either. The clubs along West 52nd fudged it, stayed open later. Terry was tipping the checkroom girl and she was giggling, helping him into the heavy camel's-hair coat. A big guy saw Cassidy, recognized him, and came bellowing over. He raised the subject of two fumbles Cassidy had made against the Bears.

"Fuckin' queer," he shouted. "Vaseline fingers."

Terry was laughing.

The big loudmouth followed Cassidy outside. It was raining and foggy. The guy wanted to fight, he was feeling good, he wouldn't remember a damn thing if he lived through the night.

Cassidy told him to get lost, turned his back on him, a

mistake, and he clipped Cassidy on the base of his skull with a fistful of car keys.

Cassidy slipped and fell forward and smashed his lip on the curbstone, tasted blood and shredded pulp, and wished he were elsewhere under a different name.

He was fumbling around trying to stand up and the next thing he saw was a flash of pale blond hair and dark brown mink. Terry had gone off down the street in the rain whistling for a cab. Cassidy looked up, swallowing blood, just in time to see Cindy Squires come at the guy from his left, smash a mink-draped forearm across his face. His nose broke, spraying blood across the mink and the rain-lashed sidewalk. She hooked her right leg behind his ankle and pushed him over backward. He went down like he'd been shot, with a bad, solid, wet sound. His head bounced off an iron grating.

Cassidy was back on his feet holding a split lip together between thumb and forefinger. "What the hell—"

"Don't talk with your mouth full, Mr. Cassidy."

"But how? What you did to—"

"I told you I had that other bloke right where I wanted him." She nodded over her shoulder. "Him, as well. I'm English, you see—"

"Ah, of course. That explains it."

"At my school they prepared us in self-defense. For a German invasion, don't you see? Then Mommy and Daddy sent me over here—"

"To work for Max Bauman?"

"Of course not. Don't be fatuous. I managed that more or less on my own." She shrugged. She looked down at the man she'd felled. "I don't suppose this could be a Nazi? No, too much to hope for . . ."

Max and Bennie came out onto the street, stood staring at them. "What exactly is going on here?"

"Miss Squires just returned the favor," Cassidy said. "Rescued me. Don't look at me, Max. It's a crazy old world." He laughed and his lip tore open again. "Shit."

"Cindy?" Max said.

"I couldn't let this numskull finish off your star player—"

"You two," Max said, starting to rumble with laughter, "have got to stop meeting this way." He punched an elbow into Bennie's midriff. Bennie offered a tolerant, pained smile, bow tie bobbing. "Howsa lip, Lew?"

"Fine. Only hurts when I laugh."

"That's good, Lewis. Only hurts when you laugh . . ." Max's shoulders shook with laughter. He put his arm around Cindy. "Nice work, baby."

Terry came back down the street from the direction of Fifth Avenue. Without a cab. He shrugged. "I saw it all, Max. She took the guy off like she was born to it."

Cassidy sat down on the wet curb realizing just how loaded he was. The whole crazy evening was landing on him like the Bears. When he stopped contemplating his undone equilibrium and looked around, he and Terry were alone with Cindy's victim. He'd missed everybody else's departure. He closed his eyes and saw Cindy watching him from behind the strands of bone-colored hair. *I don't suppose this could be a Nazi* . . . He smiled to himself. His lip came apart again. This girl, she was a new one on him. The hell with his lip. He laughed out loud.

The guy on the sidewalk wasn't moving. Once his feet in pointed black shoes twitched convulsively. "Terry, he looks dead or something."

"Do him good," Terry said. He prodded the limp bulk with his toe and the bulk groaned and said "Shit."

Terry pulled his foot back, kicked the middle of the bulk, and it jerked into a crescent shape. It sounded like it might be crying.

Terry got Cassidy home in a cab, drunk but peaceful. He laid him out on the bed like a stiff and Cassidy had a terrible dream about lying in the street all wet with a bunch of gangsters in a black Packard coming at him hell-bent and running over his hand. He woke up soaked with sweat, half convinced it had been a dream.

Jesus. What a night.

He was sober by then and the sky over Washington

Square was getting gray, wet and sad like an old winter coat you'd come to hate. Before he got back to sleep he thought some more about Karin and how it had been when the going was good. But when he closed his eyes, it wasn't Karin he saw. For the first time it wasn't Karin . . .

•   •   •

When the ball starts coming down, everything speeds up, like somebody pushed a button somewhere and you're in an old movie, running for your life with the Keystone Kops on your ass.

Cassidy kept his eye on it and for a moment the pressure of the hangover multiplied it, and there were two balls coming at him a couple of feet apart. If he muffed it, there was no Art Hannaford to cover it. Which one was the real ball?

He picked the one on the left.

It hit him like a cement breadbox, first in the hands, then slammed against his chest. It was 1:30 and the 'Dogs were being served to the New York Giants. Cassidy had the feeling they were going to put him on a roll and cover him with mustard. Fordham had never really prepared him for this. On the other hand, he wasn't in the army yet and it was a living.

It seemed like the harder he ran the slower he went. He was out of breath from the hangover and from the ball hitting him in the gut and he damn near dropped it at the fifteen. But even with a hangover he was Cassidy and that year Cassidy was the best there was . . .

Bodies were beginning to hurtle past and guys were screaming when he noticed at the corner of his vision something approaching a miracle. Danny Maidstone had just made his first block of the season. He lay on the grass with a moronic smile of surprise on his innocent mug. He'd opened a little corridor along the sidelines and that was all Cassidy needed. He cut to the right, sprinting for it, figured what the hell, so I'll have a heart attack and die

32

on the field, so what? He took off like a supercharged Buick. Fuck it, they could bury him under the goalpost.

He got past the thirty in one piece. He wondered if he was secretly hoping somebody would catch him. A ninety-five-yard kickoff return wasn't on the itinerary for the day. He'd need an oxygen tent by the time he passed midfield.

Their kicker was waiting for him at the fifty. Cassidy couldn't help himself. He was beginning to think touchdown. An opening kickoff touchdown—Jesus! He felt like laughing at the craziness of it—against the Giants! He stiff-armed the kicker and set off down the white sideline stripe, like a projectile being sucked into the crowd's roar.

Then Coogan's bluff collapsed on him.

Somebody had been chasing him from behind. Cassidy wondered what the hell had taken the guy so long—it must have been like chasing a one-legged guy with a crutch!

And suddenly King Kong was on his back. He was riding Cassidy across the sideline. Cassidy couldn't seem to avoid the long wooden bench where the Giants were politely standing aside to make way for him.

Then he was all twisted around on the ground spitting teeth and blood and that was the least of his problems.

His leg was pointing in the wrong goddamn direction. Very wrong.

CHAPTER TWO

There was a fuzzy halo of light over his head and every time he squinted it got brighter and hurt his eyes so he stopped squinting and shut his eyes altogether. He tried to check some of his other senses. He was sick to his stomach. That had to be from the ether. Weakly, he made a fist. So far so good. He tried to decipher the low murmur of voices but that was way beyond him.

When he woke up again, the light was still there, bright and fuzzy. Maybe it was God. He'd always sort of thought God was an old man with a long white beard and merry, forgiving eyes who was glad to see you at last now that you were done making a mess of your life. Like Santa Claus without the red suit and the reindeer. But maybe that was all wrong. He was no theologian. Maybe God was this bright light. Then, on the other hand, maybe it wasn't God at all. Maybe it was just a bright light. All the heavy thinking wore him out, so he went back to sleep.

Later on, a dark shape blotted out the light and someone was repeating his name. He thought he was answering but must not have been because his name kept swooping around above him.

"Jocko . . . hey, Jocko . . . you awake, Lew?"

"Shut up, I hear you, I hear you—"

Laughter. "He's coming around now."

"Feel like I'm gonna puke." Somebody pushed a cold metal basin up beside his face. He turned his head and threw up the ether and felt a little better. "It's all right," he said. "The white wine came up with the fish." He sank back, suddenly drenched in cold sweat. Then he faded out again.

When he woke up next, the shape was back, blotting out the light. He licked his lips. They were dry and cracked and his tongue felt like it needed scraping with a tire iron. He felt a hand on his arm. "You'll never tap-dance again, Fred."

"Frankly, Ginger, I don't give a damn."

It was Terry. Cassidy told him he was an old bastard and Terry tapped the cast on his leg and shook his head. Cassidy tried to look down at the cast but the effort started making him sick again so he stopped. Old Terry. Always there when needed. If it couldn't be Karin, then he wanted Terry. Terry could always take care of things. He was thinking about what a swell guy Terry was when he went back to sleep.

Later on (he had no idea what day it was), he heard two voices talking in his sleep.

Was it a dream? A kind of anesthetic-induced hallucination? They were talking about Terry, that was what he thought, talking about Terry and him, and the voices were vaguely familiar. The tones were low, muffled. Some of it was about Terry, some about him. He wanted to hear but it was hard and he couldn't seem to will his eyes open.

"Now they've done two operations on the leg, two in six hours—"

"Knee, it was his knee—"

"*Was* is right." Laughing.

"He's gonna be out for a while, damn it."

"So whassa big deal?"

"Hadda wait till Leary was on duty, he's been hangin' around here all the off-duty time—"

"I get it."

"Couldn't have Terry hangin' around, could I?"

"You think he'll go along with it?"

"He's gotta, if he knows what's good for him. They're pals . . ."

"Cassidy's pretty hot shit these days—"

"Not after this he ain't. We don't like the way he acts, we do his other knee. He'll come around. Nobody's hot enough shit for this. All these guys, Leary, Cassidy, they—"

"I know. They all think they're hot shit." More sour laughter.

"Gotta talk to Cassidy 'fore Leary gets to him, 'fore old Terry gets it figured out—"

"You think he knows?"

"Smart sumbitch, who the hell knows?"

It had to be some kind of dream. He tried to force it to make sense and he found himself back at Keen's Chop House. *Listen, pal, I may be needing your help one day soon* . . . Terry was at the top of somebody's list. But whose list? And who were the two guys talking in his sleep? He hoped it was a dream.

Two operations? *Was* his knee?

What the hell was going on?

• • •

Most of the times he woke up, Terry was there.

Sometimes the radio was on, very softly, and he remembered hearing a snatch of Nat Cole singing "If I Didn't Care" and some band music, Tommy Dorsey from the Terrace Room at the Hotel New Yorker. He'd hear Helen O'Connell or Marion Hutton singing and he'd figure he had a broken leg, like Hannaford, and he'd be done for the season but the season was just about over anyway and he'd be okay. So he'd close his eyes and his mind would wander but for some reason it always came back to Terry.

So Terry was on somebody's shit list, right at the top. Somebody was after him. Who? But, then, hell, somebody

had always been after Terry. Like that time with Tony
Morante . . .

While Cassidy had been running up and down the
gridiron at Fordham, Terry was the student manager of
the team. There was another kid who ran the milk bottles
full of water out to the guys during time-outs. Terry sure
as hell wasn't going to do that kind of shitwork. He was
more the executive manager, kept the statistics, did jobs
for the coaches, made sure the uniforms got laundered and
the balls were all put back in the big canvas bags after
practice. Opposites attracted: Cassidy was serious, took
the game seriously, hated to lose for dear old Fordham,
while Terry figured that in the light of eternity it really
didn't make a hell of a lot of difference one way or the
other. Funny thing was, they hit it off right away. Terry
was such an easy guy to get along with, had that gift for
tuning in to your personality as if it were a station on the
radio he knew mighty well. He never seemed to make hard
work of anything. It came easy for Terry.

Terry was invariably happy-go-lucky, taking risks for
the sweet, simple hell of it. He got a kick out of dancing at
the edge of the abyss. It wasn't that he was unafraid. That
would have made his whole style meaningless. Terry just
figured he could beat it while Cassidy, the athlete, always
knew there was the danger of the bad bounce, the missed
tackle, the mistake that would wind up costing you the
game. Terry had that spooky kind of innocence that scared
Cassidy, yet drew him into its orbit. Terry figured he could
beat it all, beat the fear, beat the game, beat the odds.

Cassidy played great football, was All-East his last two
seasons, was eighth in the class of '34, but he learned how
to raise hell from Terry Leary. Paul Cassidy had given him
an Auburn roadster in celebration of some movie deal that
had paid off and the car seemed to spur them on to new
exploits, further afield.

Like the time they dated the two Italian sisters from the
convent school in Providence. The four of them were
making out on the living room davenport at home when a
brother got home pretty well gone on bathtub hooch. He

didn't like it much when he got a gander at two guys he'd never seen before enjoying four of the Morante family's cute little tits.

A frantic scramble ensued. Terry's pants were at half-mast, and at first glance he didn't seem exactly ready for a fight. Lots of shrieks and buttons flying off and the two of them hopping around pulling trousers up and the girls clutching blouses and wriggling skirts down. Tony Morante had not returned alone. Four inebriated Italians undertook at once to defend the girls' honor. Cassidy was trying to crawl to the door, having had a lamp bent over his head, when he got a kick in the nuts. Things looked black. Cassidy was mourning his chances of ever fathering any children when Terry figured out a way to beat the odds.

He set the place on fire.

Lighter fluid on the davenport, a flick of the Ronson, and everybody stopped kicking Cassidy and began coughing and choking and beating on the flaring cushions.

Cassidy got up and, as a grace note, clipped Tony Morante on the jaw with a straight, pistonlike right which dropped Tony where he stood and scraped most of the skin from Cassidy's knuckles.

"Time to go," Terry said, leading an orderly retreat down the narrow staircase.

From the street they saw the orange flames flickering at the window.

"I think it's under control, don't you?" Terry saw a café a block away. It was snowing. The wind was cold and damp and driving off the ocean, the way it's supposed to be in Providence in January. They leaned into it and went to the café. The windows were steamed over.

"Terry?"

"Yes, my son?"

"Your fly's open."

They went inside and Terry ordered coffee and pie for both of them. Cassidy called the fire department.

When they were headed back down the street in the

Auburn, the fire truck had already clanged to the scene. The flames were out. The smoldering davenport seemed to be lodged halfway out the window.

• • •

When Terry decided to become a cop—this was after he'd quite possibly gotten a Broadway chorus girl pregnant and had to come up with five hundred bucks to fix it, all the time avoiding her producer boyfriend who had let it be known there was a grand in it for the guy who brought him "the balls of the son of a bitch who took advantage of Rita's warm and loving nature"—Cassidy just didn't get it. Terry the Cop seemed like a crazy idea until he sat Cassidy down and told him how the cops and the guys they chased were just alike. Well, almost.

But the odds were with the cops. The thing was, a lot of guys could go either way, be good cops or good crooks, and he knew how crooks thought. Which would make him a damn fine cop if only he could make a living out of it. The odds said that was the stickler, that you couldn't make it pay, but Terry figured those were just odds. No problem.

His uncle Paddy—the priest, not the Jersey City hooch runner—told him that being an Irish cop in New York could be a good life. Whatever that meant. Terry said he figured Paddy meant it had all the advantages of the Church but you could fuck around all you wanted to.

In those days the New York Police Department was very Irish, very Catholic, and it seemed like most of the gents at the top of the heap had initials like F. X. One Francis Xavier after another. The occasional clicking of beads was heard in the corridors of power as well as in the cells and the sweaty interrogation rooms. Father Paddy did some helpful lobbying and Terry was off the beat and into a detective's plainclothes in record time.

It was the job God had made him for, though Father Paddy had a more colorful way of putting it. He said Terry was happy as a pig in shit. Terry knew all the gangsters and gunsels. He hung around the clubs and knew the fancy women who woke up late in fancy apartments and lived mainly at night in silky dresses that draped like naughty ideas between their nipples. If that was Father Paddy's idea of shit, he hadn't thought the thing through.

So Terry knew all the Damon Runyon characters and they knew him. They understood the job he had to do and asked only that he extend them the same courtesy. Live and let live. Terry got the picture. He was a fast learner and he wasn't out to eradicate crime in his bailiwick. He just wanted to keep it under some semblance of control. It was all true, what he'd told Cassidy. There was only a nickel's worth of difference between the good guys and the bad.

Funny thing, the way Cassidy got to know more gangsters than cops from hanging around with Terry. He even made some money betting the football games, as well as the ponies and the fights, because Terry always knew when the fix was in.

Gangsters and cops, a stroll along the knife edge . . . and now somebody was after Terry again, somebody had him on their list . . . and Cassidy heard in his mind those two voices behind the curtain of ether. What the hell had it meant? Why had they seemed so threatening, so dangerous . . .

He woke up in the middle of the night, the door to his room halfway open. Every so often a nurse padded by on squeaky rubber soles. He took a sip of water, tapped the glass against the cast. Damn thing came all the way up, ankle to asshole.

He lay quietly, listening to Terry snore, sound asleep in the chair by the window. The snoring was nice and steady like the surf in the Hamptons in the summer. That was when he got to thinking about the guys watching Terry . . .

It was the night they went to see the Joe Louis fight at the Polo Grounds in October, a couple months before. Sixty thousand people on a cold fall night. He closed his eyes and it all came back to him, the roar of the crowd filling his mind the way Terry's snoring filled the hospital room.

Lou Nova was glistening under the ring lights, shuffling his feet in the corner while they laced up his gloves. Chewing his mouthpiece. He was slick and shiny with sweat, his skin pale, almost translucent, the muscles rippling. Waiting for the bell.

Everybody was there and between Cassidy and Terry it seemed they knew them all. They were sitting in the five-hundred-dollar seats and the two famous broadcasters Graham McNamee and Ted Husing were kidding Cassidy about some collegiate exploit he only half remembered himself when the ring announcer was suddenly introducing him. A lot of sporting types were trotted across the squared circle. Cassidy was up the rickety wooden steps, climbing between the ropes. "And here's the hard-driving tailback of the Bulldogs . . . the touchdown-scoring machine . . . you all remember him from his days at Fordham . . . Llleww Casss-ssidy!" There was a burst of noise, Cassidy turning and waving in the bright lights, going to each corner to wish the fighters well. Louis was looking at Nova and Nova seemed to be in a trance and Cassidy climbed down out of the ring while the jockey who had won the last Kentucky Derby was climbing up for his introduction.

They were a threesome that night: Cassidy, Terry, and a character called Marquardt Cookson, only slightly larger than Kate Smith. He must have come in at about three fifty. He was wearing roughly two hectares of blue serge and snappy gray gloves. He had little pointed feet, the kind of guy who could show them a new move or two at Roseland despite his size. Actually there was a fourth. Cookson had a little guy with him, cute as a bug in a rug, with peroxided hair, who kept handing him things. Cigarettes, a gold lighter, hot dogs, hankies to mop his streaming face. Whatever his name was, the pretty boy had a lot to do and all of it very important to Marquardt Cookson. The whole thing reminded Cassidy of the Sylvester Aubrey Bean affair and the witch-hunt for homos Terry avoided by playing down the sensational aspects of the case. Markie Cookson had been very relieved and very grateful for Terry's discretion and the fight tickets were probably just one more installment of his appreciation. Markie was said to have some drug connections. Maybe that was why the peroxided number's eyes looked funny and Markie sweat so much.

Paul Cassidy sat several rows behind his son with Max Bauman and Cindy Squires. They were flanked by Bennie the Brute, a couple of lawyers, and two other guys who were moving slowly with the weight of all the hardware they were packing. In those days the crowd at a championship fight could probably have held off the Wehrmacht. Paul Cassidy was going to Chicago the next day to testify in the Willie Bioff trial. Movie business skulduggery. Max Bauman was talking to Paul about backing a series of pictures. The guns were there because some of Bioff's hoods had gotten the word to Paul that if he went to the Windy City to testify he'd wind up in a Chicago River bridge piling. Consequently Max was sending a couple of heavyweights to keep Paul company on the train and discourage Willie's boys. Lew had heard the story the night before at Jake & Charlie's but it was all confusing, hard to keep straight when there were so many tough guys around, and he had to play the Green Bay Packers on Sunday.

It was a particularly big fight, even by the Champ's standards. Louis's draft board back in Chicago had classified him 1-A and everybody figured this would be his last fight. In May he'd struggled with Buddy Baer down in Washington but had finally felled the big ox in the sixth. Then a month later he'd gotten the scare of his life from a twenty-three-year-old kid from Pittsburgh called Conn who'd given him a boxing lesson for twelve rounds. Billy Conn was three rounds away from the world's championship when he decided to punch it out with Joe. He didn't make it through the thirteenth. And now Cassidy had five hundred bucks that said Nova would last at least five.

It was getting colder by the minute but Cookson sweat

anyway. Terry was jumpy, kept checking the crowd when he'd normally have been looking at the fighters the way he'd check out the nags up at Saratoga or the chorines on Broadway. After an uneventful second round Cassidy asked him what was eating him, anyway.

"Nothing, pal, nothing at all. Three more rounds, baby, just three more rounds." Then Cookson was tugging at his sleeve and giggling like a man who'd just done a job in his pants. He was talking to Harry Madrid, who never missed a fight, and Harry was gesturing with his right hand, telling him what Nova should have been doing. Markie was listening but the expression on his face said he was on his way to the moon. The cute blond guy handed him the hankie and Cookson wiped his face. He looked like he was thinking about patting Harry Madrid's face. That would have been something to write home about.

Cassidy shivered and watched Nova move around, jab a little, slip away, take Louis's shots on his forearms. He got through the third and nobody was breathing hard but Marquardt Cookson. The fourth went by, a stately minuet.

"Just so he doesn't do a Conn," Cassidy said.

"They're watching me, pal," Terry said, grinning. Cassidy's head snapped over. "Yeah, no shit. They watch me all the time." Terry grinned some more. "It's a compliment, hey? Ah, the hell with it. Come on, Lou baby, one more round!"

"Who's watching you all the time?"

"Somebody watching you, Terence?" Cookson inquired. He sneezed.

"Forget it, Markie. I was pulling Lew's leg. Everything's fine, just fine. Nothing to worry about. Don't get in a sweat, Markie."

"Good advice but much too late," Cassidy murmured, and Terry laughed.

Lou Nova was not only a pretty fair fighter. He practiced yoga, it was in all the papers. He had a kind of serenity and it saw him through the fifth. Cassidy could have kissed the guy.

"So Joe carried him for five," Terry said. "He made your

bet for you, pal. Now watch what happens." He winked like he knew something Cassidy didn't.

Nova came out in the sixth and tried to nail the champ with a right hook.

Cassidy at ringside heard the staccato voice of Clem McCarthy calling the fight into his mike and to a waiting world.

Louis is punching—
With all the speed and power of a Buick—
And he's down! Nova is down in the center of the ring!
And it's over! It's all over in the sixth
At the Polo Grounds!

It all came with a lethal suddenness, like getting hit by a tackle so hard you didn't really feel it. You just lay there. Feeling no pain. Nova just lay there and it was like he'd begun an unscheduled trance. It was Joe Louis and everybody had gotten used to the Brown Bomber's Special Trance. And Cassidy noticed the front of his formal shirt and the white carnation in the lapel of his tux were spattered with Lou Nova's blood.

But the thing that stuck in Cassidy's mind a couple months later wasn't Louis clubbing Nova to the canvas. And it wasn't the five hundred and it wasn't the blood on his shirt. It was Terry Leary's face, the anxious shine in his eyes, the new pencil-thin moustache that gave him the rakish movie star look, and something he'd never heard in Terry's voice before.

They're watching me, pal . . . They watch me all the time . . .

He lay in the hospital bed, leg aching, remembering what he'd never heard in Terry voice until that night.

Fear.

The night Joe Louis knocked out Lou Nova in the sixth at the Polo Grounds, Terry Leary was scared of something and he knew they were watching him.

•　　•　　•

Cassidy came all the way out of the fog on Monday. The sun was bright and it looked wintry outside, scrawny bare branches and little brown birds at the windows looking like they wanted to come in. The sheets were crisp and white and his mouth tasted like his jersey had smelled the day before.

Terry's chair was empty but his camel's-hair coat was thrown over another chair. His cigar lay dead in the ashtray. Cassidy heard him laughing with a nurse in the hallway and then he came in carrying the *New York Times*. His chocolate-colored gabardine slacks had a crease like a Gillette Blue Blade. He was wearing brown and white wing tips. The heels clicked loudly. Cassidy tried to focus on the big headlines but his eyes weren't quite right yet. He was thinking about the sports page.

"Hey, he lives! You want Nursie to bring you the bedpan? I'd hate to miss that—so how you feeling, you lucky son of a gun?"

"Some luck."

"Doc says you'll maybe have a limp for the rest of your life," Terry said cheerily. He was grinning and what he said didn't really sink in.

"Did we win?"

"I don't know but I'd be pretty damned surprised. I went down to the locker room when you went to sleep under the Giants' bench. Then came right on to the hospital with you. Then I had to go to work fighting crime for a while." He leafed through the paper. "56–14, you lost. Picture of you here being carried off on the stretcher. Not much of a likeness. There's blood all over your face. Anyway, your football days are over, Jocko. And let me tell you, nobody gives a shit about your game, not now. Sunday turned out to be quite a day."

"Terry, I don't know what the hell you're talking—"

"You got a million-dollar leg, you won't have to fight."

"Fight who?" None of it was making any sense.

He shrugged. "The Japs, the Germans, you won't have to fight any of 'em."

"Terry, Terry, make sense."

45

"Okay. Yesterday the Japs blew the shit out of Pearl Harbor—that's somewhere in Hawaii. Just about the time the Giants tried to break your leg off. There's a war on, Lew, and we're in it. You're out of it . . . and FDR is making a speech about it today." He lit a big Havana, one of Max Bauman's. It smelled wonderful. "You're out of it," he repeated. "Now we gotta get me out of it."

Cassidy was trying to make sense of everything. Mainly he kept thinking about 56–14. Jesus. Worse than he'd thought. Now this Pearl Harbor thing, what the hell was that all about?

There were flowers on the table. Terry pointed at each vase as he spoke. "Roses are from Max and that blond slugger of his, Cindy Squires. The mums are from Bennie the Brute. The guy's got a soft spot for you, Lew. I think he'd sincerely regret having to rub you out. And this lavish display of cut flowers is from the Mara family on behalf of the Giants." He slipped into his polo coat and snapped the brim of his dark brown hat. "I gotta run. I'll come back tonight after I catch all the bad guys." He flipped the newspaper onto the bed. "Read it and weep, Jocko."

When he was alone, Cassidy looked at the front page.

**JAPAN WARS ON U.S. AND BRITAIN:
MAKES SUDDEN ATTACK ON HAWAII:
HEAVY FIGHTING AT SEA REPORTED**

Then it hit him. While he'd been on the field warming up, at 1:05, the Japanese bombers had come out of the morning sun. 7:35 in Hawaii. And the Japanese army had landed on the east coat of Malaya, bombed Singapore, and marched into Thailand.

Roosevelt was going to address Congress a little after noon. It was going to be on the radio.

In Washington a crowd of more than a thousand had quietly gathered at the Japanese embassy and watched the staff make a bonfire of all its files and records. On West 93rd in New York the police had closed the Nippon Club.

There was a reprint of the editorial from the *Los Angeles*

Times. "Japan has asked for it. Now she is going to get it. It was the act of a mad dog, a gangster's parody of every principle of international honor."

Take that, you bastards! He found a little story from Berlin. The German High Command announced that they guessed they weren't going to make it to Moscow in 1941 after all.

He put in a call to Paul. He had just gotten up in Los Angeles. They talked about the war and Lew forgot to tell his father about the leg. "We're going to be at war with Germany, too, son," Paul Cassidy said. "Now what that means about Karin we'll have to see."

"I know, Dad, I know."

"I won't tell you not to worry."

"I've been worried for so long—nothing's happened to change that."

"We'll try to find out what's going on with American citizens over there. Maybe there'll be a repatriation deal."

"Look, they'll just say she's a German . . . they'll say she chooses to stay with her father. You know that as well as I do. Hell, maybe it's true—anyway, we're going to be at war with Germany right away. She's in their hands unless she can escape."

"Well, I wouldn't count on that unless life is a Jack Warner picture."

"I'm not counting on much of anything. Look, Dad, I'll call you tonight after we know what Roosevelt said. We'll have a better idea of what's going on."

"Okay, sonny. You all right?"

Cassidy laughed. "Sure, sure, I'm fine."

"Best to Terry," Paul Cassidy said, and hung up.

He'd just gotten to the sports page when he heard the most unmistakably familiar voice of his lifetime.

"Mr. Vice President, Mr. Speaker, members of the Senate and the House of Representatives.

"Yesterday, December 7, 1941—a date which will live in infamy—the United States of America was suddenly and deliberately attacked by naval and air forces of the Empire of Japan . . ."

47

The sportswriter said the final score of the game might well have been different had "the Bulldogs" scoring machine Lew Cassidy been at his customary tailback slot but the unfortunate Cassidy was injured on the opening fifty-yard kickoff return and did not return to the game. The winner, however, would never have been in doubt as the Giants unleashed a furious scoring onslaught of their own," blah, blah, blah. 56–14. Good God!

"Last night the Japanese forces attacked Hong Kong.

"Last night the Japanese forces attacked Guam.

"Last night the Japanese forces attacked the Philippine Islands.

"Last night the Japanese forces attacked Wake Island.

"And this morning the Japanese attacked Midway Island . . .

"No matter how long it may take to overcome this premeditated invasion, the American people, in their righteous might, will win through to absolute victory . . .

"I ask that the Congress declare that since the unprovoked and dastardly attack by Japan on Sunday, December 7, 1941, a state of war has existed between the United States and the Japanese Empire."

It wasn't a long speech but the man with the braces on his legs made his point.

Cassidy was sitting there in his hospital bed with his own leg throbbing, his brain still not quite up to par, shorting out, snapping, crackling, *Karin, Karin, Karin,* when there was a knock on the door.

"Are you decent, Mr. Cassidy?"

He didn't recognize the voice. "As decent as I can get," he said.

The door swung open and Cindy Squires was looking at him. She didn't look exactly friendly: There was the same quality she projected when she sang, a kind of distance between herself and the rest of the world, as if she were perpetually in two places at once and the other place was a little more important. Or maybe it was the special kind of arrogance that comes from having been hurt badly and survived. "Hi," she said, making a tiny waving gesture with one hand. She was wearing the fur coat and pearl-gray slacks and a gray turtleneck sweater. "Do you remember me? Or do you think I've got the wrong room?"

"I remember you. You're hard to forget. Beat hell out of anybody lately?"

"I retired undefeated, Mr. Cassidy." Her voice was still low and kind of hoarse. "Golly, that's quite a cast." She stared at the leg encased in white plaster. She came close and tapped it with her red fingernails, smiled slowly at the hollow sound. "How do you feel?"

"About like I look, I guess."

A playful smile crossed her solemn face. "I didn't save you from that thug just to have you get torn to shreds the next day. When I saw you go down and then they carried you away on a litter . . . it seemed to me I had a bit of a personal interest. Now I want to see how badly the goods were damaged." She gave him a teasing, appraising look.

"I'll never tango again. Those quick turns . . ." He shrugged helplessly.

"You will learn to live without the tango."

"Never. Tango is my life!"

"The injury has affected your brain. You've never tangoed in your life."

"So? Now I never will. It's the kind of news that hits a guy pretty hard. But you're making it easier to take. If you could drop by every day, who knows? A miracle recovery, anything's possible."

"You're a flirt, Mr. Cassidy. I thought that was Terry's department."

"It is, it is. I'm only a fallen warrior, carted away on his shield, looking for a little sympathy."

"Flirt."

"Come back," he said. "Visit me again. Your reward will come in heaven." Suddenly he felt like there was nothing more important than seeing her again. There hadn't been any woman since Karin, none he'd given a second thought. But the Battling Blonde—it sounded like one of his father's pictures—was a horse of another color. He simply wanted to watch her, hear her voice. "You could

49

treat it like volunteer work, Miss Squires. A good deed. You could read to me . . ."

"Mmmm," she nodded. She glanced quickly at the door behind her. There was something childlike about her eyes. Quick, darting, as if she were afraid she might be caught doing something forbidden. He wondered how old she was? Twenty? Twenty-five? He couldn't tell. Her eyes were immense beneath eyebrows that were straight, then dropped sharply down at the outside edges, fitting congruently with the bone structure. "Max is coming," she said, backing away from the cast. "He stopped to talk to some doctor he knows. That was awful yesterday . . ."

"Apparently they attacked without any warning, caught us on a sleepy Sunday morning—"

"No, no, I meant watching what happened to you . . ." She shrugged, pearls swaying across the turtleneck, beneath the mink. "Max was so upset . . . you got the flowers—"

"Very thoughtful of you."

"Oh, that was Max's idea. And Bennie, of course. He's so fond of you. I never remember to send flowers . . . Look, Terry says you're trustworthy. Is he right about that?"

"I don't know." He wasn't getting the point. She seemed to have something on her mind but she couldn't quite get it out. She looked back at the door and Max came in.

"Lew," he said, standing there shaking his head. "Lew, what a shame! A hell of a thing. Cindy. Look at this man's leg. You're going to have a limp, you know that. No more football. You know that?"

"We'll see. Thanks for the flowers, Max."

"Cindy's idea. That's the way she is, reminds me of things."

She was looking out the window. She might have blushed at Max's compliment but Cassidy couldn't tell. She turned away and went back to Max, hooked her arm through his. Her profile was all straight lines. She reminded him of Karin for a moment and he didn't want her to. Watching her made him nervous.

"We'll take care of you, Lew. You know what I mean?"

"I appreciate that, Max. But I'll be all right."

"That's what I'm saying, you'll be all right. First, we'll have to get you up and walking, then we'll see."

"I'll be fine. Everything's going to be fine, Max."

"You hear this guy, Cindy?"

"I hear him, Max."

"Take a good look at him. He's one of the great ones, give him the ball, he does the job. A real pro."

"Max," Cassidy said, "for Christ's sake. You sound like I'm dead."

"I'll have Bennie stop in every day, see to your needs. You name it, Bennie'll get it." Max started shaking his head again, looking at the cast.

"Just give in," Cindy said solemnly. "Max is going to have it his own way so don't fight it."

"You're a swell guy, Max."

"I'm only being fair, Lew. You gave it all you had. I like that. You're a gentleman and—"

"A scholar, right, Max?" She pulled at his arm. "Come on, Max, you're embarrassing Mr. Cassidy. He gets your drift, so to speak."

Max nodded. Cassidy tried to catch Cindy Squires's eye but couldn't. Pretty soon they left and Cassidy felt unaccountably exhausted. There had been way too much tension in the room and he wondered where it had come from. But he didn't wonder long. The fact was, he'd produced it himself. He hadn't been able to take his eyes off her. Once she was gone he could still see her blond hair falling across the collar of the mink. He could still hear her husky voice. *Terry says you're trustworthy. Is he right about that?* What the hell kind of question was that?

He didn't want to keep thinking about her. He literally couldn't recall the last time he'd thought about any woman but Karin. He didn't want to start thinking about Cindy Squires because . . . because it would be a rotten idea. But he wondered if she'd come back to visit him. Hell, Bennie every day. Wonderful.

Terry. He wanted to talk to Terry. He could talk to Terry about Karin. Her memory would come alive and he wouldn't think about Cindy Squires anymore. That was the ticket. He wanted to find out who was after Terry and why and how close were they . . .

But Terry didn't come back that night.

Somebody shot him.

CHAPTER THREE

It was a little past ten that night when his nurse, Sylvia of the Bedpans, came tiptoeing in with sleeping pills on a little tray and told him that his friend, Detective Leary, had just been delivered to the emergency room in a meat wagon.

"There was quite a lot of blood," she whispered, pouring a glass of water, "but I heard him talking. He was alive is what I mean to say. He'd been shot . . . he's an officer of the law, I guess things happen sometimes, but it seems a shame. He's in surgery now. I thought you'd want to know, Mr. Cassidy."

"Is he going to be all right? You can't just leave me hanging."

"Detective Leary is just hanging, Mr. Cassidy," she said with the customary officiousness of nurses. "I can't very well tell you what I don't know, can I? He went into surgery about fifteen minutes ago. Now take your pills."

"Will you find out what you can?" The news had hit him like a tackler's helmet driving into his belly. Terry with a bullet in him . . . There was a red rage of frustration building behind his eyes. Frustration about Karin, about the goddamn war, about the stupid mess he'd made of his leg, and now about old Terry dripping blood with a slug in him . . . If anything happened to Terry, he'd find a way to do something about it. Maybe he couldn't get to Germany and pry Karin away from the Nazis, but this was New York. Cassidy knew New York and he could find the rat that put a slug in Terry . . .

"Of course," she said primly. "I'll come back later."

He was groggy from the pills and his leg felt like Dumbo had been dancing on it when she came back at one o'clock. She shook his shoulder. "He just came out of surgery. He's not dead yet." She had a certain turn of phrase about her. "They got one of the bullets out of his lung. I understand there's a second near his spine but they're going to see if he makes it through the night. They didn't want to keep him under any longer. He lost so much blood . . ."

Cassidy wanted to stay awake but the pills were winning the battle. His mind was wandering. How much blood could you lose and make it anyway . . . *Listen, pal, I may be needing your help one day soon* . . . But he hadn't been there when Terry needed him. He'd let Terry down. He yawned reflexively, his fading vision turning the street lamp outside into a blur, a melting snowball of light at the window. Terry had always been there when Cassidy needed him . . . Shit. *Maybe it's a joke . . . a false alarm.* Well, it hadn't been a joke. Not with Terry shot up, a slug in his lung and another one they didn't dig out.

The two voices he'd heard from under the anesthetic floated in and out of his sagging consciousness. *Hadda wait till Leary was on duty, he's been hangin' around here all the off-duty time . . . Couldn't have Terry hangin' around . . . Gotta talk to Cassidy 'fore Leary gets to him, 'fore old Terry gets it figured out . . .*

Whoever had been after Terry sure as hell had gotten him.

•　　•　　•

The next day two detectives came by the hospital and told Cassidy what they knew about the shooting of Terry Leary. Cassidy had met Harry Madrid somewhere in the past with Terry. Bert Reagan was a stranger who said he was a football fan and it was a crying shame about the leg. Madrid said the Leary thing was all coming together because of the other guy. A punk called Mark Herrin.

"Terry's a pretty good shot, y'know, Cassidy? Puts in his time at the range." Harry Madrid wore a slate-gray double-breasted suit and brown shoes, cheap clothes that went with the cheap zircon ring that left a greenish smudge on his finger. He'd been a cop twenty-five years. He was pushing fifty. His salary was about as high as a detective's could get but he was still pushing fifty and his brown shoes weren't quite the latest thing. "Well, this Herrin character was waiting for Terry at 72nd and Park. Block from Terry's place. Terry came home, put his car in the garage underneath, shot the breeze with the attendant for a couple minutes, walked up the driveway to the street. Why he didn't take the elevator from the garage—who knows?" Harry Madrid pronounced it *garridge*. "So he's walking down 72nd toward Park, it's a nice night, he stops to light one of them stogies he smokes, decides to take a stroll. Why a stroll? Don't ask me, people do things."

"Human nature," Bert Reagan said. He was leaning against the wall, hat in hand, chewing a toothpick while his head made a grease spot on the wall. "You never know." He laughed softly. "He doesn't take a walk, he lives forever."

"But he takes this walk," Harry Madrid said, "and a little fairy shoots him. Fate, Cassidy. Bert's right. You never know what's out there waiting for you."

Harry Madrid shook his head, dug a Kaywoodie out of his pocket, and packed it with tobacco. He lit a match on his thumbnail like tough old guys in the movies. He puffed the pipe. It smelled like cherry cough syrup. It made Cassidy gag. Harry sat down, crossed his ankle on his knee. He wore high-topped brown shoes that laced up to his ankles. Then there was a band of pale leg and the gray

BVD longjohns began. Terry once told the story of how he saw Harry Madrid break a hophead's arm like snapping an Eberhard Faber No. 2. Harry took a couple of puffs, probed a huge finger into an ear bristling with gray hair.

"Fate," he said again. "It's enough to turn a man all philosophical. Terry's standing there at the corner, workin' on his stogie, and all of a sudden this little fairy prances out from behind a mailbox and starts blazing away." Puff, puff. "He hits Terry once from in front, then as Terry turns away he hits him again in the back. Terry goes down like a side of beef and our Mr. Herrin goes over to the gutter, looks down at Terry, biggest mistake of his crummy little life." He smiled reflectively, sucking the pipe.

"What happened?"

"Hell, he's lookin' down at Terry in the gutter there, gonna pump another slug or two into him. Imagine his surprise when the guy in the gutter raises up on his elbow and shoots him. Shit, I wish I'd seen that, old Terry bleedin' all over his million-dollar overcoat, two-thirds dead already, he squeezes off a bull's-eye . . . blew most of this asshole's face all over the windshield of a passing Lincoln, wham, bang, dead meat." He sighed contentedly, puffing.

"So how's Terry?"

"You know hospitals and doctors. All we hear is, he's still alive but nobody's takin' bets one way or the other. They want to go after that second slug but it's right up there against his spine and they'd just as soon not leave him paralyzed. Hell of a thing, ain't it?" He tapped Cassidy's cast with the stem of his pipe. "You two, quite a pair." He chuckled like a man who'd never found anything but death and dire straits really amusing.

"You can say that again," Bert Reagan said, still busy holding up the wall. "Cassidy and Leary, two peas in a pod." He laughed a thin, high laugh that didn't go with his build. He and Madrid made you think of a couple of trained elephants, all gray, big feet. "Quite a pair."

It struck Cassidy that he'd heard them talking before. The same two voices, the same thin laugh.

56

Couldn't have Terry hangin' around, could I?

You think he'll go along with it?

He's gotta, if he knows what's good for him. They're pals . . .

Two peas in a pod.

Damn. Cassidy looked from one to the other, the two big men grinning down at him. All bad breath and gaudy tobacco and greasy hair. A couple of cops who had been talking in his sleep. He grinned back, waiting for them to make their play, but what was the hurry? Maybe Terry wouldn't make it . . . No hurry, they seemed to say. We can wait.

But why the hell would the cops be after Terry?

It didn't add up. But then, nothing much had since the kickoff on Sunday. Forty-eight hours ago.

•   •   •

The gunning down of Detective Terry Leary went back to—and was doubtless the last act of—the Sylvester Aubrey Bean drama.

Mark Herrin, it turned out, held Terry Leary responsible for the whole sad mess. He didn't subscribe to the view that the homosexual community owed Terry any thanks for keeping the lid on. It was a complicated story but Harry Madrid, sometimes alone and other times with Bert Reagan, kept dropping in on Cassidy that week, filling in the details. Harry Madrid never brought up whatever he and Reagan had been talking about while he'd been floating around under the last of the anesthetic, but Cassidy knew it was only a matter of time until Harry came back to it.

The Bean thing had been pretty ugly, the kind of story people would have had a field day with had it all come out. Sylvester Aubrey Bean was one of the perfect aesthetes of the twenties, all silk scarves and velvet smoking jackets and brocade dressing gowns and ornate furniture and purple draperies and an art collection and more mascara than you could wink an eye at. He had aged gracefully, turning from a Beardsley drawing into a middle-aged Queen who trailed a little cloud of dusting powder, untouched by the Depression. The Bean money was very old. His family tree had been planted by the Dutchmen who settled New York back when it was New Amsterdam.

There were always rumors about Bean and his circle but most folks snickered behind their opera gloves, tolerated him as a naughty boy, a dear, dear eccentric. When it came to Bean stories, there were plenty to satisfy any taste. There were always the standard drug orgy stories spiced with a hint of necrophilia. And the inevitable satanic ritual and Black Mass tales. Sadism, whips and chains, bondage masks, sexual tortures. The works. But in the end Bean paid his taxes and contributed to all the right charities and museums and the opera and always enjoyed dressing up in his top hat, white tie, and tails for a good cause. His catamites seemed to be having a good time and didn't show any scars from rough treatment. Terry always contended that Bean and his ilk were necessary to New York. "Local color," he'd say. "Without the nut cases like Bean this city's nothing but an overgrown Dubuque."

Then one day it all came to what some figured was the inevitable conclusion. At least for Bean. One day, as the poet said, the kissing had to stop.

It all began to unravel when Bean didn't show up for a fancy dress ball down in the Village. His friends missed him right away because he'd told them he was coming as Marie Antoinette. For a while they just missed him and then they cut out the bitchy repartee and began worrying about him. But mainly it was his mother and father. They came down from their castle on the Hudson and had their driver use a crowbar to break into their son's Fifth Avenue penthouse. His father, a red-faced coupon clipper and pillar of the Methodist community, took one look and had a stroke on the spot. He went into a coma and died a week later. As it happened, he had managed to outlive his son by a full ten days. Sylvester's mother was made of sterner stuff but the scene before them didn't do her any good either.

No wonder old Hiram Bean's pump went haywire.

Sylvester Aubrey Bean lay naked on the parquet floor of his game room, his Marie Antoinette costume flung across a chairback. Beyond the windows a heat haze hung over the treetops of Central Park. The room was stifling. Sylvester Aubrey Bean had puffed up and burst. The carcass lay faceup, blackened and alive with bacteria and maggots. It lay at the center of a pentangle drawn in his own blood. At least one Satanic drug ritual hadn't been a rumor. His hands and feet had been fixed to the floor with spikes. The sledgehammer lay nearby.

Half the cops who arrived on the scene promptly added to the mess by throwing up.

Not Terry Leary, though, and not Harry Madrid. Harry looked around and fanned the air in front of his nose. "Ripe," he said, regarding the remains. "Let's call Ellery Queen."

Terry was in charge of the investigation. He set the tone and Harry Madrid did what he was told. They went about their business with dispatch. Terry made sure the details of the case were kept under wraps and far from the reporters, who were drawn like flies to the murder of such a bizarre figure. Harry Madrid wasn't shy about letting Terry know he didn't go for hushing things up to smooth the way for a bunch of queers and Terry told him he surely was entitled to his own opinion so long as he did it Terry's way. Harry Madrid had been around for a long time. He knew how things worked and he knew when to bide his time.

Terry's way worked out just fine. They pinned the murder on Sylvester Aubrey Bean's valet-*cum*-lover, a stooge by the name of Derek Boyce, who made it a lot easier by having for years proclaimed himself a witch. It didn't hurt matters that he'd once been a high school teacher dismissed for casually grabbing the football captain's dick in the locker room. Half the team had seen him do it and Boyce said he just didn't know what had come over him. Derek Boyce's prints were all over the sledgehammer. After two days of what the papers called "intensive interrogation" conducted by Harry Madrid and Bert Reagan, Derek Boyce had been reduced to one very worn-out witch. They said he confessed. All that mattered was that he signed the confession and there didn't have to be a trial to drag it all out.

Terry kept on top of it, kept the lid in place, and Harry Madrid told Bert Reagan you had to hand it to the son of a bitch. When Terry shut something down, it stayed shut. Reagan said he figured Terry had a damn fine reason, the way it looked to him.

While the Bean mess sizzled along, Terry would sometimes look across his gin and tonic at Cassidy, when the night was hot and sticky and the sirens cried like banshees in the night and people got fed up with the heat and started bashing each other for the sport of it, and say, "Thank God for DiMaggio."

The radio was always on that summer, all over town, and you couldn't avoid hearing about Joe DiMaggio. The Yankee Clipper, they called him. The rest of the American League couldn't seem to get him out. He kept hitting. Thirty straight games, forty, fifty . . . He wound up hitting in fifty-six straight. By the time Jim Bagby of the Indians finally stopped him, Derek Boyce and Sylvester Aubrey Bean were out of the papers. Terry said he wasn't absolutely sure Boyce had done it but it sure as hell looked that way and if he hadn't he'd certainly done something worse, one time or another. Or was going to. The way he looked at it, the great city had coughed up one of its ugly little perversities, belched, and gone back to business as usual. After Bagby stopped him, DiMag went right back to hitting and the Yanks continued their stately march and the world was all right again.

The story was long gone from the papers when one of his fellow cons beat Derek Boyce to death.

The truth was, nobody cared about him anymore.

Nobody but Mark Herrin, who had loved Derek Boyce with all his heart. It took him awhile to get his nerve up but when he did he knew just the fellow he wanted to kill.

Terry had been right, of course. Somebody had been

watching him, somebody had been after him. And on the night of December 8, 1941, with the whole world undertaking to shoot the works everywhere, a guy with a gun had come after Terry Leary.

But Mark Herrin hadn't been the only one watching Terry.

It was the other ones that mattered in the long run.

Herrin was just a detail.

•   •   •

Later on the doctors decided the risk wasn't worth it. They left the bullet Terry was carrying near his spine. The X rays showed it snuggled right up against the vertebrae, too close to dig it out, particularly since it wasn't bothering him. Yet. The lung was emptied of blood, reinflated, stitched up, and aside from a hellish big scar, Terry was going to be all right once his strength came back.

The first time they let Cassidy wheel down the hall to see him, Terry looked about as lively as a plucked chicken. He grinned weakly and flapped a hand. "Never turn your back on 'em, Lew. Fuckers'll shoot you every time." He coughed and closed his eyes.

It was tough for him to talk and easy for him to sleep, so Cassidy just sat quietly listening to the low voices of the radio while the afternoon lost its grip on the light. He sat through *Terry and the Pirates* and *Hop Harrigan* and *Captain Midnight* and he had the nurse bring his dinner tray to Terry's room. Then he listened to *Mr. Keen, Tracer of Lost Persons* or maybe it was *David Harding, Counterspy*, he couldn't be sure because he was thinking hard about Terry and Harry Madrid and Bert Reagan, trying to decode that conversation he'd heard from the other side of the ether. He wasn't going to bring it up to any of them. Better to just wait for it to surface again, like a treacherous log floating beneath the smooth waters. All Cassidy had to do was to be ready for it. He knew it was down there. He and Terry had always faced things together and if anybody was looking for a piece of Terry Leary he was going to have to work his way through all of Lew Cassidy first.

He dozed intermittently in the chair by the window with winter howling outside. He thought about Cindy Squires and Max Bauman and wondered why they couldn't get their stories straight about who sent the flowers and then his mind turned to Karin, who had become something like a dream in the two years since he'd seen her. Two years. Yet he longed for her more now than ever, never went an hour without thinking of her, wishing he knew what she was doing at a given moment. All the fantasies of her suddenly getting word to him that she was coming back had been thoroughly dashed by the entry of the United States into the war. Now, like so many other things you kept hearing about, the gulf between them wouldn't be bridged until the war ended. He was stuck, as he was, for the duration.

In the twilight of half-sleep he thought of her, remembering the first time he'd ever taken her clothing off, all of it, remembering how she was almost holding her breath, remembering how her stomach jerked each time she gulped some air. When she was naked he'd turned her over and spread her legs, massaged the backs of her thighs, felt the long skater's muscles, the power. She was making soft, cooing, whimpering sounds, German words he didn't understand. When he sank his fingers into her hips, trying to spread them, she resisted with the strength which amazed and excited him. Then she relaxed, as if to let him know she could have stopped him but consciously chose not to, her whole body trembling as the breath eased out of her. He kissed her ear and the soft cheek. Her breath was warm and moist. The pillowcase was damp where she'd clenched it between her teeth while he'd touched her, deeper and deeper. Slowly he slid down the length of her back, kissing the smooth rises of her spine, kept kissing her all the way down, spreading her hips, kept kissing, tasted the silky black down between her hips, hearing her accented English . . . *Don't stop, please don't stop . . .*

For two years he'd never stopped thinking about her. A lot of the time it was as if he'd seen her yesterday. He'd always heard that people forgot the faces of loved ones after a while and maybe that was true for most people. But not for him. He could still close his eyes and see her compact diamond-shaped face with the wide cheekbones, the wide diamond eyes, the short-cropped dark hair that lay sleek and close to her head when she flew across the ice, intent, ramming a hole in the air, all the world closed out but for the blades and the cold smooth ice spitting from beneath her and the fluid control of her body . . .

And he could hear her voice, thickly German at first and then growing its own American inflections, he could hear it curling around the words . . . *Don't stop, please don't stop* . . .

He hadn't forgotten a thing. Not any of it. He never would.

Sometimes he wondered if maybe he was going slightly crazy. Sometimes he thought it might be easier if she were dead, if he knew he'd never see her again.

But that *was* crazy. He was going to see her again, no matter how long it took. He was going to hold her, look into the eyes that had swallowed him, like a secret, forever.

•　•　•

One day, about a week before Christmas, with snow falling and collecting on his windowsill where pigeons left tiny tracks, he heard a woman's voice speak his name. He was dozing, floating through soft clouds the way you do in the hospital, and an angel was circling overhead. An angel actually recognized him. "Mr. Cassidy," she said, and he smiled by way of acknowledgment. The angel was growing insistent. He felt her tugging at his pajama sleeve. "Lewis . . . Lewis," she whispered. "Wake up for me."

He opened his eyes and looked into her face, the eyes like jewels, the soft down on her cheek. "Oh, God," he said, "don't hit me."

A tiny giggle escaped her cat's mouth.

"I won't hit you if you wake up. You were smiling. Sweet dreams?"

"Angel. An angel was talking to me. Knew my name."

"I didn't bring candy or flowers . . ."

He couldn't stop smiling at her. "Did you see Terry?"

"I will before I go . . . Bennie has a cold. I told him I'd do his hospital rounds today." She looked away as if she'd been caught in an indiscretion. "Max said it was all right, my coming—"

"That's a relief."

"Don't mock me. What Max thinks is important . . ."

"Goes without saying."

"I did bring you something . . ."

"Is it a secret or what?"

"Dickens, actually. People in hospital should always read Dickens."

"You remembered, Miss Squires. Will you read to me?"

"Yes."

"Pull up a chair, Miss Squires." He watched her throw the mink across the foot of the bed. She was wearing a heavy cardigan with leather buttons and a navy skirt with kick pleats. She slid a chair next to the bed, sat down, opened a thick volume.

"'The Life and Adventures of Nicholas Nickleby,'" she read, "'by Charles Dickens. Chapter One.' Stop fidgeting, get settled like a good boy. 'There once lived, in a sequestered part of the country of Devonshire, one Mr. Godfrey Nickleby: a worthy gentleman . . .'"

She read to him all afternoon, until it was dark beyond the window. He watched her from beneath nearly closed lids. He reached out and took a chocolate from a box sent by Marquardt Cookson. Cindy leaned forward in midsentence, mouth open, and he popped a buttercream between her lips. One of his fingertips brushed her lower lip.

•   •   •

Christmas came and went like a rumor. They were still in the hospital, and Christmas, the first of the war, wasn't like it used to be. He'd been without Karin for three

Christmases. He'd damn near forgotten what they used to be like.

Dr. Christensen told him what had happened to his right leg. The doctor showed him X rays and drew little diagrams on a scratch pad with a thick, marbled Autopoint pencil. It wasn't just that he was done playing football. He was going to have a limp and the doctor didn't know for how long. Six months, a year, forever, there was just no telling. And in the meantime he'd need a cane. It made him feel very mortal. He'd never undergone any kind of physical weakness. At six four, two twenty-five, he'd always chosen to run through things rather than around them. And now he needed a cane. The doctor told him to cheer up, it could be a lot worse. He could be out in the Pacific defending Wake Island or Corregidor. As usual the doctor had a point.

They got through New Year's Eve. A few of the nurses and doctors who were stuck with holiday duty brought champagne and caviar to Terry's room and they listened to the dance bands on the radio from the hotels around town. At midnight Guy Lombardo struck up "Auld Lang Syne" and they kissed the nurses and toasted the New Year of 1942. The war was going badly but what could you expect at the beginning, after a sneak attack? They toasted victory and one of the doctors swore that the Japs would be through by the time the snow had melted in Central Park. Hell, the Germans were already freezing to death in the Russian winter. The doctor said he'd heard the German soldiers were eating their own dead to survive. A nurse made a face and said enough already and Cassidy reminded them that war was hell.

•　　•　　•

Bennie the Brute came by early in January to take them home. Terry insisted that Cassidy recuperate with him at his place on Park Avenue. "Taken together," he said, "we make almost one normal adult male. If somebody else comes around wanting to shoot me, you could throw yourself in front of me, a human shield to take the fire. Or fight 'em off with your cane—"

"Or I could just go out there and wear 'em down."

"But I'm serious, Lew. I don't like the idea of being alone. They're still out there, waiting for me. I know it but I don't think they know I know—I just don't know who they are. But they're sure as hell gonna think twice if they gotta deal with you, even with the bum wheel." He was still weak and pale.

Cassidy said, "Damn right," grinning, trying to sound more confident than he really was. He wasn't sure he could fight off a crippled newsie, let alone Harry Madrid and Bert Reagan. But, then, why look for trouble? Madrid and Reagan were old friends of Terry's, weren't they? And they hadn't made a false move. The fact was Cassidy and Terry had gotten Christmas cards from both of them. Wise men on the road to Bethlehem, following a star.

So Bennie hauled them away in Max Bauman's huge Chrysler and got them settled at Terry's place, which looked like something from a George Raft picture, not like a cop's humble abode. Which made it a nice place to spend the winter, however the hell Terry managed it. Payoffs, investments from the rich ladies he dated, whatever.

Most of the time they were alone. A couple of Cassidy's teammates straggled by to sponge a drink, and a cop or two stopped in to tell Terry how life was going without him in homicide. Marquardt Cookson and his little man brought delicacies to eat, drink, and occasionally some nose candy. Bennie checked every few days to see if they were in need of anything. A few times Cindy Squires came with him, talked to them nervously and made lunch and smoked too much and left, looking neither relieved to be going nor happy she'd come. Cassidy found her puzzling, enigmatic, quite beyond his reach, and he wondered why. But he made a real effort not to wonder very hard. One day, after he'd finished *The Life and Adventures of Nicholas Nickleby*, a messenger brought *Bleak House*. No letter, no note. Nothing.

Paul Cassidy called frequently to check on their recovery and to report on his own work organizing movie star War Bond Drives. Everybody was involved in the war effort. Anyway, that was the way it seemed to the two 4-Fs watching the world go by down below on Park Avenue. The day they'd gotten out of the hospital Carole Lombard, whom Paul Cassidy had known since the days when she was married to William Powell, raised two million dollars at a bond rally in Indianapolis. Late that night she'd gotten on a plane. The plane disappeared near Las Vegas. A search began in the nearby mountains, in the deep snow and the thick forests. Her husband flew up from Los Angeles to join the hunt. By then she was married to Clark Gable. After looking for fourteen hours they found the wreckage of the plane. Carole Lombard was dead. Paul Cassidy called her Hollywood's first fallen hero, which was like him. He'd never made a picture with her but he'd liked her, always said she could make him laugh no matter how shitty he felt. Everybody was getting into the war.

It snowed outside but it didn't matter to them. They'd watch the snow drifting down in waving curtains between them and the real world, if you could call Park Avenue the real world. They'd hobble around and build a fire and turn on the new Capehart Panamuse radio and sink into their chairs like two old farts at their club. Cassidy read all the newspapers, started putting colored pins into war maps. Terry played records, as if he were trying to blot out the war. Cassidy would read William Shirer's *Berlin Diary* and Terry would play records like "Bewitched" from the John O'Hara show *Pal Joey* and they'd both smoke Max Bauman's giant Havanas.

"'You'd be so nice to come home to,'" the girl sang, "'you'd be so nice by the fire,'" and sometimes the songs would hit Cassidy a little too close to home, a little too close to Karin. Or maybe it would be the war news from Europe. And he'd grab his cane and get a fresh bottle from the bar and drink it in his room until he couldn't think about her or anything else anymore and he'd wake up with the cold gray dawn, stiff and fully clothed and hung over. Some dawns he woke in a panic, his chest tight with the fear that he'd never see her again, that he'd never watch her brush the shiny cap of hair, never feel the touch of her lips, never hear the throaty, bawdy laugh. He kept thinking: We're on the same planet, the same sun shines on both of us . . . but he couldn't get to her, there was a war between them and now he couldn't even fight the goddamn war. He took to praying, for the first time since he was a child, and he only knew one prayer.

> *"Now I lay me down to sleep*
> *I pray the Lord my soul to keep*
> *If I should die before I wake*
> *I pray the Lord my soul to take.*
> *God bless Dad and Terry . . .*
> *And, Oh God, bless Karin*
> *and keep her safe, please . . ."*

•   •   •

One night in early February somebody blew up the great French liner *Normandie* at its berth on West 48th in the Hudson. Right away everybody figured it was the work of saboteurs. The pictures in the papers showed it keeled over on its side smoking. A great prehistoric creature hounded to its death, steaming in the spray of the hoses as it lay half submerged. Twenty-four hours after it went up, the hoses still played across the smoldering ruin.

It wasn't long after that that Harry Madrid and Bert Reagan came by to see Cassidy. It was a snowy morning and Bennie had taken Terry to the hospital for another X ray of his back. Cassidy was standing at the living room window staring out into the blowing snow when the car pulled up far below. He saw both of them get out. Even from that height you couldn't miss them.

Cassidy smiled to himself. It was about time.

CHAPTER FOUR

Harry Madrid stood in the doorway in a heavy black overcoat that reached almost to his ankles. The broad shoulders were sprinkled with snow. He looked like he had a dandruff problem. He was smiling broadly, his eyes lost in the pouches of gray flesh, a pipe that was too small for the size of him stuck in the corner of his mouth. His hat was pulled down too far, pushing his ears out. Bert Reagan stood behind him sucking on a toothpick. His overcoat was plaid, like a horse blanket. They came in and stomped snow onto the carpet.

"Howya feelin', Lew?" Harry Madrid looked around, cataloguing the opulence of Terry's sunken living room and the blond bar with the slatted mirror fanning out behind it, and his face didn't give away a thing.

"I'm all right." Cassidy waved his cane in the air, shrugged. He still couldn't walk properly without it. "You guys selling tickets to the Policemen's Ball? I'm not dancing much these days and Terry just left for an X ray."

"You don't say?" Madrid shook his head. He wasn't

surprised. He probed his bristly ear with a forefinger the size of a cucumber.

"Real sorry to miss him," Reagan said. He looked out the long row of windows. The apartment buildings across Park were disappearing behind the snow. "Some view." He leaned toward the glass, looking downtown. He munched on the toothpick like a dog worrying a favorite bone.

"But the fact is we came for you," Madrid said. "Let's take a ride. Get you outa this place. Not good to be cooped up. Good for you to get out, put some color in those cheeks." The skin on his own face, once you got away from the eyes, was drawn so tight he looked like he'd swollen through the collar of his shirt. His cheeks were red from the cold but the closer you got to those eyes the less life you could find.

"Are you serious, Harry?"

"You know me, keed. I'm not much of one for laughs." He punched Cassidy's arm softly. "Come on, put your coat on."

"You guys kidnaping cripples these days? What if I'd rather stay home?"

"Come on, Lew. Don't be that way. Coupla guys want to talk to you. They're friendlies, ain't that right, Bert?"

"Sure they are. A little fresh air can't hurt, Lew."

"I don't think you guys are so friendly. I think I'll stay here—"

Suddenly Harry Madrid had moved in close, fast like big men can be, and Cassidy felt a vise closing on his arm. Harry Madrid had always been a cop who was good at the heavy work. Now he had Cassidy's arm pinned and twisted up tight and he was grinning like a Dutch uncle. "Don't fuck with me, Lew. Never, ever fuck with Harry Madrid." One jerk and the arm would snap like a twig. "I'll never fight fair if dirty will do. You got that?" The grin was stretched tight across large worn teeth. At just that moment he looked like something that fed itself by gnawing on carcasses. "You gonna come with us, Lew?"

Cassidy chuckled and shook his head like Bogart in the

movies. "Two bashful suitors. What a pair. Sure, sure, I'll come. But you gotta give me my arm back, Harry."

They all stood around and laughed like idiots stalling for time while Madrid handed Cassidy's stick to Reagan and held his chesterfield for him. "Didn't know Brooks made coats like this so big," Madrid said.

"They make 'em for big rich guys—"

"Then what are you doin' in one, Lew?" Madrid laughed.

"You're a mighty amusing guy, you put your mind to it."

"That's what the missus says." In the elevator Madrid said, "You're gonna enjoy this, Lew. You'd never guess who wants to talk to you. Never."

"You can say that again," Reagan said, making huge wet footprints across the lobby carpet. The doorman nodded to Cassidy. The toothpick was gone from Bert Reagan's mouth. Cassidy wondered where in the world it had gone.

•   •   •

The Cadillac limousine was black and shiny, like a mammoth beetle in the fresh snowfall. It looked as if it had been built on a hearse chassis and there were heavy curtains on the rear windows. Reagan squeezed his plaid bulk behind the wheel. Harry Madrid held the rear door while Cassidy gingerly climbed into the spacious backseat. The jumps were folded away. Madrid settled in beside him and lit the little pipe again, filling the compartment with cherry-scented smoke. There was little traffic and the snow blotted out all the normal sounds of the city.

"Where does Reagan think he's going?"

"Just down the street. Nothing complicated. Don't worry, the horse knows the way." Madrid chuckled, smoke trickling from his nostrils, dragonlike. He pushed the curtain away from his view. "I was a kid, there were horse and buggies on Park Avenue. Now we're driving around in a goddamn room. Tell me it's progress, Lew." He puffed reflectively, looking at the Christmas-card scene outside. Remembering his childhood. He wasn't the kind of man

who could ever have had a childhood. The thought of
Harry Madrid in knee pants, with a mother and father on
a buggy ride, took Cassidy by surprise. He'd never thought
of Madrid as, strictly speaking, a human being. He was an
old-time cop. "Times change, Lew. Now I'm thinking
about retiring, few years down the road, go someplace
upstate. My wife's people, y'know. Small-town people.
Honest, hard workers."

"Can't picture you in a small town, Harry."

"I could be sheriff, some one-horse, jerkwater place. It's
a thought, ain't it? Harry Madrid, Sheriff. Die with my
boots on. I knew Bat Masterson when he came to New
York, after all the Dodge City stuff. Newspaperman he
was. He told me the frontier was gone, it was all over. I
says, 'Bat, you're wrong, you're all wet. I been on the
frontier all my life.' He looks at me kinda slow, says I don't
know what I'm taking about. I says, 'New York's the
frontier, the original frontier town, always was, always
will be, as long as this country lasts.' He thought about it,
then he nods and says maybe I was right, come to think of
it. Well, Lew, I've been on the frontier so long I'm
beginnin' to feel like the Marshall of Abilene." He coughed
and wheezed, laughter rumbling.

Reagan slid the car to a quivering stop at the private
entrance of the Waldorf Towers, around the corner from
the main Park Avenue entrance. A man who carried
enough gold braid to be in command of a fleet or two
somewhere opened the door and they all got out, sucking
up the bracing fresh air. Harry Madrid spoke to the
doorman. Then they went inside and took an elevator
almost to the top, the domain, so far as Cassidy knew, of
movie stars, titans of industry, and big-time politicians.

"Bet you never been up here before," Reagan said.

"Well, you'd lose," Cassidy said.

"When?" Reagan sounded doubtful.

"Reception for Lindbergh. Somebody figured we'd get
along."

"Lucky Lindy?" Reagan's mouth was open.

"Himself. And his wife. She's a looker, Bert. Little dark thing."

"Yeah, I heard she's a pip."

Cassidy waited while Harry Madrid knocked. Today it wasn't going to be Charles Lindbergh. But who the hell was behind that door?

• • •

Tom Dewey was standing alone by the window watching the snow swirling down onto Grand Central Station. He must have been one of the two or three most instantly recognizable men in New York. You couldn't miss on La Guardia, for one, and DiMaggio, and then there was Tom Dewey, who really did, as he turned around, look like the groom on top of a wedding cake. The aide who ushered them in faded away into the shadowy reaches of the antique-appointed living room and Dewey came toward them with the famous thick black moustache twitching in a convivial politician's smile. "Mr. Cassidy," he boomed, the deep rolling voice not at all what you'd expect from a wedding-cake decoration with a Groucho Marx upper lip, "I'm Tom Dewey. I'm mighty glad you could stop by this morning. Come on over here, I've got some breakfast for us." He gave Cassidy a terrifically manly handshake and led them back to a table set for four. "Please, everyone, take a pew, please."

Cassidy sat down and, while Dewey busied himself with silver chafing dishes of eggs and ham and pitchers of orange juice and coffeepots, he wondered what Dewey could want with him. He knew what everyone knew about Tom Dewey. Five or six years before, he'd put aside a successful law practice and become special prosecutor in the campaign against big-time, organized crime. He was suddenly turned into a crusader for all that was right and good and a man to watch politically. He brushed off all the gangland death threats, threw himself into the fight against the mobsters. And became a public hero. Now he was a clean-cut and fresh-faced thirty-nine and his name kept coming up when people talked about a Republican to

73

run against FDR in 1944. He wasn't very big but Cassidy sensed the presence, what his father would have called star quality. He looked fit but not quite real. It was that moustache. It looked like you could reach over and knock it into his orange juice. But he was stuck with it. It was his trademark.

"Dig in, boys," he said, dishing up eggs and ham and pushing the toast rack across white linen deep as the snow outside. "It's a real pleasure to meet you, Mr. Cassidy. I'm a great fan of yours. You had quite a season—I was there the day you hurt your leg." He brushed a bit of egg from the moustache. "Pearl Harbor. I guess that day will live in infamy for you in more ways than one. How's your recovery progressing?"

Cassidy nodded, swallowing ham. It was a good breakfast. "I'm all right. Takes a long time for this kind of thing to heal."

"I've read that your football days are over. Is that true?"

"So they tell me." He sipped hot coffee. Madrid and Reagan were eating like two men afraid they'd never see another egg.

"Tell me, what are your plans? Career-wise, I mean." Dewey crunched on a piece of toast and left a little fleck of butter in the moustache. Cassidy tried not to look at it.

"I haven't really thought about it. Something's bound to turn up." He shrugged. He was wearing a black and white herringbone jacket and a white shirt open at the neck. He had an eighteen-inch neck so he didn't wear a tie all that much.

"Well, I wish you'd keep me in mind before you make any commitments elsewhere. I'm going to need some good men from now on, solid men I can depend on absolutely. You may have heard about my possible future in politics." He smiled. He was all confidence, wore it as comfortably as the blue pin-striped suit. He didn't care if Cassidy was a straight-ticket Democrat because he'd sized up the football star and decided he was smart, a man who knew the main chance when he saw it. All that came through in the smile. Tom Dewey knew he was the main chance. Cassidy

74

figured it wasn't worth arguing about. "Well, what you heard is not idle speculation. I'm going to be the next governor of New York—please, just remember that, Mr. Cassidy—and I have the feeling you're my kind of people."

"I heard you wanted to be President," Cassidy said.

"One step at a time," Dewey said. "I appreciate your candor. You *are* my kind of people."

"Is that why we're all having breakfast together? Maybe Harry and Bert could deliver campaign posters . . ."

Dewey didn't miss a beat. He laughed, turned the big smile with the black roof on Madrid and Reagan, who stopped eating long enough to roll on their backs with paws in the air. Dewey's laugh shattered all the glass in the room and when the echoes rolled away he sat staring at Cassidy until the smile was gone, too.

"You may recall that I made something of a name for myself a few years back, Tom Dewey the Racket Buster." The way he said it made you think you might as well go back to Venus if you hadn't heard. "Now I'm back in private practice—"

"Where the publicity's harder to come by," Cassidy observed. "You put what's his name, Luciano, away, right?"

Dewey nodded. "For good, I might add. Judge McCook gave him fifty years. Yes, you see I found his Achilles' heel—prostitution—and I got him on it. Think of it, fifty years, that's the same as life, and half a century in Dannemora is half a century of very hard time, indeed. It'll be 1985 by the time Lucky gets out and by then"—he spread his hands—"neither he nor anyone else will care. Have you ever had cause to visit the facility at Dannemora, Lew?"

"I'm delighted to tell you I haven't, Tom."

"It's an unhappy spot. In winter it's colder than a well-digger's heinie, the northern walls are coated with ice. In summer it's an oven. The cons up there call it Siberia. And I put Luciano in for the rest of his life." The thought perked up his appetite and he dug back into the eggs and ham.

"That's great, Tom. Hell of a job you did." Cassidy pushed his plate away. Bert Reagan, by the sound of it, was still in mid-meal. Madrid was fiddling with his pipe. "But I don't quite see what all this has to do with me."

Dewey looked up, eyes wide, as if surprised that he hadn't gotten down to brass tacks yet. He covered his mouth with a heavy napkin and came out smiling. "Ah! Why you're here! Well . . . because I'm not done with the gangsters yet, that's why. There's work that remains to be done before I rest." His face was very firm and serious now. He'd leaned back and crossed his legs and folded his arms across his chest. He was carefully modulating his voice, keeping it just short of the whine of religious zealotry. He wasn't selling *The Watchtower.* He was a man who wanted to be President with Albany a station on the line. "What I did to Luciano," he intoned, wagging a forefinger to let you know he damn well meant it, "I am going to do to . . . Max Bauman!" He blinked beneath eyebrows that made a set with his moustache. "Max . . . Bauman." He stood up and paced once around the three men at the breakfast table, his hands behind his back, and went to stand by the windows. He looked out into the blowing snow as if seeking inspiration, then turned back to face them. "Max Bauman is a very wicked man. Did you know that, Lew?"

"Well, no, I wouldn't call Max wicked, exactly. I think of Max as having a checkered past. No worse than lots of others. Anyway, I've been told all of that was a long time ago." Cassidy shrugged. He didn't know what he was talking about and he was beginning to resent Dewey's having led him down the path to a defense of Bauman.

"Well, you've been misinformed, Lew. Don't tell me, let me guess. Bauman's character witness has been Terry Leary—am I right?"

"That's right. Terry's known Max a long time."

"Indeed he has. You could hardly call him an entirely unbiased source, Lew, that's the problem."

"You want me to believe you're an unbiased source, Tom?"

"Let me tell you about Max Bauman. I'll make it brief."
He looked at his watch and shot his cuffs, showing onyx
links and an inch and a half of starched cotton. "This is a
story about four men, young immigrants, who came to
New York, grew up in the streets of the ghetto. Charlie
Luciana, who changed his name to Luciano because the
other way sounded effeminate to him. His parents came
from a village called Lercara Friddi in Sicily. Benjamin
Siegel, whose family came from Kiev. Maier Sucholjansky
from Grodno, Poland. Max Bauman from the Warsaw
ghetto. An Italian and three young men of the Jewish
persuasion. Contemporaries, more or less. They picked
pockets together as boys; they were drawn together by
their poverty, by their lack of good English, by their
determination to conquer this new, hostile country of
theirs. Early on they discovered that with money they
could control their destinies, make this new land their
home. Charlie Luciano had a Sicilian proverb he used to
recite to them. *Cu avini dinari e amicizia teni la giustizia.*
He who has money and friends has justice as well."

Dewey came back to the table and poured himself a cup
of coffee, then refilled Cassidy's cup. He went back to the
window, sipped from his cup, brushed his moustache with
a knuckle, and went on.

"These four lads robbed individuals on a door-to-door
basis, graduated to banks and jewelry stores, then developed protection rackets for restaurants, shopkeepers,
bookies. They were just hitting their stride when the
Volstead Act broadened the scope of their activities. With
alcoholic beverages prohibited, our four—along with the
other gangsters big and small—began to supply a very
thirsty populace. They smuggled whiskey from Scotland,
rye from Canada, rum from Nassau, and they ran gunboats to protect their shipments, but still they couldn't
begin to meet the demand. So they began taking over
warehouses here in the States to distill and bottle their
own stock. But there was a problem—the gangs spent as
much time fighting over territories and slaughtering each
other as they did selling the stuff. Luciano had the answer

. . . combine the gangs into one vast interlocking organization. Luciano told them the truth—the bigger the operation, the larger the profits. He called a meeting of the gangs in Chicago, taking his three Jewish lieutenants with him, and he laid out his plan. Well, it went over big; they decided to divide the country into territories. Thus, organized crime was born. They decided to resurrect an all but forgotten name for themselves, in honor of Luciano. Unione Siciliano. Funny thing was, Lucky never called it that—he used his own name for it . . . the Outfit."

Dewey paused to gauge the interest of his audience and found it pleasing. "Now they were into very big business, indeed," he said. "Twenty, maybe thirty million dollars a month. Alcohol, gambling, extortion, murder, bribery, prostitution, drugs, you name it. I don't know, maybe it was fifty million a month. Maybe there was no way to count it. Luciano was the man at the top. Maier Sucholjansky was in control of financial matters. By now his name was Meyer Lansky. Benjamin Siegel was an enforcer with a reputation for what we might call an artistic temperament . . . which had earned him a nickname. He was 'bughouse' as they say, nuts. Bugsy Siegel. And Max Bauman was still Max Bauman and his special areas of concentration were prostitution and drugs. And bribery— Max usually had acess to a million dollars in used, small-denomination bills to pay off the cops, the lawyers, the judges, the jury foremen. Max also had a reputation as an enforcer; they called him a backshooter—you never let him get behind you, that was the point." Thomas Dewey sighed and looked at his watch again. "Which pretty well brings us up to the present, Lew. Except now that Lucky's in Dannemora, Max has more of the show to himself. The war has been a godsend to Max Bauman. They say he's now in control of a thousand gas stations, Maine to Texas . . . and he's forging gasoline rationing stamps— that alone could make all this other stuff look like small change. And that, Lew, is why I'm going to get Max Bauman. I'm going to put him away for forever and a day, Lew . . . believe it!"

Dewey snapped the politician's smile back into place, erasing the crusader in an instant, and grabbed Cassidy's hand, shaking it sincerely once again. "Lew, may I say it's damn good to have you on our team? Well, it is. I know how it must frustrate you, having that bum leg when you could otherwise be in uniform, fighting for your country. But"—he raised a forefinger and tapped Cassidy's chest— "nothing you could do on some hellhole in the Pacific could do more good for this old country of ours than helping to put Max Bauman where he belongs—"

"Wait a minute, Tom," Cassidy interrupted. "Maybe I'm a little slow on the uptake here but I don't know what you think I'm going to do to help you . . . Have I missed something?"

"Lew, I'd love to stay and chat," Dewey said, "but I'm already running late. Harry and Bert have got another man they'd like you to see, then everything will be explained." His aide had appeared from the other room and was holding Dewey's overcoat. "Now, if you'll excuse me—have some more coffee, whatever you like. Harry, Bert, good of you to lend a hand." He was almost to the door when he turned back. "I almost forgot, Lew. Bauman's latest enterprise. You've read about the *Normandie*? It was sabotage. The Nazis right here in New York, on our docks. You know who did it for them? Your pal Max Bauman."

Thomas Dewey gave a jaunty little wave, put his homburg straight on his carefully barbered head, and was out the door.

•   •   •

Cassidy sat in the back of the Cadillac, unaware of the clogged, snowbound Times Square traffic, wondering just what Tom Dewey expected him to do about putting Max Bauman away. Did Dewey simply believe that Cassidy knew Bauman better than he actually did? Dewey's performance had been so carefully constructed that there had been no room or time for Cassidy to say his lines. It had been a very underwritten part, as his father would have said. Just Tom Dewey giving a lecture about a mobster. To a football player. Former football player.

And how much of it was true?

What had set Dewey off about Max, anyway? Surely none of Max's past had come as news to the former special prosecutor, so what made it so important all of a sudden? Why hadn't he gone after Max when he nailed Luciano? Was it the acquisition of all the gas stations? The forged gasoline rationing stamps? And why the hell would Max Bauman blow up the *Normandie* for the Nazis? There was something wrong with that . . . And what happened to Max's Harvard years?

The stories and rumors making the rounds about the *Normandie* were unavoidable. German saboteurs were being blamed by most people, since the huge French liner was in the process of being converted into a troop carrier capable of taking an entire division to fight in Europe. Built in 1935, it had cost an unheard-of $56 million and it was said that no liner afloat was more luxurious. The silver service for the dining rooms had cost more than $150,000. The walls of the three-story-high main lounge were fitted out with immense slabs of Algerian onyx, and the bronze doors weighed six tons. The floor was covered with the world's largest Aubusson carpet, the size of several tennis courts, and the 2,170 passengers had shopped at countless Paris boutiques ranked along promenades wide as Madison Avenue. And now, having been partially transformed by 2,000 dockyard workers hard at it in round-the-clock shifts, it lay in rusty, scorched, smoldering ruins in the Hudson.

Somebody had set it on fire and for twelve hours it had burned out of control, sending up smoke so thick it turned day into night and night into a vision of glowing, steaming, burning hell. The metal alloy superstructure melted and buckled, and molten steel ran into the Hudson. And then it had rolled over and died.

And Max Bauman was supposed to have done it?

Terry Leary had said Max was legit, that his mob days had been just an ornamentation of Prohibition. He'd never

80

said Max was a pal of Luciano, Siegel, and Meyer Lansky . . .

Terry had a lot in common with Dewey when you thought about it. The sense of style, that same kind of confidence, the presence. But his moustache was better, if you were determined to have a moustache. If Dewey was passing out jobs in his political organization, he'd have been a lot better off approaching Terry, not Cassidy, who wasn't much of an angle man. Cassidy saw the guy up ahead, ready to take you down, and his natural inclination was to accelerate and run him down. Politics was all angles and nobody was better at angles than Terry. Dewey had made his pitch to the wrong man.

Reagan had inched through the snow, slush, and traffic, and it was well past noon by the time they were heading north up the Hudson with the Cloisters up above on the right, the hilltop obscured by the heavy-laden clouds.

Cassidy came out of his reflections and looked over at Harry Madrid, who was reading a newspaper, the sports page, about a big basketball doubleheader at the Garden. He'd put his reading glasses on, and the pipe, still clenched in his molars, was forgotten, dead, cold.

"So what was that all about?"

"Dewey? Oh, Dewey needs the police to work with him on nailing Bauman. Maybe you noticed, Bert and I are cops—"

"But why you guys? Why not two other guys?"

Harry Madrid chuckled, folded his newspaper. "Hear that, Bert? Why us? Well, I tell you, Lew, it's because we're the ones know Terry Leary best." He found the thought amusing.

"Terry? But Terry's one of you. If Dewey wants Bauman, why not go to Terry? He knows *Max* best—"

"Get this straight, Cassidy." Madrid's shiny little eyes came up out of their hiding places. He yanked his pipe out of his mouth and pointed the teeth-marked stem at him. "Terry ain't one of us. Never was. He ain't our kind, y'get my drift? Long time ago he put his money down on Max. Looks like maybe he made a mistake—"

"Harry, I hate to tell you this, but you're not scaring me. And you're full of shit, too. Terry *knows* the guy. Not a crime. You really ought to introduce Dewey to Terry, not me."

"Hear that, Bert? Lew's got lots of good ideas back here. Lew, Dewey already knows Terry. A long time already. They sort of worked together once . . ." He thought better of pursuing that line of discussion. "That's why he came to you. He can't go to Terry because Terry's first loyalty is to Max. Terry won't help him nail Max. Period. Now, just stop with the questions. We're not through yet. Sit tight."

A half hour later Cassidy said, "Where are we going?"

"To see a man. Just enjoy the ride, Lew. It's a surprise, like a birthday present."

A little later they got to Sing Sing. Even through the snow, you could smell the acrid stink of disinfectant. It was the smell of prisons everywhere and it was a hell of a long way from the Waldorf Towers.

•　　•　　•

"Mr. Luciano," a prison functionary in a gray suit that matched his big-house pallor spoke softly, like someone approaching a prince of the Church, "this is Mr. Cassidy. Of course, you know Detectives Madrid and Reagan."

"Sure, sure," Luciano said. He clamped Cassidy's hand in his own and offered a bitter smile, the kind that turns down in irony at the corners. "Tough about your leg, kid. I heard the game on the radio. Tough." He was almost a foot shorter than Cassidy, thick and muscular—like a pit bull with broad shoulders that wouldn't give an inch even if he were overmatched. Cassidy took one look and was glad they weren't climbing into a ring to fight it out. Luciano had a slightly triangular face with a pointed chin, a long nose with flared nostrils, and thick black hair with a widow's peak like Dick Powell's. In middle age he had laugh lines at the corners of his mouth but they'd soured a bit with time. Cassidy wondered what made Lucky Luciano laugh. But it was always the same: You heard about a guy, all the things he'd done, good or bad, whether

82

it was Lucky Lindy or Lucky Luciano, and then you met
him and he was just a guy. Maybe they had that stage
presence, maybe they had a look about them that filled the
room, but then you sat down and started shooting the
breeze and they were just guys. Cassidy knew what made
Lucky Luciano laugh. Amos and Andy, Jack Benny, Fibber
McGee and Molly, Groucho. The same things that made
everybody laugh.

"You guys have lunch yet?" Luciano asked.

"Not yet, Lucky," Harry Madrid said.

"Well, they brought me down here from Dannemora this
morning, crack o' dawn, and I had some oatmeal before it
was light and I'm so damn hungry I could eat a horse and
chase the rider." Luciano was ushering them from an
anteroom into a private interview room that had been set
up with a dining table, chairs, and a sideboard. There was
a small dark man in a business suit who was introduced as
one of Luciano's lawyers. Luciano turned to the man who
had made the introductions and spoke softly, patting his
back. "Okay, Al, take a hike. You, too, Tony. I'll let you
know when we're through." The two men nodded and left,
closing the door to the dining room behind him.

"So I hear you guys had breakfast with Mr. Dewey."
Luciano was just making conversation as he inspected the
lunch arrayed on the sideboard. The table was set with
starched linen and the platters might have come from the
Waldorf catering offices. "How was Tommy?" There were
three opened bottles of Chianti and crystal goblets, china
service, and at the head of the table, two bottles of Dr.
Brown's Celery Tonic, obviously intended for the host.

"He was fine," Harry Madrid said. "All in a lather, of
course—"

Luciano's laugh was soft, tolerant. "So what else is new?
He's in a permanent lather, our Tommy. Well, if you'll
excuse me, I'm not standing on ceremony here." He took a
plate and began to load it with lobster, rare roast beef,
cold sliced chicken, linguine with white clam sauce,
crusty bread, butter, salad. He filled two plates and made
way for the others to follow suit.

When they were arranged around the table and he had taken the edge off his appetite, Luciano took a deep swig of his Dr. Brown's and leaned back in his chair to let his digestive juices put in some hard time. "It's not always like this," he said, "in case you guys are gettin' any ideas. This is special. We owe it all to you, Cassidy. It's like you're the state's key witness in an Edward G. Robinson movie." He chuckled softly again. You didn't see them at first but they were there, all the scars on his face, all the stitches holding him together from the old days.

Cassidy said, "I feel like I'm being fattened up for the kill."

"Naw, nothin' like that. But the way we got it figured, you're a key man and Tommy and I, we thought we'd ease you into the picture, nice and gentle. Make it fun. You having fun, Mr. Touchdown?" His eyes were large, liquid, dark, like Valentino's. They were filled with a peculiar mixture of cruelty, humor, and wary distrust.

"I'm not actually beside myself," Cassidy said, "but it beats sitting around all day listening to *The Romance of Helen Trent—*"

"Hey, one of my favorites," Luciano said. "I got a lotta dead time on my hands. That Helen Trent, she must be a looker. A little stiff but a tiger in the raw.

"Look, I been inside six years now. It's not a great life, Cassidy, not even if you're Lucky Luciano. Mainly it's boring. No action. Do I still run things on the outside, you wanna know—I say, a little yes, a little no. The Outfit's big; some days it runs itself, like General Motors, y'know." He speared a chunk of lobster, drizzled some mayonnaise over it, and ate it thoughtfully.

"The name of this game is I gotta get outa here. There's a lot of things I can do to help my country in this time of war. Like dock security. You heard about this *Normandie* thing. I'm gonna level with you, Lew. I did that. Yeah. No shit, Lew. Ya wanna know why? I needed an angle. I control the docks still. Nazi saboteurs loose on my docks? That's a laugh, kid. But I hadda make 'em come to me. I do the *Normandie*, they come to me, 'Lucky,' they say, 'can you do this favor for us, for your country? Can you tighten up security on the docks?' Sure, I tell 'em, no problem." He winked at Cassidy. "That's the end of Nazis on my docks." He chuckled at the idea of his own ingenuity. "And the government boys owe Lucky one, a big one. Guy stuck in fuckin' Dannemora makes the docks safe . . . They know Lucky's word is good. I wouldn't shit ya, Lew. From Lucky you get the truth, the whole truth, nothin' but the truth.

"I can help back in the old country, too. Mussolini, he's made it real bad for our people there, but when the time comes to invade Italy, believe me, I can help clear the way, I can mobilize an army inside the country to join up with the Allies . . . I want to get outa here, though, see? It's tit for tat, like they say." He finished the first bottle of Dr. Brown's, buttered a piece of bread, and talked while he chewed. "Now, how do I get out? I'm in here for fifty fucking years, Mr. Touchdown. Long time. Man my age, I can kiss off gettin' out. I need a parole, is what I need. Only one way to get a parole now these bastards got me in here. I need my own man in Albany. I need the governor to lean on the parole board. You follow me so far, pal?"

Cassidy nodded. Madrid and Reagan were continuing to eat like a pair of starving Armenians.

"Now, the only governor I'm likely to get is Tommy, the same guy who framed me and put me in here. We understand each other, Tommy and me. We musta read the same rule book when we were kids. He's a shitheel, you understand, but he's a shitheel I can understand. We need each other. He's a sharp little guy, not as dumb as he looks with that stupid moustache. Tommy, he comes to me a while back, he says he's got a deal he thinks I'm gonna like, I should listen to him. Okay, I listen and he tells me he wants to get Max Bauman and Terry Leary, am I interested? I says sure, I'm interested—"

"*You* want to get *Terry*?" Cassidy shook his head. "I think I just missed a chapter—"

"Listen to me. Am I some jerk you interrupt? Just eat your chicken and drink your wine and listen to Lucky, Mr. Touchdown. *I want Bauman and Leary.* You wanna know why? You ask Luciano for reasons?" Suddenly the ferocity that had been building stopped. His shoulders relaxed, his face unfurrowed, and he shrugged. "Okay, so Leary's your pal, I'll give you reasons. Ask anybody, Luciano's an honorable man. There are things I do, things I don't do. Lansky and me, we decided a long time ago, no whores, no drugs. Whores are more trouble than they're worth, drugs are bad, a man of honor doesn't sell drugs . . . it's like selling poison gas. Any of my boys get into whores or drugs, they know what happens when I find out. What happens ain't pretty, Mr. Touchdown. So when Tommy decides he's gonna put Luciano away, what does he do? He can't make a case, an honest case, that'll even get him an indictment, let alone a conviction . . . so he's gotta frame me, he's gotta fix it. Tommy's good at that, he knew where to go—he went to my fancy Harvard friend, Maxie Bauman. Maxie, says Tommy, it's you or Lucky gonna do a long time in the slammer, who'd you rather have it be? Maxie guesses he'd rather have Lucky do the time. That's good for Maxie, it works for him no matter how you look at it. Maxie's got the whores and he's got the muscle. He puts the squeeze on sixty of his bimbos to testify against *me* . . ." His voice had begun to tremble, his fists white-knuckled on the table. "Me, Luciano, they frame . . . and the world thinks Luciano . . . runs . . . whorehouses!" One perfectly manicured fist slammed down on the table. The empty bottle of Dr. Brown's bounced off and shattered on the floor. Bert Reagan blew about half a pound of roast beef up his nose and Harry Madrid looked nervous, like a man who'd just noticed he was locked in the gorilla cage.

"That's why I want to get Bauman and Leary. You get that? Okay. I was framed, I want to get even. I'll help Dewey get Bauman if he throws Leary in . . . but that's just the beginning of the deal. Tommy and I both want him—I mean Dewey—in Albany. When he came to me with his plan for Max, he asked me something else." Luciano paused to open his second Dr. Brown's and wet his lips. "Dewey's a Republican, and any Republican who wants to be governor is scared of New York City. There's only one sure way he can carry the city and guarantee a win—he can get me to put the Outfit behind his campaign. I can carry the city for him, no ifs, ands, buts, nothin'. Getting Bauman gets him all over the papers again, makes him the big hero again . . . and the Outfit carries the city. Now, what do I get? You don't have to be a college man to figure that out, eh? As Governor Dewey, he paroles me." Luciano sank back in his chair. He was wearing a white shirt with the collar open and now it had begun to wilt. Sweat stains were spreading from his armpits.

"Sounds like you got yourself a deal," Cassidy said, "but I don't hear anything that sticks to Terry . . ."

"Oh, that," Luciano's voice was so soft Cassidy leaned forward. So did Madrid and Reagan, three men on a single string. "Terry was a young cop and Max bought him, put him in his pocket for keeps. Terry was the guy muscled the hookers for him, for him and Dewey. All three of them in on the frame. Two hoods and Dewey. Dewey is the only one who can do me any good now. Fuck the other two."

"Terry Leary's my friend," Cassidy said. "You? You're just a con I don't know from Adam. So, Lucky, fuck you."

Harry Madrid said "Aw shit," under his breath, and looked at the remains of his lunch. Bert Reagan went into another coughing fit. Lucky Luciano stared at Cassidy. Cassidy stared back and couldn't keep from smiling.

"You got some mouth on you, Touchdown," he said at last. "A real smart mouth. Figure you're a big tough guy. I don't know. You're a cripple, too."

"You're a little greaseball punk," Cassidy said. "In here for the duration. We could sit here, call each other names all night. But I didn't ask to see you and as far as I'm concerned I've seen about enough. Unless there's a hell of a dessert, I'm for wrapping this up and getting back to civilization. Harry? Whattaya say?" Cassidy pushed his chair back, stood up.

"Don't be a cornball," Luciano said. "Who you tryin' to impress? Any ladies here I hadn't noticed? So you're loyal to your pal. You're a Boy Scout." Slowly he began to clap his hands, applauding. "You're a nice wholesome boy.

Loyalty's a nice quality, as long as you're loyal to the right people. I'm suggesting that Leary's not quite as worthy of your loyalty as you think he is. I'm asking you to think about it." He sipped from his Dr. Brown's again. "Come on, kid, siddown. We're almost done, anyway. I get gas when people get mad at me, I really do. I'm a real easygoing guy. Siddown."

Cassidy slid his chair over, sat down. Madrid sighed deeply and closed his eyes.

"Y'know," Luciano said, "this war ain't gonna last forever. The Krauts are so dumb, they don't know it but they're all wet, they're pissin' in the wind and getting it back in the kisser. They didn't have a chance once the Japs bombed Pearl. Once we were in the war, the meter started running on the Krauts. Couple, three years, there won't be enough Germany left to fill your cat's shitbox. It's gonna be bad over there. We'll either turn Germany into one big farm or we'll have to build the whole damn country again to keep the Reds from taking over all of Europe. Either way, the Krauts get the shit beat outa them in this war. And when it's over, there's gonna be a boom over here like you never dreamed of. There's gonna be more money, more people wanting to spend it, and I'm gonna get my share. Casinos, travel, resorts, airlines, money just layin' around waiting to be picked up—"

"Look, I don't know why you're telling me all this—"

"I'm thinking of your future, Touchdown. Once we get Max and Terry where they belong, you're still gonna be a smart, mouthy, bright-eyed young guy. You many not like me yet, but I think you're okay. You're gonna help me, I'm gonna help you. Say the war's over, all this is behind us, I might put something in your way . . . a casino maybe, or the travel business, or something else. You know what's gonna be big? Pro football. Maybe I'll buy me a football team, it'd need a top man, wouldn't it?"

"Everybody wants to give me a job—"

Luciano laughed. "Don't listen to Dewey, he's a double-crosser."

"So what's to keep him from double-crossing you on the parole?"

"Because I'd let it out in detail how he came to me to get elected. No, don't worry about Luciano. But remember, you can trust me to do what I say, you can't trust Dewey at all. I'm an honorable man, that shitheel wants to be President . . . that says it all. Tommy Dewey in the White House." He shook his head and laughed more loudly. "This is the moment of truth, Touchdown. You're lookin' right down the barrel of the rest of your life. You can go in the crapper with Bauman and Leary. Or you can grab the brass ring, go with Lucky and Dewey. That little squirt gets to be President, I'm gonna be King for sure. Think about it, Touchdown."

Cassidy nodded. "Okay, okay, I'll think about it. But in the meantime, you haven't said a word about what you want from me."

"You're close to Leary, Leary's in bed with Max. I want to know what Max is up to. I don't care what it is, forged gasoline stamps, bribery, homemade twenties, war prof-iteering . . . Leary's got to be in it, too. You find out. You can't help but find out if you pay attention . . . and we'll get back to you, Harry and this guy with the toothpick, we'll be in touch. Simple."

"What if I don't do it?"

"Think of yourself as a spot. Think of me as the spot remover. Like I say, it's simple."

He smiled at Cassidy as if he were genuinely pleased, finally at ease knee-deep in a murder threat.

• • •

The snow had stopped falling but it was still blowing across the highway, blowing hard off the Hudson. Bert said he wanted to stop and get the chains put on before they slid off into the damn river. He pulled into a garage and café where the blowing snow hovered around the lights like swarms of gnats in the summertime. They went inside for coffee while the kid started in on the chains.

Harry Madrid ordered three coffees. They sat in a booth

by a window where a neon sign cast a red glow across their faces. They all took their hats off but left their overcoats on. Cassidy stared quietly into the last fading shreds of daylight. Headlamps poked nervously along the snowy highway. He was trying to make some sense of the day. The more he thought about it the less he liked it. He felt like a man being crammed into a very small cage. Every time he made a move he hurt himself.

"So, Lucky, fuck you," Harry Madrid whispered. "If that wasn't the goddamnedest thing I ever did see. Jeez, Cassidy, you haven't got the brains you were born with . . . so, Lucky, fuck you! If that don't beat all . . ."

"You're lucky he was in a good mood," Reagan observed.

"What was he gonna do, shoot me?"

"Oh, Lucky's got ways," Reagan said. "Remember the *Normandie*? Like he said, though, you're okay with him. You can trust him. Like he said, Dewey's a liar."

"Where does all this crap leave you guys?"

"Up to our chins in crap," Harry Madrid said, "as usual. But Bauman's going down, any way you slice it."

"But why drag me into it?"

"Because Max's operation is real tight. We can't get a guy inside. Max don't trust many people. Terry, he trusts Terry—"

"So go to Terry—"

"For one thing, Luciano wants Terry, too. And Terry won't bite the hand that feeds him."

"Give Luciano Max and he'd forget all about Terry."

"Lucky's got a long memory," Reagan said, shaking his head.

"You guys think I'm going along with this?"

Harry Madrid put a match to his pipe. "Yup, I think you will. If you don't, you heard what the man said. One spot gets removed. And he still gets Terry. There's no percentage in that, chum. It's a mug's bet. Who knows, you give Dewey and Luciano a hand here, Bauman goes inside, maybe you can deal for Terry's ass." He cupped his hand around the bowl of the little pipe and puffed mightily. "No other way, Lew. They've got you by the balls. And if Lucky blows you away, don't think Dewey'll give a shit. He won't. He needs Lucky." He shook his massive head. "Nobody blowin' smoke your way today. Truth time, all day long."

•   •   •

The rear chains were starting to bang at the inside of the fenders and the wind was pushing the big Cadillac around the road like a toy. Up ahead the clouds had begun to blow away and the glow of the city had come into view.

To pass the time Harry Madrid told Cassidy how Charlie Luciano had gotten his nickname. It was 1929. A smart Sicilian colleague of his called Salvatore Maranzano wanted Luciano to kill yet another Sicilian, a gang leader, Giuseppe Masseria. Maranzano set up a meeting at an empty warehouse on Staten Island.

The thing was, Luciano was just as smart as Maranzano: He knew the Sicilian Mafia tradition that a man who killed a superior could not then immediately take his place. Luciano wanted to be top man in the Outfit and saw through Maranzano's scheme to prevent his accession. He told Maranzano no dice.

Before Luciano knew what was happening the warehouse was full of Maranzano's boys intent on mayhem.

They strung Luciano up against the wall and had at him with clubs and belts. They ground cigarette butts into his back. They took turns slicing his face with razors. Maybe now, Maranzano suggested, he'd reconsider and ice Masseria. But no, with what little strength Luciano had left, he said he didn't think he would.

They finally cut him down. He looked like a butcher's mistake. They piled him into the back of a car and threw him out onto the road once they'd reached top speed. They figured the pavement would not only kill him but make such a mess of the corpse that nobody would notice the torture scars.

The cops found the body later on. They didn't think the poor bastard would live until they got him to the hospital but they gave it a try. It took fifty-five stitches to put just his face back together. And somehow he lived.

Meyer Lansky came to visit him, asked how he felt.

Luciano whispered through the bandages, "Lucky to be alive."

"Lucky," Lansky marveled. "Lucky Luciano, that's you."

And so it was.

CHAPTER FIVE

Winter turned to a cold, wet spring. The snow melted and the ice was gone from Central Park and the Japanese hadn't given up, which only went to show you that even doctors can be wrong. Insofar as Cassidy and Terry went, the doctors were doing fine. They both were slowly rounding back into something like their old form. Terry was thinking about testing his tender back by returning to work and Cassidy was getting used to maneuvering with his cane. The strength in his leg was hinting at a revival but it was going to be a long, slow process. He was still living at Terry's and the days were long and quiet. Terry had turned off the flow of female admirers who'd gotten into the habit of dropping by. It was as if he needed solitude to think but he never brought up the subject of the people who were watching him. Cassidy wondered if just possibly he'd forgotten about it, but no, that wasn't like Terry. What was happening was more like the celebrated "Phony War," which had occupied Europe while Hitler had rested, waited. Cassidy and Terry were both waiting out an interlude, waiting for all hell to break loose again. There was too damn much time to think, so far as Cassidy was concerned. It was almost as if Tom Dewey and Lucky Luciano had appeared to him in a crazy dream. There was no word from Harry Madrid, nothing. He thought of Luciano, back at Dannemora, listening to *The Romance of Helen Trent*, thinking about settling the score with Max Bauman and Terry Leary. He wondered if Lucky was growing impatient. The prospect was not a comforting one.

The failure of Harry Madrid to press him left Cassidy free to avoid facing the issue of Max and Terry. Nobody had asked him to produce information, so the dilemma remained at one remove. One thing he knew for sure: He couldn't betray Terry. With luck, no one would force his hand. But what if he had to betray him to save him?

He watched the papers for war news, read everything, and never missed the correspondents' reports on the radio. All in the hope of finding something which might shed any light on what could be happening to Karin in Cologne. The bombing of Germany had so far ignored Cologne, thank God. It was a fruitless search and he knew it. But he kept looking. He didn't know when he might stumble across some ray of hope, however faint. Some news. Anything. But there was nothing and he knew that was the best he could hope for. When Cologne made the papers, it was bound to be bad news. That was the only kind of news coming out of the fatherland these days.

She was over there, that was all he knew. So he went to sleep every night thinking of her, praying that she was all right.

But when he closed his eyes, it got worse. What he'd feared most, what he'd told himself could never happen, was beginning. It felt like a dreaded disease, long in remission, now beginning to run its course. He couldn't see her as clearly anymore. The memory of her was doing the one thing he'd known, *known*, it could never do. It was beginning to fade. Very slowly, but it was fading. Only he knew it. When he spoke of her to Terry, the words were no different. He loved her as much as he ever had. That wasn't the point. He loved her but time was stealing her away. With each day the worst thing happened, kept happening. Karin was slipping away from him. Every night he faced the darkness and the fact that love's fire was dimming at last. It wasn't lessening, only receding. He began to realize he was no longer in love with a woman. He was in love with an abstraction called Karin. A symbol . . . Karin just wasn't real anymore. He didn't know what to do about it. Maybe there wasn't anything he *could* do.

•　•　•

The Bataan Peninsula fell to the Japanese early in April. They took 36,000 prisoners. Cassidy figured the lucky ones had died in the fighting.

The war news was bad and both Terry and Lew had begun to grow weary and restless with their isolation. Cassidy was confronted by too many frustrations. He'd decided he'd waited long enough on Harry Madrid: What did the silence mean? Had they decided to proceed against Bauman and Terry without him? That was the worst possibility because it would deprive him of the chance to keep Terry out of it. Cassidy didn't care what happened to Max Bauman, not in the final instance, not if what he'd been told was true. But Terry . . . he had to keep Terry from going down aboard Max's ship. To complicate the issue, if he told Terry what was going on, God only knew what Terry might do . . . One thing was sure. Terry couldn't find out what was going on. It would be like lighting a stick of dynamite while you were locked in a closet.

One evening Terry casually mentioned that it would be fun to throw a party announcing their return to the land of the living. Cassidy leaped on the idea. When contemplating the guest list, the name of Harry Madrid came up: Cassidy observed that Harry had certainly paid enough hospital visits to earn an invitation. Terry agreed, threw in the names of a couple other homicide dicks, including

Bert Reagan, who invariably seemed to go where Harry Madrid went.

Paul Cassidy was in town for the first time since the Louis-Nova fight the previous autumn. Terry made sure Max Bauman and Bennie the Brute were there. And Max made sure that Cindy Squires got a night off from Heliotrope. Charley Drew took a night away from the Tap at the Taft to come by and play the piano. Terry arranged for several highly decorative, unattached women to join the group. Paul Cassidy brought a couple of wandering screenwriters and a publicist who'd been working on the Jane Russell campaign which had made her one of America's most famous stars, though no one had ever seen her act. It was the triumph of tits, according to Herman Redwine, the publicity man who'd introduced the special cantilevered brassiere, designed by Miss Russell's patron, Howard Hughes, to the waiting world. "Those tits don't have to *act*," Redwine observed with the bemused confidence of a man who has seen the future and recognized it as tits. "They just sort of have to sit there and look alert. This brassiere will do it, believe me." His shirt was too tight but the collar was too big and he talked with a smoke in his mouth. His eyes were bloodshot. Paul Cassidy said that between Hughes and Miss Russell's breasts Herman Redwine was not the man he'd once been.

There were thirty, maybe thirty-five people working their way through the White Horse and the Old Granddad and the ribs and all the chafing dishes full of stuff Terry had had sent over from Longchamps. Some of it was brown and tasted like chili. Some of it was yellow and tasted like lobster Newburg. It was all very festive. Cassidy tried not to think about Karin and the 36,000 guys on Bataan. Unfortunately, the first rank of alternatives—Harry Madrid, Tom Dewey, Lucky Luciano, and Max Bauman—was no great improvement.

•　　•　　•

Harry Madrid came early but immediately attached himself to Terry near the bar, putting back bourbon neat, and embarked on cop stories. Harry's face was getting red and Terry was laughing and two more cops joined the group and Cassidy stood watching them and wondering at all the camaraderie. Harry was quite an actor.

Paul Cassidy had brought along a movie projector and the Robert Montgomery picture *Here Comes Mr. Jordan*, which he was getting ready to show in the master bedroom. Lew gave up watching Madrid buddying up with Terry and went with his second drink to the bedroom, where his father was threading the film. Paul winked at him, kept talking to the pretty women who had clustered around him, wondering just how big a deal he was when it came to getting you into the movies. Cassidy smiled, remembering how his late mother had always enjoyed watching her husband charming the hopeful ladies. He'd always been good at it but she'd known he was a one-woman man, producer or not. When she'd known she didn't have much time left, she'd held her son's hand and smiled past her pain and told him to grow up to be a man like his father and she'd know it, she'd look down and be proud of him. She told him to understand if his father ever fell in love again, because a person needed someone to share his good times and his bad times. She'd made him promise and he had, but Paul Cassidy had never fallen in love again. "I'm lucky, Lew," he'd told him years later. "I'm in love now, see, son, I've always been in love with one woman and it'll just be a while before I'm back with her. So don't worry, kid. I'm fine."

Now he was telling the ladies about Hollywood's idea of a wartime crisis. MGM may have had more stars than there were in heaven but they also had an Eleanor Powell musical called *I'll Take Manila* and consternation had swept the executive suites.

A pretty blonde batted her eyes and pouted: "What's the big deal, vanilla, chocolate, or butter brickle?"

Paul looked dolefully at his son. "Manila. In the Philippines, my child. Not vanilla as in Schrafft's. See, Eleanor Powell isn't going to take Manila anymore. The only people likely to take Manila now are the Japs," and the blonde laughed like Billie Burke. She didn't know what the hell he was talking about. Maybe she hadn't heard about the war.

He told them that Gable had taken Lombard's death very hard. He expected Gable to enlist any day now. Female eyes filled and shone moistly at the thought of a grieving Rhett Butler. Cassidy kept thinking of those poor bastards on Bataan. But Paul was doing all he could, salvaging the family honor. He was putting together another Bond Tour with a bunch of stars, Bogart and Tracy and Mary Astor and Loretta Young and a lot of others. Remember Pearl Harbor, that's what everyone was saying.

• • •

"Sorry to hear about the leg, Lew."

He turned around and saw a man wearing an officer's uniform, perfectly tailored, a brown coat, and immaculately creased officer's pinks with a wonderful break at the top of his gleaming cordovans. He was tall, thick, and filled the doorway. He was smoking a cigarette in a black holder and carrying a lowball glass. He was tight-mouthed but smiling with pale green eyes. His name was Bryce Huntoon. He'd been a Harvard fullback when Cassidy was in his last year at Deerfield. He'd tried to model his running style on Huntoon's. Lots of stiff-arming. Cassidy hadn't seen him more than a few times in the past five years but he made the society columns from time to time. Part-time ladies' man, a full-time hotshot Wall Street lawyer.

"Occupational hazard, Bryce. That's what I get from running around with a football. Glad you could come. What the hell kind of getup is that?"

"Oh, this," Huntoon said, shaking his head of wavy hair. "I don't like wearing this, it makes me feel like I'm fighting the war, or trying to look like someone who is, and I'm not." He was a stuffed shirt but not a bad guy. The cigarette holder was a little much, though. "False pretenses. But I'm a soldier for the duration, officially anyway. They insist I wear this monkey suit—"

"They give you a gun?"

"Are you kidding? No, no gun. No basic training either, thank God. I'm in the army but mainly I sit at a desk doing what I do best. Shuffling papers. What I've always done. Contracts for war material. Right now I'm working with Mr. Bauman. Scrap metal, trucking . . . everybody's got to pitch in these days."

They walked back toward the music. The living room was crowded and smoky. Charley Drew was playing "Don't Sit Under the Apple Tree."

"What's your rank, Bryce?"

"Colonel. Don't ask me why—"

"Uniform make you lucky with the ladies?" Terry asked the question, smiling, surveying the party with satisfaction.

"Terry, old man, I'm always lucky with the ladies, hadn't you heard?"

"Well, good luck tonight," Terry said. He went off to greet Max Bauman, Bennie the Brute and Cindy Squires. Their coats were wet with rain.

"Why, there's Mr. Bauman now," Huntoon said. "Who's that with him?"

"The gentleman who would blot out the moon, were there a moon, is known as Bennie the Brute—"

"No, no, the girl. The frail, as Terry used to say."

Cassidy looked back. She was getting her bearings, casing the joint, looking a little uncertain, the way she had at the door of Cassidy's hospital room.

"Cindy Squires. She works at Max's club."

"And? Go on."

"Singer," Cassidy added.

"Well, luck don't fail me now."

Cassidy watched him head across the sunken living room. The man had a damn fine tailor.

•   •   •

Cassidy had drifted past some couples who were dancing slowly near the piano and was making himself another drink when he felt Harry Madrid settle in at the bar beside him. His gray hair was plastered down and his blue suit was pulling across his broad meaty shoulders. He grinned crookedly and spoke out of the corner of his mouth, like a man confiding a dirty story. "Fancy," he said, nodding at the room. "Can't say old Terry doesn't know how to live." He pulled a cigar from his breast pocket. "Terry gave me this, one of Max's. The Babe coulda hit a homer with one of these babies. Light me, will ya, Cassidy?"

"Light yourself, flatfoot. I don't seem to hear much from you these days, Harry. You give me the dog-and-pony show, then it gets real quiet. Not nice, Harry."

"What are you all of a sudden, some kinda tough guy? Tough guy with a cane?" He frowned and lit a match.

"I've always been a tough guy. Be careful. I might stick this cane right up your nose." He sipped the Scotch and soda and looked into Harry's little black eyes. It was hard to believe they were windows to the soul or any other damn thing. They were like mirrors where you saw all the bad things about yourself.

"Relax, Lew, we're all friends here. It's a party."

"I'm a little itchy, Harry. Ratting on my best friend always gets under my skin. The way it strikes me now, it's all your fault."

"You haven't done any ratting yet, Lew. Relax. Hell, maybe you wanna forget the whole thing, let Terry go into the shitter with Max . . . it's all the same to Harry Madrid." The match was burning his fingers and he dropped it. It smoldered on the pale carpeting.

"Pick it up, Harry."

"Aw, for the chrissakes—"

"Pick up the fuckin' match, Harry." Casually he placed the point of his cane on Harry Madrid's shoe and leaned on it a little.

"You're being a prick, Lew—"

"The match . . ." He leaned a little harder.

Harry Madrid's face got red when he bent down and dug the match from the carpet. It broke and made his fingertips black. He puffed and dropped the match into the ashtray on the bar.

"You pull this shit, Lew, you're gonna go right off the high ledge." He struck another match and got the cigar lit.

"Sure, sure, I'll watch it, Harry. Terry hasn't said a word about Max, not a word about gas stations or rationing stamps. What can I do? I can't make him—"

Harry Madrid interrupted. "You haven't let on to Terry about any of this?"

"Are you kidding? I tell Terry what Dewey and Luciano and you are up to, he'll get his gun and use you guys for target practice."

"That's what I mean." He nodded vigorously. "He's a touchy sonuvabitch."

"Touchy? You want to put him in the big house and you don't want him to get touchy about it? You ask too much, Copper. But no, I haven't told him. You'll know if I do."

"We'd have to kill him. And you'd be responsible, Sunny Jim. He shows one sign of knowing what Tom and Lucky have got planned . . ." He raised his eyebrows, a paradigm of injured weariness. "He's deader than Lindbergh's baby, get me? Mum's the word."

"And so cleverly put," Cassidy said.

Harry Madrid shrugged, looking hard at the room. He was sweating. "We got other sources. You're not the only one. This is big stuff, Lew. You're just a little piss-poor part of it . . . We're gonna get Max—"

"You're smoking Max's cigars, you're drinking Terry's liquor. What kind of guy are you?"

"Thirsty guy who appreciates a good smoke. What kind of guy are you, Lew?"

"Still tough," Cassidy said. "Did I hurt your foot, Harry?"

"Yeah, you bastard."

"Good. That's good. That was the whole point."

"You're makin' a mistake here, Lew. I'm your buddy's only chance—if we nail Max, just maybe . . ." He shrugged. Anything was possible, maybe even saving Terry's ass.

"Then I'd say he's in trouble."

"That's as may be. Slim chance is better than none."

"Better be," Cassidy said. "For your sake."

"I'll be all right, don't you worry about Harry Madrid. And Terry—he stays in the dark. Ignorance is bliss."

"Don't be out of touch for so long this time, Harry. Let me know what's going on." He smiled at Madrid, who looked momentarily confused. "Relax, Harry. We're in this together, you and me and Lucky and Tom Dewey. I just got a little touchy a minute ago. Hey, let's see a smile, it's a party, remember?"

"You're way outa line, Lew." He began moving away.

"Enjoy yourself," Cassidy said. He'd have to watch his temper. It was always lurking in its cave, occasionally rattling its chains, needing exercise. Football was a help. But there wouldn't be any more football. He watched Harry mingling, moving through the crowd. He didn't look like he belonged. He looked like a security man hired for the night. *We got other sources. You're not the only one.* What the hell was he talking about? Somebody else close to Max Bauman? Max wasn't close to anyone. Maybe Harry was blowing smoke, just whistling "Dixie."

• • •

Marquardt Cookson always had to be the center of attention, which, given his size and high-pitched voice and the constant beacon from his vast, sweating, domed forehead, was inevitable anyway. That night he arrived wearing a crimson-lined opera cape, carrying a large rectangular package about four inches thick. His little friend carried the oversize rain-slick umbrella and a magnum of Dom Pérignon '27. He surged through the crowd, grabbed Terry in a great moist hug, then made a place for himself on the big cream-colored couch. He held out his hand for the handkerchief, dabbed at his forehead, then looked down at his patent-leather dancing pumps. There was no way he could reach them. He pointed at them, handed the handkerchief to the pretty boy, who dropped to his knees and whisked the rain spots from the glossy finish. Terry placed a silver bucket of ice on the coffee table and rotated the champagne, screwing it down into the cracked ice. Cassidy moved closer, watching. Harry Madrid stood at the edge of the circle, scowling intently at the unfolding scene.

Cookson took the bottle of champagne from the bucket and quickly worked the cork up with his thumbs. It rocketed out and glanced off a long mirror with a chromium frame. He ceremoniously filled several glasses, passed them around. He motioned to someone to come closer, offered a glass. Harry Madrid accepted it blandly. It hadn't seemed to Cassidy at the Louis fight that they'd known each other, but now they did. Harry Madrid seemed to get around.

Cookson lifted the glass. "To me! And to my greatest acquisition!" He tapped the package. Everyone drank. The group made a little island in the center of the party, which had lost interest and was racketing along on its own.

"What is it, Markie?" Terry asked.

"A copy of the *Necronomicon!*"

Harry Madrid laughed. "Like he said, what is it?"

Marquardt Cookson explained, his pudgy hands cradling the new possession. He lived entirely in his own world, where there was no war, no Bataan, no real life. In his world there was only the timeless, eternal vastness of Marquardt Cookson.

Charley Drew was playing "Tonight We Love," courtesy of Freddy Martin via Tchaikovsky, very loudly right behind him, but from what Cassidy could tell this *Necronomicon* was some kind of ancient Book of the Dead, full of witchcraft spells which, if you did them right, were capable of summoning up the dead and all the scary powers of the Darkness Beyond. Cookson nattered on and the champagne flowed as champagne does and Cassidy began to get a headache. He was slipping away from the nuttiness when he felt a hand on his arm. It was Harry Madrid again.

"Florida," he said.

"What?"

"Florida. Supposed to be some guys comin' up from Florida. Keep your ears open, you hear anything, let me know. Could be Johnny Rocco's boys . . ." Harry Madrid was back to scowling at Cookson. "The fat man's higher than a kite. Guys like that worry me. I look into my crystal ball, nothin' there. No future. Sylvester Bean was like that. He'd been on borrowed time for twenty years, you ask me." He blinked at Cassidy. He looked tired, older than he was. He dug a finger into his hairy ear. "You use dope, Lew?"

"Nope."

"Atta boy." He leaned close, took the cigar out of his mouth. "No hard feelings, Lew?"

"No hard feelings, Harry."

"Man's gotta do what a man's gotta do," Harry Madrid said. "Florida? You lemme know, you hear any talk.'

• • •

Charley Drew had switched to "Cabin in the Sky," a Vernon Duke song. Terry had once told Cassidy that Vernon Duke's real name was Vladimir Dukelsky. He knew funny things like that, couldn't forget them. He said it was a curse.

A woman spoke from behind him. "Don't you find that man rather—how to say it? Creepy? Scary?"

He looked at her. A cat's face with an upper lip that didn't move much when she spoke. Her hair was like white gold, which she raked from her eye with a long fingernail painted brownish red, like dried blood. She wore a low-cut black cocktail dress. Her breasts were tiny. Her shoulders with the stringlike straps were frail, delicate, fine-boned. Her eyes had that faraway look, shining as if they were full of tears. They were almond-shaped, like a cat's.

"Harry?" he said. "Yeah, I suppose. Scary, anyway. He's a little hard to be creepy. Hard men are scary. I didn't know you knew him."

"Max knows everybody," Cindy Squires said. "But I didn't mean Harry Madrid. That one"—she inclined her head—"the fat one. With the boyfriend. Look into his eyes sometimes. He's drowning in drugs, killing himself—"

104

"Oh, Markie." Cassidy smiled. "He gets a little tedious, but he has his good points."

"Really? Somehow I doubt that. I wish Max didn't know him so well."

"They do seem an odd pair. Max probably just knows him in passing."

"Oh, you think so?" She shrugged. "Max knows everybody," she said again. "That's what they'll put on his tombstone. 'Here lies Max Bauman. He knew everybody but didn't have a friend.' Somebody he knows will be the death of him, too."

"I'd say Max is pretty careful," Cassidy said. He lit her cigarette, watched it tremble in her fingers. Her lipstick smudged the paper.

"Not careful enough. Someday when he least expects it . . ." She made a pistol out of a pointed forefinger and a cocked thumb. "Pa-choo, pa-choo," she said, firing the gun. "That'll be all for Max . . ."

He followed her eyes and saw Bauman standing in his tuxedo by the fireplace talking to Terry. They looked serious. Were they talking about Rocco coming up from Florida? Rocco had a place on Key Largo, a gunboat or two, ran girls and money and dope in and out of Havana. Everybody knew about Rocco, one of the old Chicago gang. He'd been in the papers using his gunboats to hunt for German U-boats off the Florida coast. Somebody had suggested giving him a medal. Was Rocco coming up from Key Largo to see Max? Was Max cutting him in on the gas stations and the stamps?

When he turned back to Cindy Squires, one eye had overflowed and a large teardrop clung to an eyelash, losing the struggle against gravity. She stuck out her lower lip like a little girl looking for a fight.

"Are you all right?"

"Of course. I always cry at parties."

"Listen, I can't tell if you're serious or pulling my leg or what. You'll just have to slow down on the curves if you want me to follow you."

"Who said I wanted you to follow me or anything else?

105

Why don't you go pour your fat friend some more champagne, play the host, get him some cocaine . . . Oh, damn!" The tears were streaking her face. He took her arm gently. "No, no, you mustn't touch me. He'll see . . . I'll be all right." He withdrew his hand, watched her helplessly. "Look"—she swallowed a sob—"are you really trustworthy? Like Terry says? Do you run to Max with everything you hear?"

"You keep asking me that."

"Don't be silly. I know Max, that's all. He's the poor guy who owns the Bulldogs and as such I feel sorry for him. Come on, smile at that."

She sniffed, smiled. "It's not such a hot team," she admitted, dabbing a knuckle at a wet eye. "I need to talk to someone I can trust . . . I'm scared. Oh, damn, I can't stop crying. He's going to see me—where's the bathroom?"

He led the way down the hallway, past the movie in the large bedroom, to his own room. The rain was blowing at the windows and it was dark in the room except for the street lamps' glow. The bed was piled with coats. He pointed to the bathroom door.

She started across the room, then turned back, sobbing, her guard down, and stood against him with her head on his boiled shirtfront. He felt her shaking and he put his arms around her. She made herself small, he smelled her hair and kissed it. It tasted blonde.

"Cassidy," she whispered several moments later. They hadn't moved. He felt lulled, holding a woman, feeling her body and her warmth. Her crying had stopped. "I'm sorry about this. There's something so sad about everything—I don't even know you and yet you're the person I come crying to when I'm scared . . ."

"What are you scared of?"

"I can't talk to you now. He's going to wonder where I've gone, I've got to get back." She stood at the bathroom door. "Can we meet somewhere? I need to talk to someone, to you, I guess . . . I need help." She came back and took his hand. "Please . . ."

"Sure, we can talk. And when it comes to help, there's always Terry—"

"No," she gasped. "Not Terry, anyone but Terry. You mustn't mention any of this to Terry. Promise me—"

"All right. No Terry."

She squeezed his hand. He didn't let go, pulled her toward him, kissed her. Felt her warm breath in his mouth, her moist tongue, the membrane hidden beneath her tongue. She trembled against him and finally he released her. She turned quickly away, fled to the bathroom. He waited until she came back.

When they stepped out of the darkened room into the hallway, a huge figure, taller and wider than Cassidy, loomed over them.

"Ah, there you are, Miss Squires." It was Bennie, looking concerned, almost wounded, behind his spectacles. His tuxedo fit perfectly because Max's tailor did him, too. He wore his usual polka-dot bow tie. His eyes moved from her to Cassidy. His huge nose twitched, as if he were smelling a rat. "Lew," he said.

"What is it, Bennie?" she said.

"Mr. Bauman wants you. I couldn't find you." He was slightly out of breath. It was his job to find people for Mr. Bauman and it bothered him when he couldn't do it.

"Mr. Cassidy showed me the ladies' room, Bennie. I wasn't feeling well. I'm fine now."

"I waited to make sure she was okay." Cassidy explained himself to Bennie because no one wanted Bennie or Max upset with them. He smiled at Bennie.

"Let's go find Max," she said.

"Good idea," Cassidy said.

Cindy Squires moved away, back toward the party. Bennie looked at Cassidy. He was frowning. He took off his spectacles and began polishing them with his folded handkerchief.

"Having a nice time, Bennie?"

"Lew," Bennie said, checking the lenses and fitting the glasses over his huge ears, "you've got lipstick on your mouth." He handed Lew a perfect white handkerchief.

Bennie shook his head slowly. "You better be careful, Lew. You better watch yourself. Know what I mean?"

"It's always a pleasure being threatened by you, Bennie."

"I'd never threaten you, Lew. We're friends. I was just thinking out loud, so to speak." He looked sad, almost mournful. It was mainly in the eyebrows. "There's so much pain in the world, why add to it?"

"I see your point."

"Be careful, Lew." Bennie turned away. "I better go see Miss Squires doesn't get lost again. Women, Lew, never trust 'em."

Cassidy went back into his bedroom, stood in the spot where Cindy Squires had held herself against him. He summoned up the smell of her hair, the faint memory of lilacs. There had been sapphires and diamonds at her throat, and her earrings had been sapphires matching her eyes, almost iridescent blue.

•   •   •

When he went back to the party, Bennie was standing with a plate of food, eating and watching Max Bauman, who was talking with Marquardt Cookson. Cindy stood quietly at Max's side.

"Having a good time, Bennie?"

"Very enjoyable, Lew. A lovely gathering in every way."

Bauman and Cindy Squires came over to where they stood. Bennie looked from Max to Cindy. "Mr. Bauman was wondering earlier if you'd do a song or two with Mr. Drew . . . could you do that, Miss Squires?"

Max looked fondly at Bennie like a man proud of a well-trained pet.

"Oh, gosh, Max, I don't know—"

"I'd appreciate it, darling," Max Bauman said. "Charley said he'd love to play for you."

"All right," she sighed. Her eyes caught Cassidy's, the light behind the sapphires dimming as if her wattage were running low, her resistance ebbing.

She went to the piano, where Charley Drew was waiting

108

for her. Terry stood morosely across the room, by the windows, watching the rain lashing the terrace. Bennie stood beside Cassidy, watching Bauman drawn once again into a peculiar conversational triangle with Marquardt Cookson and Harry Madrid. Bennie was staring straight ahead when he spoke. "Mr. Bauman is very fond of that girl. You might say he's taken a deeply personal interest. Know what I mean, Lew?"

"Hey, Bennie, who do you think you're talking to? This is Lew. A college man. Not a chump. I got eyes, I see what's going on."

"Glad to hear it, Lew. She's living out at the house now, y'know. That's how it is. I knew you wouldn't let me down. Mr. Bauman, he takes a real personal interest in you, too."

Cookson had begun reciting some kind of ominous-sounding chant. Max Bauman shook his head. Harry Madrid looked on as if it were feeding time at the zoo. A buff-colored envelope was working its way out of Cookson's pocket and his boyfriend pushed it back in.

Charley Drew's fingers began stroking the keys, and Cindy Squires sang "Fools Rush In," her blue eyes anchored someplace where she was all by herself. The emotions only barely hinted at in her voice were somehow palpable, reaching across the room toward Cassidy, lapping at him. She sang "The Nearness of You."

> *It's not the pale moon that excites me*
> *That thrills and delights me*
> *Oh no, it's just the nearness of you.*

She was so delicate, so fragile, but her hips were broad and female and strong, her sturdy legs planted wide apart when she sang. She hardly moved a muscle while she sang. No histrionics, no flailing arms, no fluttering hands. It was all in her voice. She didn't really have much range. She was no songbird, no liltin' Martha Tilton. But her reading of the lyrics was impeccable. Cassidy wondered where she'd come from, how she'd learned to do what she did, submerging her own personality in the song, transforming the song and herself into some new, third thing. She sang "I'll Remember April" and Cassidy couldn't watch anymore.

He wanted her.

She was the first woman he'd wanted, deep in his gut, since Karin, and the realization hit him with a truckload of sudden guilt and sorrow and longing. Since Karin had gone, there hadn't been anyone. Oh, some quickies on road trips, but nothing real. Now he needed to hold someone and be held and it couldn't be Karin and he wanted it to be Cindy Squires . . .

•   •   •

He stood just inside the doorway of the darkened room. Seven or eight people were sprawled on Terry's bed or sitting on the floor while the projector's light beam poked through the filter of cigarette smoke. He sipped the Scotch and water and held the cold glass against his forehead. The rain drummed on the window. Robert Montgomery was caught in a wonderful fantasy of life and death, love and the power of memory. He was dead by accident, a mistake, and had been allowed to come back as someone else and met the girl he'd once loved in that other life. She was a stranger, but, still, there was a spark of something . . . as if he'd known her, or someone very like her, once before . . .

He stood in the dark trying to get Cindy Squires's face and voice and scent out of his mind, failing. She was out of bounds. She was Max Bauman's girl. That made her more dangerous than Axis Sally and Tokyo Rose put together. And how many ways could you betray a man? You could betray him to the will of Harry Madrid, spy on him, rat on him . . . and you could betray him with his girlfriend. Lots of guys had doubtless done both.

But not to Max Bauman. Not guys who lived to tell the story. It was a dangerous fucking game is what it was.

And Cindy Squires brought with her, like the perfume, a fill-the-room-with-danger quality. There was something about her that made him want to put on the old armor and

110

mount his steed and charge on it, something about her, like theme music, that made him want her even while he knew there were people who wouldn't survive, whose blood would overflow the scuppers. Maybe he just didn't care. The world was dripping with blood, why should he be immune? He closed his eyes and there she was, the sapphire eyes, the way she raked the sharp nails so near her eye . . . the way her body had quaked against him when she cried . . .

Then he heard two men talking behind him, out of sight in the hallway.

• • •

"So tell me, Harry, what's bothering our Terry? He's not himself, not atall, not atall." It was Father Paddy, Terry's uncle.

"Can't say as I know what you're talking about, Padre." That was Harry Madrid, all right. Cassidy got a whiff of the cherry tobacco. He must have been lighting up the little pipe.

"He's mighty worried, our Terry," Father Paddy said.

"Somebody just put a couple slugs in him," Harry allowed. "Makes a fella kinda peaked, I reckon, don't you?"

"It's not just that. He kept saying people had it in for him long before his misfortune. Well, I thought it'd stop—y'know, thinking it was this Herrin who'd had it in for him, but no, he's still worried. Not that he lets on to the world in general. But, hellfire, I'm the lad's old uncle Paddy, not much he keeps from me . . ."

"But he never says who, that it? You'd tell me, wouldn't you, Padre? If Terry said anything at all, you'd let me know . . . a man gets shot, sometimes he gets funny ideas afterward, don't make no sense, I've seen it happen before." Harry Madrid was puffing, the scent turned the corner, seeped into the bedroom. "There might be something I could do about it. You know what I mean, Padre?"

"Aye, and you're a fine fella, Harry Madrid." They had begun moving off down the hallway. "I'll let you know if I

111

hear him leaving hints behind him. I appreciate your concern, Harry. I'll be lighting a candle for you."

Harry chuckled. "Much obliged, I'm sure." And then they were gone.

•　　•　　•

When the movie was over, Cassidy went back to the living room. Bryce Huntoon was standing at the bar talking to Cindy Squires. He was one of those guys burning up the tracks between New York and Washington. They seemed to have all the answers, leaping upon them like hounds gathered around a medieval dining table snapping up scraps. Gossip was the valuable currency of the day and everybody had a source somewhere. He wondered if Cindy Squires was impressed with Huntoon and his uniform and his connections. He hoped not. He was already feeling jealous and the poor bastard was just talking to her. But he was also a ladies' man . . .

Later on people started to leave. The party was over. It was past midnight. Terry and Cassidy were patting people on the back, standing by the door. Terry's face was pale and drawn. Lew figured his back was giving him trouble.

Paul Cassidy, with the screenwriters and the publicist and a couple of girls in tow, stopped to tell his son he was hoping to get into film production for the army. It would mean he'd be going overseas. Maybe North Africa where Rommel's Panzer Korps was working the desert like they owned it. He was excited at the prospect.

Charley Drew kept playing the late-night tunes and then almost everyone was gone. Cassidy made a last drink, leaned on the bar with his back to the mirror, looking out over the room. Cindy Squires slowly circled the place snapping off most of the lamps until it was restful and dim. The piano went on softly. The rain streamed down the French windows overlooking Park Avenue in the fog below. Bennie the Brute leaned back in a deep chair, crossed his long legs, tugged at his bow tie until it was dangling down his shirtfront. Cassidy casually touched the smudge of lipstick on his own shirt. Max Bauman's

112

face had collapsed. He looked old suddenly, staring at the rain. Cindy Squires sat down on the floor, her legs underneath her, leaned her head back against the couch, and closed her eyes. Her rounded thighs were tight against the black dress and her belly was imperceptibly rounded. Cassidy watched her and sipped his drink and tried to figure out what he should do, how he was going to go about it. There was Rocco coming up from Florida, there was Max up against Dewey and Luciano and Harry Madrid. There was Lew Cassidy with a wife he couldn't get to . . . and unable to take his eyes off Cindy Squires . . . who was scared and wanted to believe he was as trustworthy as Terry said.

In the stillness, with the piano tinkling forlornly, Charley Drew hunched over the keys, exploring a world of his own, Max Bauman began to talk.

"Well, it's quite an old world, isn't it, folks? Nice party, Terry, Lew. Very nice." He looked around at their faces and put his hands up, squeezed his temples. "I got a call today, I haven't told anyone about it yet. Not even Bennie, Cindy here. From a navy friend of my son Irvie's. Another officer. Quite a story he had to tell. Irvie . . . quite a boy, my Irvie. Lotsa guts, you said that, Lew. Guts."

Cassidy nodded but Max didn't see him. He wasn't looking at anybody. He sat on the couch, his hands clenched on his knees.

"Communications officer. Ship got torpedoed in the bow . . . Irvie was down in the communications office with a buddy of his when they got hit . . . hell of a mess, according to this fella. Fire. Ship started to heel over . . . see, thing was, they couldn't get out, Irvie and his pal. So they started playing poker. Poker! Can you believe that? Cool under fire. You know how this fella knew? I'll tell ya. He was on the flight deck and they could talk to Irvie and his buddy down below . . . all the time they were trapped in the communications office they were talking to the guys on the flight deck. Guts, Lewis . . . Guts! There wasn't any way to get them out, see, they all knew it, they weren't going to make it . . . the ship kept

113

heeling, the water coming in, the pressure building on the bulkheads, the air getting thin, hard to breathe . . . and Irvie and his buddy just kept playing poker . . . they *knew* they weren't getting out but they didn't panic, they kept on talking to the guys topside . . . then it was time to say good-bye . . . Irvie was the last one to talk, he said tell my dad I'm not afraid, I know what's going on, it's time for us to sign off now, tell Dad I love him, tell him I'm going out ten bucks to the good . . . and then there wasn't any more talk . . . ten bucks to the good, that's quite a boy, my son Irvie . . ."

Tears were welling up in the creases of Max Bauman's face, spilling over, but he wasn't making a sound.

Charley Drew hadn't heard the story. He was playing a pretty song, singing softly to himself. "I saw you last night . . . and got that old feeling . . ."

Cassidy set his drink down on what he thought from the corner of his attention was a bar towel. It was instead a buff-colored envelope. The same one he'd seen in Markie Cookson's pocket. It was thick with no name on it. Cassidy slid it off the countertop and opened the loose flap. Everyone was sitting quietly in the semidarkness, thinking about Irvie Bauman. From the envelope Cassidy slid ten one-thousand-dollar bills. His throat went dry and he took another sip of his drink. He put the currency back into the envelope and replaced it on the counter, set his drink on it. Cookson had casually left ten grand behind. For Terry. Which was a hell of a way to say thanks for a pretty fair party.

Cindy Squires slowly turned her head until she was looking at Cassidy. Her face was expressionless but her eyes lingered until he returned the stare. Max Bauman reached forward and folded her delicate white hand in his.

Lucky Luciano said Max was doing the Nazis' dirty work on the docks. And the Nazis were turning Max's family in the old country into soap. And Johnny Rocco might be coming north to get his cut of a wartime racket of Max's. Everybody was after Max and Cassidy wanted his girlfriend and Harry Madrid was standing like grim Fate in the shadows and Terry had ten fresh ones from the fat man . . .

But in his mind Cassidy saw a different kind of headline.

GANGSTER'S KID DIES A HERO

CHAPTER SIX

A couple weeks later Bennie the Brute arrived with an invitation from Max Bauman. "He said to tell you he's sorry about burdening you that night with his private grief," Bennie announced by way of preface. "He said to tell you it was a fine party and he hopes he didn't put a damper on it. He'd like to have you join him for dinner down on the Jersey shore. Day after tomorrow."

Terry nodded and looked at Cassidy. "Sure," he said, "that's fine by me."

"How's Max holding up?" Terry asked.

"He's having a tough time," Bennie confided. "It'll be good for him, taking a little outing. Can't get his mind off what happened to the boy. Wakes up in the night shouting to the kid. He thinks he's on the flight deck and he can't get below to save the boy and he keeps hearing Irvie begging him to help . . . Frankly it gives me the shakes when I hear him screaming like that." He shook his head at the thought and so did Cassidy. The idea of Bennie the Brute with the shakes gave you pause. "He's got something he

116

wants to show you guys. Fireworks, he calls it. But you've got to go to Jersey for the full effect. I'll tell him you're on, then, both of you?"

"Anyone else in the party?" Terry was clipping the end of one of the big Havanas.

Bennie shrugged. "Small party. That's all I know—"

"Is Max really bad off?" Cassidy said.

"It's a bad time for him, that's all. It was bad when the missus went back in '34, too, but at least he had Irvie and the daughter to help him through it. Now there's no Arlene, the daughter's married and in Phoenix for her husband's asthma, and all of a sudden Irvie's never coming back. It's a bad time for Mr. Bauman."

"Well," Cassidy said, "he's got Miss Squires. That must be some consolation."

"Tell him we wouldn't miss his fireworks," Terry said.

When Bennie left, Cassidy sat for a long time in the gathering darkness of a murky afternoon thinking of the house overlooking the waters of Oyster Bay. A house fit for Jay Gatz. And Max Bauman waking up screaming for his dead son in the depths of the night. Bennie's slippered feet echoing and flapping along the hallway as he hastened to his master's side. Together they might sit in Max's library, surrounded by volumes purchased by the running yard and never read, sipping Scotch, waiting for first light. He wondered where Cindy Squires fit into the picture. And he wondered why she hadn't called him, hadn't come to him as she had wanted to . . .

•　•　•

But the next day Max had developed pleurisy and was laid up. He'd been out patrolling the shoreline with a shotgun in the cold and rain. All over Long Island the citizenry had formed themselves into squads patrolling at night, looking out for German saboteurs coming ashore from U-boats. It was no joke. A few had been caught and no one knew how many had gotten through and lost themselves in the canyons of the city. Max had undertaken his patrol with great enthusiasm and the inclement weather too many nights in a row had brought him low.

Bennie showed up with the news that Max wasn't coming but the fireworks expedition was still on. It was still dank and clammy, like a bad November, and Cindy Squires was wearing a heavy, belted trench coat and a beret that made her look like a beautiful French Resistance fighter. Or rather, Paul Cassidy's idea of such a creature in the movies. Paired with Errol Flynn, blowing up bridges and ammo dumps.

The big Chrysler wore an *E* sticker on its window, now that rationing was in full effect. An *A* got you only one stamp, which was worth five gallons of gasoline a week. A *B* was for commuters. *C* was for cars used in the line of work by salesmen and such. *E*s were hard to get. You still had to use stamps but you could get as many as you wanted. They were for emergency vehicles. Reporters had them, tow-truck drivers, cops, politicians with pull. And, apparently, gangsters.

Terry rode in front with Bennie; Cassidy got in back with Cindy Squires. Bennie kept glancing in the rearview mirror, nervously, as if he didn't really want to catch Cassidy kissing her but had his responsibilities to his employer to consider. He needn't have worried. Cassidy and Cindy sat in opposite corners, staring out the windows.

When Terry turned on the radio, she seemed to pull herself back from her thoughts, started to talk. She told him that Max had told her about Karin's being trapped in Germany. She wanted to hear all about it and Cassidy told her. She asked him if he had a picture and he slid a snapshot from his wallet. She said, "She's beautiful. She looks sad, though."

"She had a toothache that day. She's not normally sad."

"You must be lonely—"

"I miss her, if that's what you mean."

"I guess that is what I mean."

"In that sense, yes, I'm lonely. I've always been a loner but she changed that. It's good, loving someone."

"It must be," she said.

They talked about the war. It turned out that her father was English, her mother American, and they were both still in London. "My father is at the Foreign Office and Mummy works in her garden. And arranges the church jumble sales and she's a fire warden. She kept a very stiff upper lip when the bombing was bad. They sent me over here in '38 because war was coming and they didn't want us to be in it. My brother Tony and me. He's fourteen and I'm twenty-two. There's my sister Gillian, she's living in the Cotswolds with our aunt, safe enough, I should think. She's twenty-three. Tony goes to school at a school called Deerfield. My mother's family is from Boston. We stayed with them for a time. What about you, Lew? Before you played football?"

"There is no before, not really. I went to Deerfield, too."

"Really? What a small world! But you must have been born somewhere—"

"Los Angeles. My father's in the movie business. My mother died before I got to college. We lived in New York, too. No brothers or sisters. Football, Terry, Karin." He shrugged. "The war."

They had crossed into Jersey. Looking back across the Hudson it was a shock to see how dark the city looked with the new dim-out laws in effect. The lights of Broadway were already a memory. There was a war on.

She was looking back across the river, too.

"I was there," she said, pointing, "the night the *Normandie* burned."

"You were?" He flashbacked on Luciano, the smells of the disinfectant and the lavish lunch mingling in memory. "Why was that?"

She moved away from the window and he smelled her, saw her profile in the darkness, forgot the prison and Luciano. Then he saw Bennie's eyes flickering in the mirror, watching.

"Max wanted to see it so we drove down to the pier. You know how everybody knows Max, we got close . . . it was like a peek into Dante's last circle. The hull was red-

119

hot . . . *red*. And all the hoses were spraying it and the water just kept hissing and turning to steam. The fire crackled, it was loud, and this incredible hissing sound, like a million snakes. The fire was so bright in the night and there were all these searchlights trained on the ship . . . it was like nothing anyone could imagine. There were all these beautiful rainbows—"

"In the middle of the night?"

"That's what made it so unearthly. The lights were so bright the hoses made rainbows with the water. Then it just turned on its side and sank." Her voice trailed off.

They didn't talk much the rest of the way. There were no references to their previous conversation. He saw her pale hand on the seat between them. He put his hand over it, closed his fingers around hers. She made no attempt to move away, just kept looking out the window. The silence made Bennie nervous. He damn near ran the car off the road while trying to keep track of the backseat in the mirror.

•   •   •

There was a dinky little police roadblock on the way to the roadhouse. One cop car, two overage officers huddled inside out of the wind whipping off the water. Bennie waved a piece of paper at the one who got out and came over to have a look. He was wearing a yellow slicker. Sand pelted in through the window Bennie opened. Then he walked up ahead in the headlamps and moved the sawhorses blocking the lonely road.

"All these roads are closed off now," Terry said.

"Why?" she asked.

"German saboteurs. They're landing them from U-boats all along the coast. Miami Beach, Cape Hatteras, all the way up to Nova Scotia. I sure as hell pity any of 'em run across these two hardcases." He laughed sarcastically, nodding at the guy holding the sawhorse, waving them through.

They turned off the road onto a sand-blown path leading up to a jutting promontory which hung over the beach like the prow of a derelict sailing ship. The wind blew cold and salty and the sand rattled against the side panels. There was a dim red bulb over the once brightly lit entrance. The windows were hung with blackout curtains. The Chrysler was the only car in the lot.

Terry got out, pulling his hat brim down against the wind. He held the door for Cindy Squires and Cassidy slid across with his cane and got out behind her.

"Must be tough staying in business," Cassidy said, surveying the emptiness.

Terry said, "He's got a very special, very loyal clientele. Max, a few other businessmen." He winked at Cassidy. Cindy had gone on past them, taken Bennie's arm, and was leaning into the wind, heading for the doorway. A man was standing there, wiping his hands on a voluminous white apron. "They use this place for special meetings. Like a club, you might say."

"But not like the Elks and the Rotary," Cassidy said.

Terry's laughter blew away on the wind. The surf was pounding on the beach below like the planet's slow, steady heartbeat. There was a constant tremor underfoot. Cassidy half expected to look up and see the Giants bearing down on him. Terry threw his arm around Cassidy's shoulder.

"Watch out for my cane. What are we doing here, anyway, Terry? What fireworks?"

"We're getting sand in our shoes, that's what." He coughed, a staccato little sound, like a muffled gunshot. "Showtime later. First we eat." He coughed again. "Damn lung." He winced. "Back's acting up, too." He grabbed Cassidy's arm and they soldiered onward.

At first it was quiet, like showing up for a party on the wrong night.

Even the jukebox playing "O Sole Mio" was quiet, making the place seem even emptier. The fat man in the apron gave Bennie a two-handed shake, said to Cassidy that he was Giuseppe, his voice so thick with an Italian accent he could barely make it out. Giuseppe waddled about greeting everyone, then showed them to a large round table by a side window facing seaward. The window was covered by a heavy black drape. He told them they were the first to arrive but he'd had a call from the others who'd be along later. There must have been thirty tables, each with a red-and-white-checkered tablecloth and a candle in a wax-drenched Chianti bottle. The room was the repository of half the world's known reserves of candle wax. It was spooky as hell, just the four of them at the big table set for eight. All those flickering candles, the rest darkness, the windows shrouded, like an empty church, the funeral of an unloved man.

Giuseppe insisted that they begin their dinner without waiting for the rest of their party. Fried calamari, clams Casino, fettuccine in a red sauce, veal Marsala, on and on the plates kept coming. It was the goddamnedest dinner Cassidy had ever seen, all that food, all the Italian music sobbing away, all that shadowy emptiness, Giuseppe trotting back and forth from the kitchen working up a sweat. And nobody having much to say.

Then, over the wind whining at the windows, Cassidy heard the sounds of another car arriving, doors slamming, men shouting to each other. Bennie stood up quickly, his tweed jacket falling open, the butt of the forty-five automatic showing above the holster strapped across his shoulder. The door burst open and four men squeezed through, brushing sand from their trench coats. "Bennie! Brute, you old son of a gun!" The biggest man came across the room and grabbed Bennie in a mighty hug. Bennie looked embarrassed, smiled self-consciously, said, "Leonard, the same as ever." He backed away and Leonard pumped his hand, turned to the three men fanned out behind him. Their faces were shaded by their hat brims. "Bennie, you remember Artie and Marvin and Chicago Willie—"

"Sure, I remember," Bennie said. "How are you, boys? You've had a long drive. You must be hungry." He looked like a teacher addressing a bunch of delinquents. "Take off your coats, make yourselves comfortable." The smallest man, Marvin, put a large attaché case on a table and slipped out of his trench coat. He was wearing a brown suit nipped in at the waist.

"Havana, last time I seen you, Brute," Chicago Willie said, his voice a hoarse whisper, as if he didn't have quite all of his throat. "You're still one helluva big guy, Brute."

They all laughed and Artie said, "Still a helluva big guy," his face an unmoving, thin, hollow-cheeked mask.

Leonard beamed. "Man ain't been made can take Brute in a fair fight."

Marvin said, "Last time I saw a fair fight was in Pocatello, Idaho, 1919."

"Pocatello, Idaho, 1919," Artie said.

They came to the table and Bennie introduced them. Artie had a moustache like Terry's, thin and carefully tended. All four of them were deeply tanned, darker than Terry's sun-lamp job at its best. Leonard said, "Cassidy? Lew Cassidy? Well, I'll be damned! You won me some money last fall, Lew. That touchdown spree of yours, I kept puttin' money down, sayin' you'd keep it up and sure as shootin' you did! Damn good to see you . . . sorry about that leg, Lew."

"Don't be sorry," Cassidy said. "I had a good run. Lotta guys get hurt before they get to the good times."

Artie looked at him across the candles. "Lotta guys get hurt before they get to the good times. Lew's a regular philosopher, Lennie."

"Comes in handy," Cassidy said. "You oughtta try it."

They all sat down and Giuseppe began doing his number all over again. Cassidy sat quietly listening to the byplay, watching the four tanned faces, wondering what was the occasion. Terry seemed to know them slightly and joined in the general conversation which concerned itself mainly with sports. Cindy Squires leaned back in her chair, looked into the coffee. Lennie said they were going on to Montreal in the morning with a shipment. Tonight they were going to stay at the roadhouse. "Giuseppe's got rooms for us upstairs," Lennie said, "that is, if we don't stay up all night lying about the old days, hey, Brute?"

Lennie liked talking about Havana in the old days. It was like his needle had stuck there, in his favorite passage.

"So how's Johnny these days?" Terry lit a cigar and watched the smoke drift across the table into Artie's face. "I hear he likes hunting for U-boats—"

"Johnny," Lennie said. "He wants to know how Johnny is! He's great, he's Johnny!" All the food and wine had given his face a shine.

"He's in the pink," Marvin said.

"Yeah," Chicago Willie whispered through a mouthful of veal, "Johnny's in the pink."

"I thought he was coming with you this trip."

"Well, he came as far as Philly," Lennie said, "then he had to go into New York to see a man. Do some business. He's sorry he missed you, Brute, he told me personally to pass that on."

Bennie nodded and Terry said, "No great tragedy, not since Max couldn't be here either. Funny, both of them changing their plans like that." He grinned.

Artie said, "Funny. Two ships that pass in the night."

After the zabaglione and the coffee Terry looked around the table. "Whattaya say we hit those slot machines? Bennie? Why not, Artie? You feel lucky tonight, Willie?"

"Sure," Chicago Willie whispered. He was a thin man of indeterminate age with thick reddish hair parted in the middle. He looked like a hick. "I feel lucky." None of Johnny Rocco's boys were hicks, however they looked.

Cassidy shook his head. Cindy Squires yawned. Bennie said something to her, she nodded, and everyone else got up and headed back through an archway toward a back room. Somebody turned on the lights and Cassidy saw the slot machines. They began to whir and ring their little bells, the fruit spinning. Marvin had taken his attaché case with him. They sounded like rowdy kids.

"Have you figured this out yet?" Cindy Squires looked at Cassidy, something like fear, or maybe dread, in her eyes. She turned nervously to the blackout curtains, began tugging at the corner to peek out.

"I'm not sure there's any point to it."

"You don't seriously think this is just a casual get-together, do you? You weren't born yesterday, were you, Lew?" She gnawed momentarily at her thumbnail. "Max has some kind of business deal with these guys but then at the last minute he and Rocco don't show up."

"He can't help it if he gets pleurisy."

"Is that what he said? He doesn't have pleurisy." She sighed. "It's as if he wanted us all out of town for the night."

"What kind of business has he got with these guys?" Cassidy figured the hell with it, he'd ask. "Does he talk to you about that stuff?"

She gave him a long look, then ignored the question. "I worry about him, isn't that the limit? He's got guns all over the house, big guns, little guns. And he's been so blue ever since he found out about Irvie . . ." She worried at the thumbnail some more, chipping the paint. "I'm afraid he might . . . you know." She pointed her forefinger to her temple like a pistol. "Listen to me—why should I worry? It would solve everything . . ."

"Cindy, you wanted to talk to me, you wanted to see me alone—"

She rushed on, shaking her head. "He's so blue and he thinks he's getting old. He says he sees signs, he's not as young as he used to be . . . I tell him he's crazy, what he's so worried about, it can happen to anyone, including young guys. I wish you'd tell me to shut up, Cassidy. I shouldn't be telling you this." She had that flat, solemn way of speaking that caught you off-guard, robbed you of your own sense of humor because she seemed to have so little herself.

"Are you talking about his depression or his sexual capabilities?"

"What's the difference? When a man's so sad and blue it's not surprising he can't get his penis to stand up. Oh, what do I know about men? Pay no attention, I'm raving . . ." She smiled hopelessly.

"He's got Bennie. And he's got you. Bennie's loyal to the

last drop. You're so beautiful . . . Well, what more could a man want?"

"A wife he's loved all his life, a son he had all his hopes in, a daughter near enough to visit and show him his grandchildren . . . he could want all those things." She stared into her empty coffee cup. Her expression, her voice, he had the feeling they wouldn't have changed if she'd just come in to announce Judgment Day. Maybe she was, in some weird way. Max's Judgment Day. "What do you mean, he's got me?"

"You can answer that better than I. You're the one who's so familiar with his penis."

She looked at him and he thought she might slap him. Her face didn't show anything but there was something in her eyes.

"Fair comment," she said at last, "and I brought it on myself. I brought his penis up." A hint of a smile teased at the corner of her mouth. "Or didn't, which is more to the point. Have I just made a joke?"

Cassidy nodded. "A small one."

She laughed, covered her perfect white teeth with her hand. "Now you've made one. Oh, poor Max. Poor Cindy." She sighed. "You held my hand in the car. Why?"

"I'm not sure."

"Do you want me?"

"Yes, I want you."

"I knew you did," she said. "That's one of the reasons I wanted to know if you were trustworthy. If we made a bargain, could I trust you."

"What kind of bargain?"

"You could do whatever you wanted with me but you'd have to help me in return . . . but it only works if you're brave and trustworthy."

"I don't think I want it so easy, not that way—and I doubt if you really do, either."

"I know exactly what I want. And if you think it would be easy, you'd better think again. You're right, Max has *got* me, I'm his. So nothing at all about me would be easy. I guess it all comes down to how much you want me—"

"I hadn't contemplated such a businesslike arrangement—"

"It's all I can offer." She bit her lip and looked away.

"I suppose there might be problems. Like Bennie. Every time I look at you Bennie practically goes for his gat. I'd hate having Bennie unhappy with me—"

"Well, maybe you're better off forgetting me. You can get out in time, write off the deal, your virtue intact. Anyway, you're a married man—"

"That's unnecessarily cruel."

"I know. I'm sorry. It was a rotten thing to say. I'm an expert at saying hurtful things, even when I don't mean to. And I really don't mean to hurt you." She looked up, caught his eye. "Really, truly, I don't want to hurt you, but I will. I always do. I've hurt Max, I'm going to hurt him some more before it's over. I know that. I'm Max's steady whore, do you understand that? He gave me a job I wanted because he wanted me. It was all very straightforward at the beginning. He listened to me sing, then took me into his office, told me the job was mine if . . . if . . . He told me to undress right there. He told me he was having a little trouble and he felt sure I could cure him if I really tried. He wasn't brutal, I don't want it to sound that way . . . he was nice, sort of sad. When I was naked he asked me to do certain things while he watched me and then I knelt in front of him and worked on him for an hour and at the end of the hour I knew I had the job *and* Max . . . Max and I had each other, we were bonded in a way, but now, no matter how I try, I can't help him anymore, but he says I have to try, he needs me, he says without me he has no hope . . . so I do . . . but I hate it now, I hate what he makes me do, I hate myself for doing it, and I hate myself for failing, and I hate him . . . but he won't let me go. It's his *need* I can't break away from. Do you understand? God, I'm trusting you too much already. *He won't let me go.* Oh, Cassidy, I *am* a whore, I really, truly am. And that's the only kind of bargain I can make, all I have to offer . . ."

She sat quietly for a while, her hands clasped in her lap.

127

The guys playing the slot machines were still making a lot of noise. "Sometimes," she said eventually, as if she'd been mulling it over in her mind, "I think it's just my nature. Maybe I should be the one who dies, uses one of those guns of his. Maybe I'd be better off. I don't know."

"Cindy . . ." It was as if she were in the confessional and he, a worldly priest, heard her reciting her sins and couldn't help her or himself, wanted her more the more he heard, wanted her in all her calculation and despair.

"That's what it is. I need to be a whore." She shivered. "You mustn't think I talk like this—I've never said these things to anyone before."

"Why me?"

"You're just lucky, I guess." She smiled tentatively, wondering if he still wanted anything to do with her.

"This will all pass, you'll see."

"You're an optimist, Cassidy. You don't want to see me for what I am. The fact is, there's something cold in me that rather enjoys being a whore. It takes all the risk out of things. I was one, I think, the very first time. I was seventeen. He was the choirmaster at the little church . . . I wanted to see if I could break through his propriety. It was so easy. Oh, my goodness," she said, pointing at the wine bottle. "*In vino veritas.*"

The slot machines whirred and jangled. Occasionally someone would shout gleefully.

"Let's get a breath of sea air," Cassidy said. "I wish I knew why the hell we're here—"

"Fireworks."

"Yeah, fireworks. Well, you've done your part. I don't get it. If Max isn't sick, why did he send us out here alone?"

She was slipping into her coat and putting on the beret. "Max always has his reasons."

"Did you know ahead of time he wasn't coming?"

She shook her head. "It was news to me."

• • •

They stood on the balcony off the dining room, at the top of a long flight of stairs leading down to the sand. The

128

wind whipped off the ocean like it had a personal grudge. Stray arrows of rain and bits of sand nipped at them. She pulled the collar up around her face, turned to shelter against him. He felt the damp wool of her beret on his cheek. Dogs were howling and yapping somewhere down below where the surf furled and rolled in the darkness. A couple of low-intensity red flares were stuck in the sand like sparklers on the Fourth of July. From time to time the shadow of a man with a large dog at his heels would pass across the faint red gloom. Volunteer coast guards on their nightly rounds.

Her compact weight pressed against him. "War is bloody," she said, sounding English, using *bloody* for *rotten*. "I can't believe they don't just stop it . . . Irvie Bauman, blackout curtains, saboteurs landing by dark of night, people getting marched off to war. It's all so utterly ridiculous, if you want my opinion." She burrowed her fists against the front of his trench coat. "War is bloody damn nonsense."

She was trembling and he put his arm around her, holding her tight. The gale whistled in the eaves of the roof's overhang. Awnings flapped like they were trying to lift Giuseppe's off the runway. Out of nowhere a Jeep snarled through the cocoon of darkness below and sped past the flares, was gone again.

"Cassidy, do you ever feel pointless?"

"Everybody does," he said. "Sometimes. Comes of thinking too much."

"Like there's no design behind our existence? That it's all just random and that time blunts all the little personal tragedies and that none of it matters for very long? Not the living, not the dying . . . that's all just for now and now just lasts a minute, before it's gone, just gone."

"Look, it's a universal fear."

"Well, that's the excuse I use for everything. What difference does any of it make? As a little girl I used to sit in the cemetery in the little village in the Cotswolds where we summered. And I'd wonder, who were these people who slept beneath me now? Their lives were important to

129

them—my God, Hardy wrote his novels about them—and then they were gone and a little girl was sitting on their gravestones . . . what difference had their lives made? Well, what difference does it make if I'm a whore and Max is a gangster and your leg is all torn up and Irvie's dead? We're all going to be dead and forgotten so soon . . . Anyway, I feel like an imbecile telling you all this rubbish. It's all my excuse for being no better than a cheap tart. Let's pretend I didn't say it, is that possible, Cassidy?"

"Probably not."

"No, I suppose it isn't. Well, hard cheese for me."

"It's not important."

"Who says?"

"Writer, Scott Fitzgerald. He said there aren't many things that are important. And they're not very important."

"I must remember that."

"Why? It's not important."

She laughed. "He was right. It's all pointless."

"It's the war," he said.

"I wish that's all it were."

"You know, I really do think I'm in love with you, Cindy."

"I suppose you are. It's not me. It's the war."

"I'm afraid it's you. I've known it for a while. I think I was lost from the day you came to my hospital room and lied about the flowers being Max's idea . . . I think maybe I started loving you right then."

"You're going to be sorry, you know that."

"Oh, I don't think so."

"Your judgment is clouded now. You're in love with a worthless little tart."

He grabbed her, turned her to face him, stared into her pale, wounded face. He hadn't realized she was fighting back tears. He kissed her cheek, tasting the salty warmth, then kissed her mouth and she opened herself and took him inside.

Breathless, he leaned back, still holding her. "Don't talk that way anymore. I've got to think about what I'm going to do . . . But no bargains between us, no business relationship. Anything we do for each other, we do. No strings attached. No deals, no bargains. Got that straight?"

"Forget me, Cassidy. It's bound to turn out badly. It'll all go wrong and why should you get dragged down, too—"

"Shut up, Cindy. You don't scare me—"

"I'm just trying to warn you—"

"Why? None of it's very important—"

"Because if I could love anyone, I'd love you."

"You can. You already love me—"

"I know, I know," she whispered. "Kiss me once. It won't make any difference soon enough. Just another little girl someday, thinking in a cemetery, sitting on a gravestone, wondering who we were . . ."

He held her and wanted to hold her until they were no longer afraid, until whatever was going to happen happened and they had taken their places in the long procession and the story was told and he kept holding her and he felt himself crying for the first time in years and years and years, since his mother had died, and just for an instant he thought it was the biting wind in his face or maybe it was the war but, no, of course, he knew what it was. It was Cindy Squires.

●   ●   ●

The door behind them banged open and Terry and Giuseppe came out, followed by Bennie, who looked at Cindy, then at Cassidy, blinking behind his lenses. Giuseppe was pointing out into the darkness. "Keepa watchin' out there, you'll see the fireworks. Not every night, mosta nights." He shrugged palms-up, as if it were not his responsibility. "Justa keepa lookin'." He went back inside. Cassidy wished they'd all go back inside and leave him alone with Cindy. His heartbeat was racing. He couldn't let himself look at her, not while Bennie was there.

She pulled away from his side, leaned on the railing. Terry produced a pair of binoculars and scanned the night. "Hell," he said, "this could take hours. Let's mount watches. I'll take the first. An hour. Then you're up, Lew."

Bennie held the door for Lew and Cindy. Back in the dining room the others were setting up a card game. Bennie sat in with them, facing Cassidy and Cindy. She wrapped herself in her coat, curled up on two chairs, and went immediately to sleep. Cassidy watched her. Her mouth dropped open about half an inch and she began to snore very softly, like a child. He watched her for an hour and thought about what had just happened between them and about what he ought to do about it and then Terry came in and handed him the binoculars. They felt like ice. "Let us know if you see anything," he said. He went to join the poker game.

It came about half an hour into his watch.

At first it looked like a magician's pinkish-orange paper flower popping up, unfolding in the black void of ocean and the night. For a moment he forgot he had the binoculars, simply strained to see what was going on out there. The ball of color grew larger and brighter, glowing, creating a halo around the darker center.

He brought the binocs to the bridge of his nose and adjusted the focus now that he had something to focus on.

Fire. An immense explosion of fire, so far away as to be soundless against the surf and the wind.

He banged at the door. "Get out here!"

They came through the doorway in a rush. Cindy was rubbing her eyes with her fists, like a child awakened on Christmas Eve to see Santa passing overhead.

"Judas Priest!" Lennie whispered. Cassidy handed him the binoculars.

"What is it?" Cindy yawned into her fist.

Bennie leaned his huge hands on the railing and whistled. He slipped his fedora off, passed his hand over the high dome of his balding head. "Extraordinary . . ."

"What is it?" She sounded sleepy and impatient.

"Merchant ship," Terry said. "One of ours. This is the war, right off New York City. The U-boat wolf packs are hunting all along our coastline."

"The Nazis," she said in wonderment.

"Well, they're keeping it pretty quiet," Terry said.

"People would go nuts if they realized just how bad it is. Better than a hundred ships have gone down so far."

"It's a gauntlet," Bennie mused.

The fire had flattened out and was burning along an imaginary line. The waterline. Not so imaginary. The line between one kind of death and another.

"There must be men in the water out there," Cindy whispered. "Drowning and burning . . . and screaming . . ."

Cassidy held her arm, pulled her close in the darkness.

"That's right," Terry said.

"Why don't we do something? What about our navy?" Her voice was small, shaking.

"There isn't enough navy," Terry said.

There was another silent explosion. Two merchant ships.

Voices were calling on the beach.

"Coast Guard patrols. Can't have the public coming out for the free show—"

"Like us," she said.

The fires were burning unchecked, spreading as the oil and gasoline drifted on the water.

An hour later they were still burning.

Cindy went inside and Cassidy followed her, leaving the rest of them passing the glasses back and forth. It had begun raining steadily but they couldn't tear themselves away.

She sat with her head on her arm on the table.

"Damn it, this is all insane, Cassidy." Her voice was muffled. "Fireworks. Men out there filling up with saltwater and burning oil. And we drive down for a casual outing to watch. It's like my grandparents crossing Europe to get to the Crimea. Making camp on the hills above the battle. Women in fine dresses. Servants setting up the trays for tea. They could hear the screams of the dying . . . Take me home, Cassidy, or get me drunk. This whole night is just too crazy."

"I don't think our friends want to go yet."

"Oh, well, then God knows we have to stay. While Terry

133

and the Immovable Object and their creepy gangster pals get their kicks. Fuck them. Fuck all of us . . ."

He sat down beside her to wait. She probably didn't know it but she needed company. Or was it that he did?

Well, as Fitzgerald said, it wasn't important.

•　　•　　•

Morning came gray and harsh and raining. The slate cloud cover merged at the eastern horizon with the iron sea and a great fogbank was out there, moving inland. Giuseppe made coffee and his wife bustled in with baskets of hot rolls and bread with slabs of cold butter. The blackout curtains were rolled up and secured on hooks. Cindy's eyes were red and she sipped her coffee, staring blankly at the fog. She'd come back from the bathroom looking scrubbed and girlish. She made a face and said, "I brushed my teeth with toilet paper. Aren't we ever going home? Are we stuck here for eternity? Like *Outward Bound*?" The jukebox was playing "Come Back to Sorrento."

With morning's light the poker game broke up. Lennie stood and stretched long simian arms. They'd all taken off their coats, showing guns in shoulder holsters. Marvin gnawed on a roll after dunking it in his coffee. Artie wore a lemon-yellow tie with a dark blue shirt and yellow suspenders and didn't look any different than he had upon arrival. His beard hadn't even grown, while the others had stubble darkening their faces. Artie was something else.

Cassidy watched Artie and decided he was the one hardcase in the bunch, the real ice man.

"Come on, you guys," Lennie said, waving his arms at the thick miasma of cigar and cigarette smoke. "Let's get some fresh air. Bring our bags in so we can at least get cleaned up. Come on, up and at 'em."

Lennie swung the door leading to the parking lot wide open and took a deep breath. "Come on, come on," he said, and the other three followed him across the damp wooden porch. The rain had eased off and the fog had reached the shore. Bennie and Cassidy stood in the doorway enjoying the chilly damp breeze. Cassidy took a step through the doorway, then felt Bennie's hand tightening on his arm. The cane slipped from his grasp and clattered on the floor.

"Wait," Bennie said softly, "wait a minute . . ."

Like robots, several heads, then shoulders, were rising up out of the sand-blown scrub brush rimming the parking lot, rising almost in slow motion, as if they were a lost legion coming like phantoms from the sea. Their hats were pulled low against the streaky rain and mist and their trench coats were soaked through. They came without a sound, five of them ranged along the final rise of the dune.

They were carrying Thompson submachine guns.

Halfway across the lot toward the long, gleaming Lincoln Continental, beaded with rain, Chicago Willie saw them, yelled something inelegant, hey, who the fuck are these guys . . .

Lennie turned to look and in a blur he had his gun in his hand, had dropped flat on the ground with the automatic out in front of him, had fired once, a roar that split the morning stillness . . .

A puff of sand rose in front of one of the men from the sea.

Artie made a dash, like a sprinter kicking for the tape, got to the Lincoln, yanked the door open, pulled a shotgun from the front seat . . .

A burst from one of the tommy guns took Chicago Willie off at the knee, dropping him where he stood, screaming in a widening pool of blood. He got his gun free and another quick burst stitched his epitaph across his chest . . .

Marvin tried to scuttle back toward the doorway and another of the men with the tommy guns raised the muzzle . . .

Bennie slammed the door shut a millisecond before it was raked with slugs. Marvin let out a frightened yelp and they heard him slammed heavily onto the wooden porch, heard him battering weakly at the door, trying to get in . . .

Cassidy got to the window in time to see Artie pull the

trigger on the shotgun and blow one of the tommy-gun men back over the lip of the scrubby dune, his gun rattling off a salvo into the gathering fog . . .

A large square-shaped man appeared for the first time from below the crest of the dune as if he'd waited for the opening volleys to pass and opened up on the Lincoln, ripping curling holes across the long hood, filling the fog with an explosion of glass, ripping huge gaps in the fabric top, blowing a row of holes across the door shielding Artie and his shotgun . . .

Chips and slivers of parking lot were flying all around the prone figure of Lennie, who fired back, having to know it was hopeless, having to know it was all over . . .

It had taken five or six seconds so far.

Terry stood beside Cindy, his face ashen, leaning on her chair. She had her hands over her ears.

Bennie stood stock-still by the window, the huge .45 looking like a gambler's derringer in the massive fist . . .

Cassidy said, "Come on, everybody, it's time to get the hell out of here." He grabbed his cane, yanking Bennie away from the window just before more slugs tore into the roadhouse's wooden siding and the window exploded back across the table.

Cassidy grabbed Cindy, pulled her upright, and headed toward the door onto the rear balcony from which they'd watched the burning ships. Terry, weaker than he'd expected, gamely followed, his face almost blue with weakness and pain. He looked at Cassidy. "It's my back . . . let's go, Jocko, I'll make it." Bennie followed.

Cassidy turned back, saw Marvin's precious attaché case on the table, pushed the others ahead, dashed back in to get it. They were still firing in the parking lot. He heard Artie let fly again with the shotgun. Very soon Artie was going to be dead. Men were yelling out there. He took the case and went back out the door. The rest of them were down the steps. He limped downward, hard on his knee, and fell the last three steps. But Bennie was there to catch him.

They ran across the wet sand, angling off toward the

first dune between them and the water. Each jolt was an agony for his knee and the cane was useless in the sand. He flung it away into the fog. Terry fell over a half-buried piece of driftwood, Cassidy stopped, helped him up. "Come on, beautiful," he said.

"A day at the fucking beach," Terry gasped.

Bennie had swept Cindy over the top of the dune and rolled down the other side with her.

Cassidy staggered onward, Terry's arm around his neck, holding on, and then they too had crested the dune and he was lowering Terry as gently as he could.

"Put a fork in me, momma," Terry whispered, "I'm about done. Leave me here, I've got a gun, Jocko. I can slow the bastards down . . . you go ahead."

"No, this is all right," Cassidy said, sinking down beside him on the wet sand. "Listen, pal, I'm not feeling too damn chipper myself." He sat quietly, gulping air and smelling the fog which had engulfed them. He peered into the mist. Bennie and Cindy were scrambling up the slope toward them. Driftwood, wet sand, dune grass, fog blowing thickly off the water. "Let's just dig in here and see what happens. The fog's on our side. Hell, I don't think these guys are after us."

"Who are they?" Terry asked, gritting his teeth, shifting his weight, trying to ease the pain in his back.

"I don't know . . ." But Cassidy had seen the last man up, the big square man who'd waited, and he'd have sworn he'd recognized him. He was almost sure. Almost.

He held on to the attaché case. Cindy huddled against him, shivering. Bennie leaned over Terry: "Are you okay?"

Terry nodded slowly, eyes shut. "Not quite up to par yet, I guess." He laughed softly, opened his eyes, and winked at Cassidy. He reached inside his coat and came out with a .38 Special. "Here, Lew. You'd better take this. I'm weak as a cat . . ." Cassidy took the gun.

They sat listening to each other breathe and the rolling, lapping surf. Cindy said, "It's stopped." She cocked her head, brushing her hair away with a sand-covered hand. "Listen, the shooting's stopped . . ."

"They're all dead, then," Bennie said.

As if to punctuate the gun battle there was a muffled roar, like something suddenly blowing up, a whooshing sound and a crack, then nothing.

They waited another five minutes, then Cassidy said he was going to have a look. They couldn't sit there on the wet sand forever.

Cindy sighed. "Please be careful."

He looked down at her, trying to convince himself that last night had really happened. She smiled tentatively. He got up and limped up over the rim of the dune and kept on going. When he looked back, the dune was gone in the fog. He was caught in the middle, plodding onward, no longer able to see where he'd been, not yet able to make out what lay ahead. For a moment he thought he smelled smoke, an oily fire. What the hell was he going to do? Was he going to start shooting people? Was he going to keep on playing footsie with Dewey and Luciano and the cops? Was he going to keep telling Max Bauman's girl he loved her? He was wandering in the goddamn fog . . .

The outline of the roadhouse loomed suddenly above him. It rested on stilts sunk into concrete pilings and there were the stairs they'd descended. He leaned against one of the stilts to catch his breath and rest his knee. There were no sounds coming from above so he went to the last set of stilts. The voices finally reached him, filtering through the wind and fog. He couldn't make out what they were saying. He held his breath, listening, trying to identify just the one. He edged closer to the corner of the building. The parking lot was above him now, the dune curving ahead of him, nothing to protect him but the fog.

Suddenly the voices came clear, just ahead, and he froze.

They were breathing heavily, slipping and sliding down the steep wall of wet sand. He waited until he'd heard them pass, heard the heavy metallic slapping of the tommy guns jostling. He edged forward again and saw the shapes of the men from behind.

They moved like ghosts in the fog.

The big square man was bringing up the rear. He could hear the crackling burning of something in the parking lot. One of the others turned, called back through the fog, "You coming? You all right?"

"No, you dumb shithead, I'm gonna stay for breakfast! 'Course I'm coming . . ."

The sound of a motor launch firing its engine sliced through the fog.

"Where the fuck's the dock?" the big square man yelled, stopping, turning, trying to get his bearings.

"Over here, follow the sound of my voice . . ."

Then they were gone, faint sounds of the tommy-gun men clambering from the dock onto the launch.

He was right about the square man but it didn't make things any better knowing that he'd been mowing down gangsters in the parking lot.

Harry Madrid.

•   •   •

Cassidy limped back across the stretch of beach, following his own tracks, climbed the dune, and there they were, Bennie standing guard, Terry and Cindy huddled halfway down the dune. Cassidy sat down beside them, keeping his leg straight before him.

Terry had recovered somewhat, though the pallor beneath his tan gave him away. He leaned on an elbow, fumbling in his coat, brought out a leather case, slid off the top to reveal three of Max's Havanas. "I take it the danger has passed. Calls for a cigar. Bennie," he called over his shoulder, "you want a cigar?" Bennie ambled down the dune and squatted beside them. "Don't mind if I do," he said. Terry cupped his hands around his lighter and waited until all three had their cigars going. Cindy leaned against Cassidy, making herself small.

"They're gone," Cassidy said. "Motor launch."

"So what happened?" Terry asked. "Could you see anything?"

"Oh, yeah, I saw them . . ."

"So? Who was it?"

"It was Harry Madrid."

Terry scowled. Bennie, who'd stood up and taken a few steps away, turned from his contemplation of the sea, slowly being revealed by the breaking up of the fog.

Cassidy said, "Harry Madrid just came out of nowhere to wipe out one of Johnny Rocco's divisions, rat-tat-tat. I wonder if Max will be happy . . . Maybe, maybe not.

"The question is," Cassidy persisted, "how did Harry know they'd be here? And did he know Max wasn't coming?"

The fog had drifted away and the sun began to glow timidly behind the low-slung rain clouds. It gave a watery light, a weak yellow wash over the gray ocean.

Bennie was pointing toward the shoreline. "What's that? Coming in with the surf?" He polished his glasses on his handkerchief and hooked them back over his ears.

Cassidy stood up, gave Terry a hand. "How's the back?"

"It's eased off. It's that slug, it moves around."

Cindy got up, holding her high heels in one hand.

Bennie had struck off down the shingle of sand, making for the water. They set out after him, stragglers from a battlefield, wandering through the wind and mist. Cindy walked in stockinged feet, leaving tiny prints.

The smell of oil was thick, the slicks from the merchant ships washing ashore, staining the cementlike sand. A couple of dogs had come from nowhere, barked angrily at the wheeling gulls above them, at the dead, blackened fish fetching up at their feet. Bits of junk began to bob up in the foaming surf and stick in the sand with the froth curling around them, sucking at them as if the sea had thought better of it and wanted to reclaim them. Footlockers, wooden slabs from lifeboats, a lifesaver riddled with bullet holes. The U-boat had surfaced to machine-gun the survivors in the water. Oil cans floated in like gravestones marking the ends of things. The stuff kept coming in waves.

It looked as if logs were coming next. Bumping one another, riding the waves among the oil drums and the blankets and shredded planking.

When they floated closer, you could see the truth.

The logs had arms and legs and faces. They were soaked in oil and blood and saltwater. Had they felt any better in the last moments, unarmed, knowing they were dying for their country?

Cindy Squires gasped and turned away. "That's it," she said. She set her jaw firmly, turned her back on the sea, and set off back up the beach toward the dunes.

Bennie and Terry were standing at the edge of the water, staring at the bodies washing up at their feet.

Cassidy looked down into one of the faces. The flesh was bluish white and rubbery. The eyes were still open. Water dribbled at the corner of the man's mouth. One side of the face was burned and raw and white, all the blood drained away from the wound. Cassidy turned away to keep from vomiting.

He'd counted six corpses already. It was a hell of a show, all right, but probably nothing more than just another day for the guys overseas, island-hopping in the Pacific. The rain had coarsened again and was dripping slowly off the brim of his hat.

Bennie and Terry had moved on. He watched them, wondering when they'd have had enough. He was just about to turn back and go find Cindy Squires when it happened.

A disproportionately large lump of body, like a prehistoric sea creature, crested a wave and came flopping onto the sand. It was blackened with oil, like the others. Terry walked toward it. The gulls were gathering, screeching at the dogs, trying to get at the dead fish. The dogs howled, dashed at them.

Terry stopped abruptly, looked back for Bennie, then moved closer to the monstrous body.

He bent down, hands on knees, staring into the face. Then he stood up, looked out at the ocean and the diving gulls.

Then he went. He just toppled over. Crumpling.

Bennie plucked him out of the air as if he were a

tumbling leaf. He never hit the wet sand. Bennie held him in his arms like a child.

Cassidy got to them as quickly as he could.

Bennie pursed his lips, said from a great height, "He swooned, Cassidy. You saw him." He might have been speaking of a maiden lady in *Barchester Towers*.

Cassidy looked down at the oversize mound sprawled indelicately on the sand.

It wasn't a man.

It was two men. They were roped together. A good part of each head was gone. And they weren't sailors. It didn't make any sense. But, of course, it had made some kind of sense to someone.

They'd been shot in the head, tied into one large bundle, and dumped somewhere offshore. As he watched the bodies rocking in the foaming eddies a tiny, nervous-looking sand crab crawled timidly from the larger corpse's slack mouth.

Cassidy felt his stomach dropping down an elevator shaft.

He knew both of them.

Markie Cookson and his little blond lad.

With the sailors at last.

CHAPTER SEVEN

When Cassidy awoke at four o'clock that afternoon, the inside of his mouth needed a shave and his bad leg was as stiff as W. C. Fields on Saturday night. He lay in bed for several minutes trying to sort out the dreams from the reality of what had happened at the shore. The dreams couldn't compare. Then he hobbled into the bathroom, turned on the shower, brushed his teeth eight or nine times with the last of the Ipana, chugged a bottle of Listerine, and stood under the hottest water he could deal with. Pretty soon he sat down on the little three-legged wooden stool in the glass shower stall and coaxed himself back to life. Sen-Sen. He needed a mouthful of Sen-Sen more than anything in the world.

Marquardt Cookson's half-exploded head loomed at him when he shut his eyes. He smelled the stench of the blackened, oil-soaked mound of blubber on the beach. Then Terry was toppling through space, his hat drifting away into the water, then Bennie was catching him . . .

Bennie hadn't recognized the corpse. The two corpses. It was easy to forget the prettyboy, a kind of lady-in-waiting.

143

Bennie had been far too busy grabbing Terry to register the identity of the fat man. But Terry had gotten a good look at poor sweaty old Markie and had fainted dead away. He'd come to while Bennie was carrying him away from the bodies. He'd insisted he could walk, so Bennie had put him down gently as if he might shatter. Terry wobbled a bit, then pulled himself together and grinned at Cassidy, running a finger along his moustache as if it might have fallen off while he was out. "One look at a stiff," he said, "and old Leary passes out." He shook his head. "I can't afford that kind of talk." He frowned. "Keep it to yourselves, gents."

Cindy Squires was sitting on the Chrysler's running board staring at her nails. It was better than looking at the parking lot which was splattered with dead gangsters. The Lincoln Continental was burning, a grace note Harry Madrid hadn't been able to resist. A column of black smoke twisted away in the mist. Flames crackled, tongues of orange fire poking up through the frame of the rag top, like pictures coming back from the desert war in North Africa.

Nobody had much to say on the ride back to the city. They were all sealed in their own little compartments of shock and weariness, but Cassidy was thinking too hard to grab a nap. There were too many angles to pull together but what struck him as important was the certainty that recognizing Markie's face was what had caused Terry to faint. Had it been just the surprise coupled with his general physical weakness? Looking at dead merchant seamen, you didn't expect to see your everyday dead aesthete. Maybe it was because you didn't expect to see a friend.

Or maybe it was something else. Maybe it was the envelope on the bar, all that money . . . Markie wouldn't be paying the piper anymore.

The connection between the two men had always puzzled Cassidy but the envelope on the bar looked like a lot of explanation. Markie, however, still remained an enigma. What had he and his boyfriend done to get washed up with the sailors?

And what had Harry Madrid been doing out there, anyway?

And if Max Bauman wasn't really sick, then he and Rocco must have gotten together somewhere else . . . and the trip to the shore had been an elaborate piece of misdirection. Which made him wonder if anybody had known what the hell was going on last night . . . Maybe everybody had been bitten in the ass by the unexpected. Hell, maybe Max had staged the rub-out. But no. Harry Madrid didn't do Max's killing for him . . .

Finally he figured he was as clean as he was going to get. He dried off, primped for a while, gave that up as too little too late, got dressed, and ventured out of his room, wondering what was coming next and knowing it would grab him by surprise.

• • •

Terry had already gone out. Cassidy made fresh coffee and sat in the breakfast nook staring at the attaché case he'd kept in his room while he'd slept. A battered leather case, scuffed and scraped, with brass fittings. A single lock. He sighed, gave in to curiosity, and got a screwdriver from the catchall drawer in the kitchen. He stuck the business end in under the hinged brass flaps and pried until it popped open.

He looked at the contents, paced around the kitchen, and turned on the portable radio next to the breadbox on the counter. He went back to the case and stared.

There was no point in counting it. Stacks of twenties, crisp and new, looking like the ink was still wet. Twenty, twenty-five stacks in paper wrappers, forty or fifty of them to a bundle. Maybe $25,000. Snappy as Dick's hatband, as the old codgers used to say.

Somebody down in Florida had a printing press.

From the looks of it, Rocco was doing a nice business in twenties. And Cassidy had walked away with the sample case. Was Max Bauman in the market for twenties?

He closed the case and took it back to his room. One more loose end.

• • •

When Terry got back, his dark blond hair was freshly trimmed, slicked straight back, and his thin moustache had survived another trip to the Terminal Barber Shop. His pallor had also had a sun treatment. Cassidy came into the kitchen and saw him sitting in the breakfast nook smoking a cigarette, looking out the window into the air shaft. Cassidy poured himself coffee and slid in across the table from him.

"Got any answers, sport?"

Terry looked up. "How the hell should I know? It's all Greek to me."

"Has it occurred to you that neither Markie nor his chum was a member of our Merchant Marine?"

"It's a dumping ground out there, Lew," he said impatiently. "People who kill people take the stiffs out there and drop 'em off. Sometimes they get a cement necktie, sometimes they just let 'em wash up on the shore. That's if they want to send a message to somebody."

"But why take the bodies out there?"

"Lew, Lew, what is this, a test? Maybe they saw it in the movies. Maybe it's a grand old tradition. A union rule. I never asked. They just do it. Thing is, if this is a message, it's going to take awhile to get it delivered. It's all pretty confusing out there, all those bodies." He unplugged the percolator and filled his cup again. He started ladling sugar into the cup.

"What kind of message?"

Terry shook his head. "That's what I'm thinking about. Who's supposed to get scared when word gets out? Or when Markie doesn't show up for his regular whipping?"

"What kind of enemies would he have?"

"Guys like Markie could have dozens. Fairies fight all the time. Jealous little pricks." He was thinking aloud.

"You going to report it?"

He looked at Cassidy from the corner of his eye. "Oh, I

don't think so. They got their hands full without worrying about the Jersey shore. Let's just wait and see what happens." He inspected his nails, bit at one. He never did things like that. He was strictly a weekly manicure man. "Listen, Lew. Let me be frank. I'm getting one helluva message. Me. Personally. Maybe the message was for old Terry . . ."

"What are you talking about?"

"Don't ask me to explain. Just listen. If it was meant for me, I sure wasn't supposed to get it so soon. Just dumb luck I was there. But it means I've got an edge. And that's all I need." His eyes were shining, almost bubbling with excitement. It was his element and he was in it up to his ears. It seemed as if he *knew* the message was for him and now the abyss of danger beckoned irresistibly and he was feeling alive again.

"Why kill Markie to send you a message? I don't get it."

"You don't have to get it, Lew. Just take my word for it." He looked across the steaming coffee. "I can handle this, I can beat this game, any game in town. All I need to lock it up is a little edge. No contest. They're coming after me now, Lew, I know it . . . you ever have a feeling? You *know* something? Somebody's out there breathin' hard, watching me . . . Well, now it's starting . . . I'd like your help, sport."

Cassidy shifted, poured coffee so he wouldn't have to look at Terry and show the confusion he felt. Dewey, Luciano, Madrid, they wanted his help. Cindy Squires wanted his help. Now Terry. And Terry had the oldest claim, the strongest. It was like the old days. But helping Terry wasn't as simple as it once had been. There were too damn many angles.

Terry kept talking. "There's something I gotta do. Tonight." He batted his eyes at Cassidy. "I'd like a backup man. Somebody to ride shotgun."

"So what's the deal?"

"Come on, Lew. Friends don't ask. They just start bailing."

147

"Sure, Terry. Don't worry. I'm your man."

"Tonight we ride, amigo."

•   •   •

It was raining again by nightfall. The Yankees had managed to squeeze their game in during the afternoon. They'd beaten Connie Mack's Athletics, 11–2, and Cassidy had been looking forward to going out to the Stadium the next day but the radio had said New York was in for several days of rain and cold. Well, it was a long season and he was reading *War and Peace*, which couldn't get rained out. He was enjoying General Kutuzov immensely, making all the connections between Hitler and Napoleon that were on everybody's minds in those days. He felt as if he'd once played for Kutuzov himself and the old bastard had never heard of the forward pass. Coach Kutuzov had believed you let the enemy keep coming at you in little chunks of yardage because it was a very long field and sooner or later they'd fumble the damn ball. Reading the novel, then reading the daily papers, you got the feeling it was all happening again in Russia.

Twenty-four hours before, they'd all been on the way to the Jersey shore and the impending fireworks and Cindy Squires had told him about the rainbows of the *Normandie* and now everything had changed. Cassidy felt as if someone had been tinkering with all the dials and he was hearing a bunch of stations he hadn't known were there. He kept hearing Cindy Squires's self-hatred, going on about how she was a whore and wanted to make a business deal with him and had to get away from Max . . . and he heard himself telling her he'd fallen in love with her . . . and now he wondered what the hell had been going on out there. And Harry Madrid with a Thompson sub wasting a battalion of Rocco's foot soldiers . . . and the fat body sprawled on the sand . . . Too much had happened. He was having trouble getting it all straight. And there was a bag full of counterfeit twenties and where were the gasoline rationing stamps Dewey'd been so hot about? And what had Cindy Squires done to warrant so much of her own hatred? And what had she really offered him? Was she serious, would she remember? Did he love her, for God's sake?

Then Terry said it was time to go.

•　•　•

At the first drop of rain all the cabbies had remembered pressing engagements elsewhere so it took forever to flag one down. He was headed home to Brooklyn and consented to drop them on First Avenue at 51st rather than turning up into Sutton Place. Cassidy swung his bad leg out, stood in the rain, and tipped him a dime.

It was raining hard. Rivers gurgled in the gutters. The traffic lights reflected in the wet streets. Very pretty. They crossed the street, collars of their macs turned up, hat brims low, and headed into Sutton Place where the door knockers were polished lion's heads and the old money lived happily ever after.

The late Marquardt Cookson had lived on the east side of the street. The building exemplified the High Moroccan period which hadn't lasted long but had left its mark all over the East Side. There were three arched entryways with thick oak doors crisscrossed with black iron straps, carved confessional windows like the old speakeasies, and wrought-iron hinges not much larger than Aunt Fanny's picnic hams. Terry picked the lock.

The lobby was dim and quiet, resting. Wrought-iron sconces on the swirled stucco walls held electric bulbs that flickered like torches. Heavy beams overhead made you want to stoop when you didn't have to. Moorish designs winked like harem girls from the designs on the walls. Long mirrors shot through with veins of gold looked like a bad accident at Tiffany's. In just a minute the Sheik of Araby was going to flounce out from behind a potted palm and start having a go with his assegai. There were some chest-high pots at the end of the hallway by the elevator cages. Ali Baba and the Forty Thieves maybe? Terry dropped his cigar into one of the pots. Cassidy waited for the scream but the elevator came first.

149

Markie Cookson had enjoyed his money. Aside from the fact that he probably had to be greased down to get in and out of the elevator, he had his own elegant little fiefdom looking down on the East River. The rooms weren't big but there were a lot of them. And a balcony with the tugs and harbor patrol boats cruising along like toys far below. Queens and Brooklyn and the bridges were speckled with only a handful of lights. They'd never been so dark before. There was a war on.

Terry put on gloves. He went to a desk that would have just fit in Delaware and began going through the drawers. Cassidy watched, wondering what he was looking for. He was beginning to prefer it that way. He wasn't sure how many laws they'd broken already but he figured they were nowhere near done.

The main room was fitted out with chairs like thrones, heavy beams with wrought-iron chandeliers at just the right height to bean you if you weren't paying attention. Real candles. There was a pair of very large paintings devoted to devils and goblins crawling out of people's heads and mouths, like the crab emerging from the hole in the middle of Markie's dead face. Gilt frames. The fire-place could have housed a family of four. A big black statue of an Egyptian cat goddess. Cassidy recognized her from a Boris Karloff movie.

While Terry rummaged through Markie's papers, Cassidy headed down the dark hallway and switched on a light in the bedroom. Immediately he wished he hadn't. A huge round bed encircled by a heavy beaded curtain squatted in the center of the room. The requisite round mirror hung from heavy chains over the bed. What it had seen didn't bear much contemplation. An immense photograph of the bullet-domed master of the occult, Aleister Crowley, dominated one wall. There was a kind of altar in front of it. Goblets, candelabra, a variety of doodads, all looking sort of tacky and sad. An old-fashioned movie camera on a tripod was trained on the bed. Cassidy prayed he'd never have to sit through that double feature.

There were some African tribal statues with very large

150

dicks. Markie had puckishly draped several Sulka ties over the mammoth erections. Also a pair of handcuffs among the silks. The lighting was all blue and dim and indirect. There were fat jars of Vaseline and various other lubricants and unguents on a nightstand. On one shelf someone had left a plate with the crusted remains of a liverwurst sandwich, some gherkins, a crumpled napkin, used toothpicks. Whatever you did, you had to eat.

Painted on the floor, with the circular bed at its center, with the points stretching away into the corners of the room, was a huge pentangle.

Cassidy was backing out of the room when he saw something else. He felt the hair on his arms sitting up and yelling for help.

There was something funny smeared all over one wall. He went closer. There were pieces of stuff stuck to the wall. And it was sort of hairy. It had dripped down the wall in a few places.

He went back down the hallway. He smelled something sweetish and sickening. Maybe it was old incense clinging to the walls. Markie was just the type.

Then he smelled dope.

Terry was sitting behind the desk dragging on a reefer. He pushed a cigarette box with a top of inlaid pearl dragons cavorting in a devil-may-care fashion at Cassidy. "Markie's private supply. Not bad stuff."

"Let's get on with this—"

"Keep your shirt on. You look funny—"

"I think I just found the rest of Markie's head."

Terry sat straight up. "What?"

"It's stuck to the bedroom wall."

"For chrissakes!" He got out from behind the desk and went down the hall. Cassidy picked out a throne and sat. In a while Terry came back, nodding. "That's what you found all right, amigo. They killed him here. But dumped him way the hell and gone out there." He looked at the trees on the balcony swaying in the wind. "I think maybe Markie wasn't supposed to be found at all. Same message gets sent but there's no body, no evidence, no slugs. Except

151

for this one." He flipped Cassidy a mangled nub of lead. "Dug it out of the wall."

"Somebody had a sandwich while they worked him over," Cassidy said. "Jesus. Did you find what you're after?"

"No such luck. But he had something I need. Got to get it, amigo."

He went through the rest of the apartment. Cassidy sat in the living room leafing through Markie's prized copy of the *Necronomicon*. The sweetish smell wouldn't go away. It wasn't the reefer. It was something else. He paced the room looking at the renderings of devils and goblins. The only sound was the tapping of his cane.

Who killed Markie?

What did Markie have that Terry needed?

And what was that goddamned smell?

"Okay, Lew, let's get out of here. Only one other place to look. Come on."

"What is it, Terry. What are you looking for?"

Terry just smiled.

•　•　•

The hand-lettered sign said *Pendragon: Rare Books, First Editions, & Incunabula*. The shop nestled between a couple of very tony art galleries on East 57th in a sliver of freshly tuck-pointed red brick four stories high. It was Marquardt Cookson's place of business. Terry used a key to get in. Closing the door behind him he said, "The money's in the incunabula, if you know what I mean."

The light from the street filtered through the rain-streaked windows, cast jittery shadows. Tables were neatly arranged with piles of books. Gilt edges, morocco bindings. The walls were lined with dark wooden shelves and there were Tiffany lamps on low tables. A bronze bust of Dante was catching some shut-eye on a fluted pedestal. There was a gold-tooled escritoire at the back for the rude business of commerce. Framed Aubrey Beardsley prints. Bright clouds of flowers in large vases and copper pots.

Terry pulled the chain on one of the Tiffany lamps, sat

down at the escritoire, began shuffling through the contents of the drawers. There wasn't much. A petty-cash drawer, bundles of receipts, book orders, bills, catalogs. He looked up, frowning. "Upstairs. He keeps all the serious stuff on the second floor. For his special clients and friends."

He turned off the lamp and they went up the narrow dark wooden stairway, found themselves in the second of the two rooms over the main shop. The larger room overlooking the street was shadowy and dim and the rain beat on the mullioned windows. The smaller room contained another desk, this one a plain schoolteacher's number for use not show, two filing cabinets, a drinks table, a couple of cracked-leather armchairs. One of them was dribbling horsehair stuffing.

It didn't take long. What he wanted was in the lower drawer. The first item was a leather-bound volume with the words *Cash Ledger* stamped on its cover. The other was a desk diary. He leafed through the diary nodding to himself, whistling occasionally under his breath. He put it aside and opened the cash book, ran his fingers down a few pages while he moved his lips. Cassidy picked up a book from the stack on the floor at his feet. Photographs of men having sex with adolescent boys, girls, and the odd collie. One picture was much like another. On the whole, Markie may have gotten more or less what he deserved. He put it down and wanted to get the hell out of there.

The old floorboards were creaking, the kind of sound you don't pay much attention to in such buildings. Terry closed the books. "Well, it's all here, Lew. Meticulous record keeper, our Markie." He spoke affectionately.

Cassidy knew what was in the ledger and diary by then. A record of the payoffs. Markie Cookson with a cop on his team. Terry's manner of living was a mystery no more. When you had Max Bauman and Markie Cookson donating to the cause, you were the only Park Avenue homicide dick in town.

There was the sound of a footfall in the darkened front

room, and in the instant, Cassidy put it together—what he'd noticed at the Sutton Place residence.

A sweet, sickish smell. A plate full of gnawed toothpicks. Harry Madrid's cherry-scented tobacco and . . .

Bert Reagan was standing in the doorway with a toothpick in the corner of his flat miser's mouth and a Smith & Wesson Police Positive in his hand. His wet trench coat looked like he'd picked it out of a trash can and he was dripping, standing in a puddle. His wet Dobbs snap-brim was straight on his bony forehead and he needed a shave. His brown wing tips still bore caked sand, a souvenir of the Jersey Shore.

"Where's your keeper, Bert?" Cassidy said. "Lost in a good book?"

Reagan didn't take his eyes off Terry when he spoke. "Stay the fuck out of this, cowboy. You're not part of this. But you," he said, shaking the gun barrel at Terry like a teacher's admonishing finger, "you're something else again."

"Shop's not open, Bert," Terry said, leaning back in the squeaky swivel chair. "Come back tomorrow." He smiled. "Hell, Markie'll give you credit. You don't need the heater."

"Funny," Reagan said. He wasn't laughing and he didn't look happy. "What are you doin' here? How did you know . . ." He caught himself and the toothpick hot-footed it from one side of his mouth to the other.

"How did I know what? That you and Harry iced Markie Cookson over on Sutton Place yesterday?"

The color drained away leaving two pink spots on Reagan's face, as if he'd scraped his cheekbones. The toothpick made it halfway back and his Adam's apple bobbed like something going down for the third time.

Terry began to laugh. "Honest to God, you and Harry, the Keystone Kops. You oughtta be in pitchas!" He wiped his eyes. "What are you doing here, Bert, old pal?"

"I don't know nothin' about Cookson. Fat hophead, whatever happened to him wouldn't surprise me—"

"A fine moral tone," Cassidy said. He was beginning to

worry about Reagan growing too talkative. About Tom Dewey and Lucky Luciano and Lew Cassidy looking like a snitch. The atmosphere in the tight little office didn't seem to be right for explanations.

"I'm warning you, Cassidy—"

"Bert, give it a rest. You sound like a George Raft movie. Where's Harry?"

"Harry asked me to come by, check a coupla things—"

"Like these?" Terry nodded at the two volumes on the desk.

"Wouldn't be surprised," Reagan said sourly.

"I hear you and Harry been out to the shore, Bert. Shooting up some of Rocco's boys. Was that smart?"

Reagan scowled. He was a man who didn't know his lines, not any of them. He was on one page, the whole damn team on another.

"Bert doesn't have much to say, amigo. Maybe you should shove off, whattaya say, Bert?"

"I think I better take you guys to see Harry. Yeah, let's all shove off. This is Harry's game. You shouldn't of been here, you guys . . ."

"Where is Harry?"

"Oh, he's in his—what's he call it—his operations room, that's it. He's playing with the big boys now. Hotel room, down at the Danbury in Times Square there—"

"Operations room? Beautiful—he's got a little game on his own. Everybody's got an angle—"

"He's gonna nail you, Leary!" Reagan's temper snapped. He bit through the toothpick. "He's gonna have your balls. You can kiss it all goody-bye, Park Avenue, the broads, he's gonna bury you—"

"Bert, you're nothing but a dumb errand boy. Fuck you. You're too goddamn pitiful to deal with." Terry stood up. "I oughtta make you use your piece . . . would you like that? Think you've got the guts? Are you fast enough to squeeze one off 'fore I got you?"

Reagan decided not to wait.

The gun cracked like a bullwhip and the slug burrowed into the desktop an inch or two from Terry's hand. Terry didn't move. Splinters sprayed across his sleeve. While the sound died away Terry worked at producing a smile. Cassidy contemplated hitting Reagan from the side, wondered how fast the cop's reactions might be. Thought better of it.

"Real jumpy, Bert," Terry said.

"You get under my skin, Terry, smart-mouthing me like that."

"Well, you've had a long day. Killing Markie, staying up all night, probably getting seasick, hauling those bodies around in the dark, an amphibious landing in the fog, shooting up all those gunsels . . . you look like you could use forty winks."

"After we go see Harry," Reagan said.

"One-track mind," Cassidy said.

"Harry's not going to like this, Bert. I'll have to tell him you spilled the beans about Markie—"

"You son of a bitch, I didn't spill nothin'."

"Well, maybe Harry's feeling forgiving—don't worry about it."

"I ain't the one who's worried. Now up, both of you, we'll go see Harry. Right now! Gimme your piece, Terry, or so help me god I'll drill you where you stand."

Terry handed the books to Cassidy, then slowly took his revolver from his shoulder holster, gave it butt-first to Reagan.

"Okay, gents," Reagan said, "let's go."

Cassidy went down the stairs first, leaning on his stick. Terry followed, then Bert. Cassidy had to negotiate the descent in the dark with painstaking care.

"Move it, Lew," Reagan said. "We ain't got all night."

Terry said, "Be nice, Bert."

"Shut up!"

Halfway down the stairs where it was darkest, where you couldn't see anything, Cassidy leaned to one side, steadied himself. "My leg," he said. "It's still weak . . ." He couldn't see Terry but sensed him inches away.

"Come on, come on!" Reagan was all impatience.

Cassidy sucked in a deep breath and pitched the two

books of Markie's records back at Reagan. He couldn't tell where they hit him but he heard a cry of surprise, heard Reagan lose his footing. There was a hell of a noise and a muzzle flash and plaster falling from above. Terry made a move. Reagan grunted again in the dark. Somebody moaned in pain. Both of them came crashing against Cassidy, one hurtled past, the other grabbed at the railing and it came out of the wall in his hand.

Cassidy sat down hard, bouncing on the edge of the steps. Pain exploded in his leg. Gritting his teeth he tried to straighten it out with both hands. The stick had rolled away.

Someone at the bottom of the steps was struggling to get up. There was a lot of heavy breathing going on.

There was another muzzle flash from above.

The shape jerked backward. There were three more shots. Cassidy squeezed his hands against his ears. The shape was driven to its knees, then hammered into the floor like a spike with each shot.

The noise kept blasting in Cassidy's head. The smell of gunpowder filled the tight stairway. He was choking on it.

He tried to get down the stairs, had to get to him.

"Terry! For Christ's sake, Terry!"

When he reached the body, he got his hands sticky with warm blood.

He looked back up the stairway where slow footsteps were coming toward him. He was yelling and he couldn't see a damn thing. He was trying to stand up and the leg wouldn't hold.

"You'd better kill me, too, you bastard!"

The footsteps stopped near the bottom of the steps.

Cassidy looked up at the void and waited for the slug.

"Now, why the hell would I do that, amigo?"

It was Terry.

CHAPTER EIGHT

The plaster hand with the scarlet nails hovered above the playing cards, the head with its thick black hair in braids rocked back and forth with indecision, then hand and head stopped, the yellow light bulb snapped off, and a small blue card dropped from the slot. The plaster eyelids clicked shut.

> *Life may seem humdrum at the moment but cheer up! The future holds many interesting moments. You have a romantic disposition which may have gotten you in trouble in the past, but you are about to find a new love who will be your TRUE love! A friend wields a great deal of influence in your life. Changes coming soon. You have fine taste in clothing, causing many people to envy you. Drop another nickel in the slot and I will tell more.*

Cassidy read the card. How much more could there be, anyway? He dropped it in his pocket, finished the hot dog, wiped a mustard stain from the clothes everybody envied so much, and looked back at the traffic and sunshine on 42nd Street. Half the men were wearing uniforms. He felt suspect without one, like a secret Section Eight who had long conversations with lampposts and the angel Gabriel. The pinball machines clanged and rang and banged all around him. The arcade was full of sailors, a day's shore leave. Kids. Killing time, waiting. He stood on the sidewalk, watching the Danbury Hotel across the street. It wasn't the Waldorf. There were full-time residents, who made book out of the lobby, and the room-by-the-hour crowd who liked to gum up the sheets and give the springs a workout.

And then he saw him moving like a tollbooth through the sunlit, blinking crowd—there was Harry Madrid in a double-breasted gray suit and a Panama hat which had seen a lot of first summery days since coming north. He passed the pawnshop, turned into the lobby of the Danbury, and went to the elevator cage unwrapping a King Edward. The tiles on the floor were chipped and the dust on the potted palms was thick enough to autograph.

Cassidy crossed to the desk and paid the counterman five dollars for the double-breasted gray suit's room number. He went upstairs knowing too late he'd have gotten the number for a buck. But he was new to this and had to go by what he'd seen tough guys do in the movies.

Madrid was still wearing his suit coat when he answered the knock. The hat was on the bed. The telephone was off the hook. He looked at Cassidy through the smoke from his King Edward, squinting, eyes small and shining, piggish. "You," he growled, "I wanna see." He turned back to the telephone, said something, slammed the receiver down. "How'd you know I was here? Nobody knows I'm here."

"Just wanted to stop by, tell you how sorry I was about Bert. Do they know who did it?"

"Don't kid a kidder, Lew. Bert was just one more fart in a very big windstorm. A popgun in the big war. The hell with him."

"Softie."

Madrid ground out his cigar and tugged a pipe from his pocket, then a yellow oilskin pouch. "Bauman's cigars ruin all these other things for you." He fingered tobacco into the bowl; the first puff filled the room with the cloying cherry smell.

"Too bad about Markie Cookson, too."

"Yeah, I heard about that," Madrid said with a shrug of his massive shoulders. "Heard he's gone missing . . . he'll turn up. His kind always turn up."

"Not this time, Harry. When you and Bert kill 'em, the bastards stay dead. Like Rocco's boys down on the shore. You've been up to mischief, Harry. I want to know when and where it's gonna stop . . . you and me being partners with old Tom and Mr. Lucky. I get worried the way you're killing people, setting up your own little operation here. All of a sudden I'm getting all faint and girlish at the thought of you free-lancing from a posh place like this . . . I'm wondering if maybe I'd better remember who my friends are—maybe I'd better go tell Max and Terry what this looks like to me. Dog's breakfast, Harry. Feel like I'm stepping in it . . ."

"Your mouth," Harry Madrid said, "it's running overtime. You could talk yourself into an early grave—"

"That's my Harry."

"You knew I was here. You get the idea somewhere Cookson's croaked . . . you're beatin' your gums about Rocco's hoods . . . You come here and throw a spitter like Bert at me, think I'll go for it. So Bert shot off his yap to you before you and Terry kill him—hell, it's a sorry old world, Lew. Football players should stick to being heroes. Take an expert's word for it. Siddown, Lew."

A warm breeze fluttered the curtains ten stories above 42nd. He sat in the ancient Morris chair while Harry Madrid poured Old Crow shots into a couple of glasses.

"It's too late," Cassidy said. "I'm not a hero anymore. The heroes are all gone now, busy elsewhere; hadn't you heard?" The bourbon didn't sit so well with the hot dog.

"Nobody left but us villains, is that it?"

"I think Bert's death was an accident," Cassidy said.

Madrid chuckled through the smoke. It circled around his broad fatherly face. A cop of the old school. A flatfoot, Terry used to call him. "Why not? Shot himself three, four times and keeled over. Sounds reasonable. I guess Markie's death was an accident, too. Let's say for the sake of argument that Markie's dead . . ."

"Let's," Cassidy said. "That must have been quite a scene in Markie's bedroom, Harry. The blue lights, the mirror over the bed, the movie camera, the handcuffs on the big pecker—did you think to film it? Big round bed, all his doodads. So you got fed up with him, maybe you couldn't break him, so you rammed him up against the wall and blew his head off, very messy; you should have cleaned off the wall. You dumped him off the Jersey shore."

"Lemme tell you about Markie, Lew. For the sake of argument, y'know. You got a minute?"

"For you? Sure."

"I been watching Terry for a long time. Watching and thinking about the way your pal Terry lives, how he operates. Then Luciano starts going on about him . . . now Terry's playing this big part in my life. And I want him out of it altogether, see. But I can't quite catch him at the bad stuff. When I get him, I gotta get him good. He's a cop on the take but half the cops in this town have a Max Bauman somewhere. I hadda do better than a gangster with a fat roll for payoffs . . . well, Terry never shoulda hooked up with the fat man. I could see him playing ball with Max, but with a pansy like Cookson? Unnatural. Then that kid plugs Terry and I smoke my pipe and keep thinkin'. If this little bumboy Derek Boyce had really killed Sylvester Aubrey Bean, Herrin might have hated Terry for screwing up the course of true love, but he wouldn't of shot him like that. So I get to thinkin' maybe Herrin *knew* Boyce was innocent, the fall guy that Terry set up to spare the real killer the aggravation of going to the chair. I investigate a little on my own time like and it turns out Markie was not only screwing around with this

161

Boyce character . . . but Markie was also the main pur-
veyor of dope to the queers—how 'bout that! sez I to
myself. It hits me that Markie was tight with all these
guys, particularly with the very rich Mr. Bean. But old
Terry's investigation skips all that, settles right on Boyce.
But there were all sorts of links between the fat man and
Bean . . . turns out Bean's place was full of Markie's
fingerprints, even some mash notes he'd written Bean
. . . and there were some pictures of a fat man in a mask
whipping the shit out of Bean while Derek Boyce watched
like a retard. Well, it don't take Holmes and Watson to
figure out that Bean was the victim of what would you like
to call it? An excess of enthusiasm, boyish high spirits?
They were all hooked on dope, on this creepy witch stuff,
all boys together—following me, Lew?"

"At a safe distance," Cassidy said.

"Terry figured the fat man was too good to waste on the
'lectric chair, doncha see? So he gave 'em a nutsy little
fairy like Boyce and kept Markie out of it. Let's say the fat
man was no ingrate." Harry Madrid tamped the hot ash
down into the bowl with a thickly callused fingertip.
"Now, Lew, you gotta admit that sending Boyce to the
lion's den was a bad thing to do . . . I had a damn good
case, hypothetical I know, on Cookson, and Terry was right
in the middle of it . . . so I kept gnawing on it, like this
bull terrier I got when he gets after a juicy soupbone, and
whattaya know, I'm only part of the way home . . . Terry's Max Bauman's boy. And what's Max's big crop? Dope.
Reefers, coke, heroin . . . and the fat man was the sup-
plier to the queers. Which makes Terry the middleman
taking a helluva cut from Markie's cost. Now I know for
damn sure that Terry wants Markie out of jail . . . and
there's a chance that Markie has kept a record of his
payoffs to Terry so he can bargain with the coppers the
day everybody comes knockin' at his door. Everybody's
ass-deep in this and Markie's got his own little insurance
policy against the rainy day." Harry Madrid smiled
comfortably like a man who has seen the light after a
long time in the darkness with everybody else. "Terry's a

bad man," he said, puffing. "Now, if I can figure out Markie's having an insurance policy, then so can Terry . . . but why did Terry decide to pick up that insurance policy now? You got me there—"

"A sixth sense," Cassidy said.

"Terry must of found all the records of the payoffs because I sure as hell didn't. And I figure Terry killed Bert because Bert was there following my orders—to bring me the stuff that would incriminate Terry. Don't tell me a shitload of lies, okay? Life's too short. So Terry's got the evidence and I'm back where I started . . . it's a game for chrissakes, Lew, don't look at me like that. You know about games. Look at your leg, that was a game. Well, this is our game, Terry's and mine, and Terry's losin'. He may not think so, but he's losin' and the other guys have got the ball. You'd do well to remember that, Lew. I want Terry. Lucky wants Terry. He's a dead man . . . and you're the only guy with any chance, *any chance*, of getting him out alive. Want me to be honest with you? I don't think you can do it, kid. Now, what the hell do you want? You didn't tell me how you got here."

"I'm just trying to figure out what's going on," Cassidy said. "I have to hear everybody's lies. What was that number you pulled with Rocco's boys—"

"Don't look at me. Gangland massacre. I'm clean."

"You, Harry? Clean?" Cassidy shook his head.

Madrid stood up, knocked his pipe out on the windowsill. The wind whipped the ashes out into space. "Everybody's dirty so far as I can see. You're not getting any cleaner yourself, Lew." He grinned. "Forget Rocco's boys. Look at it this way, the world's a better place without them. Whoever killed them, he oughtta get a medal." The grin turned into a small laugh.

"I saw you kill 'em," Cassidy said.

"Did you at that? Well, you know what I think? I think it was a vision, Lew. Or the DTs maybe."

"You came in a motor launch, you came up out of the dunes to the parking lot and opened up on 'em. I saw it happen."

"No kidding? Anybody else see me do this?"

Cassidy stared into the hard little eyes.

"I mean, hell, Lew. Uncorroborated testimony . . ." Madrid shrugged. "People, they're seein' things all the time, things that never happened . . . it's just one of those things." His hand was on the doorknob. A sepia picture hung on the flowered paper beside the door. A frontiersman was standing up in a canoe while an Indian paddled. At least *he* had a paddle. "I'll be in touch. We're still counting on you, Lew. Give us Terry and Max, we might throw Terry back." He held his pipe in his hand, chuckling as he closed the door.

Waiting for the elevator, Cassidy wondered just where the interview had gone wrong. Sometimes you had the feeling that you were the only one who ever got surprised. He was glad to get through the musty lobby. But he was standing in front of the pawnshop, staring at a team photograph of the '07 Yale footballers without really seeing it, when he felt a very large paw on his shoulder.

• • •

Bennie the Brute said, "Lew."

"Well"—Cassidy looked at the polka-dot bow tie—"I don't know why I should be surprised. How are you, Bennie?" He felt like something caught in a powerful vortex he could only partly control. He could beat his tiny fists on the windowpanes, make a noise, pretend it made a difference, and then a hand as big as his head would drop on his shoulder. Nothing surprised him anymore. Except the belief that he still had some control.

"Don't be alarmed, Lew."

"All right, Bennie. I won't."

"You looked alarmed for a second there, Lew. Mr. Bauman would like to see you." He nodded back along the curb where the Chrysler sat like a huge cream puff. He gently touch Cassidy's elbow, the slightest pressure. "We been following you, Lew. You shouldn't hang around with guys like Mr. Madrid."

"That's good, Bennie, really good. Harry thinks his Danbury office is a secret."

"Looks like Harry's wrong again. He's all wet about a lot of things." He opened the rear door and Cassidy got in beside Max Bauman. Bennie waited patiently until Cassidy's leg was tucked in, then closed the door with a heavy solid click.

They were slowly heading uptown after Bennie had made a left. Horns were honking and children were holding balloons and the pretty girls were out in their summer dresses.

Max Bauman shook Cassidy's hand, leaned back, and looked out at the crowds of girls on their lunch hour and soldiers and sailors wandering through the city most of them had never seen before. They were only at the beginning. They were going to see a lot of things they'd never seen before and die in places they'd never dreamed of and maybe some of them would even get back to New York someday and try to remember the young men they'd been so long ago.

"I'm a direct man," Bauman said, "when it comes to business. But let me ask you a question before we get down to cases. What business do you have with a rascal like Harry Madrid?"

Cassidy was waiting for an elaboration on the question. None came. "Condolences about Bert Reagan. That was my business with him."

"Strong feelings to inspire you to go to his little undercover headquarters. He's working with the FBI now. Isn't that amazing, Lew?"

"Amazing."

"How did you know where to find him, Lew?"

"Bert mentioned it once, I think. Look, what the hell is this, Max?"

"Take my advice, Lew. Wash your hands of this man, this Harry Madrid. He has a bad history."

"I don't get the point of this—"

"Harry Madrid is tampering in my business, Lew. He is trying to upset what I like to think of as the natural order of things. I will not stand for it. I refer, of course, to the cold-blooded murders of my associates from Florida. Terry tells me you personally saw him . . . after the shooting was over. A massacre—"

"Harry said I was having a vision—"

"He knows you saw what happened?"

Cassidy nodded.

"And how did he come by that information?"

"I just told him."

"You told him. Now, that is amazing." Max stared out the window. He didn't sound amazed. "In a way, it would be possible to make a case for Harry Madrid believing he was only doing his job. Perhaps I should give him the benefit of the doubt. Do you think I should give Harry Madrid the benefit of the doubt?"

"I don't feel all that warmly toward Harry."

"I am sincerely glad to hear this from your own lips, Lew. Because I have no intention of giving Harry Madrid anything but possibly a cement necktie. So you wonder why don't I do it? It would be child's play. I know about his hotel office, I know about his connection with Mr. Hoover's bureau, I know about his friendship with certain criminal elements . . . You may not believe this, Lew, but Harry Madrid was a bagman—yes, as God is my witness—a bagman for a fellow I've known a long time, a man who has grown twisted and evil with the years . . . Lucky Luciano! Yes, Harry Madrid would do anything for Lucky. Until Lucky ran into some bad luck . . ." He leaned forward, tapped Bennie's shoulder. "Through the park, Bennie. Lovely day. Trees leafing out." He reached across and tapped Cassidy's knee. "That's the kind of man Harry Madrid is. When he murdered my associates from Florida, the thought crossed my mind—he is doing this terrible thing for Lucky Luciano. Luciano torments me from his prison cell!"

Bennie swung across 59th and glided into the park. The racket of the city faded. "Look at those squirrels, Lew. They planned ahead, they stored up nuts for the long winter, and they survived. They were vigilant. Survival is all. Goddammit!" His calm burst like a ruptured blood vessel. His face splotched with anger; saliva welled in the corners of his mouth. "Rocco, a man I've done business with for twenty years! Rocco thought I had his men murdered—me! It's like one of the Bard's bloody histories! Well, Lew, I convinced him it wasn't me . . . he bought something from me, a first order of some of my goods, you might say, and he paid me a million dollars . . . well, I let him keep the goods and I gave him back the million! Just to show him I had nothing to do with the massacre— that we were still pals! Now," he sighed, struggling to control himself, "you'd think that would be bad enough, wouldn't you, Lew?"

"Bad enough," Cassidy agreed.

"But the worst is yet to come." He took a deep breath, a man going off the high dive. "Somebody told Madrid those men would be there . . . *somebody told him I would be there!* Harry Madrid could have killed me. And Rocco, for that matter. If we hadn't changed our plans at the last minute. Listen to me, Lew." Veins pulsed in the forehead and Cassidy looked away, found the bloodshot eyes. Not a great improvement. *"I have been betrayed! The fucking serpent is at my bosom, Lew."*

Cassidy nodded. He didn't want to ask the name of the serpent. The car seemed full of them.

Bauman whispered, "Did Terry betray me, Lew?"

"You must be joking—"

"Do I strike you as a man who's joking?"

Cassidy shook his head.

"I want to know if Terry is betraying me. I want you to find out . . . don't spare my feelings, Lew. If a man has a cancer, he wants to know. The cancer must be cut out. And if Terry is true to me as ever, well, I'll make it up to him. Lew, I'm at a loss . . . there was no one else I could come to." His tongue flicked along dry, cracked lips. It was his lizard impression. "You've played ball for my team, you've given everything. I trust you, Lew."

"All right. I'll see what I can do, Max."

167

"You don't sound happy. But do your best. I'll do something nice for you, Lew."

Cassidy got out of the car near the Metropolitan Museum. He said he wanted to do some walking, give his leg some exercise. Once he leaned down at the window.

"Max, you're forgetting someone else who could have set you up."

"Oh? Now, who would that be?"

"Who benefited most?"

"What are you saying?"

"Rocco himself. Gunsels are a dime a dozen. Kill expendable men of your own to prove your innocence."

Bauman's face grew pinched and red again, as if he'd just swallowed something with hair on it.

"Just a thought," Cassidy said, stepped back from the car, watched it slip into the Fifth Avenue traffic. He didn't know who had tipped Madrid. But there were a great many possibilities, Rocco being merely the one he thought Max would find most confusing.

Jesus, he wished people would stop asking him to spy on Terry . . .

*　　*　　*

"Here's to you, amigo." Terry lifted his glass. "You saved my life on that staircase. Reagan would have iced me without batting an eye." Night had fallen on Park Avenue, the lights were shining in the windows, and you could smell summer coming. Terry was looking like a millionaire. He wore a maroon-and-blue-striped robe with padded shoulders from Sulka. Navy blue pajamas. He got Cassidy settled on the couch with his leg up on a hassock and brought him a hefty Scotch. There was something comforting about watching him play with the silver ice tongs and hearing the solid clicking of the cubes in the crystal. Everybody was after Terry but Terry didn't know it. Ignorance was bliss. But he knew *somebody* was after him. Harry Madrid was always out there, barking, clawing. Which one of them, he wondered, watching Terry enjoying himself, was in the cage? Remembering Harry's remarks, watching Terry, you began to realize how raw Terry must have rubbed the old copper.

"You got me out of the soup, amigo," Terry said again, tilting his glass at Cassidy once more.

"So you owe me an explanation," Cassidy said. "We'd better get it out of the way."

He sat on a stool at the bar. He was grinning in a lopsided way, making a major production of clipping and lighting one of Max's cigars. It was built along the lines of a rifle barrel. Glenn Miller was stringing the pearls on the record player.

"All right," he said. "Fella risks his life for you, fella gets an explanation. Reagan and Madrid had some of this figured out, I don't deny that. Markie was a generous, grateful soul when it came to services rendered. Technically I was on the take . . . but that's not quite as bad as it sounds. What Harry's been doing—hell, guys have been telling me this for months, you can't keep a secret among a bunch of cops—he's been poking around the Sylvester Bean murder, trying to pin it on Markie . . . and on me for covering up for Markie. Well, the fact is Markie didn't have a damn thing to do with Bean's murder. He had a crush on him at one time but that didn't come into it. Harry was adding two and two and crapping out. Derek Boyce killed Bean, though my own guess is that he was too hopped up to know what the hell he was doing. Raggedy Ann and Andy time, y'know? I figure Bean got Boyce high as King Kong on the Empire State Building and said he wanted to be tortured in a nice genteel way. A little gentlemanly sadism, that's what Bean enjoyed."

"Masochism," Cassidy said.

"All comes down to the same thing. Anyway, Boyce was listening to voices from out near Jupiter somewhere and got carried away. That's my guess. Boyce's brain was a piece of green cheese by the time we got him. Anyway, he was the right guy. Harry was chasing the wild goose.

"Markie was questioned during the investigation, no favoritism. But I treated him like a human being—not Harry's style—and he appreciated that. I could have turned the whole thing into a Page One Extra. I mean, hell, Markie and Bean were old pals, belonged to the same coven of witches, probably had their robes run up by the same mysterious gypsy woman. Yeah. I peeled the scab off all this witchcraft stuff but what was the point in scaring the pants off everybody? Hell, they're just a bunch of harmless loonies. Markie knew I could have blown the gay world to smithereens if I'd been out to grab some head-lines. But he watched and he saw me keep my word. I didn't make the poor old fairies the scapegoats, I sat on the lid and made it tight.

"Markie was a sweet guy, really. He told me he'd like to show his thanks. You think I'd turn him down?"

Cassidy interrupted: "You did take it, then? And the drug side, Markie supplying the gay community?"

"Markie moved some reefers, some coke, sure. I put him in touch with Max on that. It was between them. Look, Markie was buying a friend on the inside and I let him. He felt better and safer. And I sure put the cash to good use. What the hell? Nobody got hurt, amigo."

"What are you talking about, Terry? Nobody got hurt? What about dear sweet old Markie?"

"You know what I mean. Nobody got hurt in my deal with Markie. Sure, Harry killed him but that's different. Harry's psycho. He's obsessed with me. With getting me. Markie was a natural victim, Harry's a predator."

"He's a monster."

Terry nodded philosophically, watching the Havana grow an ash. "Well, you gotta know Harry. Personality quirk. He figures some guys are expendable. And Markie was expendable because he was a hophead and a fairy. Harry's sort of old school about that. Traditionalist. The way old Harry looks at things there's only one thing worse than fairies and that's cops who get above their station, a show-off cop . . . like me. Not a cop on the take—just the show-offs. A cop who thinks he's smarter than the system. Well, hell, I *am* smarter."

"But Markie's dead," Cassidy said. "The money tree's been cut down."

"Well, the same thought occurred to me, believe it or not. And I've been thinking. I can't make a living being an honest cop. This lousy job has forced me into taking money from people to create the illusion that they have a tame cop . . . and I can't even give them honest value. So"—he slid down off the stool and began changing the stack of records on the changer spindle—"so I've decided to rethink the situation. I want to hear your thoughts about the future. What should the kid do with his life?"

"Punt."

Terry laughed. He was so damned happy, so intensely alive, dancing along the abyss. For a moment Cassidy couldn't grasp it, couldn't share it. But he kept laughing at all the beasts in his dark night, his eyes twinkling, moving around the room, reflected in the mirrors, swirling an imaginary girl to the Glenn Miller records.

Bean, Boyce, Herrin, Markie, his little nameless boyfriend, Irvie Bauman on the *Yorktown*, five gunsels blown to shit in a parking lot . . . They were all dead but there was a war on and people were dying everywhere. And nothing was the way it had been once and it would never be again. Karin was fading, the love-light fading like a beautiful song, and he'd told another woman he loved her . . .

Terry lifted his glass again, managed to stop laughing, tears on his cheeks. "To absent friends!" he said and began to laugh again.

Without quite realizing why, Cassidy heard himself laughing along with Terry, as if there were some great joke.

•　•　•

One morning in May, walking in Central Park with the city's towers rising in a balmy haze around them, Cassidy asked a question that had been on his mind since Max had made his crazy suggestion about Terry's betraying him. There hadn't been any contact with Max and Bennie for a couple of weeks. Max and Cindy were said to have gone to

171

Los Angeles on the train. If they had, Bennie had certainly gone with them.

"Somebody had to tip Madrid so he could stage his little wake-up party in the parking lot. Who would you bet on?"

Terry leaned on a railing, staring down into a lake, staring at the man he saw looking back. He was still drawing his NYPD check and probably a retainer from Max. But he was looking around for something else. Maybe the face in the lake had an answer.

"Well, it all depends, doesn't it? If they figured Max and Rocco were gonna be there, then you gotta ask yourself who wants to climb over Max and Rocco . . . if it was a question of putting away some of Rocco's infantry, it'd look like Max was the source. Whatta you think, sport?"

"I think whoever did it set it up thinking Max was going to be there, then it was too late to change it."

"Narrows the field," Terry said thoughtfully. "Who's got a motive? Motive and opportunity, that's all a cop ever thinks about. Well, we don't really know who had opportunity 'cause we don't know who all might have known about the meeting . . . but it's not so hard to think of motive. Money's a motive, power's a motive; that's what matters to guys like Max and Rocco. And, believe me, Lew, the plot hardly ever changes. Thing like what happened in Jersey, it's always some guy who figures it's his turn, he's waited long enough. The serpent in the bosom." Terry grinned.

It was the second time Cassidy had been told about the serpent in the bosom. "So who are you nominating?"

"Obvious," Terry said. "But none of our affair—"

"Who?"

"It's always the closest person to you, the Judas. The traitor is always the one you trust the most . . ."

"Who?"

"Bennie," Terry Leary said.

•   •   •

It was all a puzzle and the problem was you couldn't be sure what was really important. Cassidy could identify the players without a program. That wasn't the problem. What mattered was getting a picture of the connections. But they were all blurred.

Terry and Harry Madrid were both cops, had worked together, you'd think they were on the same side. But they weren't. Terry had already killed one cop with the gun strapped inside his pants leg and it looked like Harry was willing to do damn near anything to put Terry down.

Terry worked for Max Bauman . . . but Max thought Terry was betraying him . . . to Harry Madrid, of all people. And Harry was working with a hotshot politician like Tom Dewey and the biggest mobster of all, Luciano, to bring Max Bauman down, to put Dewey in Albany, and to get Luciano out of the slammer. And Luciano was in line to get Terry, too.

Max thought Harry Madrid was a scoundrel, at least partially because he'd been a bagman for Luciano in the old days. Conversely, Max's good right hand was Bennie the Brute . . . and Terry figured Bennie was in fact the serpent Bauman felt writhing at his bosom.

And Cassidy was supposed to be watching Terry for Madrid *and* Bauman while he was in fact the only player on the field who was betraying Max . . . and Max trusted him. Betrayal—because Cassidy had fallen for Cindy Squires, who belonged to Max. But even that hadn't gone unnoticed. Bennie the Brute had seen it coming all along.

It was a puzzle.

And in Cassidy's eyes nothing was more puzzling than Cindy Squires and his feelings for her. He hadn't seen her or had word from her since the night at the shore. The longer her silence, the more he thought about her. He played their conversation again and again in his mind, all of it, so often sticking on her harsh judgments of herself, or on the image of the little girl sitting swinging her legs on the country gravestone, or on her pleas for help, the arrangement she'd suggested . . .

He spent too damn much time thinking about her, which was dumb in several ways. She was Max Bauman's girl. Which made all the other reasons unimportant. But he thought of her adolescent's breasts and the sturdy width of her hips and the sapphire eyes and the voice that stayed on one note so much of the time. After a while he began consciously trying to push her out of his mind, exercising what passed for his will. He didn't mention her to Terry, didn't ask Terry if he'd seen her. Sometimes he'd find a matchbook on the coffee table and Terry'd have been to Heliotrope. But Cassidy didn't ask and he didn't go to Heliotrope. But he read his *Bleak House* . . .

And he'd think about Karin, too. He'd think about the downy hair on her tan arms and he'd get out the photo albums and look at them for hours. Karin on the ice back in '36. Karin with Paul Cassidy outside the Beverly Wilshire. Karin, Lew, and Terry on the Boardwalk at Atlantic City . . . a great many pictures. And he'd close his eyes and see her on the day she'd left to go back to Germany, all dressed up in a navy blue suit with white piping and blue and white spectators. He'd taste her lipstick and her tears and kiss the hair at her temples and kiss her delicate ears and she'd whisper things in German and then he'd fall asleep and dream of her and wake up afraid he'd never see her again.

As summer crept up on them, the last day of May was no different from any other day that spring. The flowers were in bloom and the trees green, just as if there were no war at all. Bing Crosby was in great voice on the radio and Gabriel Heatter tried to find something hopeful in the war news but night after night he came up with the sentence that was becoming his trademark and part of the American landscape. *Ah, there's bad news tonight* . . .

Cassidy went to bed that last night of May thinking of Karin.

He didn't know she was already dead.

CHAPTER NINE

Monday, the first day of June, 1942. The three-layer headlines stretched all the way across the front page of the *Times*.

**1,000 BRITISH BOMBERS SET COLOGNE ON FIRE;
USE 3,000 TONS OF EXPLOSIVES IN RECORD RAID;
GERMANS ARE HURLED BACK IN BID FOR TOBRUK**

Centered under the headlines was a photograph of an RAF bomber crew sipping tea before their airplane after the raid. The caption read: "Tea After the Greatest Air Raid in History."

Cassidy's breathing had just about stopped.

He began reading the stories, gulping down the words, choking on them. The ninety-minute raid had demolished the city on the Rhine where Karin had grown up, where she had returned to her father's side.

He read the report beneath another headline: "Cologne 'Inferno' Astonishes Pilots." It was datelined May 31, London, from United Press.

Seven-eighths of Cologne, a city the size of Boston, was in flames, an inferno "almost too gigantic to be real," when the history-making raid was over last night, pilots who took part in it said tonight . . .

"Cologne was just a sea of flames," said Squadron Leader Len Frazer of Winnipeg, one of the more than 1,000 Canadian airmen who had a hand in the epic raid.

"I saw London burning during the Battle of Britain and it was nothing compared to Cologne," Pilot Officer H. J. M. Lacelle of Toronto, gunner in the tail of a bomber, contributed.

These reports were typical of the thousands being sifted tonight and compiled into a record of the mightiest piece of destruction ever devised by man.

The lurid sky over Cologne for ninety minutes was as busy as Piccadilly Circus as the great Lancasters and Halifaxes, Stirlings and Manchesters, streaked in at the rate of one every six seconds to unload their total cargo of steel-cased death . . .

"It was almost too gigantic to be real," said the pilot of one Halifax. In every part of the city buildings were ablaze. Here and there you could see their outlines, but mostly it was just one big stretch of fire.

"It was strange to see the flames reflected on our aircraft. It looked at times as if we were on fire ourselves, with the red glow dancing up and down our wings . . ."

He went to the kitchen and drank a glass of orange juice, stared out at the air shaft and the sparrows who came down to eat bread crumbs from the windowsill. Terry was still in his room asleep.

Karin.

. . . the mightiest piece of destruction ever devised by man . . . it looked as if we were on fire ourselves . . .

The sparrows were going on about their breakfast.

Karin. He found he couldn't take a deep breath. He

176

closed his eyes, flattened his hands on the tabletop. There was no point in kidding himself.

He went back into the living room and picked up the *Times* and began pacing, reading as he toured the room, trying to control the movement of his eyes, unaware of time or where he was or anything but the bombs raining down on Cologne, the sea of fire.

There was no point in kidding himself. Karin had been in Cologne with her father. Maybe she survived, maybe she'd gotten to the basement and had lived through it in the debris, maybe she'd been out of the city and maybe it was all a bad dream . . .

But no, it wasn't that way at all. No, it was one of those things you heard during the war and you knew the news was bad, it was meant for you, it was inescapable and you couldn't pretend. You'd never forget the moment you heard it, where you were and what you were doing. You'd never forget that frozen instant when you got the bad news. It was the worst news you could imagine and maybe you were having a piece of apple pie and a cup of coffee in the kitchen and the Western Union man was slowly coming up the walk and you knew, you knew for sure. Or maybe you were listening on the radio and you heard your husband's ship had gone down or your boyfriend was on Bataan and you just knew you'd never be the same again, that the last of your trust and innocence had been used up. It was always the worst news you could imagine.

On an inside page was the story released from Berlin by official radio. They admitted serious damage to Cologne due to "terror attacks" with incendiary bombs on the civilian population. But they said it wasn't such a big raid. They said seventy RAF planes had gotten to the city. They said 111 people were killed.

Among the dead they named an actor well known to the German public. And a prominent scientist, several times mentioned for a Nobel Prize. Herr Professor Richter. And his daughter, the famous Olympic skater and film star. Karin Richter. Karin . . .

She was a German and the Germans were beginning to

177

die in large numbers and they were the enemy and when he turned on the radio everybody was pretty happy about the thousand-bomber raid, about the mightiest piece of destruction ever devised by man. Karin was just an unimportant casualty. In the inferno of Cologne she wouldn't be missed. A woman who hadn't ever done much but ice-skate and fall in love and get married. No kids and she hadn't had time to grow old. She'd been merely another frightened speck beneath the falling bombs.

Karin was dead.

The telephone rang and it was his father.

"My God, son, I'm sorry. You've got to be strong, Lew . . . it's the goddamn war," his father said, calling from the Shoreham Hotel in Washington. He sounded as if he'd been crying and when he hung up, Lew broke down.

When Gabriel Heatter came on that night, he finally had a legitimate reason to make America feel good.

"Ah," he said, "there's good news tonight. History's first thousand-bomber raid, more than twice as many RAF bombers than Reichsmarschall Göring's Luftwaffe ever managed to put in the night sky over London, struck at the heart of Hitler's Reich last night . . . ah, yes, there's good news tonight . . ."

Karin was dead.

• • •

It was a long mean summer for Cassidy. His thirtieth summer. When he wasn't wandering in a daze of helplessness and sorrow, he was fuming in the furious frustration of not being able to get into the service. He hated his leg and he drank too much and when he was drunk he wanted to die for Karin and for his country. Some nights he just wanted to die. He sought the punishment he believed he deserved for falling in love with Cindy Squires, for letting Karin slip away even before she died. He sailed on a stormy sea of bourbon, tried to fill the unfillable empty blackness at his core with booze and self-pity. He limped around with his cane and fell off the occasional barstool.

And Terry Leary was always there to catch him. Stinking drunk and maudlin and full of anger and yelling and screaming and crying—and still Terry Leary was there to catch him when the trapdoor opened and the hungry monsters beckoned.

Cindy, on the other hand, was nowhere to be seen. He began to think of her as a phantom, an illusion. She'd never happened at all and he'd never told her he loved her and he'd never spoken her name. And Terry set out to bring him back from the mists of the dead where he seemed to hover like one of the bad spirits from poor Markie's *Necronomicon.*

Terry bought all the new records everybody was playing. He made sure Cassidy had all the new books to read. Every so often the gloom lifted. *See Here, Private Hargrove* left them both on the floor helpless with laughter. *The Robe* wasn't as funny.

They went to see all the new movies and some days they even stood in line. They saw Noel Coward in *In Which We Serve* and Ronald Colman and Greer Garson in *Random Harvest* and Spencer Tracy and Katharine Hepburn in *Woman of the Year* and Walter Pidgeon and Garson again in *Mrs. Miniver.*

Terry was still ruminating about what he was going to do when he left the Force. Paul Cassidy kept calling Lew offering him jobs which he knew, even as he procrastinated, he should have taken. Make movies, his father said, win the war on a Culver City back lot and chow down at Musso & Frank's or the Brown Derby. Help with the war bond tours. Take your mind off things, there was plenty to try to forget. . . .

August was brutal, the dog days. They killed a lot of time at Yankee Stadium. They'd keep score and eat hot dogs and soak up the sun and lose themselves in the flow of the games.

In the middle of August there was a doubleheader with the Senators, what they called a War Chest Benefit. It was hot, the kind of day you just had to wear seersucker slacks and your shirt stuck to your back and you found your old straw boater and wore it at a jaunty angle over your eye. Karin had bought Cassidy's for him but he tried not to think about that. He was trying to discipline himself. Two and a half months had passed since Cologne had been reduced to rubble. He hadn't seen Karin in nearly three years. He told himself he'd never see her again. He told himself he had to get on with life.

There were seventy thousand people at the stadium that afternoon. It wasn't just the doubleheader. It wasn't just the War Chest and the patriotic fever, though people were feeling a little better about things. The battles of the Coral Sea and Midway were victories that began the summer, and Doolittle's incredible raid on Tokyo had perked people up as far back as April. A week before they went out to the stadium for the doubleheader with the Senators, some German saboteurs who'd been landed on Long Island from U-boats were sent to the chair. By God, don't fuck with us, the Americans seemed to be saying.

Still, the fans weren't coming out just because the news was good. There was something special that day. Between games Walter Johnson, now fifty-four but with a name that was still magic, the greatest fireballer of them all, was going to try to throw a lamb chop, as the sportswriters were saying, past a wolf named Babe Ruth. The Babe was forty-seven and had last been to bat in 1935. Johnson had retired in '27, that greatest of all years when Lindy flew the Atlantic and the Babe hit sixty. Big Train Johnson and the Babe, again, after all these years. The whole thing sent shivers up your spine.

The Babe looked pretty much the same. The belly was a little bigger but the legs were still spindly, the bat still an extra heavy the size of a tree. Johnson looked to be in good shape, too. The papers said they'd both gotten into their old uniforms and, what the hell, maybe they had.

The crowd was going nuts when old Walter wound it up and started throwing. The Babe hammered the fifth pitch deep into the right-field seats and Johnson stood frowning at him from the mound. Pandemonium. Then there were twelve inconclusive pitches, two of which were swinging strikes triggering all the old-time oohs and aahs. On the eighteenth pitch he did it again. The battered baseball made a tiny hole in the sky, soaring high and far, back into the seats in right again, and this time he trotted in that pigeon-toed way around the bases with his elbows tucked back like a man doing an impression of a duck.

That was it. They walked off the field together and Terry threw his hat in the air and it bounced from hand to hand out onto the emerald grass. Seventy thousand people had seen the Babe hit a couple off Walter Johnson and life was simple and wonderful again. The war was far away. But only for a moment.

It was beginning to dawn on everybody that summer of '42 that things were changing forever, that the world of the Babe and Walter Johnson was receding into the shadows, that there would be no going back to the world they'd grown up with, not even when the damn war was won . . . It was a brief good-bye to the past that afternoon; it needed about as much time as it took to throw eighteen pitches and circle the bases for the last time.

•　　•　　•

They wound up that hot sticky night in the lobby of the Algonquin where the fans struggled against the muggy heat. A big old cat checked them out while they drank Tom Collinses. Munched on peanuts. Bob Benchley was holding forth in a corner looking just like he did in the movies. Cassidy was watching him, and Terry was tapping his arm with a finger salty from peanuts.

"I said I'm going into the private-eye business. Whattaya think of that?"

"It sounds like a movie. Are you serious?"

"Hell yes, I'm serious."

"Can you make any money at it?"

"If I do it right. Corporate clients, missing persons, rich missing persons only need apply. Maybe a big divorce.

Maybe a little security work. Bodyguarding the rich and famous."

"You're gonna have your hands full."

"I'm staffing up with some former cops. It'll work, Lew. Only I need a partner. I've been thinking about that." He was grinning wolfishly, popping peanuts into his mouth.

"Sounds like a fella could get hurt."

"Don't worry about the boss."

"All the same . . ."

"But I'll need a steadying hand. A partner I respect, a guy I'll listen to. Somebody who can back me up when I need it. That make sense to you, *compadre*?"

Cassidy nodded.

"Well, there's this guy I know. I want him. I wondered what your reaction would be—"

"Who is it?"

"Only man I can trust. Only man I'd trust my life with. You, Lew. I want you to come in as my partner."

Terry was beaming, feeling good, figuring it all out. The Babe had put a couple in the seats and the war in the Pacific was looking up. He'd had his own personal sneak attack the day after Pearl Harbor and he'd survived. Now he was ready to get out there on his own and start fresh.

He was going to be Humphrey Bogart.

He was going to be Spade of Spade & Archer.

He wanted Cassidy to be Archer.

Only Archer had gotten killed. Miles Archer got shot down by Bridget O'Shaughnessy on a foggy San Francisco night. Everybody knew that. Never trust a woman.

Terry was smiling, smug and happy, waiting for Lew to say something.

"I need another drink," Cassidy murmured.

• • •

Cassidy was still having a bad time of it and he felt like he was dragging Terry down. The depression that had flowered with Karin's death wouldn't relent. Neither would his desire to see Cindy Squires, who had herself, with Max, retreated into a kind of abstract lunar distance.

Bennie came around occasionally and he'd drop news of Max and Cindy but they were always out of town, always out of reach. But Cassidy's state of mind wasn't bothering Terry, who was optimistic and excited and planning the opening of his detective agency. He was a blur of fast talking and high hopes. He resigned from the NYPD, a fact the columnists duly noted in the papers, and had begun following up on his connections with lawyers who could provide clients. He leased space in the Dalmane Building on Madison at 43rd, just a nine iron from Grand Central Station, which he kept calling "the crossroads of a million private lives." He seemed to think that augured well for the detective business.

He hired a couple of old pals he'd served with on the Force. He got the telephones put in, hired a secretary/receptionist, had the name painted on the door. *The Dependable Detective Agency.* The legend beneath the big letters read: *Discretion Our Watchword.* The letterhead was delivered, very simple, elegant, no little magnifying glass, no deerstalker, no open eye, nothing cute. All very uptown. He was patient, waited for Cassidy to give him an answer about the partnership.

One night in late September Cassidy told him he was moving back downtown to his own place in the Village. He told him he had to get pulled back together on his own time, not on Terry's. And finally he told him he didn't have a detective somewhere inside himself crying to get out.

"I think you're wrong about that, old sport," Terry said, hooking his thumbs behind suspenders decorated with a pattern of chubby naked ladies. "You'll come 'round later. I'll bet you a dollar you do. But sure, you need some time to yourself. I understand that. Just remember, whenever you need me, or want me around, I'm ready. Dependable, that's me." He grinned, all Irish charm. "And the day'll come when your name gets painted on the door, right next to mine. Trust Terry, sport."

He went behind the bar and brought out a long thin package, wrapped in gift paper covered with little blue and pink babies. He handed it to Cassidy.

"Shower gift?"

"Only paper I could find. Sort of sweet, really. Go on, open it."

Cassidy stripped the paper away, feeling something hard and knobby. He sat on the couch staring at it.

He was holding a long, heavy, gleaming blackthorn walking stick. It was polished, smooth yet brutal, lethal. Elegant. It was topped by a leaded brass knob that fit firmly into the palm of his hand. There was a gold band which had been engraved. *Lew Cassidy. 1942.* Below the name in small lettering he had to squint to see. *The Best of the Backup Men.*

"Jesus, Terry . . ."

"Here, gimme that thing."

Holding it so Cassidy could see what he was doing, he pointed at a tiny black button beneath the knob. He pressed it with his fingertip.

Without a sound the heavy knob leaped into his grasp. In one swift motion he withdrew a thin gleaming blade.

Cassidy damn near jumped out of his shoes.

"Finest Sheffield steel," Terry said.

Terry lowered the blade first onto Cassidy's right shoulder, then onto the left.

"Go in peace, Lew," he said. "But use your steel if you must."

Terry Leary winked at the best of the backup men.

CHAPTER TEN

The tip of his blackthorn stick made a reassuring sound as he walked across Washington Square toward the massive arch so reminiscent of the Arc de Triomphe. The park was empty but for the occasional bum sleeping under a canopy of newspaper on a bench and the pigeons ignoring them. It was ten past six, a gray misty morning with the colored leaves littering the grass and the pathways, with the curtains still drawn in most of the windows facing the Square. Cassidy stood by the arch, stamped his feet against the early morning chill. Fifty years earlier Henry James's characters had peered at the park from behind heavy draperies, hearing the clip-clop of the horse-drawn milk wagons making their rounds. In the middle of World War II you could hear the clatter of the milk bottles being delivered and see the early risers out walking their dogs. William Powell and Myrna Loy and Asta were nowhere to be seen but, when he looked up empty Fifth Avenue, he saw the big man in the light topcoat coming toward him, past the hugely solid apartment buildings which gave the bottom of the avenue its status and weight. Harry Madrid fit right in, oddly enough, heavy and solid, one of the pillars on which the everyday order of the city rested. The last thing you'd have thought, watching him that morning, was that only one thing separated him from all the other homicidal maniacs in town. His badge.

He crossed the street and cast casual glances right and left, stopping beside Cassidy.

"Nice morning, Lew," he said. He pulled a black pipe from his pocket, packed it as he spoke. "Does a man good to start the day at the start of the day. Where's your place?"

Cassidy nodded toward the west side of the square.

"Nice, very nice. Feels good to be home, right?" He struck a match on the concrete arch, cupped his hands around the flame, and lit the tobacco.

"What do you want, Harry?"

"Why, I thought you liked to have me stay in touch. Say, Lew, I'm mighty sorry about your wife. Even if she was a Kraut."

Cassidy stared at him.

Harry Madrid nodded, agreeing with himself. "So, you got anything for me, Lew? We figure you've had six months, better than that, but who's counting? You haven't come up with much, have you? So Tom Dewey asks me how we're progressing on your friend Max, he wants to know what you've come up with . . . I hated like hell to disappoint him. Thing is he says Lucky's pressing him for action. Thinkin' about another winter or two in the big house makes Lucky sulk. Lucky wants Dewey to get moving, put Bauman away in a big show trial, and get old Tom on the road to Albany. You got any ideas what I could tell him?" He puffed reflectively on the cherry tobacco. "They're breathin' down my neck, pal."

"I got bad news for you, Harry. I figure Terry's not a cop anymore so you can stop hating him for being a bad cop. What Terry's being a bad cop makes you I hate to think—"

"Watch it, Lew—"

"So you can leave Terry to heaven, okay? And I gotta tell

you, I've had an attack of conscience. I don't think Terry needs my help to save his ass from Luciano and you. I think he can take care of himself because, frankly, Harry old stick, you're kind of a stumblebum. You killed Markie and you fumbled the ball, you didn't get your proof Markie was paying him off for services rendered. I don't think you're going to do anything to Terry . . . so I quit—"

"You're forgetting Lucky's spot remover. Remember? You're the spot—"

"Forget it. Do your own dirty work. Am I getting through to you at all, Harry?"

"You're whistlin' past the graveyard, Lew, and we both know it." He laughed easily. The confidence was making Cassidy nervous. "But I'll tell you how to fulfill your obligation, your promise, to Dewey and Luciano. Two guys it'd be bad to have pissed off at you, by the way. And I can keep you from getting yourself removed. You satisfy them and, what the hell, maybe everybody'll forget about Terry."

They were walking through the park, damp leaves clinging to their shoes. The squirrels were already up and gathering the winter's stores. The city was just waking up and it was still quiet in the park. The blackthorn stick had lost the sound of reassurance. Now it sounded more like a blind man feeling his way across dangerous ground.

"Lucky'll be inside for a while, Dewey's gonna see to that. And I guess I don't give a shit what happens to Terry . . . but, believe me, Lew, you don't want to give us any trouble on this. We're giving you an easy way out. Don't blow it."

"What's this easy way out?" He didn't want to listen but he remembered Luciano's face, the sound of his voice telling him about the spot remover, Markie's bloated body on the sand.

"We're back to the gas rationing stamps. It's a huge operation, Lew, bigger than we'd thought. They're all over the eastern seaboard, the Midwest, California, the Deep South. Counterfeits. Tens of millions, hell, it's like printing money. But"—he puffed contentedly, led the way to a bench where they sat down—"but we haven't been able to tie Max to any of it." The sun was starting to glow, turning the clouds to a faint hint of blue sky.

"Maybe he's just plain not involved."

"Don't make a damn bit of difference. He prolly is but we don't give a shit, not anymore. Get it? We're gonna get him on the stamps whether he's involved or not. We're gonna get him good." He smiled at Terry and dug a finger into his bristly ear. He took his finger out, regarded the tip, flicked the wax away. "Hoover's behind it, all the bright boys at the Bureau—you know what those buggers did? I'll tell ya, in thirty years I never seen anything so beautiful. Hoover had 'em print up his own goddamn counterfeit stamps, floated a bunch of them around the marketplace! No shit . . ." He was chuckling to himself, his hard little eyes disappearing in the folds of flesh. "Hoover! I don't give a damn if he is a pansy, he knows how to play this fuckin' game!" His girth was shaking under the topcoat. "We're gonna plant our counterfeits on Max! We're gonna salt the fuckin' mine shaft! Max ain't gonna know what the hell's going on and we're gonna put him away . . . Hoover, Dewey, Madrid . . . and Lew Cassidy!"

"You don't need me."

"Oh, hell yes! You're the guy's gonna plant 'em on Max."

"Oh, shit . . ."

"You're doin' the honors, Lew. Piece o' cake."

"What about all these other sources of yours? All these sources close to Max? What about the guy tipped you to the Jersey shore?"

"You're my guy, Lew. You got the most to lose if you fuck it up."

Harry Madrid began laughing again.

•　　•　　•

The summer was dying a peaceful death, a gentle good-bye full of tranquil beauty, shedding a slow, easy life for a more demanding, vigorous one. They were raking the leaves in Central Park.

Cassidy had gone uptown with the intention of telling Terry the whole story. Madrid, Dewey, Luciano, Max, the threats and the phony twenties and the counterfeit gas stamps. Particularly those damn stamps! They sat now in sealed cartons in Cassidy's hall closet. Harry Madrid and a silent man, one of Hoover's hard-asses, had brought them down one night. "Plant 'em, any damn way you want to," Madrid had said, puffing his pipe. "Hell, use Terry if you want. Just plant the bastards and tell us where they are and we'll take it from there." So they sat in the closet like a ticking bomb. He'd have to do something soon.

But he'd gone uptown, had stood across the street from the familiar building on Park Avenue, and in the end he hadn't been able to do it. Better to keep Terry out of it. Handle it yourself and Terry's off easy and never had to know and . . . Max Bauman. He knew how to take care of himself. And he wasn't exactly the Citizen of the Year. Cassidy had all sorts of reasons for turning around and walking away.

He walked down Fifth Avenue, listening to the solid clicking of the new stick's ferrule on the cement. He stopped for a moment to lean on the brick wall and look across the park at the nannies wheeling children in baby carriages and strollers. Dogs ran around rolling in piles of leaves and barking at the squirrels. The sun was still high but it was riding down the southern sky and the shadows were lengthening.

It was late October and you could smell the burning leaves. It was the smell of burning memories for him, all the memories of all the things he'd lost. Burning leaves and football games and walking in Central Park with Karin and making love on the rug before the fireplace, warmed by the dying embers . . . Well, there wouldn't be any more football, no more Karin in his arms, but there would always be the smell of leaves and the clouds of memory.

He was beginning to get used to the ache in his chest and the gaping wounds in his memory where Karin had gone to stay forever. He didn't look at the photo albums anymore. He knew every picture by heart. Maybe he'd never look at them again. Never want to, never have to. There was no little Karin to show them to and say, look, honey, there she is, she was your mommy . . .

But he still had to play out the hand, live his life, risk the pot. He was going to have to make it work so that at the end when somebody up there said well, that's it, pal, zip-zip, that was your life, hope you had a good time, mate, you pass this way but once . . .

He strolled on down Fifth Avenue, crossed Central Park South among the horse-drawn hacks, and went into the Plaza. The Oak Bar was sparsely populated and he sat at the long bar and ordered a weak bourbon and water. He was feeling like a Hemingway hero, a kind of Jake Barnes for World War II, lonely and tragic, only he knew he was a fake, of course. Hell, anybody eavesdropping inside his head would have thought he had a war wound. The gridiron war, a paltry tragedy. Order of the Purple Shoulder Pads.

People would see him with his cane, he'd see them watching and whispering among themselves, wondering if he'd been at Pearl or Bataan or Wake Island or Corregidor. Every so often some fat old guy in a bar somewhere would come up to him and shake his hand with tears in his eyes and tell him how he'd got it at the Battle of the Marne or the Somme and Cassidy didn't have the heart to tell him he'd gotten his at the Polo Grounds.

But for the moment he wanted a drink or two while he thought about the future, where nothing much awaited and anything might be possible. He didn't want to get drunk. He'd spent enough mornings through that summer holding his head as if it were the last known egg of the last known giant auk while he left the previous night's ration of experience in the toilet bowl. He was finished with all that. He was getting straight and maybe he'd drop by and see if the team could use him as an assistant coach or as one of the old bums who sold programs outside the stadium for a dime . . .

First, however, he'd have a drink or two and then go home and take a good clear look at the future. Figure out what he was going to do with the gas stamps. So he sat at the bar, watching the barman polishing glasses.

He should have skipped the drink. He should have gone home then, before she found him . . .

• • •

She sat on the stool next to him. All those empty stools but that one had her name on it. He saw her face in the mirror behind the bar. Her perfume was so faint you almost couldn't smell it. It pulled you toward her, like a whisper. There was just enough to make you want to smell a hell of a lot more of it.

She was short of breath, like she was nervous or had been hurrying. He felt her brush against him, wiggling her rear end on the stool. She took a deep breath. It was nerves. Her cigarette case clattered when she dropped it on the shiny surface of the bar. Then she spilled most of the Camels trying to pry one loose. Her hand was shaking. She wouldn't catch his eye. Her voice was low and a little hoarse and there was a tremor in it.

"Light me, please?"

He struck a match and watched her lean forward to meet the flame. She was wearing cream-colored gloves and a casual suit the shade of tobacco. The jacket hung open. There was a cream silk blouse.

"Thank you," she said. "Don't you smoke?" She seemed becalmed now that she'd sucked the smoke down into her lungs and blown it across the bar at their reflection.

"No, I'm in training."

"Oh, dear, how serious. In training for what?"

"For living as long as possible. Those things'll kill you."

"Well, what's to worry, then? I won't live long. So I might as well smoke. So many things can kill you these days. But, then, maybe I like living dangerously."

"Then it's your style."

"I followed you for the last ten blocks. Wondering if I

191

dare do this. Scared of the consequences. Then, of course, I'd remembered that I'm an adventuress. It's a good thing, too. The world's a pretty inhospitable place these days. Like the lady in the operetta, I laugh in the face of my own mortality, tra-la, tra-la." She told the barman she wanted a perfect martini.

He nodded. "Coming right up, Miss Squires."

She finally looked at Cassidy. "Billy makes a perfect martini. All gin. Sort of passes the vermouth over the glass. A ritual."

"Sounds like you're a regular here."

"I'm a regular lots of places."

He watched the bartender with his black leather bow tie and the lonely strands of dyed black hair carefully stretched across his shiny scalp. "He would."

"Would what?"

"Make a perfect martini."

Billy placed the glass in front of her, centered on a cork coaster. Her long-fingered hand flicked the pale curtain of hair back from her face. She sipped. "Dutch courage. I need it."

"What's the problem?"

"Well, I haven't seen you for a long time. I didn't like that. And . . . and I heard about your wife. I'm so terribly sorry. You must feel helpless. It's all so bloody awful."

"I'm getting used to the idea now. You know what they say."

"No, I don't think I do."

"About war. It's hell. But that's not why you followed me."

"True. I was going to see Terry and then I saw you. I knew you'd be better for me than Terry . . . you're not one of them. *Them.*"

"Who?"

"Oh, all the ones I need to get away from. Max and Bennie and all of Max's other happy elves. And Terry, too, for that matter. And all the people at the club. Heliotrope. Where, I notice, your face is ne'er seen anymore. I can't move without their knowing everything I do." She was twisting a sapphire and gold ring she wore on her right hand. "They're smothering me . . . Max, all of them, I feel like a little adopted refugee who also happens to sleep with her new father—"

"That ought to appeal to your sense of danger."

She sipped the last of her drink and waited for Billy to place another one before her. There was a long blond hair on her tobacco-colored lapel. She lit another Camel. Her lips left a dark red smudge on the paper. Cassidy was drowning in her.

"You know what I told you that time?"

"You've told me quite a lot."

"You know perfectly well what I mean. Well, I really am . . . a whore. Through and through, it's my nature."

"It's all part of living dangerously."

"I think it's something a woman's born with, something that goes all wrong inside her—"

"Like being born with one brown eye, one blue."

"Like being born crippled." She stared at Billy and he moved off down the bar, polishing, polishing. "Apparently I can't belong to any one man, can I? I feel like I'm going crazy—"

"If she finds the right one, then it all calms down. She's a whore no more. She's in love and it's a well-known fact that love conquers all. It can even change people's natures."

"What a dope! What an innocent you are!"

"Just a romantic."

"Nothing changes one's nature. It's a well-known fact, the leopard and his spots."

"You're a youthful skeptic."

"No, Cassidy. I've told you what I am. And Max is driving me crazy. I'm Max's girl. Max's property. He gives me everything I want but he doesn't want me, doesn't understand about me . . . He's my father but he also does it to me, that's his fantasy. And I'm little Bo Peep. I want to get out . . . but I'm afraid. He doesn't understand I have to be available."

"What the hell are you punishing yourself for?"

"Don't tell me you're a disciple of Dr. Freud."

"No, just a smart guy with a winning Ipana smile."

"Oh, you poor guy." She touched his hand. "Is it your winning smile that makes me unload all this baggage on you?"

He shrugged. "Soul mates. We did watch a bunch of guys get murdered together."

She ignored him. "So I escaped this afternoon. Max was at a meeting with his lawyers and Bennie went off on an errand and no one was watching me. So I just left." She shivered with the daring of it.

"So why were you afraid to follow me?"

"When you belong to Max you get to thinking there's always somebody following you, watching you . . . it's like one of Dali's paintings, eyes watching you, clock faces melting, time running out. Or that movie, the razor slicing the eyeball. Sometimes I'd like to take a slice at all the eyes watching me. I'd like to hurt them . . . and all they're being is kind, taking care of me, but always for Max—oh, well, why don't you tell me your troubles?"

"Women always seem to have better troubles . . ."

"No, they just make a bigger deal of them."

"Well, Cindy, I'm going home now. It's been very nice psychoanalyzing you again."

"Mind if I walk with you?"

They walked all the way down Fifth Avenue and his leg felt okay. Almost a year, and a good day with the leg was an event. She didn't say any more about being a whore, thank God. It was getting to be an old story. As they walked, he noticed that he was beginning to feel like a human being. He wasn't thinking about the war. He wasn't thinking about Karin. He was listening to her talk about her childhood in England and her brother Tony's letters from Deerfield and the music she liked and where she liked to shop and her love of Dickens. She admired his blackthorn stick and she read the inscription and he told her about the sword.

Standing in front of a church on the corner of Eleventh Street, she said, "Can I see your sword?"

"Just press the button below the knob."

She grinned, felt for it. The knob rose solidly into the gloved palm. "Can I take it out?"

"It's your funeral."

Slowly she slid the blade out. Her eyes were shining. "It's beautiful," she said slowly.

•　　•　　•

His living room seemed so bookish and unfamiliar, so humble, after all the months at Terry's. Out past the trellis at Washington Square they were burning leaves, and the aroma of autumn was seeping into his apartment. The late afternoon was darkening. The clouds of leaf smoke hung over the square like the mists of Avalon.

Cindy said she didn't really feel like another drink so they sat talking, watching the last of the sunlight wiped away by dusk. She excused herself and went to the bathroom. Cassidy closed his eyes, leaned back. Max Bauman's girl was in his bathroom. He hoped to hell nobody actually had been following her.

When she came back from the bathroom, she'd taken off the gloves and the suit and the blouse and the brown and white pumps and the stockings and her garter belt and her panties which dangled from one finger. All she had on was the slip. It clung to her nipples as if it were soaking wet. She wriggled her toes, the nails red as precious stones arranged on the rug. She went around the room turning off the two table lamps so the light from the street left the room in gray shadows, enough light to see her by. She stood in front of him with her feet apart so the dim light haloed around her and between her legs. "Well," she said, half swallowing the words, "you know what I told you." She slid the straps of her slip down over her shoulders. Her eyes were cast down upon herself as if she were as interested in what would be exposed as he was. She pulled the slip down until the top caught on the points of her nipples. Right about then it occurred to him that her nipples were the only things in the world worth living, dying, or fighting for.

She tugged the slip down until it slid over them, making the tight erectile tissue twitch, and he saw the soft outline of her tiny girlish breasts with the distended dark tips. She eased the slip down over the swell of her broad hips and let it drop to the floor. Her belly was flat, actually a slightly concave dish pouring the dark flood of pubic hair from its rim. Her breath caught in her throat. "I'm going to feel awfully foolish," she whispered, "if you don't want to fuck me."

She took his hand and led him past the bathroom into the bedroom. She lay down on the bed. The light from the bathroom lay like an icicle across the foot of the bed. He slipped out of his shirt and slacks and stood beside the bed watching her. She reached up with one hand and gently pulled his stiff penis out of his shorts. She moaned when her fingers closed around him. "Oh," she murmured, "you're slippery already, aren't you . . ." She placed her other hand slowly and carefully between her legs and parted her thighs, bending her knees slightly. He watched transfixed by her deliberate movements while she probed in her pubic hair with her middle finger until she located the labia touching one another. Then she slowly parted the thick hair, spread the lips wide with her forefinger and ring finger. The darkness inside of her glistened.

"Come to me," she whispered. "Hurry. I want to take you in my mouth before it's too late."

He lay down on the bed beside her, rested his face on the solid, smooth fleshiness of her inner thigh, smelled the richness of her sweat and the lubrication of her vagina which was quickly matting the hair. Her tongue was licking at him, he heard it and felt it, and he felt what came out of him thickening as her mouth slid over him, engulfed him, pulling at the center of him as if she would willingly do him injury if it would fill her mouth, satisfy her need, but she couldn't hurt him, she could only try, and he licked at her fingers as she worked them in and out of herself, licked at the viscous saltiness as she removed them and smeared them across his mouth, and he pulled her open with both hands and leaned into the darkness

and the flood of her and tasted her and plunged his tongue
into her and worked his finger into the tightness, circling
his finger within her anus, felt her hips arch off the wet
sheet, heard her mouth sibilantly sucking his semen,
gagging and choking and pulling him in again, felt her
fingers tightening rhythmically around his testicles, milk-
ing him efficiently, familiarly, an expert at work, but when
she felt his finger work its way to the hilt between her hips
and felt his teeth nibbling at the tiny wet bud hidden
behind the folds of her inner lips, the thrashing and the
deep growling in her chest was more primitive than any
performance, a cry of pain and release and vulnerability,
and for just that moment she was the helpless little girl
she sometimes parodied and for an instant at least he
knew she was his, not someone born a whore doing her job
or acting out a man's fantasies, but a creature slipping off
the high ledge into uncharted darkness and she pumped
her belly and her thighs and her hips spasmodically, out of
control, all the gears stripped, in fast forward for what
seemed a very long time . . .

When he pulled her around so that her face was near his,
she quickly clamped her legs around his thigh and
continued the slow gentle lapping of her internal sea,
soaking his leg with the endless flow. And before he kissed
her he saw the saliva and the clots of semen in the corners
of her mouth and drifting in streaks across her soft, downy
cheek and she was crying.

An hour later she moved around on the damp, sticky
bed, said, "I want it all again, Lew, all the same things.
Don't leave any of it out," and she began. They clung
together with all the same results and his mouth was
rubbed raw by the thick hair between her legs and she lay
gasping on her back, holding the back of one hand to her
forehead, collecting semen on her fingertips from the
corners of her mouth and absentmindedly massaging it
into the bulging nipples while he looked up the length of
her past the dark sodden mass of hair licked flat against
her thighs and groin. There was nothing left anywhere, no

197

desire, no strength, no need to be a whore. Not for a little while, anyway.

Another hour passed and this time it was Cassidy waking, wanting her again. She was breathing deeply, asleep, her head down by his knees. He had to touch her, explore her again. He pulled her nearly dead weight across him, her belly wet and sticky on his chest, her knees on either side of his shoulders, and she moaned, a mixture of exhaustion and desire coming alive. He looked up into the wet darkness again, opened her again and she sobbed. "It hurts," she whispered sleepily, "I'm sore . . ." He stroked her with his tongue, tasting it all again. She sighed and giggled deep down. "I think we could be arrested for everything we've been doing . . . nothing but unnatural acts . . ."

He took his mouth away from her and picked a strand of hair from his lip. "I know, I know, ain't a life of crime just grand . . ." And soon she was rocking back against his face and from beneath her he flicked his tongue across the fingers she'd worked back between her thighs and she wouldn't stop until they'd both struggled over the top yet again. He was smiling in his own darkness. Not a natural act since they'd started. His kind of girl. They'd watched men die . . .

• • •

She was dressed, leaning over him where he'd collapsed. She smelled like powder and perfume again. It was a quarter to ten. In half an hour she'd be singing at Heliotrope.

She spoke insistently, battering at his weariness. "Listen to me, darling. I don't know when I'll see you again. Whatever you do, don't call me. You're going to want to talk to me and do all this again but you mustn't call me. And don't send me a note. Barely remember me if we meet." She leaned down and kissed him. "I used your toothbrush. I needed it." She sighed and touched his tiny, helpless, limp penis. "Take care of this brave little soldier."

"He's a private," he said.

She pressed her fingers when he tried to say something else. "Hush. No questions, no little endearments. My only answer is, I don't know. I've got to be careful. If he found out, he'd . . . he'd kill me. Now go to sleep."

He heard her leave and sat on the edge of the bed. The sheets smelled of sex. He inhaled deeply.

Once she was gone, he felt as lonely as it was possible to feel. The fun was elsewhere. He couldn't believe she wasn't coming back to him. Later. After she was done singing.

He waited awhile, then went to take a shower. He was deep in the lather and steam, she'd been gone for half an hour, and somebody was banging on the door. He turned off the shower, wrapped himself in a thick terry-cloth robe, and hobbled to the door trying to shake soap and water out of his ear. He almost expected her to be standing in the doorway, like Claudette Colbert coming back to the guy she really loves in the movie, ready to tell him she'd fallen under his spell and she was a new woman and wanted him and what were they going to do about it?

As so often happens in life, however, he was mistaken.

Bennie the Brute was standing there staring at him and what he saw in the eyes floating behind the thick lenses was definitely not love.

It wasn't even like.

CHAPTER ELEVEN

"Gee whiz," Bennie said, slowly removing his soft homburg, "I'm so disappointed in you, Lew." He shook his massive head sadly and came inside. "This is just terrible, Lew." He looked as if he hoped Cassidy had a miracle explanation.

"You've been following her?"

He nodded. Human nature was such a sorry affair. "We knew she was seein' somebody, Lew. We gave her a little rope." He shrugged like a Galápagos turtle shifting its shell.

"Probably wouldn't do any good to tell you this was the first time?"

"Probably not. What difference does it make? Once you break an egg it can't get any more broken . . ."

"Voltaire?"

"Not to my knowledge, Lew."

"This," Cassidy said, toweling his hair, trying to be casual, "is the time when men of goodwill sit down, have a brandy and cigar, and reason together. There's a way out of this situation."

"I'm not quite so sanguine about the prospects," Bennie said. He put his hat on the table in the front hall and followed Cassidy into the living room. Her smell was everywhere. "On the other hand, we should exhaust all the peaceful options before resorting to . . . well, you know, the less peaceful options." He sat down in a chair by the windows, crossed his legs, smoothed his mackintosh across his knee. The polka-dot bow tie peeked out at the collar.

Cassidy poured two snifters of calvados and took two Havanas from the box he kept in the refrigerator. He clipped the ends, held the match for Bennie, and they undertook to be reasonable adults solving a moderately sticky problem. The trick was to keep Bennie calm while Cassidy tried to think of a way to bribe him without his taking offense. He wondered if Terry had it figured: Had Bennie tipped off Harry Madrid? Did Bennie figure it was his turn to be Max now?

"Miss Squires was right, then," Cassidy said. "She really is being followed. I call that damn bad form. She's a grown woman, she should come and go as she pleases. Without being watched."

"That would seem to be true," Bennie observed judiciously. "Normally I'd be the first to agree with you. But"—he shook a finger at Cassidy—"Miss Squires is not a normal case. She has certain problems. For instance, she is a loose woman—no, don't deny it, Lew. She is. We must save her from herself. Let's face it, Lew, her base nature has gained the upper hand. The rest of us have an obligation to protect her from that flaw." He puffed and regarded the cigar like an old friend. "These are just like Mr. Bauman's."

"They are Mr. Bauman's. Terry gave them to me. Now, listen, why the hell weren't you saving her from herself when you saw her come in here? You could have saved me this problem with you—you would have if you were really my friend—and you could have saved her virtue."

"Oh, come now, Miss Squires's virtue is long past saving, I'm afraid. My job is to protect Mr. Bauman from

201

the sordid truth and the unhappy effects of her weakness. It's a big job, too. Hell, Lew, sometimes getting all my jobs straight confuses me." He unbelted his mac and opened it. He was wearing his customary tuxedo. He'd be at the club later when he and Cassidy had had their little talk. Cassidy felt like he'd been summoned to the principal's office. If the principal was King Kong.

"We're all confused," Cassidy said. "Everybody. Let's just simplify our lives and forget tonight ever happened. What the hell difference does it make?"

"Ah, that's the question, isn't it, Lew? Well, I'm afraid it does make a difference. I gotta live with myself, for one thing. I have my morals. Try to understand that, Lew."

"The concept of morality is not entirely foreign to me."

"Well, I'm glad to hear that. You couldn't prove it by your behavior tonight. Now, I could keep all this from Mr. Bauman, I could wink at you and figure you just serviced a bitch in heat. I could hope that you'd never repeat this deplorable lapse of manners—"

Cassidy was beginning to worry. He was sweating under the robe and his heart had speeded up. "Bennie, you must really understand that I didn't make a play for her." Bennie was watching him through the lazy swirls of smoke, his eyes shining, his mouth working the cigar. His hands were huge, fingers thick, fists like wrecking balls. "She found me, she came down here . . . listen, you know I'll never let it happen again." Now he was feeling clammy under the robe. Bennie was getting restless in his chair. Bad sign.

"Lew, don't kid me. How will I know you'd be able to resist her attractions? Hell, she's tried it on me, leaving the bedroom door open while she was naked, doing her exercises—I mean, Lew, I saw it *all* . . . and she knew it, she loved having me watch her. Jeez, Lew, I can't trust myself, how the dickens can I trust you?" It would have been funny if Bennie hadn't been so serious. He was working it all out and his face showed it, a map of consternation.

202

"You can trust my words, Bennie. You can trust my fear if not my word. You think I want you to work me over?"

"I don't know." He sighed. "I'm not so hot on this trust malarkey. Take all the trust in the world and a nickel, it gets you a cup of coffee. You might forget how I could hurt you, or you might think I'd get soft and not hurt you, and first thing you knew you'd be sticking your thing in Miss Squires again—" He shuddered at the thought. "And then where would we be?"

"But what's it to you? Who really cares?" He was cold but sweating. Bennie was like a natural disaster waiting to happen, a great big dark cloud getting ready to rain all over Lew Cassidy.

"Well, I care, Lew. What I can't have is that Mr. Bauman has any more pain. He's lost too much and I don't want him to lose Miss Squires. I may not think she's so much but that doesn't matter. He's crazy about her, she's young and beautiful and he cares. I like you, Lew, you know that. Always liked you. But I'm loyal to Mr. Bauman. I *owe* him. It comes down to that." He stood up leaving his snifter behind, still smoking the cigar. Cassidy was too scared of what he might do to move. Bennie stood in the doorway to the bedroom looking at the messy bed, then turned back to him and whistled softly. "I don't know," he murmured, "maybe it was worth it. She really something, Lew?" Cassidy nodded. "Oh, Lew, I'm afraid I'll have to do something to make you remember to behave yourself . . . y'know, this is nothing personal, I wouldn't care what you and Miss Squires do, you make a nice couple for all I give a shit, but it's Mr. Bauman, I worry about him . . ."

Cassidy stood up. "You're not worried about him, you're scared of him. I don't blame you—Bennie, get the hell outa here. You're not going to hurt me, we're friends, for God's sake. Now, take me at my word, I'll stay away from Cindy, you get your big ass up to the club—forget all this, it never happened . . ."

"Is that the way it is, Lew?" His voice was so soft Cassidy could barely hear him. He picked up his hat, put

203

his cigar down in the ashtray. He placed the hat straight on his head and came to stand beside Cassidy.

"Of course it is," Cassidy said. He opened the door. "I'll be a good boy."

He was filling the doorway when he turned back with a perplexed expression on his large pale face. The eyes swam behind the glasses, then stopped abruptly.

"No," he said, "no. I'm sorry about this, pal."

A fist the size of Bill Dickey's catcher's mitt and heavy as a bowling ball slammed into his gut. His eyes went black as the inside of the bat cage and he doubled over unable to breathe. He was going to die like a fish on the dock.

Bennie's knee came up and he felt the two-by-four hardness of his thigh breaking his nose. His teeth rammed into the pulp of his cheek and his mouth suddenly filled with blood. Bennie let him fall. He lay on the floor gagging on the blood. He wished the bastard would just shoot him and be done with it.

He blinked, looking up at Bennie. It was like lying at the bottom of a dark mountain. "Lew, I feel like hell doing this but . . ." Pain was blurring his vision. Bennie held out a hand to help him up. He took it. Bennie pulled him halfway up, then sank his boot into his ribs. Something cracked, snapped. There wasn't going to be much left that wasn't broken, the rate he was going. "But you've got to learn to keep your hands off Mr. Bauman's things." He sank back onto the floor, gagging, trying not to choke, trying not to vomit from shock and pain.

Bennie hadn't even broken a sweat. His bow tie wasn't even askew. His hat was still straight. Everything about the guy was suddenly a personal insult. And he kept telling Cassidy how much he hated having to kick the shit out of him. There was a shifting blur as he drew his foot back again. Cassidy tried to turn and roll away, anything to keep him from driving ribs into a lung or into his heart. The boot got him in the kidneys. He kept coughing and spitting blood and felt a loose tooth wobbling against his tongue. "Well, Lew, I think that's enough, don't you? Now, you promise you won't forget why we had to go through this."

"I promise," Cassidy croaked.

Bennie left him huddled on the floor and went to the kitchen. "You want a nice drink of water, Lew? I sure can use one." Cassidy heard him puttering around with glasses and the jar of cold water from the fridge.

Cassidy began crawling across the floor toward the couch. He wiped the tears out of his eyes and tried to ignore the blades of pain in his chest. "That wasn't a fair fight, Bennie," he said.

Bennie laughed softly in the kitchen. He was cracking ice cubes out of the trays. "It wasn't supposed to be fair. It wasn't even a fight. It was punishment."

Cassidy hoisted himself up on the arm of the couch and got his blackthorn stick. He stood up, steadying himself, waited for his head to clear, and then hobbled to the kitchen. "Yeah, I could use a glass of water."

"Sure thing." Bennie handed him a glass and clicked his against Cassidy's. "Better times ahead," he said. "Understood?"

"Right. I've learned a valuable lesson."

Bennie smiled. "That's good to hear, Lew."

Bennie turned and was going through the archway back toward the living room.

Cassidy lifted the blackthorn stick high, ignoring the arrows of sheer agony in his chest and the explosions of light behind his eyes and the weird sounds in his nose and throat when he breathed, and hit Bennie in the head with the leaded end, with all the strength he had.

He staggered against the wall. "Gee whiz, Lew—"

Cassidy swung it again and got him behind his left ear. He went forward on his knees.

"It's not a fight, Bennie. It's getting even."

Bennie was holding his head with one hand. Then he was trying to get up and Cassidy was wondering what the hell he'd done. *What am I going to do when he gets up and is mad at me?*

Bennie turned toward him and raised up on his knees

like Porgy about to tell Bess she's his woman now and Cassidy did a real Babe Ruth, caught him on the temple over his left eye and his skull collapsed like a ripe honeydew and he went over sideways and let out a sigh like a blown-out Firestone and didn't move a muscle except to jerk his limbs a few times.

Bennie didn't get up anymore.

•　•　•

Terry Leary stood looking down at Bennie. It was eleven o'clock.

"Boy, Lew, I've seen Bennie look a lot better."

"I've seen *me* look a lot better." The blood kept oozing from his nose into his throat. He couldn't move without feeling like he was having a heart attack.

He regarded Cassidy thoughtfully. "But you at least got laid, old-timer. I hope it was worth it."

"I haven't decided yet. But I think it was."

"You've got guts," Terry remarked. He dripped some more cold water from the towel he held over Bennie's head. "More guts than brains, messing around with Max's lady. Not smart, Lew. You could catch your death of dumbness like that."

"Look at the other guy."

"That is quite true. But a word to the wise—she's all trouble and a mile wide—"

"Shut up about her, okay?"

He looked up. "You like her?"

"Let's just drop it, Terry. I got problems breathing here."

"Bennie's not exactly at the top of his game."

"Is he dead?"

"Naw. He sort of quivers every so often. Look. See? Naw, he's not actually dead." Terry smiled. "That's the good news and the bad news." He pointed at the stick. "You better clean off the knob. It's all sticky."

Cassidy went to the kitchen and ran water over the knob and wiped it with a dishtowel. He went back to the living room.

"What now?"

"Well, when Bennie wakes up I'd say he's gonna make you eat your stick and then he's gonna yank it right out your asshole."

"If you can't say something nice, don't say anything at all."

But when Bennie came to, he lay there blinking at them. It took him a long time to focus. Finally he said, "Hi, Terry." He paused and licked some foam from his lips. "Hey, Lew . . ." There was a mild sense of wonder and confusion in his voice. "What the heck's going on, anyway? Boy, I don't feel so good, you guys." He threw up on the rug. "Gee, Lew, I'm sorry about that . . ." Terry wiped Bennie's mouth with the wet towel. "Where am I?"

"You're downtown. Lew's place."

"Lew's place?" His face was gray. He pulled himself up and leaned against the back of the couch. Cassidy made himself look at the mess above the left eye. It looked like maybe bone was showing through. He looked away fast. "Why Lew's place?" Bennie asked.

"Listen, Bennie, pay attention to me now. Watch my lips. I don't know why you were downtown but the point is you were. You got rolled—Jesus, don't touch your head!" The thick fingers were fumbling toward the raw, wet hole.

"Me? Rolled?" He dropped his hand. He couldn't believe it. "Me? Are you sure we're talking about me?" The words came slowly, his lips forming each one with a determined effort. He began to reach for the wound again.

"Hey, come on, Bennie! Don't do that." Terry batted the hand away. "You got a nasty little . . . ah . . . cut up there. You got beaten up. Lots of guys. Real big guys, Ben."

"It figures," Bennie grunted softly. "Lotsa big guys. I never saw 'em, Terry. They musta got me from behind—"

"Absolutely. The only way. You were lucky Lew was just getting home. He went after them with his cane. They beat hell outa him, too, broke his nose, banged him up pretty good . . ."

Bennie tried to focus on Cassidy, lifted his hands weakly.

207

"Whatta guy, Lew . . . gee . . . boy, my head's killing me. You got any aspirin, Lew . . ."

"Not now, Bennie," Terry said. "Lew got you into his place here and called me. You were laid out for damn near an hour, I guess." Terry was kneeling down looking at Bennie close up. "Don't go back to sleep, Bennie. Gotta stay awake—"

"I'm real sleepy, Terry."

"I know. But we're taking you over to St. Vincent's, have 'em take at look at that head. We're gonna have to get you on your feet now, Bennie. Slow and easy does it . . ."

Bennie was like a great big baby, not in full control of his arms and legs, and he leaned on his friends. When he was upright he hugged Cassidy, his huge arms weak. "Thank God for you, Lew. Thank God . . ." He started to cry.

"It's okay, Bennie," Cassidy said. He hugged the big son of a bitch. He'd always liked Bennie and now it all seemed sad, like scraping the bottom and not knowing if you could make it back to the top.

Before they went out to the car Terry whispered, "Lew, leave that goddamn stick here. Take one of your wooden canes. No point some smart-ass in the emergency room making a match on Bennie's head and being a genius at your expense. Just play along, amigo. Trust Terry."

•　　•　　•

The emergency room doctors took Bennie away, muttering to themselves about the dumb bastards not calling an ambulance. Bennie waved to them from the stretcher and then his arm just hung down with the knuckles on the floor. Another doctor came and looked curiously at Cassidy. "You look like a plate of Spam yourself, fella," he said. He was a big guy with a paunch that stretched the buttons on his white coat. He was wearing a full complement of bloodstains. He sat down on the edge of his office desk and shook a Lucky out of a flattened pack, lit it with a Stork Club match. He coughed and stared accusingly at the cigarette. There was only one dim light in the room and the tip of the cigarette glowed like a stoplight. "You want me to fix your nose?"

"No, no, I've had it busted a dozen times. I'll go to my own doctor tomorrow."

"Shoot yourself, it's your nose. But it's gonna be a long night without breathing. You got bad ribs, too."

"No, I'm okay."

"You're far from okay, sport. Let me put some tape on those ribs. Be nice if you didn't puncture a lung tonight." Cassidy winced and gave in. Even tough guys listened to reason once in a while. When the doctor had finished he peered at the broken nose. "I could do something with that schnozz . . ." Cassidy shook his head.

"No, it's okay. Tomorrow's fine."

"You're the doctor," he said. "Well, your large friend got a whole load kicked out of him, gentlemen. Somebody beaned him three times with . . . I don't know, a ball bat or something. Mean, real mean." He sucked on the Lucky. "Goddamn animals out there. They come out at night. Which is why we've got emergency rooms."

"Is he going to be all right?"

"Well, it's all relative—"

"But he'll live?"

"I suppose so. If he were going to die, he'd have done it by now."

"What about his memory, Doc?" Terry asked.

"His brain's been bounced all over the south forty. That can throw a man's memory out the window. Chances are he won't ever remember what happened to him tonight. He's lucky he's not dead . . . or maybe he's not so lucky, time will tell."

Lew said, "What's that supposed to mean?"

"We don't know how badly everything's scrambled up in there. But let's just say his brain has been rearranged, so we'll have to see. He might start trying to drink coffee through his ear and take a crap out of his belly button. We'll just have to wait and see."

He took down a lot of information from Terry while Lew sat on a straight-backed chair and stared out the window onto Seventh Avenue. Then Terry dropped Lew at home and said he was heading up to Heliotrope to give Max the bad news.

•   •   •

The doctor was right.

When you're used to breathing, a broken nose and a chest full of cracked ribs louses up your whole routine. Cassidy felt like he was drowning and the four o'clock cold was making him shiver, which rattled his ribs, which made him want to forfeit the game, run up the old white flag, and go home. And then he thought about Bennie and how the front of his forehead had collapsed and he felt like a bastard, until he remembered how his nose and ribs had gotten into their present shape and then he figured Bennie just got run down by the odds. He'd picked on the wrong guy, which was bound to catch up with you sooner or later when you spent enough time beating the shit out of people.

It was hard work carrying the two suitcases and not breathing. The ribs were screaming for mercy. Each step with the suitcases seemed to be sliding his arms out of the shoulder sockets. He put them down at the corner and looked down the empty street. The cream-colored Chrysler was parked near the corner of Fifth Avenue and Washington Square. He gritted his teet, hoisted them once again, and set off on the last leg of the journey across the park.

He put them down again, fished in his pocket for the keys he'd filched from Bennie's mackintosh, and opened the trunk. It was very neat in the trunk. Carefully he stacked the two suitcases, closed the lid, yanked it to make sure it was locked.

Slowly he hobbled home across the park. He'd had to use both hands on the cases so he didn't have his stick and it wasn't so good without it. He threw the keys into a flower bed well off the path. Max was bound to have another set of keys.

In the morning he'd call Max, tell him where he'd seen the car parked. Max would send somebody to pick up the car.

And Max would have a couple of suitcases full of counterfeit-counterfeit gas stamps.

The rest was up to Harry Madrid.

• • •

After the call to Max and the commiseration about what had befallen Bennie, he went to the team doctor who'd put his nose back together a few times in the past. He packed the nose and whistled "Pretty Red Wing" while he was doing it. "Lew," he said, "when are you gonna grow up?"

"You should see the other guy."

"Juvenile, Lew." When he finished with the nose he played a xylophone concerto on the ribs, said the doc the night before had done a good job. "You look just like the guy in *The Mummy*." He kept chuckling at Cassidy's agony and trying to whistle at the same time. Then Cassidy went to the dentist, who pulled two teeth and got the smelling salts when he mentioned how much the bridge would cost.

• • •

Cassidy heard nothing more about the trunk full of faked evidence. Nothing from Harry Madrid and no word from Max's camp, which had the whole Bennie crisis to deal with.

Everything was quiet on the Luciano front and no one was pressing Cassidy to come up with anything on Terry. But maybe Luciano had been at work behind the scenes, as he'd promised Dewey.

Because Tom Dewey climbed down off the wedding cake and made his run for the state house. He was swept in with a landslide plurality of 600,000 votes. He'd done it without prosecuting Max Bauman. But the word around town was that the Outfit had busted a gut getting out the vote for him.

Luciano had done his part.

Now it was Dewey's move.

211

● ● ●

That pretty much took care of 1942.

Bennie was in and out of the hospital all fall and they put a plate in his head and he wore a white turban of bandages up through Thanksgiving. He lost a lot of weight as well as the memory of that one very bad night. The tricks his memory played could be cruel. He never knew when there'd suddenly be a hole and he couldn't finish a sentence because something would be gone. Sometimes he couldn't finish the sentence because he didn't have any idea how it had begun. But some of the time he was okay. By the end of the year he discovered he could remember all the Christmas carols he had ever known. Bennie smiled at that and sang "God Rest Ye Merry, Gentlemen" to his heart's content.

The week before Christmas, with snow drifting softly down on Washington Square, Cassidy went to his mailbox and found a Christmas card. On the front there was a reproduction of a painting by Cézanne. Inside it read: *Cézanne's Greetings.* Beneath that in a girlish hand: *Get it? Cindy.*

It was the only word he'd had from her since the night they'd made love.

● ● ●

Terry threw a New Year's Eve party.

It seemed a very long time since the previous April when he and Cassidy, roommates recovering from their various injuries and wounds, had given that other party. This time Cassidy arrived early and made himself at home while Terry dressed. It was like watching a slide show, sitting at Terry's bar, staring into the mirror but seeing the reflections of that other party when Markie had arrived out of the rain to show off his prized *Necronomicon* and Cindy Squires had bent to Max's wishes and sung some songs and Harry Madrid and Lew had stood together drinking champagne and being tough with each other and Charley Drew had played the piano and they had ended the evening sitting around the dying fire while Max had told them about his son going down with his ship. He was deep in memories of that night's party when the new one began with a trickle of guests.

Cindy was bound to come with Max. Waiting for her to appear was like standing at the five and waiting for the kickoff to come down. He remembered asking her if she wanted to go into the bedroom to see the movie his father was showing, remembered her response, her misunderstanding of the kind of movie it was. Then she had sung "The Nearness of You" and he had realized she was filling his mind the way only Karin ever had . . .

She was still on his mind as the room filled up and Charley Drew began tickling the ivories and the chatter got going. Bryce Huntoon was one of several men in uniform. He surveyed the party, came across the sunken living room, and settled in at the bar beside Cassidy. He was spiffy as ever, like a recruiting poster. They talked about the war news, mainly about the speech the British foreign secretary, Anthony Eden, had made to the House of Commons shortly before Christmas. "It's about time," Huntoon said. Eden was the first official to address the subject of the Nazis' extermination of the Jews. A great many people had known about it for a long time but now it had gone public and the shock waves were beginning to be felt. "This isn't just another European war," Huntoon said, "like all the other wars Europe has staggered through. This is wrong, this is satanic. Mankind at its very worst." He looked at Cassidy sheepishly. "Didn't mean to make a speech, Lew. But, blast it, this thing has got my blood up! Max had it right all along, what's been going on over there."

"Evil," Cassidy said. "People are going to have to get used to the idea that there is such a thing as Evil. Pure and unadulterated Evil that is its own reason for being. If you accept it as a given, it's a very simple concept, really, isn't it?"

"Say, Lew, that's mighty well put. I'll have to tell Max what you just said. I'm impressed."

"Sounds like you see quite a bit of Max these days."

"Oh, here and there. He's been a big help to us. He really is a very public-spirited gentleman. It's funny, the way some people think of him as a gangster. A fine gent, really."

"Relax, Bryce. He is a gangster. Face facts." Huntoon frowned at this.

"Well, you'll never hear anyone say that to me," Huntoon said, jutting his Dick Tracy jaw.

"Well, I just did."

"I mean anyone else."

"Stout fellow," Cassidy said. "There he is now."

Max Bauman had just come in with Bennie the Brute beside him. For an instant Cassidy's eyes played a trick and Bennie looked the same as always but then he took Max's coat and he moved slowly, almost let the black coat with the fur collar slip from his grasp. Cindy Squires was wearing sable. She looked pale and delicate, bare shoulders, a black dress with some kind of little spangles that made her shimmer. Cassidy couldn't look away. Then he realized that Bryce Huntoon had left his side, made his way across the crowded room. Cindy smiled her cat's smile at Huntoon and he shook hands with Max and they moved away together with Bennie following. He was shambling, shuffling, and Cassidy went in search of another drink. To see her, not to be able to go to her, to see Bennie and know how he'd gotten that way—it all left a bitter sinking in his belly.

His father arrived shortly thereafter. He was in uniform. When he got to the bar, Cassidy asked him what was going on with the fancy dress.

"Listen, go easy on your poor old father. Our government moves in mysterious ways its wonders to perform. None more mysterious, my son, and less wondrous than turning me—at my age—into Major Cassidy. It's humiliating. No campaign ribbons. God, I need a drink." The night's bartender poured a double Scotch neat.

"What do they have you doing?" His father looked grand. He was in his mid-fifties. His gray wiry hair was cut short and he looked trim, ready to go out and win the war.

"I think I'm in military intelligence and don't tell me that's a contradiction in terms. Old joke. For a while I thought I was in the Signal Corps, no, I don't know why, but later when I said so to one of my many bosses he looked at me like I'd peed on his shoe and set me straight. It's all academic. I spend most of my time watching German movies. Commercial movies, documentaries, propaganda crap. Looking for keys to the essential Teutonic character. It's crazy, we already knew they don't know from funny. So what's left? How many times can I watch *The Cabinet of Dr. Caligari* and *Triumph of the Will* and *The Blue Angel*?"

"You never heard about any movie Karin might—"

"No. You think that wasn't my first priority? But my not finding anything means nothing. I was talking to my boss, a general yet, who used to be a producer who worked for me, I asked him if there was any way I could find out anything about Karin. He said he'd look into it, which is better than saying no. He was actually kind of interested that I had a German connection, so you never know." He took a slug of Scotch and licked his lips.

"Well," Cassidy said, "she's dead."

"Yeah." He stared across the room. "Speaking of dead, have you seen Bennie? Wow. A zombie. A head of cabbage. What's the story?"

"He got rolled. Down in my neighborhood. I tried to break it up and got my nose broken again. But Bennie got it pretty bad." The lies came so easily.

"Somebody said he's got a plate in his head."

"Steel plate. Terry says it picks up the CBS news if you're standing close to him. You can hear all the war news coming out of Bennie's head."

"Convenient. Well, I'm going to circulate, see who all's here." He squeezed Cassidy's shoulder and moved away.

Cassidy turned around and came face-to-face with Cindy and Max.

"Good to see you, Lew," Max said, pumping his hand.

"You don't come 'round the club much lately. We miss you, kid, don't we, honey?"

"How are you, Miss Squires?"

"Why, I'm fine, Mr. Cassidy." There was a mischievous light in her blue eyes. "And we do miss you. Is your absence a critical judgment on my singing?"

Max laughed indulgently.

"Not at all."

"Then you'll come back? I hope so."

"It's a personal favor," Max said. "Lemme buy you a dinner, Lew. Bring your girlfriend, everything on the house. I can never thank you enough, what you did for Bennie that night. Really."

"How is he these days?"

Max tapped a finger to his skull. "Some days there's just nobody home in there."

"Did you have a nice Christmas?" Cindy asked.

"Nothing to write home about."

"I'm sorry to hear that."

Max had turned away and was talking to Father Paddy, who never missed a party. Cindy caught Cassidy's eye, and her impersonal smile was gone. Her lips formed a word quietly. *Lew.*

Bennie came up behind her. Cassidy tried not to look at the triangular dent where his left temple had been. They had built it up when they put the plate in but it didn't look right. It made his whole head look like something a mad scientist had stapled onto his shoulder as an afterthought.

"Bennie. You're looking good."

"Thanks, Lew." A smile twitched. He'd put some pounds on but they were puffy. "I'm feeling pretty good, too. I have my good days, I have my bad days. Boy, Cindy, you know how Lew here saved my life—"

"Yes, Bennie, you told me all about it."

"I guess I have at that. I forget things—Lew found me down in Washington Square, he lives down there—"

"I know, Bennie."

"Still don't know what I was doing down there . . ."

His voice trailed away and he stopped talking, looking off at the party.

Max turned back and put Cindy's bare arm through his and the three of them drifted off. Terry had been listening and shook his head ruefully. "Funny, seeing the big guy like that. It's like he's punch-drunk. That was some night, amigo."

Later on Cindy stood beside Charley Drew at the piano and the party got quiet while she sang a couple songs. She finished with the big new song of the season. Bing Crosby had sung it in a movie and now Cindy was dreaming of a White Christmas, with treetops glistening and the sound of sleigh bells, just like the ones all of them used to know.

It was wartime and a lot of people hadn't made it home for the holidays and it was late on New Year's Eve and some of the guests had a faraway look, remembering people they loved and wouldn't be with and remembering Christmases long ago.

Cindy was standing at his side just before midnight. Bryce Huntoon was looking at her longingly from across the room. She smiled out at the crowd but she was speaking softly to Cassidy.

"I think about you," she said. "Did you get my card?"

"Sure."

"I thought it might appeal to a smart guy with a winning smile."

"It did. But not as much as you do."

"I know, I know. There's nothing I can do, Lew. He holds me so tight—and Bennie's always with me . . ."

"My tough luck," he said.

"Mine, too, you know. I keep trying to think of ways to reach you. I've wanted you . . . oh, I should shut up. It's about midnight. Here they come."

They were all together in a little group with the party going on all around them. Cindy and Max and Terry and Bennie and Paul Cassidy and Lew. Terry had a bottle of champagne wrapped in a white towel and he filled all the glasses.

"Happy New Year," Terry said softly. "May 1943 bring

217

us all the good things of life . . . and may we deserve them."

"P-p-peace to all men," Bennie said.

They lifted their glasses and toasted the New Year and somebody across the room began to sing "Auld Lang Syne."

Max had his arm around Cindy's shoulder, pulled her close, and she turned to kiss him. Bennie spilled the rest of his champagne, his hand shaking violently. He looked around and mumbled his apologies. Terry pecked Cindy's cheek and Bryce Huntoon showed up to kiss her. Cindy came to Cassidy and gave him her sober, serious look while Max watched her. "Mr. Cassidy," she said, "would you like a New Year's kiss?"

"Why not?" he said.

She leaned forward and brushed her mouth against his just a fraction of a second longer than was necessary. Then she kissed Bennie, standing on tiptoe to reach him, and he blushed like a schoolboy.

Later Cassidy was standing in a quiet spot and saw Bennie alone, looking out the window at Park Avenue. It didn't seem like there was all that much left of Bennie. He was a big dumb animal now where once he'd been something else, something whole. All because he'd picked on the wrong guy. He was staring out at the snow falling on Park Avenue in the first hour of 1943. His face was working, a symphony of tics and twitches, but he didn't seem to be aware of anything, not the tics, not the snow, not the party, nothing. One eye was closed, as if he were winking at his reflection. The thing was, the eye stayed clenched shut.

Cassidy's last memory of the party was watching Max and Cindy and Bennie leaving. Bryce Huntoon joined them at the door, left with them.

Terry looked at Cassidy and said, "Are you thinking what I'm thinking?"

"I don't know," he said.

"Well, thinking of your happiness as I invariably am"— he winked—"it occurs to me that nobody may be keeping track of Miss Squires anymore. I doubt if Max has another watchdog he trusts like Bennie. Maybe she's on the loose."

The thought took Cassidy by surprise. "That's not what she says," Cassidy said, wanting her more than he could believe, wanting to relive that one night.

"Maybe she's just afraid, amigo. I don't see Bennie as a big problem anymore."

Cassidy nodded. "Not anymore," he said.

Once again, tapping his stick in the carpet of snow, he walked all the way home. The sun was shining behind the snowfall by the time he reached Washington Square.

CHAPTER TWELVE

Sometimes he thought it would eat him up. Sometimes, rarely, he gave in to a momentarily appealing girl, but he never gave her a thought the next day. There was only one he wanted. The desire never left him, but . . . but . . .

Cassidy let 1943 pass without trying to reach Cindy Squires. He thought he saw her once sitting on a bench in Washington Square but he was a long way off and decided he'd be better off not making sure. Terry kept asking him if he'd seen her and Cassidy kept telling him no, he hadn't. Cassidy didn't know if Terry believed him. But he didn't have the stomach for seeking her out, not when he thought of Bennie. Or what was left of Bennie. When his mind turned to Cindy, Bennie was always there in the shadows. None of it seemed right.

Neither did he ever go back to the team for a job. The past was past. He did shuttle back and forth to Washington for a few months when his father got him onto his civilian staff as a consultant, which meant he spent a lot of tedious hours in overheated smoke-filled rooms watching incomprehensibly boring German movies. A couple months of that and he gave in to Terry's nagging. His name went up on the door of the Dependable Detective Agency right next to Terry's. Dependable Detective. Sounded like one of the pulp magazines he sometimes read while soaking in the tub. It was summertime, the living was easy, and Cassidy was a gumshoe. Terry saw to it that he got a license, a gun permit, and a gun, which Cassidy put in his desk drawer, safely locked away so he couldn't do himself any harm.

He didn't do any real detective work, God forbid. He sort of managed the office. Elmo Andretti and Herb Contreras were the two operatives Terry had hired. There was a secretary, Olive Naismith, who typed, filed, and billed. Cassidy interviewed prospective clients, set up the open files, made sure Elmo and Herb were attending to business, and sat around watching Terry put his Bostonians on his desk while he smoked cigars. Terry was working his way through a variety of girlfriends, none of whom Cassidy ever actually met. He kept urging Cassidy to enjoy some feminine companionship himself, even if it wasn't Cindy Squires. Cassidy couldn't bring himself to explain how he felt, stretched so tight between the longing for Cindy and the haunting memory, the ghost of Karin. One day Elmo was listening to Terry chiding Cassidy about being too reclusive and said, "Listen, Terry, old Lew here's got the right idea. Sugar's sweet and so is honey, fuck your hand and save your money." Elmo was not only Dependable's poet but its wit, as well.

•   •   •

How did '43 creep past? Ah, he could count the ways.

He read Ayn Rand's *The Fountainhead*. That took quite a while but absolutely everyone was doing it. *Amos 'n' Andy* went off the air when it was still the most popular show on the air. Campbell's couldn't afford to keep it going because they couldn't sell enough soup because all the tin for the cans was going to the war effort. Exeunt *Amos 'n' Andy*, which only went to show you there was indeed a war on.

221

He read somewhere that World War I had cost America thirty-five billion dollars. The price tag on WWII was running eight billion a month. An old pal of his father's was killed in February when the Pan Am Clipper taking performers to entertain GIs crashed near Lisbon. He saw the play about the little Nazi kid raising hell in the American family, *Tomorrow the World*, at the Ethel Barrymore, and *The Voice of the Turtle* at the Morosco and *Oklahoma!* at the St. James. J. P. Morgan died at seventy-five and Edsel Ford fell to cancer at forty-nine, which brought old Henry himself back to run the family business. He read Wendell Willkie's *One World*, which broke every sales record everywhere. Everybody read Ernie Pyle's accounts of the foot soldiers' war, everybody saw *Casablanca*, and up at Heliotrope Cindy Squires made quite a name for herself singing "As Time Goes By" and "Speak Low When You Speak Love" and "I'll Be Seeing You" and "Comin' in on a Wing and a Prayer." The Russians stopped the Wehrmacht and began the long counterattack, which just about bled the Nazis dry in the East. FDR called in federal troops to put down the race riots in Detroit. He met with Stalin and Churchill at Teheran; he and Churchill and De Gaulle got together in Casablanca—the town, not the movie. Mussolini and the Fascisti called it a day in Italy and by October the new government in Rome had declared war on the Germans. Fats Waller sold more records than either Crosby or Sinatra, and Terry and Cassidy kept catching a young singer who'd graduated from the chorus of Ethel Waters's Cotton Club show, one Lena Horne. Of course Terry's favorite song of the year was Al Dexter's recording of "Pistol Packin' Mama." The pistol packin' general, George S. Patton, was in the news a good deal, but General Eisenhower got the call to be the commander-in-chief for the invasion of Europe. Terry and Cassidy were there, too, on a freezing January night when Duke Ellington took the top right off Carnegie Hall for a good cause—Russian relief. The band wore long gray coats with jet-black carnations in their buttonholes.

• • •

A year after his one night with Cindy Squires, a year after he'd just about put Bennie down for the big sleep, a year after Tom Dewey was elected governor of New York, a year after all that, Cassidy ran into Harry Madrid drinking quietly and alone at Costello's. It was a raw night with the wind blowing sheets of cold rain along the deserted streets. Harry Madrid stood at the end of the bar staring into his beer; the joint smelled of cherry tobacco.

Cassidy shook the rain off his trench coat and went to stand next to the big, fatherly-looking cop. It just went to show you about deceiving appearances.

Cassidy ordered a beer and Harry Madrid looked up.

"Well, if it ain't Mr. Touchdown," he muttered.

"How are you, Harry?"

"You don't wanna know, Lew . . ."

"Aw, hell. What's the matter?"

"D'ja ever notice," Harry said, as if he were continuing aloud what he'd been contemplating in solitude, "that things never turn out the way you expect?"

"I've noticed that, Harry."

"The man's noticed that," Harry said deliberately. "You prolly figured you had some more years playin' football—then, wham, it's all over. You figured you had a wife—then, blam, that's all over. You just never know." He banked the pipe into an ashtray, dug the last bit of dottle from the bottom of the Kaywoodie with a penknife. "Nothin' ever works out. Like me and the wife, gonna get that sheriff's job upstate, live to a ripe old age . . . funny how nothin' ever works out the way you think . . ."

Cassidy drank his beer, staring down the almost deserted bar.

"I just left the hospital, see."

"You sick, Harry?"

"Well, tell the truth, I ain't feelin' so hot—"

"Come on, Harry, what's the matter?"

"It's the wife, Lew."

"She sick?"

223

"Oh, no. Ethel ain't sick. Not no more. She's dead now. She was sick right up until a couple hours ago."

"I'm sorry, Harry. I had no idea—"

"Cancer of the stomach. Worse 'n bein' gut shot, Lew, lot worse. I been takin' care of her, y'know, for months. Six, eight months. Takes a long time, cancer of the stomach. Long time Ethel spent dyin'. Wasn't much left of her, little wisp of a thing, ended up about seventy pounds or so . . . Anyway, she's gone now." He sighed. His face was stony and impassive as ever. "She's better off dead, but it sure fucks up our plans, y'know?"

"Harry, I don't know what to say."

"Not much to say. I wouldn't of recognized her, I went out for a hamburger and a piece of pie, I come back . . . nothin'. She's dead. Nobody even knew it. Not 'til I told 'em. Ethel just went and died on us." He blew his nose loudly and stuffed the handkerchief up his sleeve. "Nothin' ever works out, Lew. Ya know all them goddamn phony gas stamps we laid off on Max? Remember that?" A ghostly smile. He shook his head.

"I remember."

"Big fuckin' FBI operation, war effort, gonna get those goddamn war profiteers like Maxie . . . well, shit!"

"Whatever happened with that? It was like I dropped 'em down a rathole, never heard another word . . . now Dewey's governor and what's happening with Luciano? Is he in or out? What about the parole?"

"Fuckin' Hoover backed out, that's what the fuck happened! Tells me to forget it . . . just forget it, Harry old shithead, just forget it!" He blew himself out and his whole body sank lower. He signaled for another beer and a shot. He downed the whiskey in a quick, practiced motion. "Somebody up there put the fix in for Max. That or Hoover just couldn't make it stick to Max. Or they had somebody else to go after . . . and I'm left holding my pecker like the last guy in line at the cathouse. I can't figure it out, Lew, and nobody's gonna tell me. What was the point, I ask you? All that trouble for nothin'." He wiped the head of beer off his upper lip. He was wearing his specs and looked older, tireder. Cassidy couldn't look at him, though, without seeing those shapes rising out of the fog with the tommy guns rattling and the gangsters dying.

"What about Luciano?"

"Dewey's gonna drag his feet. Willkie just beat him out of the Republican nomination in '40. Dewey wants it in '44 and he'll probably get it. I figure he don't want some smart-ass pointing out he paroled Luciano between '42 and '44. Just my guess . . . and what the hell's Lucky gonna do? He's gotta stay on Dewey's good side if he ever wants to get out. Anyways, I hear they moved Lucky to Great Meadows Prison in Comstock, just to keep him calm. Great Meadows is a lot like freedom, Lew. The cons call it the Country Club, for the chrissakes. He can have his meals sent in from good restaurants, all the visitors he wants. Hell, they'll let him spend evenings out on the town, get him laid." He frowned into his beer. "He'll be fine. But you can bet on one thing, Lew . . . I'm gonna get that bastard Max, one way or another . . . I'm gonna get everybody, get 'em all . . . I got nothin' to live for anymore but I can still raise some real hell. Believe me, Lew, I can do that . . ."

• • •

A few days before Christmas Terry and Cassidy left the Dalmane Building about one o'clock in search of lunch. The thermometer was in the twenties and the wind was working its way across town and up the canyons like something with a personal grudge against Gotham. Snow eddied across the sidewalk, snapping at their ankles. It was nasty enough to stop the clocks on Cassidy's socks. The crowds out rounding up the last Christmas presents leaned into the gale, held on to their hats and shopping bags. Taxis and buses snarled at staggering, wind-driven pedestrians. Newspapers blew apart, whipped along the gutters.

They were standing at 42nd and Fifth waiting for a traffic light when Cassidy saw a guy, a well-dressed bumly sort, who reminded him of the bankers and stockbrokers you used to see a few years ago selling apples on the same corners, when they weren't landing on them from great heights. This was a big guy, stooped, with rounded shoulders, wearing an expensive black herringbone overcoat from Brooks. He wore a stocking cap. He was partly sheltered in a doorway, demonstrating a toy he was selling from a grocery sack.

It wasn't much of a toy and he made a sad, yet comical figure. It consisted of a cardboard tube he held in his mouth and blew into, like a New Year's Eve noisemaker. When he blew into this thing, the air traveled through the tubes which arced upward around his face to a point on either side of his head where two rolled paper horns would then unfurl, leaping wildly outward from his forehead. Each time he blew, zap, the horns shot outward. It was driving two kids in sailor suits and coats into spasms of hysteria. They were pulling at their mother until she finally came up with the necessary quarter and bought a couple. When the man took the quarter, he looked up and Cassidy saw his eyes, huge and watery behind his round spectacles.

It was Bennie the Brute.

Cassidy poked Terry, who looked over and nodded. "Yeah, I saw him yesterday. I didn't have the heart to tell you."

Bennie saw them and walked over, smiling like a man who was hearing jokes everybody else was missing. The horns kept shooting out and recoiling until he stood beside them and the tube dropped from his mouth. "Merry C-C-Christmas, you guys," he said.

"Come on," Cassidy said, "let's go have a sandwich, Bennie. You look cold as hell."

"Pretty n-n-nippy out here," he said. "Lemme get my inventory there." He went back to grab his sack and they all went to a little bar on a cross street a block away.

He ate two hamburgers, a bowl of chili, fries, cole slaw, and two glasses of milk. Then he had a piece of mince pie with ice cream melting on it. Finally he looked up shyly like a big friendly creature from a child's storybook. "Get hungry standing out there. Job's not as easy as it l-l-looks."

As they talked, Cassidy kept trying to catch his eye but it was always slipping away. He wore a small white bandage taped across his left temple but Cassidy didn't ask why. He'd asked once before and Bennie had said he sometimes picked at the scar tissue. Oh, boy.

It turned out that he'd told Max Bauman he couldn't take his money anymore, couldn't take it for doing nothing. "Heck, I'm no damn good anymore," he said. "Nothing I c-c-can do for Max amounts to a damn. I can't even remember things so good, sometimes he tells me to go get the early editions of the papers for him and I'd find myself standing there alone on the street . . . and I wouldn't know why the dickens I was there. It's gettin' worse, too." He seemed to be taking it all pretty philosophically. "Max, he didn't want me to go but I figured mainly I was sitting around listening to *Ma Perkins* and *Helen Trent* and playing gin with Miss Squires. Who needs a guy like that? So I got my own little place and I sell these toys—"

"Wise up, Bennie," Terry interrupted. "Go back to Max. Take a lifetime pension. The guy loves ya, for chrissakes, Bennie. Does Bennie the Brute belong on the goddamn corner selling the dumb crap in those sacks?"

"I don't know, Terry," he said slowly. "I think they're sort of c-c cute. Bennie the Brute ain't so tough anymore, he gets these headaches—"

"Bullshit!" Terry was scowling with anger. "I hate to hear you talk like this. You're giving in, you're going soft. Pull yourself together, you're okay—"

"Oh, I'm not so sure of that, Terry, I think maybe you're wrong there. The doctors, they say my b-b-brain isn't all there anymore. They say I'm real passive now and, y'know, I think they're right. Fight's all gone outa B-B-Bennie." He smiled, a look of something like surprise on his face. "Some ways, y'know, it's a l-l-lot easier this way. But I miss Max and Miss Squires and some of the guys. Look, nothin' I can do about it, I am what I am."

Terry laughed and punched him on the arm. "All you need is, go out and ice a couple guys for Max, pretty soon you're the old Bennie."

Bennie's face grew very somber. "I didn't like doing that stuff, icin' guys, Terry. Never. But I had my job to do. You won't believe this, but I used to get to w-w-worryin' at night about going to Heaven! I used to think I'd never get into Heaven 'cause I iced a lotta guys, mostly bad guys but still they was alive and well before they met me. Now, y'know, maybe God, He'll forgive me my trespasses. You think?" His watery eyes settled on Cassidy, questioning all the verities.

"I don't think you got a thing to worry about, Ben," Cassidy said. "It's all gonna be okay. There's a spot for you in Heaven, kid."

They drank another cup of coffee. Over the bar there were individual letters strung on a sagging string against the mirror. M-E-R-R-Y C-H-R-I-S-T-M-A-S. They were very old and somebody had glued dangling strings of tinsel to each red letter. Bennie rattled his cup back into the saucer. "Look, it's great seeing you guys," he said, wrapping his muffler around his throat and chin, pulling his cap down hard but leaving enough room for the toy to work. "But I gotta get back out to work. Thanks for lunch and everything." He stood up and shook hands.

"Take my advice," Terry said. "Go back to Max, Bennie. He'll welcome you with open arms, the return of the prodigal."

But Bennie was already heading toward the street, carrying his ratty old sack of toys.

"Let's go back another way," Terry said. "I don't want to see him doing that. Jesus. Bennie . . ."

Cassidy nodded and together they went back into the cold.

• • •

Another New Year's Eve. Cassidy was measuring out his life in sips of champagne, to the strains of "Auld Lang Syne," and glimpses of Cindy Squires, who never changed

228

much, never seemed to adopt new hairstyles or funny clothes, always sang the best songs. The party this time was out in Oyster Bay, at Max Bauman's mansion.

About one o'clock on the first morning of 1944 Cassidy was getting into his velvet-collared chesterfield and fondling his new homburg, about to get into the 1938 Ford convertible he'd bought from an old guy in Princeton whose son had bought it new and then been killed in North Africa. The hallway was very dark and it seemed that the party was very far away. Max was playing billiards with Terry and Bryce Huntoon a cab ride from the front hall. Cassidy figured he was alone, making a quiet getaway.

She had come up very quietly. When she spoke he practically fell over.

"Nerves," she cautioned. "Where's the tough private eye?"

"I left him in my other suit."

"It's been fifteen months," she said. "I didn't think I could stay away from you so long, not after that night. Somebody should turn our story into an opera—"

"A very short opera."

"But, then, I didn't think you could stay away this long, either. You're a tower of restraint, Lew."

"That's what everybody says. I grieve over my restraint on long winter nights. Besides, you told me not to "

"I know what I told you. I'm sorry . . . but I had to. I thought Max might have Bennie do something awful to you if he found out."

"How good of you, how good, how kind . . ."

"But Bennie isn't so tough nowadays . . . please, don't be cold to me, Lew. I was thinking—hoping—maybe we could . . . you know—"

"I'm not so sure. Maybe the moment's passed. It happens sometimes. You've been with Max a long time. That makes a difference."

"You're telling me you're the last of the honorable men?" She pouted slightly, nervously. Pouting wasn't her style.

"We're a dying breed. Like the bison. Time has passed us by."

"I want you inside me. My knees are shaking, I'm shaking all over. I feel like I'm going to boil over. I mean it, Lew. I haven't had anything, not anything, with Max in almost a year. He says he just can't and I don't blame him, he can't help it . . . but he won't let me go. Do you understand? He won't. He said he'd kill anyone else . . . and he means it. Oh, Lew, what am I going to do about everything?"

"Why ask me? Leave Max, take your chances. Then?" He shrugged. "I'm still in the book."

"Why are you treating me this way? Do you hate me, Lew?"

"I'm afraid—"

"Of Max?"

"Anyone in his right mind is afraid of Max. But, no, I meant I'm afraid of you."

"I don't believe you're a coward, Lew."

"I'm getting older. I no longer think I'll live forever. But that's another story. I am afraid . . . of what I might feel for you. When you're not being a smart-mouth."

"Look, if it matters to you, I don't feel like a whore anymore."

"Must be all this enforced celibacy."

"Maybe you are just a bastard! But maybe I'm crazy . . . come on, will you fuck me? Please? Right here, on the steps, nobody would—"

"You're right. You are crazy."

"And you call yourself a sport!"

"I don't recall ever calling myself anything of the kind."

"Can I come to your place? Next week? I'll make you forget the last time."

"I don't think so, Cindy." He smiled into her eyes. "I don't want to forget the last time."

"Are you saying you don't want me?"

"I want you way too much—"

"Do you mind if I persist?"

"I admire a woman who knows her own mind. Anyway, it's your nickel, Cindy."

He put his gloves and hat on and reached for the doorknob. He had his stick under his arm like a man reviewing the troops. He could smell the same perfume. She never changed anything.

"Wait," she said.

"I'm going home now."

"Lew?"

"Yes, Cindy?"

"Kiss me once."

He did.

•   •   •

About a month later Terry left a scrawled note on Cassidy's desk. He wanted him back at the office at ten o'clock for an important meeting with a client. It was a brutal night, early February, snow crunching underfoot and the wind damp and cutting. Cassidy had dinner alone at Keen's and was back at the office going through a stack of photographs taken of a wife making nice-nice at a Jersey roadhouse with some lug who was doubtless a lot of things but definitely not her husband. He was rescued from this impoverished pursuit by Terry's arrival. He slung his polo coat over a client's chair, wiped a smudge of lipstick—he always called them "campaign ribbons"—from the corner of his mouth, and lit a cigar.

Max Bauman came in at 10:10. He was with a stranger, a man in his late forties, gray hair, expensive gray suit with a faint red thread in it, a little overweight, paunchy. Small feet. He'd be fast, a good dancer. He looked like a lawyer. Max introduced him as an "associate," which could have meant just about anything. His name was Bob Erickson and he said he'd wait in the outer office for them to conclude their business. When they closed the door he was thumbing through the morning's *Wall Street Journal*.

Max was wearing his tuxedo, just like the gangsters in the movies, the same gangsters who always owned a nightclub. He took off his soft slouch black hat and he looked very different. He was wearing another pound of salt-and-pepper hair. Looked like the rug on his swarthy scalp cost as much as the big Persian in his study at home. He settled himself in the chair as if he were looking to come clean. He looked distracted. And different. Somehow. Maybe it was the new hair that made Cassidy see him fresh. His Levantine features—lips, nostrils, eyebrows—seemed thicker, larger. There were deep ridges etched in the corners of his mouth. His ears seemed heavier, with droopy lobes close to his skull. The skin of his face was dark and leathery and, uncharacteristically, the collar of his shirt was loose. His face was thinner. He looked older. He'd lost the stocky solidness, which could have meant a lot of things. Maybe he'd gone into training. Lost some weight, glued the new piece onto his dome so he'd look cute for Miss Cindy Squires . . .

Maybe he figured it would make up for not being such a hot lover anymore. The more Cassidy looked at him, the more he thought Max was a man with woman trouble, but maybe that was only because he knew Max had all the woman trouble in the world, the only kind that mattered, whether he knew it or not. And then Max began talking about it.

"This isn't easy for me, boys, so let me go about it my own way." He crossed his legs, lit a cigar about eight inches long. "It's about Miss Squires. That is, Cindy." He blinked as if he expected an argument. Terry just nodded and told him to go on.

"You know how I feel about this girl. It's like my feelings for you, Terry—deep, abiding. You're like a son to me, Terry. You introduced me to Cindy. You were the matchmaker, you son of a gun." He smiled briefly, in a fatherly way. "Well, Cindy's a very complicated woman. And she's a lot younger than I am. And the fact is that I'm dependent on her in certain ways. You're intelligent boys, men of the world; I can speak openly here. She is my mistress, yes. But she's also like a daughter, a youthful friend. She's my

232

lease on my own youth. She keeps me young. She keeps my illusions intact—don't laugh, even I have some illusions. A man must have an illusion or two. She makes me feel good, better than I have since I was a young man kicking around Harvard Square. My illusion is that the girl loves me. Maybe she does, maybe she doesn't. But the illusion is what keeps me going. My son dead, my wife dead . . ." He puffed his cigar, eyes flickering from Terry to Cassidy.

Terry said, "Max, you love her?"

Max waved his hand, the smoke moving slowly, like the music at Toscanini's command. "Love, love, what is love? Love, love, hooray for love! But what is it? It's a recent arrival on the scene of Western culture. But I've told you I need her, I derive many benefits from her presence in my life. You may think it odd, you being young men, but I don't even have to touch her flesh . . . I can just watch the miracle of her naked body as she moves through a Sunday afternoon, every minute, sipping her coffee, reading the *Times*, looking out at the water . . . I can just sit and watch her naked as the day she was born. And then I feel as if all this utter, total shit of life is all worthwhile. It is a miracle, you understand? I sometimes look at her fanny or her toes or the muscles in her thighs, and I wonder is there any point in life without her? Is there any point in ever thinking of anything else in all of life? So, you ask me, is that love? If it is, then I love her . . . oh, yes, I do love her. And she makes all the sewers overflowing around me worth living through. Do you get my drift, boys? The hounds of hell are nipping at my heels, boys. I'm up to my ass in hounds, in fact, and I don't mean Mr. J. Edgar Hoover . . . he's a puppy compared to my fucking hounds—"

"What the hell are you talking about?"

"Traitors, Terry. Nameless, faceless traitors!" Max's face was going an unhealthy scarlet, eyes bulging with the effort to control his temper. "You boys don't know about this and you shouldn't be burdened . . . Hoover's trying to stick some insane war profiteering crap on me. Me! Max Bauman! A gold-star father with a son dead in the fucking Pacific! Some counterfeit gas stamps, planted in the Chrysler, the Feds tipped off . . . My lawyers can outtalk his dumb bastards any day, but it's the principle here. Somebody's trying to put me under! Christ, I was set up, somebody had the guts to set me up! Max Bauman! Just like that mess at Giuseppe's over in Jersey back in '42 . . . somebody tipped that off, too—and I still don't know who the hell the triggermen were!" He sank back into the chair, shriveling in his tuxedo, looking almost vulnerable. Almost. "It's all shit, boys. And that little girl . . . I'm telling you, she keeps me going . . . without her I don't know what I'd do. If she went, boys, I might lose my grip on things, on everything . . . oh, hell yes, I love her, need her, give it any name you want. But I will not lose her . . ."

Terry sighed and slid an inch of ash into an ashtray set into a small version of a tractor tire. "Max, I don't know about this Hoover thing, but it sounds like you're getting all worked up over nothing. She's nice to you, you're nice to her. She's got a world-class fanny and you're rich as Croesus. Everything sounds top hole to me, Max. We should all be so lucky. So why muddy the waters? Why come to us—and why *have* you come to us? I don't get it—"

"Ah, Terry, Terry. Try to understand me. All is not well in this earthly Eden. A serpent—call it jealousy. Or more to the point, call it another man. Yes, let's call it another man . . . I'm afraid she's seeing another man."

"Every man fears that the woman who happens to be the answer, his own personal answer, is just possibly unfaithful." Cassidy shook his head sadly at Max. "Hell, Max," he said, "everybody's afraid of that."

"I watch her. She pines, for God's sake. She's pensive, wistful, sad. She's pining for someone. Give me some credit—I'm not a total novice when it comes to women. She leaves the house or the apartment. She goes to the library, she goes to the movies, she goes to bookstores, she walks the streets aimlessly—you understand? That's what she says she's doing . . . but all the time I know goddamn well she's . . . she's thinking of *him*. Goddamn him! She walks for hours in this city. I even tried to follow her once . . . she went to Washington Square and sat on a bench like she was waiting for someone who didn't show up." He shook his sleek head and ran his palm across the hairpiece, puzzled. Cassidy swallowed hard and acted like he was taking notes. *Washington Square.* "Then she walked all the way up Fifth Avenue to the Metropolitan. I thought I'd keel over! And then she looks at pictures for four hours. Now, that's an art lover, boys! Or a woman thinking damn long thoughts."

Terry said, "So you caught her at it. Going for a long walk and looking at pictures. Forgive my saying so, Max, but this is not a problem. This is not a woman to worry about." He looked at Cassidy for confirmation. Cassidy said it all looked pretty innocent to him. He knew damn well what Terry was thinking. Washington Square.

Max nodded impatiently. "Look, boys, I didn't come here for a debate. I need a tail on the young lady. I want to find out who the guy is. I want a name. That's all."

"We're not going to find anybody. She's clean, Max."

"Terry, Terry, you're having trouble with this concept. If you're right, think how relieved I'll be. Cheap at twice the price. But . . . there *is* a guy. I *know* that. Sometimes I just know things." Listening to him was like looking at a blueprint of his mind working. He wasn't giving her sex so he was sure she was getting sex somewhere else. It was like a geometric proof. It allowed no other possibilities. Cassidy didn't say anything about the job Max was proposing. Terry already thought the mystery guest was Cassidy and the fact was Cassidy didn't even want to imagine her with another man, though the odds said she was. The odds said Max was right. She'd told him what she was, even if she wasn't so sure anymore. She was the kind of woman who'd always have a guy stashed some-where in case of emergency, when the itch got too bad and she couldn't control herself, when she had to have a nobody, an anybody, a nothing at work between her legs. Cassidy knew her, too.

"I want this gentleman," Max said calmly.

"And what if we come up empty?" Terry asked.

"You won't, son. You won't come up empty. Trust me. Just do your job and when I have his name and some proof, there's a bonus. Ten thousand dollars."

"What are you gonna do when you have the name?" Terry looked at Cassidy from the corner of his eye, through the fog of cigar smoke. He was sure Cassidy was the name; they'd need a sacrificial lamb, a patsy. The wheels were spinning, the gears meshing. Next there'd be smoke coming out of Terry's ears.

"I'll tell the gentleman to take a long walk on a short pier—"

"Not to be indelicate, Max . . . but no cement galoshes, okay?"

Max frowned at him as if such loose talk were unworthy of comment.

"And what about Cindy?" Cassidy said.

"She'll know nothing about any of it."

"You want to marry her?" Terry asked.

"You want the truth?" Max puffed gently, squinting at them, the obsidian eyes gleaming beneath the heavy lids. The leathery jowls made him look infinitely old just then, a tribesman contemplating eternity beyond the endless sand and sky. "Let me tell you the truth. It's hard to believe but believe it. I've asked her to marry me. How old you think I am?"

"Fifty, fifty-five," Terry suggested.

Max smiled. "Sixty-five. I was born in 1878. In Constantinople. A Turkish-Polish Jew. I don't even remember the name I was born with. I've had six names, think of that. But I've had aspirations. It's damn near impossible to stop me getting what I want. I wanted America. I got it. I helped that punk Luciano . . . He could be my son! I wanted Harvard. I wanted money and power. I wanted to marry a woman of breeding. I got it all. And now at the end of my life I want this beautiful blond girl . . . and I work up the nerve to ask her . . . and she tells me no, she won't marry me. *But* . . . you'll never guess why, not in a million years. She says she'd rather show me how much she cares for me without a piece of paper, without any legal claims. She says if she married me I'd finally get to wondering if she married me for my money. This is the kind of woman she is. Do you doubt I want her? This way she says I'll always know she's with me because she cares. This is an extraordinary woman . . ."

"Then why not just trust her?"

He shrugged. "Never trust a woman."

"Max, you amaze me," Terry said.

"I probably do," he said.

"Look, Max," Cassidy said, "have you thought she might simply be lonely for friends her own age? Quite innocently, I mean—"

"You're a nice boy, Lew. But there's nothing innocent about this girl. She's the daughter of Time. She's a thousand years older than I'll ever be. She, like Evil, *is*. She is all of it, this woman. She is goodness and kindness, she is depravity and wickedness, the Whore of Babylon, yet she is an angel. She is cruel and dark as the pit. And she is my joy. Try to understand. I'm not raving. She is everything a woman can be. She'd be willing to die to protect her children . . . then devour them without a second thought. Do you wonder I love such a creature? So just do it, do what I ask, leave the rest to me."

He stood up and slipped back into his overcoat. He put on the slouch hat.

"Be careful," he said. "She's the spirit of the light and the dark. Both of you, watch yourselves."

When he and Bob Erickson were gone and the sound of the elevator grinding downward reached back into the office, Terry looked up and shrugged. "Well, he was wrong. He *was* raving."

Cassidy stared back at him, wondering. "Seems to me he just told us what love is. Exactly what love is."

"If," Terry observed, "love's a fatal disease." He stood looking out the window into the night, staring down at Grand Central. "Somebody tipped Max to the boyfriend. Somebody tipped Harry Madrid to the meeting in Jersey. Somebody planted those stamps in the Chrysler . . . You know what, Lew? Max must have offended a god or two, because the gods sure as hell are fucking with Max's life . . ."

Chapter Thirteen

Something—call it human nature, call it a tip from a friend—something had taken Max's mind, had diverted it from the idea that Terry had sold him out and set up the ambush at the Jersey shore. One obsession had been replaced by another: his certainty that Cindy Squires was unfaithful to him. In a way Cassidy found it all baffling but, looked at another way, it struck him as part of the inevitable illogicality of life.

Lucky Luciano was still in prison, Dewey was governor, and Max Bauman was still a free man. Harry Madrid and J. Edgar Hoover had gone to a lot of trouble to get Max and then when they'd had trouble making it stick, it had all sort of petered out . . .

Cindy Squires. Cassidy had fallen in love with her for no better reason than people ever fall in love, then his wife had been lost beneath the RAF bombs and Cindy had evaporated. But she'd come back for one passionate evening, like a reward . . . and the joy of having her had exploded with Cassidy nearly killing Bennie and she'd slipped away again, leaving only a Christmas card . . .

But the thing was, nothing was ever over. The story was always in progress, which was, of course, what set life apart from art. Life just kept on going, running over you again and again to make sure you got the point, and you couldn't make it stop and nothing would stay the same. Once you had all that figured out, you'd look up feeling a little better and all of a sudden the long black shadow fell across your path and all you could do was duck and cover your path and pray.

Cindy Squires was a story being told, ever shifting and changing as time went by, never quite what you thought she was. It was true of all of them. Max. Bennie. Harry. Terry. Lew Cassidy . . .

Only the dead were complete.

The rest of them were all still flailing away. Coming and going. Trying to figure it out. Trying to know whom you could trust. Changing. Caught in the whirlwind.

Somebody had tipped Harry about Jersey. Somebody had planted the gas stamps in Max's car. Bennie had had Lew dead to rights on Cindy—and suddenly the slate of his memory had been wiped clean. Cassidy had a briefcase full of funny money stashed under his bed and had no idea what to do with it. He had a cane with a sword in it and memories of a dead wife and he had a pain in his belly called Cindy and somehow he'd managed not to betray Terry Leary . . .

The point was, you just never knew what life was going to throw at you next. Whether it was Pearl Harbor or a bad leg for the rest of your life or Markie Cookson pouring you champagne one day and the next time you see him he's a piece of garbage on the beach. You just never knew when you were supposed to laugh. There was always something funny going on. Life wasn't a movie. Life was kind of random and it could always get a lot worse than you'd ever imagined.

So 1944 was upon them.

•   •   •

Terry put Herb Contreras on Cindy for two weeks. He used his Leica and collected a lot of pictures of her minding her own business. She went to an afternoon string quartet concert; she browsed Scribner's bookstore for hours, bought a dozen current novels; she had her hair done, facials, manicures; she bought clothing; she lunched. Almost always alone. No girlfriends. Only one man. What emerged from all those black-and-white glossies was a portrait of a very lonely woman.

The man she met twice for lunch was Colonel Bryce Huntoon, who looked more like a movie hero's best friend every day. He was in uniform both times and the luncheon spots were hardly hideaways. Once they met at "21" and once at the Algonquin. If they'd been trying to attract attention they couldn't have chosen more wisely. There were pictures of Cindy smiling wanly at some comment, accepting a light for her cigarette, sipping a martini, eating sole and chicken, always in repose while Huntoon did everything but wear his napkin for a hat to amuse her. He never seemed to get more than the pensive, vaguely detached smile.

One afternoon Cassidy went with Herb and she met Huntoon down on Wall Street. They took a cab and Cassidy flagged one, followed. This was a break in her pattern. They got out down at the tip of the island and took the ferry to Staten Island. Cassidy was thinking: love nest on Staten Island, and the thought made him sick. He didn't want her to sleep with Bryce Huntoon. He didn't want her to sleep with anyone. He wanted her to want him. He wished to God he had the nerve to have the affair with her that Terry figured they were having.

It was cold and windy on the ferry. Herb seemed to be taking pictures of everything but Cindy and Huntoon, but they were all he was shooting. Cassidy lurked far away, huddled inside his coat, stealing glances. He needn't have feared exposure. Huntoon couldn't take his eyes off her and she just listened to him and stared off across the choppy water. Cassidy felt his eyeballs freezing but when they went inside he was afraid they'd see him if he followed. His death of pneumonia would be on her head.

All they did was ride to Staten Island and turn around and come back. Whoopee.

Huntoon? What the hell was he supposed to be doing? All the time he watched them they never touched each other. He asked Herb what he made of it after two weeks.

"Damned if I know, Lew," he said. "The way she looks, the guy must be a homo. But whatever he is I'll bet he's not her Valentine, y'hear what I'm saying? Chemistry ain't there. No sparks. Whose fault, I dunno. But, God, is she built or something! No knockers but there's something about her. I break out in a sweat."

On the fifteenth day of surveillance Herb followed her to the Waldorf, where she met a different man for lunch.

Terry Leary.

Herb was a real soldier. He said he felt like a fool but he just kept shooting.

When they parted, Cindy Squires kissed Terry's cheek. In the photographs Herb developed that night Terry looked very pleased with himself.

•   •   •

When Cassidy got to the office the next morning, Olive Naismith looked up from her Underwood and stopped beating up on it. Clacking away, Olive was a furious typist. She was a pretty girl, very dark with a perfect oval face, like a cameo, hair so brown it might have been black, and large teardrop breasts hanging provocatively from narrow shoulders. He figured Terry probably slept with her from time to time and bought her the occasional fancy dinner. It was a cinch she wasn't working for Dependable Detective to get her hands on a vast salary. Terry also supplied her father with gas stamps from some private supply.

"You won't believe this," she whispered, casting her huge soft eyes toward the inner office, "but Himself slept in the office last night. He was working when I got here at eight to catch up on my typing."

"Tell me the truth, Olive. You volunteered to stay with him, comforting him with apples through the night—"

"Mr. Cassidy! Really!"

"I can't accept that as a denial, Olive. Sorry."

He found Terry in his shirtsleeves, with an overnight growth of stubble, and his perfect slick blond hair mussed from scratching his head. His fancy suspenders even looked slack, tired. He had the Max Bauman file open on the desk and a couple hundred eight-by-ten glossies strewn about. He was scribbling on a Big Five tablet and there were four cigar butts in the tractor tire. Never had a room smelled worse. Worse than old jersey and shoulder pads ever smelled. Cassidy threw open both windows and let the snow blow in off the cement ledge.

Terry looked up and yawned. "Little close in here, is it?"

Cassidy poured himself a cup of coffee.

"I had lunch with Cindy yesterday."

"I saw the pictures."

"Well, I got an earful from the woman in the case. She thinks Max is going nuts."

Cassidy sat down on the edge of the desk and began sorting through the photographs without really seeing them. Lunch at the Waldorf. They made a handsome couple. "He didn't seem so nuts when he came to us."

"Oh, I'm not so sure. I thought the Daughter-of-Time-Whore-of-Babylon routine came from the general direction of the moon—"

"Point taken. But that's talking crazy, not acting crazy. Acting crazy is eating breakfast out of your underpants. He's not sick," Cassidy said, "he's just in love."

"Not to hear her tell it. She's scared, right down to her shoes. Says he flies into uncontrollable rages. He smashed a Chinese vase worth ten grand—maybe *our* ten grand, for chrissakes—when she told him she *wasn't* having an affair with anyone. Then he fainted in the middle of dinner one night—scared her half to death; just fell into his apple pie in the middle of a sentence. She said this Bob Erickson character was there and carried him upstairs and put him to bed. Max didn't remember it in the morning. The thing is, Lew, a lot of his rage is directed at her . . . I'm thinking maybe she's right, maybe Max is headed 'round the bend. I've been trying to figure out what to do; that's

243

why I never got around to going home. I'm freezing my ass off, Lew."

Cassidy closed the window most of the way.

"Did you tell her we've been tailing her?"

"Yep. Mainly because Max hiring us fit right in with what she was telling me."

"And what did she say?"

"She was a little numb, didn't say much."

"You mention Huntoon?"

"Nope. Should have, I guess, but it seemed irrelevant by the time she'd gotten the load off her chest. I've got a plan, y'know."

"What am I gonna think of it?"

"Damned if I know, amigo."

•　•　•

She stood in the doorway with the lights of Washington Square behind her, snow falling hard, twinkling like diamonds in the mink. The collar was turned up, framing her face. She was so pale and immaculate she reminded him of the nuns of his childhood. Her mouth was tight, teeth behind the harsh lipstick chattering. She wore a beret tugged down on the almost white pageboy. She managed a small smile. "Lew," she whispered, and brushed past him into his darkened living room. "No, don't turn on the light. They could get here any moment, they could be watching—make me a drink . . . hurry, Lew . . ."

She was unsteady on her high heels, clung to the refrigerator door while he splashed Scotch over ice, then made one for himself. It was past midnight. She took the glass with both hands and drank deeply.

"I've run away, Lew. From Max, from Heliotrope, from all of it . . . I left my dressing room, out the back door, nobody saw me but they're bound to be looking for me by now . . . kiss me, Lew, hold me . . ."

He put his arms around her, felt the cold melting snow on his face. He held her, whispering to her until she stopped shaking.

"Lew, I didn't know where else to go; there wasn't

244

anybody but you I could go to. I love you, Lew, and now it's all up to you. I'm so scared . . . we can't let him find me, he'll kill me . . . you've got to hide me, take care of me." She finished her drink and sat down, staring at him. "Please, Lew. Say something—"

"Thinking," Cassidy said. "I've got just the place to stash you for the time being. Give us some breathing room—place in Connecticut, belongs to friends of mine who winter in Palm Beach. They always leave me a key so I can hide torch singers running away from gangster boyfriends—"

"We've got to hurry, Lew. He'll think of you and Terry. He'll be here looking for me."

Cassidy had just gotten into his coat, located his keys and gloves, when the telephone rang. He picked it up, faked a hearty yawn.

"Lew, sorry to wake you. This is Bob Erickson. I'm calling for Max—"

"Max? Max isn't here—what can I do for you, Bob?"

"No, Max is here. We've got a crisis on our hands, frankly. Max is pretty worked up. We can't find Miss Squires. She just disappeared from her dressing room. Damn strange . . . you there, Lew?"

"Sure, sure. Max think she was kidnapped maybe?"

"Why, I don't know—"

"It's possible, y'know, Bob. Max has enemies—"

"I think he's worrying about something else altogether."

"You do? Like what?"

"Hell, you know, Lew—another man. That's all he thinks about, another man." Erickson's voice had fallen to a whisper. "Max thinks she's got a boyfriend, Lew . . . he's going crazy with worry right now. He wants her back. He's going to find her, Lew, wherever she is—"

"What a mess . . . and nobody saw her leave—"

"She must have grabbed a cab . . . or had someone waiting for her. He says she's capable of anything." He sighed heavily beneath the weight of his problem. "Level with me, Lew. I know the kid's been wanting to make a break for it . . . she might turn to you for help—you or Terry Leary. If she came to you I think we can calm Max down, get her back—"

"Well, she hasn't come to me. I've been in bed for an hour. What's Terry say?"

"Max is trying to get hold of him right now."

"Look, more than likely she cracked under the strain of things with Max. Probably checked into a hotel for the night just to be alone and think things over. Or maybe she caught the late train up to Boston. She's got a kid brother at Harvard—"

"Say, that's a lead! Jesus, I hope you're right about that—that'd be perfect. She goes to see her brother. Can't get more innocent than that!" He sounded like a man who'd just noticed that his parachute had finally opened.

"Check up on it tomorrow," Cassidy said. "Keep Max under control—"

"Easier said than done. But thanks for the tip." He was about to hang up. "Oh, Lew. A word of advice—"

"Always welcome."

"Play straight with us on this, Lew. Max would be awfully disappointed if you didn't."

The line went dead.

•   •   •

She put her arm through his while they walked to the little Ford. She was still a little unsteady, wobbling on her heels. There were a few flakes of snow blowing around, landing in the mink. She held tight to his arm. She was scared. When she tried to talk, her voice shook and her teeth chattered and finally she gave it up. He kissed her and told her everything was going to be all right.

They were on the highway with New York disappearing in the darkness behind them. The Ford convertible had a few wind leaks so even with the heater on full blast it was cold in the car. They were playing Glenn Miller on the radio. She was toying with the blackthorn stick, withdrawing the sword a few inches, pushing it back in, again and again and again.

"Damn it," she said. "This isn't quite the way I wanted us to get together."

"Well, it wasn't going to happen at all—"

"Don't say that, I don't want to hear that. Anyway, you don't know. You can't know. I'd have figured out something else, sooner or later." She popped the button and the knob released on its spring. She pushed it back down, until it caught. "I feel terrible about Max. I don't know if I did the right thing . . . Would I have done it if you hadn't been there for me? Has Max really acted all that crazy? Or did I exaggerate just to make this happen . . ."

"I don't know. You sure convinced Terry."

"Is it too late to change it back? Undo it?" She gnawed at a gloved fingertip.

"Getting there."

"I don't know what I'll do. If I don't go back to Max . . . and I'm not, I'm out of that now. Out of Max's life, out of a job, I won't have much money."

"You'll get another job."

"Lew, you're not getting it, are you? Max is going to kill me when he realizes I'm not coming back."

"You're right, I'm not getting it. I thought we were getting you out of the way while Terry calms Max's nerves—"

"I suppose that's what Terry *does* think. He thinks I'll go back then. I'm telling you, I'll never go back. Do you get it now?"

He shook his head, watching the road disappear beneath the blowing snow.

"I want you, Lew. I couldn't wait any longer." She too was staring ahead into the night where the headlights stopped abruptly in the shifting wall of snow. "This is the only way I could think of, that's all." She sighed, bit at the thumbnail. "There's one problem, though—"

"At the very least," he said.

"Either I'm going to get killed . . . or Max is. The only way to keep me alive is for Max to die. If he lives, Lew, he'll kill me for leaving him. That's it. I'm just telling you how it is."

Listening to her, he saw in his mind the little girl sitting on the tombstone, swinging her legs.

• • •

The house was set at the top of a long sloping hill, on the crown of a rolling meadow which lay under a crisp, clean, deep snow cover. The snow shimmered, blue in the moonlight. They turned off the road and fit into the shallow ruts leading nearly a mile, a single lane, between two rows of stripped, wraithlike poplars. There was a barn behind the house. Cassidy got out, staggered in the blast of wind, and forced open the huge swinging door which stuck in the snow. He was just able to squeeze the car inside. The smell of cold hay and packed earth made him sneeze in the silence. She waited while he got her suitcase out of the trunk. Together they tramped across the driveway, hunched against the gale. The key worked in the side door and they went into the kitchen. The house was still, frigid, waiting.

The electricity worked. A long, two-story, lodge-style room had huge fireplaces at either end. There were several oil lamps with thickly smoked glass chimneys, colonial pine cabinets and tables, and hooked rugs the size of battleships. The firewood in the buckets was dry, the bark pulling away from the hard wood. The pantry held lots of cans. The caretaker who lived in town kept the refrigerator stocked for friends of the owners. All the faucets were running.

Cassidy built two fires and they sat before the flames waiting for the cold to leave them in peace. There were Grandma Moses and Currier & Ives prints, some other flat, depthless colonial paintings on the knotty-pine walls. Also a rack of guns on one wall above an antique cupboard with a marble splash back. The fire threw dancing, hypnotic shadows about the long room. She leaned into his arms. He kissed her and she held him longer than he'd ever been held. She was crying, the tears mingling in their mouths.

"Oh, God," she whispered, "I didn't know I'd be this

248

scared. It's been a game almost, planning how to get away from him, thinking about not having to face him every day and every night, thinking about how I wouldn't have to be afraid of his rage . . . it's the sex, that's what's done it to him. He's lost it, it's over for him and when he looks at me the humiliation he feels . . . it's driven him crazy." She sniffled, blew her nose, blinked at the tears. She laughed softly. "I'm pretty crazy, too. I haven't made love for so long, Cassidy . . . will you take a long time with me, go very slowly? Oh, I don't feel like a whore anymore, Cassidy, I feel like a little girl . . . oh, my, that's good, keep doing that, do that for a long time, oh, your teeth, I can feel your teeth, Cassidy . . . nibble me to death . . ." Her fingers were in his hair, holding him between the soft thighs, her flesh warmed by the flames and by the fires deep in her belly. After she'd come the first time, she lay panting, licking the taste of her orgasm from his mouth, whispering again and again, *I don't want to die, Cassidy, please don't let me die . . .*

Somewhere in the night their bodies joined again and voices were saying *I love you, I love you,* and he couldn't say who was talking, it didn't make any difference. By that time they'd become one, one voice, one creature, and they lay shivering despite the roaring fire. Those words . . . And now he knew he was scared, too. He had so damn much to lose.

In the shadows she whispered, "Let me be a whore for you now, just for you, just for a moment, I want you to do something for me . . ."

She led him to the bathroom. She sat on the toilet and parted her thighs. She was breathing hard, through her mouth. She pulled him down to kneel before her, half moaning, told him what she wanted. And he leaned into the heat of her, felt her fingers spreading the matted, damp hair, peeling herself open until he could put his mouth where she wanted. She was trembling, gasping, her soft little belly quivering, rocking back and forth, then she screamed down deep in her throat, said *I can't hold it, I can't hold back, oh, God, love me, love me no matter what I do, please love me*, and her orgasm seemed to tear her apart, tore the breath from her, and she came and came and her bladder emptied into the toilet and she pulled his face into her belly while she bent forward over him, her hands flat on his back, convulsing against him until she was empty and spent and he leaned back covered in sweat, hers and his, and rested against the wall. She dabbed tissue between her legs, flushed the toilet, and stood up, making herself small, huddling against him, burying her head on his chest. He felt her lips move against his flesh, "I'm so embarrassed," and he almost couldn't hear her. "I never did anything like that before . . . I never felt anything so violent inside me. Like I was coming apart . . . Are you disgusted?" He covered her mouth with his, picked her up in his arms, and carried her back into the shadowy room. He limped on the bad leg but he felt like the strongest, best man in the world. He put her down on the great rag rug before the fire and pulled their heavy coats over them. She fit herself against him, curled within his arms. "Cindy," he breathed into her delicate ear, "there is nothing, not one single thing, you could ever do, or ask me to do, that is anything but what I want . . . Nothing that is you could ever be other than what I want . . . nothing." He kissed her ear and she gave a deep sigh of contentment. He touched her mouth with his fingertips and felt her smile.

• • •

Cassidy woke first in the morning. The fires were still glowing, giving off warmth. Cindy lay on her side, mouth open an inch, wedges of white teeth peeking out, snoring softly like a little girl. He covered her back up with the mink and his heavy ulster, got dressed, and went out to the vast country kitchen. He made coffee and found some fresh bread, butter, strawberry jam, sugar, milk, and thanked God for the caretaker. Staring out into the gray, low-slung day, he sat at the rough-hewn kitchen table and drank the morning's first two cups of coffee. He checked his Hamilton against the ticking Regulator on the wall. It was 10:30.

Everything had gotten very complicated since yesterday. He hadn't thought he'd ever be involved in any way again—beyond longing for her like a lovesick fool—with Cindy Squires. He'd thought the surveillance of her would convince Max she wasn't running around on him, whether in his crazy jealousy he wanted it to or not, and now that had been blown to hell by her running away. He'd thought the war news was the most exciting thing in his immediate future. Like everybody else, he was thinking about when and where and how the Allies under Ike were going to invade Festung Europa. And he'd grown used to the thought that Karin would always be there, the central ache within him.

But all that was yesterday.

Now Cindy Squires had taken everything into her own hands and was raising all kinds of hell in all of their lives. He had to get it all clear as he could before he got run down in the panic.

First, Max loved but didn't trust Cindy, was sure she had another man. Either he was right, she was a liar, and the evidence of Herb Contreras's two weeks was worthless, or Max was obsessed by not being able to service her sexually. Or maybe it was all true—fair proof that there was no God.

Second, Cindy said Max was crazy, positively chewing the carpet, out of his head. She said she was scared of him and had to get away from him. But . . .

Third, Cassidy knew Cindy was scared. She was scared because she was convinced that Max was going to find her and kill her . . . precisely because she had made her own decision to leave him for good. So that made the question of Max's recent behavior oddly academic. He'd either let her go, sanely, wih a hearty good luck, which didn't sound like the Max who'd visited Dependable Detective . . . or he'd exact his revenge.

Fourth, there was Cassidy himself. He had no choice but to admit that she'd nailed him down, made him remember what he'd been trying to forget. He had fallen in love with her in the first place because of her looks, then because she appealed to his romantic nature in all the old ways. Love, sex, passion, her own kind of vulnerability, her open and savage eroticism. She seemed lost and of course he knew he alone could save her.

But could he trust her?

Hell, what did it matter? He loved her . . .

She'd never been anything but straight with him. He couldn't have lived with himself if he hadn't trusted her. Maybe she was using him, maybe he didn't know quite how. But everybody always used everybody. That was life. And love was love and he was stuck with it.

It had been a hell of a long time.

• • •

"What's the story with you and Bryce Huntoon?"

"That's right," she said, remembering. "You've been following me."

"Max is convinced you're having an affair with someone."

She nodded. They were sitting in a dim little Italian restaurant down the road toward the nearest town. The day had passed in the manner of days in love. He'd called Terry, told him where he was, that he'd be in town the next day. In the meantime Terry could handle Max, present him with the Boston scenario. Now they were finishing the linguini with clam sauce and a bottle of wine and were sitting over coffee, smiling, trying to enjoy being in love with the shadows of gunmen hanging over them. There was so much beneath the surface, an undertow they had to fight.

"Bryce is just a guy," she said. "Somebody to talk to. His biggest attraction, I suppose, is that he's not Max. He's working with Max on some defense effort stuff, or he was, and I kept seeing him. At the club, sometimes at the apartment or out at the house. So I was in a kind of frantic heat—there's no point in my lying to you, Cassidy. I haven't lied to you about anything and after last night it's

252

just too late to start now. I was in heat and Max was no use to me and I was afraid to drag you into the mess I was in. And, besides, I didn't think you'd do it. That's the truth. Anyway, Bryce was the only guy I could get to so I put quite a bit of pressure on him. I didn't beg him to take me to bed . . . you're the only man I've ever begged, ever wanted to beg. But I let Bryce know that I wanted it." She shook her head sadly. "He's such a regular Joe, sort of pompous, pretty innocent. And when he got the message he sat me down and told me that he would enjoy enjoying me, that's exactly what he said, but he told me a man has a code and one of the things in the code was that you didn't betray a friend. And he looked upon Max as a friend. He said it was simply impossible. He was always shaking hands with me. Very sweet man. So I respected all that and asked if we could be friends and he said of course. And I stopped thinking of him as a potential lover . . . and I knew then that he'd only have been a poor substitute for you, knew then that I had to get away from Max and my time was running out. I was serious, I knew I had to make you understand that what I felt for you was real, that I wasn't just a whore . . . and to do all that I had to be alone with you. Oh, Lew, I was a whore with Max . . . but I wanted to be a woman. I had to be a woman with you, you wouldn't have settled for anything less." She took his hand across the table and squeezed it. "Get it?"

"Got it," he said.

The next day Terry called and told Cassidy to get back to New York. Everything was falling into place and he needed his partner.

CHAPTER FOURTEEN

The big pearl-gray cat was blinking slowly, bored by the pre-cocktail hour lull. The lobby bar of the Algonquin was quiet, no glittering crossfire of sarcasm from the famous wits who always had their names in the columns. Cassidy was nursing a Rob Roy and playing mind games with the cat, Hamlet. He was losing because he was too proud to admit he was pitting his will against a cat's. Hamlet was winning because Hamlet just plain didn't give a shit. You could learn a lot from Hamlet if you were smart enough in the first place. Cassidy wasn't, so he read the *Mirror* until Terry showed up.

He ordered a martini, filled his mouth with peanuts, and leaned back, red-eyed and weary. "Lew," he said, "I'm not absolutely crazy about the way this one's working out. I'm having to think too damn hard, it's complicated. When it doesn't come easy I'm always suspicious. Thing is, I'm trying to save your ass and everybody else's, too, but it's . . . sticky. Still"—he took the drink directly from the waiter's tray and had a healthy slug—"I've got it figured.

Absent friends," he said as always, lifting the glass. "How did it go out there?"

"Fine. She's just fine. Scared, worried. She says she's not going back to Max. Regardless."

He lit one of his long Dunhill cigarettes. "She in love?"

"Let's not have another seminar on love—"

"Just asking, don't get shirty with me, Lew. I'm on your side. She in love?"

"Says she is."

"Anyone we know?" Terry grinned beneath the sleek moustache. "What's the matter with you, anyway?"

"Maybe I'm getting my period . . . or maybe I want to know what Max is planning."

"Huntoon—she saying anything about Brother Huntoon?"

"They were friends, that's all. She thought he was sweet and pompous."

"So she was half right. Hmmm, friends." He thought about that and sipped the martini. Hamlet had strolled over and was smelling Terry's cuffs. Hamlet had always liked Terry. "You believe her?"

"Yeah, I believe her. She was straight with me. She tried to seduce him but he wasn't in the market."

"No kidding? Hard to believe. Don't you find that just a tad unlikely? A little saintly for Brycie-boy?"

"He said it would violate his code."

Terry laughed. "You kidding me? You gotta be kidding me, amigo. When it comes to women, as it often does with our Bryce, his code is 'Get 'em while you can' and it always has been . . . but that's what he told her?"

"That's it."

"Well." He took his turn staring at Hamlet, who did a coy number, licking the long tail. "Makes me think I'm right. About human nature."

"Come again?"

"About people. Cindy and Huntoon. They were having an affair."

"You're wrong, Terry. Dead wrong."

"You romantic devil, you," he said. "Funny how a really

beautiful woman can convince a guy she's honest as she is beautiful."

"Terry, you're right on the edge—"

"That's where it's best. That's where you can really live, amigo, out there on the edge." He was grinning. "Come on, relax! I'm just thinking out loud. Maybe you're right. I like Cindy, don't get me wrong. But I think we'd better check, just to get our ducks in a row. Like I told you, I've got this plan. Want to hear it?"

"Sure, sure." Terry was getting under his skin. Maybe it was just Cindy, she was the one who was getting at him, making him jumpy. "But let's leave her out of it."

"As much as possible, of course." He ran a knuckle along that thin moustache. "We're going to check out Huntoon's little *pied-à-terre* up on East 62nd. I think maybe they were having an affair. You say no and you're probably right. But I'd like to ease my mind. So I want to know if she's spent any time at his place. You grant me that?"

"Waste of time."

"Maybe. But we gotta have some results for Max. I've thought it over and we're gonna have to give him old Bryce."

"I'm not surprised you don't much like your plan. I don't like it either."

"No. You wouldn't. But my point is, if we have to give Max someone, and that someone happens to be Huntoon, it might be nice if he's actually guilty. See?"

"Nobody's innocent, Terry. You know that."

"Ah, the voice of experience. But if there's stuff of Cindy's at his place . . ." He shrugged. "And if there isn't anything, you might as well get used to the idea that we'll have to salt the place."

"Like salting a gold mine? When there isn't any real gold?"

"Such a smarty."

"I can't let you do that, Terry—"

"Ease up, will ya? We'll cross that one when we come to it. Just remember, Max said he wanted some proof—"

"We're not going to plant evidence incriminating Cindy

. . . and, anyway, you've got the photographs of them together. Give those to Max if you have to—"

"We may need something better than that. And we don't *have* to incriminate Cindy, amigo. Max has already decided she's guilty. We're incriminating Huntoon . . . instead of letting Max figure out it's you she loves. Get it through your head—Max has decided about Cindy! All we can do for a first step is fill the other opening. And don't forget the ten grand . . ." He munched another handful of peanuts.

"This is bad. I don't like it—"

"There are worse things, amigo. Like we don't give Max what he wants and he decides to go looking for himself. And sooner or later he comes down on one very scared Lew Cassidy. We really wouldn't want that, would we?" The place was filling up. Soon the *bon mots* would be filling the air. Hamlet had already slouched away in search of safety. "Max can be a very uncivilized fellow when the going isn't so good."

"So what about Huntoon? You're setting him up to be killed!"

"Hey, come on. This is Terry, remember? I'm one of the good guys."

"Then give me the rest of the plan."

"Huntoon won't have any trouble with Max. He can just lay low in Washington for a while. Max'll get interested in something else. Lew, I'm gonna *warn* Bryce. Whattaya think I am, anyway?"

"And what about Cindy?"

"We'll work that out, too."

"She says Max'll kill her—"

"No, no, he's not gonna kill Cindy. He may be crazy but he's not that crazy. He loves her. I can talk him out of that, if I have to."

"Cindy says Max dies or she dies, no other way."

"So who says she's the big expert all of a sudden? I know about these things. She's just being overly dramatic—"

"It's no act," Cassidy insisted.

"Well, I've got Elmo glued to Max—"

"You've *what*?"

"Andretti. I've got him on Max so we can head off any trouble. So far all I know is that this Erickson character never leaves his side. Who *is* he?"

"I can't imagine."

"I want to find out," he mused.

That night Terry told Cassidy he'd arranged to have lunch the next day with Bryce Huntoon, just two friends getting together at Costello's to catch up on things.

While they lunched Cassidy would use Terry's lockpick and go through Huntoon's place. Cassidy told him it was a fool's errand, a waste of time. Terry asked him to humor him, go have a look, just in case. "What's to lose?" he asked as they parted back on 44th Street. It was a cold and windy night and he thought about Cindy, alone in the country, in front of the fire he'd laid for her before returning to town. When he got home he called her to say good night. She was already asleep but she whispered sweet nothings into the phone. He damn near got in the Ford and drove out there.

He should have. He should have gone and taken her away and never come back, headed west until they hit the beach at Malibu. He'd have saved all those people who were right on the verge of getting killed because of her . . .

But, of course, he didn't. You just didn't do things like that.

• • •

He dialed Costello's from a telephone booth on the corner of 63rd and Lex. Terry came to the phone and said that Colonel Huntoon was at that very moment awaiting his corned beef and cabbage. "I'm not going to find anything," Cassidy said. "You know that." But Terry told him just to pop in, have a look around, check the drawers, closets, and particularly the bathroom.

It was a small brownstone, chopped into eight tiny flats. He checked the number on the mailbox, let himself into the front hallway, climbed the stairs to number six. The wallpaper was striped and the carpet flowered.

Inside the apartment the shades were drawn. The room was neat and clean, devoid of any sense of life. A clock ticked. The room and its contents might have been purchased directly from a shop window. The carpet was pale and thick. The lamps were sleek ceramic ladies on tiptoe, reminiscent of the twenties. The couch was soft and blotched with big hungry-looking flowers. Lots of blond wood curled around them and held the package together. It didn't look as if anyone had ever actually sat on it. A couple of standard reproductions of vaguely jungle-ish scenes with big cats staring out hung on the pale gray walls within their blond scrubbed wood frames. The kitchen gave the overall impression that no one had ever eaten a meal in the flat, either. A couple of bottles of Scotch, a White Horse and a Black and White, stood on the counter. In the fridge he found cheese, apples, a bottle of champagne, some butter. A carton of Camels. A bottle of milk.

In the bedroom everything began to fall apart.

The double bed was unmade. One pillow was smeared with dark red lipstick. A woman's nightgown, black and filmy, lay across the rumpled sheet. It was hot in the bedroom. A pair of panties and a slip hung on the back of a chair. Saks and Bergdorf's. On the bedside table there was a box of Trojan rubbers, opened. On the table at the other side of the bed was a jar of hand cream.

The bathroom. A pair of woman's stockings hung over a towel rack. Under the sink a box of Kotex, almost empty. In the medicine cabinet a tube of dark red lipstick, new. A thick tortoiseshell comb lay on the washstand. A strand or two of long, almost white hair, soft and silky, was entwined among the teeth.

There was a small bottle of perfume on the back of the washbasin. He withdrew the stopper and held the bottle to his nose. It was the kind of bottle a woman carries in her purse, an amber glass bottle encased in elegant silver filigree. She would transfer her perfume to such a delicate container, using a miniature silver funnel. He stood smelling the exquisite, familiar, unmistakable scent . . . remembered seeing the bottle somewhere before . . .

He stayed in the bathroom for a long time. He tried to take it like a man, tried to be tough-minded and realistic. Then he went to the toilet, leaned over, legs shaking, and vomited.

•   •   •

Back at the office Terry found Cassidy at his desk staring out the window. "You, my friend," he said, "look like hell." He went to his desk, looked back as if he'd felt a sudden twinge from the bullet he carried around. "Uh-oh," he said.

"You can say that again," Cassidy said.

"Okay, I get the picture. Buck up, come on, come on. We're going out for a bracer. Rub o' the Brush."

Cassidy had to smile at that, no matter what. Terry the movie fan, quoting one of his favorites. Walter Brennan as Judge Roy Bean in *The Westerner*. Gary Cooper took a drink at the judge's bar, asked what the judge called the stuff. *Rub o' the Brush*. He had to smile.

Ten minutes later they were sitting in a dark little dive just below street level, in a black leather booth, and Cassidy had a fiery brandy burning in his belly. He'd muttered the story of Huntoon's flat during the first brandy and Terry had had another one set up for him.

"Believe me, Lew. I'm sorry as hell." He sighed philosophically. "Max's Law. Never trust a woman. Love 'em, hate 'em, worship them . . . just don't trust 'em."

"I believed her," Cassidy said. "I was so damn sure."

"You can't hold it against her. Well, it didn't make any sense that he turned her down—I mean, my God, amigo, just look at her. Look at a woman like Cindy just once and you get cracks in your walls, look twice and the old code's straight out the window." He fished one of the huge cigars out of his pocket, clipped the end, lit it.

"But why would she lie to me?"

"Come off it," Terry said. "She loves you. She's made a

260

hell of a big deal out of getting you. Now she wants you to trust her, love her back. She doesn't want you sitting around thinking about Huntoon humping away on her. She knows men, she knows it'd eat at you. So she told you half the story—the half that strikes her as important, her real misbehavior—but had to stop there, leaving out what's for her unimportant."

"Bullshit. Looked like she'd been there recently. But we had Herb on her . . . so when?"

Terry shrugged. "The point is now she's made her move with you, she's done with her military service." He grinned at that. "Count on it. Take her at her word—"

"I did. And she lied to me—"

"Not that word. The other word. That she loves you. That's the word that matters."

"It doesn't work that way. She used to tell me she was a whore. Now she says she stopped, but she hasn't. She had to have somebody and she picked Huntoon. It could have been anyone, he happened to be handy—"

"Look, grow up, Lew! She's a woman. Everybody's got woman problems. They're like that. They're frightened, they're confused, they need someone to hold them, sometimes it doesn't matter who it is. Sometimes it's easier if it's someone they don't care about—"

"But you were right. You said she was having him and I said impossible, can't be true, not my Cindy. And you were right, goddamn it!"

"Drink your brandy, Lew."

They sat in the booth quietly drinking, watching the feet kicking through the slush at eye level past the window, listening to Helen O'Connell sing "Green Eyes" and Bing sing "Where or When." Somebody kept feeding nickels into the box and Bing kept singing the same song over and over again. A couple of navy officers were sitting at the bar calmly getting smashed. Terry said they were drinking because of women. An army officer was sitting in a booth across the way, holding a girl's hand. Her hair was piled on top of her head and she was wearing pearls and one of those sad wartime smiles you saw everywhere, in every bar in town, on every railway platform, on the faces of the women looking over their guys' shoulders on the dance floor. Terry and Cassidy should have been at war, doing something to help win the damn thing, whip the Huns and the Nips so all the boys could come home again. They should have been off doing their bit somewhere, scared out of their wits but still getting on with it. Fate, or destiny, had kept them out of it and most of the time Cassidy tried not to dwell on it, most of the time he was glad, way deep down. But just then he didn't much like it. Not just because of Cindy but because of Cindy and Karin and her father and . . . Mainly because he felt like a piece somehow misplaced on the game board. Nothing but the war seemed to make any sense or any difference about much of anything and he thought about what Bogart said to Bergman at the end of *Casablanca*, the movie everybody was seeing and crying over. Bogey was right. The problem of a few little people didn't amount to a hill of beans in this crazy, mixed-up world . . . but Cassidy was stuck with this particular hill of beans, no way out of it. And the crazy part of it was this: It was getting dangerous and scary, just like the big war outside. They had their own little war to deal with and it occurred to him that it didn't matter where or when you got killed. Fate had spared them the war. Maybe because fate had something else just as bad in mind. Whatever it was, you'd be the same kind of dead. Dead was dead. Going, going, gone.

• • •

He sat at his desk and listened to Terry's end of the conversation.

"Bryce, it's Terry . . . yeah, great seeing you, right, we oughtta do it more often . . . look, Bryce, I just heard about a little problem that's come up; I thought I'd call you right away . . . well, to be frank, it's about Max . . . oh no, he's well enough so far as I know, but he's in something of a bad humor . . . yes, not good, I agree, not good at all, he needs time to cool off . . . yes, well, you see it does concern you in a way . . . no, more directly than that, I'd say . . . ahhh, sure, of course . . . well, it all comes back to Cindy, surprise, surprise . . . thing is, he's gotten the idea that you and Cindy, Cindy and you, have been seeing each other . . . look, Bryce, I'm talking about an affair, sleeping together . . . don't ask me, but he's dead certain and he's loaded for bear . . . look, I'm not accusing you of anything, believe me, old man, I'm just telling you what Max is saying and thinking. It's Max and you know how Max gets . . . oh, I understand, it's all a terrible mistake, it's just that Max gets a little unpredictable . . . yes, okay, but I don't advise trying to make him listen to reason right this very minute, if you know what I mean . . . sure, in fact that's why I called. My advice is to get back to Washington and lay low for a while; it'll blow over. Lew and I are going to see him and try to talk some sense to him . . . oh, Good Lord, don't thank us, it's the least we can do . . . well, maybe you're right about that but I have my doubts; if I were you, I'd take it pretty damn seriously . . . I'm aware that this is the twentieth century, Bryce, but I'm also aware that Max doesn't figure the number of the century has much to do with you and Cindy . . . okay, old-timer, think about it mighty long and hard . . . my advice is Washington and don't spare the horses . . . sure, Bryce, you're very welcome, right, right, I'll be in touch. Adios, Bryce."

Terry looked at Cassidy and stroked his moustache. He shrugged. "He'll go, once he thinks about it. Can't say he hasn't been warned." He stretched, worked his stiff shoulders. "On the other hand, I'm not his keeper. I did what I could." He looked at his watch. "Come on, we got work to do, Lew."

• • •

The wind was whipping furiously, blowing the snow in sheets from the heavy boughs of the evergreens, blowing tumbleweeds of snow across the icy black driveway. Cassidy turned the Ford between the stone gatehouses and headed up toward the mansion, which glowed merrily in the dark—like a wonderful doll's house, full of joy, a child's dream. He parked at the front and followed Terry up the steps, across the balustrade to the sliver of light where an English butler called Bivins held the door ajar for them. "Mr. Bauman is in the game room," he intoned while he took their coats and put them on thick wooden hangers. "Please, follow me," he said, vastly dignified. He was tall, ramrod stiff, a fair-haired version of Arthur Treacher playing Jeeves. All his life Cassidy had dreamed of having a Jeeves or a Bivins of his own. Cindy Squires had had one within her grasp and had thrown it away. Following Bivins he imagined her in this house, catered to, feared, Max Bauman's wife; it would all have been hers. And she'd run out on him. And screwed the Colonel and screwed Cassidy and lied to him and driven Max nuts and got Cassidy to beat Bennie so badly he'd have been better off under a marker at Mount Olivet.

"This way, gentlemen." Bivins took a sharp left and pushed on toward a doorway beyond which a billiard table sat like an oasis. Cassidy hoped Max wasn't in the mood to kill the bringers of bad tidings.

They went in, drawn by the clicking of the balls on the emerald felt. Max was leaning on his cue. He was wearing a wine-red velvet smoking jacket. An ascot of paisley design was knotted at this throat, a white shirt, the black trousers to his dinner clothes. He was smoking one of the gigantic Havanas. His hair was carefully in place. He nodded to them, put a finger to his lips for quiet. He looked a hundred years old.

Bob Erickson was leaning over a shot. He made an easy, gentle stroke, a bank shot which turned out well. He looked immensely pleased when Max said, "Bravo," very softly.

In the shadows a figure moved, someone Cassidy hadn't seen. Terry saw the shifting figure, too, turned, almost startled by it. The man moved into the penumbral light cast by the lamps hung low over the table. He wore a vast formal shirt like a glacier drifting in the darkness, crossed by the black harness of a shoulder holster. He moved slowly like a dream of death. Max was smiling as if he'd remembered a much-loved old joke which just might be on his visitors.

"Hello, Terry," the big man said, turning. "Lew."

It was Bennie the Brute.

He wasn't selling toys anymore.

"You're looking good, kid," Terry said. "Back in the ice business. Took my advice, I see."

Max said, "Bennie's come home. Back where he belongs. A loyal knight. There's always a place for Bennie here. Isn't that right, Bennie?"

Bennie's eyes were wide and innocent behind the round lenses. The big nose like a zucchini and the polka-dot bow tie, what the well-dressed knight was wearing that season. With a shoulder holster. "That's right, Mr. Bauman."

"Good to see you, Bennie," Cassidy said.

Bennie's eyes, like ice cubes, turned. "Is it, Lew?"

There was one of those endless moments while Cassidy's life passed before his own eyes making faces at him. The gun in the pocket of his jacket felt much too heavy to lift.

Max broke the spell.

"So you've come with a report for me. Bob, some of that fine old armagnac for Terry and Lew, please."

They sat with their glasses at a round poker table.

"Please, Terry, you may speak freely with Bob and Bennie, they know the situation."

"You're not gonna like it, Max."

"I didn't expect to like it."

The wind sprayed dry snow, rattling like sand, at the windows. Cassidy's hands were sweaty and cold. Bennie leaned on the billiard table, arms folded like oars across his chest. Watching the men at the table. Watching. What was left of his memory, what had come back to him? What was going on behind the plate in his dented skull, in what was left of his brain?

"It's Colonel Huntoon," Terry said.

Max sighed, leaning back in his chair, propping his fingertips together on his smoking jacket, beneath the ascot.

"Proof?" he inquired. "Is she with him now?"

"Photographs of them out on the town together. Her things in his apartment." Terry shrugged fatalistically. "She's done a fade . . ."

"Colonel Huntoon enjoyed my confidence," Max reflected. "Even my friendship. What kind of world is this? Is trust dead? Is honor a rotting corpse? Let me tell you, it makes me want to weep for the death of trust and honor . . . even among men, friends . . ."

Bob Erickson looked from Max to Terry to Cassidy, his forgettable face bland and objective like a banker considering your loan application and deciding how best to give you the bad news. Bennie was breathing through his mouth like a man who should have had his adenoids fixed in childhood.

"Look, Max," Terry said, "give it a couple days. Cindy's just a kid when you stop and think about it. Kids make mistakes, you gotta make allowances." There was sweat beading on Terry's forehead. "And Huntoon? He's nothing, just a big jerk in a fancy uniform. Tell him to get his ass down to Washington and stay there. Cindy? Hell, Max, forgive and forget . . . she's a kid, forget her, she's not enough woman for a man like you—"

Max put him out of his misery. "Be quiet, son. I know you're trying to help. But you've done your job, I appreciate your efforts. And yours, Lew. But you're not my spiritual adviser, Terry. You'll have my check tomorrow. Now I think you'd better go. Just go. And thank you, both of you."

He didn't stand up. Bob Erickson made to see them out. Bennie nodded as they passed. His eyes never left Cassidy.

They were halfway down the hall when there was a god-awful scream behind them, then the smashing of glass on glass, a window being broken, then the splintering of a cue on wood. The scream grew into an animal howl of anguish. Cassidy turned to look back, saw Bennie standing in the doorway, slowly closing the door.

Bob Erickson hastened them along. "Mr. Bauman's just not himself tonight, I'm afraid. We're going to have to find the girl. I don't think she went to Boston, Lew . . . but Max says he wants to go up there himself and look around—he's in a bad way."

At the front door there was no Bivins. Erickson found their coats and held them. "Allow me," he said, good-naturedly, worry showing through. Cassidy slid his arms into the sleeves while Erickson held the blackthorn stick in one hand. "I once knew a man who had a stick like this. There was a flask concealed inside. Ingenious. Do you have a flask in yours, Lew?"

"Not in mine, I'm afraid."

Terry said, "Tell me, Mr. Erickson, who the devil are you?"

Bob Erickson gazed at him, a flicker of surprise crossing his plain, solid face. "Why, you might say I am merely a hewer of wood and carrier of water for Mr. Bauman. Thank you for coming, gentlemen. Your efforts are much appreciated." He opened the thick front door and a blast of wind swept in like the souls of the dead looking for peace or maybe a game of billiards. "Good night, drive carefully," he said.

They got into the convertible, felt it buffeted by the gale. Cassidy turned the wipers on and they whisked the thin layer of dusty snow from the windshield. He started the engine. Terry let out the sigh of a lifetime.

"Get us the hell out of here," he said.

• • •

They were back at the office by ten o'clock. The lights were all on. Elmo Andretti was drinking coffee from a chipped mug, making small talk with Olive, who was always willing to work late and hard.

"What's going on?" Cassidy said to Elmo. "You're supposed to be keeping an eye on Bauman."

"Well, boss, since you guys went out there I figured I'd have a decent dinner for a change, meet you back here, then go pick up on Max at the club. I got something I thought you might want to know."

267

Terry was already at the coffee, warming his hand on the cup. "Like what, Elmo?"

"I think Bauman is sick or something," Elmo said.

"Do tell!" Terry had regained the ability to grin, which had been in eclipse on the ride back into the city. "Psychotic would be more like it. We left him just now. Smashing up the furniture and howling at the wind. Bennie's back as Official Keeper so far as I can tell . . ." He whistled and started pouring sugar into his coffee until it thickened.

Cassidy said, "What's the story, Elmo?"

"Well, it's like this. He's been going to this building way up on Madison. Every day, see. I figured he was seeing a friend or something, it's an apartment building. But just for the hell of it I went up and looked at the tenant list and there's this doctor, one Maurice Epstein. So I called him from the corner as soon as I saw Bauman and his shadow, that Erickson character, leave. I just asked the nurse if Mr. Bauman was still there, I had a message for him . . . bingo, pay dirt! She said what a shame, I'd just missed him." Elmo smiled at his audience. "Not so bad, right? So I figure the guy's sick. It's the only interesting thing I've found out about him—oh, except last night, he and Bennie were at the club having a heart-to-heart—get this—with none other than Harry Madrid! And damned if Max didn't start crying . . . they helped him back to the office. I'm telling you guys, this is one sick gangster—"

"Damn fine work, Elmo," Cassidy said. "Now, what kind of a doctor is this Maurice Epstein?"

"Expensive, I'll bet," Olive said.

"I figured you could just look him up in some directory. I think it just said M.D."

"It's okay, Elmo." Terry looked at Cassidy. "The night is young. We ride, amigo!"

•　•　•

Forty minutes later they were standing in the cold across Madison from Dr. Maurice Epstein's office. The doorman was finishing a thermos of coffee, shaking the last few drops into the silvery tin cap which had a handle and served as a cup. Nobody had gone in or out of the building in the twenty minutes they'd been pretending to have a friendly chat in the middle of the screaming wind. Cassidy kept thinking what it must be like in the house in Connecticut with the wind whistling across the blue snow. He hadn't called her all day. She must be wondering what was going on and for a moment he forgot about Huntoon's apartment, the panties and the lipstick and the rumpled sheets and the perfume. And then he got to thinking about Max crying on Harry Madrid's shoulder. Harry Madrid and Max. The idea made him colder than the night. Why had Harry Madrid gone to Max . . .

"Won't be long now," Terry said. "This guy has got to take a leak soon. All that coffee. I gotta piss just watching him."

Ten minutes later the doorman laid down his *Journal-American* and went into the inner lobby, passed from view. Terry was leading the way across the street, clapping his gloved hands to warm them up. He picked the door lock in maybe eight seconds and they were inside. It was quiet. The doctor's office was at the end of a hallway leading off to the left from the core of elevators. The office door lasted four seconds, tops.

It was like every doctor's office in New York. A receptionist's desk, a bank of filing cabinets, a stack of *Collier's*es and *Saturday Evening Posts* from six months ago, a couple of prints of gondoliers in Venice, a potted fern that looked like it needed the doctor's help, like it wouldn't last out the night. The file cabinets were the old wooden variety. They had locks but they probably hadn't been used in twenty years. There were even little cards with letters of the alphabet taped to the drawers. Max Bauman was in the first drawer.

Terry sat on the receptionist's desk and read the notes, all neatly typed, and handed the pages to Cassidy as he finished each one.

A lot of it was mumbo jumbo. A lot of it wasn't.

The previous October Max Bauman had gone to see Dr.

Epstein complaining of dizzy spells, extremely painful headaches, fainting spells, short-term memory lapses, loss of his sense of taste, increasing loss of the sense of smell. The symptoms had been coming on for six months or so. Dr. Epstein had run a torrent of tests and diagnosed the problem. A Dr. Wagenecht had even done a little digging in Max's cranium while his friends had thought he was on a sudden, urgent business trip to Arizona right before Halloween. The hairpiece must have been used to cover the scars. He hadn't been thinning down for Cindy Squires. He was losing weight because he was dying. An inoperable, malignant brain tumor in an advanced stage.

According to Maurice Epstein, Max Bauman wasn't going to see the spring of 1944.

According to Maurice Epstein, Max Bauman's brain was in a kind of violent convulsive state. He'd prescribed a couple of drugs which might calm him down but Epstein noted that he was afraid Max wouldn't take the medication since it might also turn him into something indistinguishable in all the ways that mattered from a Hubbard squash. The doctor's fear, he confided to his file, was that Mr. Bauman could possibly—given the nature of his personality and the symptoms already observed—lose himself in erratic, uncontrollable, violent rages . . .

Maurice Epstein sure had Max's number.

If Max was about to go, he might just as well take as many folks with him as he could.

CHAPTER FIFTEEN

Fate is funny.

Olive Naismith woke up early and couldn't get back to sleep. Her job interested her and she realized she could start rearranging the files if she went into work right away, before anybody else got there, so she was the first person to arrive for work in the Dalmane Building the next day. Because she was so conscientious she killed a man before she opened the office door. She did it but the crazy part of it was that she didn't know she'd done it. It was all a bad joke.

• • •

Midmorning. Terry was already on his second cigar and the office was thick with blue smoke. They were trying to devise some plan to deal with Max. They weren't having much luck. Cindy was still safe in the country, if not in Cassidy's heart, which felt like the A train had run over it, and maybe Max was still hoping she was in Boston visiting her brother. But, inevitably, he would start look-

271

ing for Bryce Huntoon . . . Soon. Very soon. Terry was blowing giant smoke rings.

"Everything's different now, that's the problem," Cassidy said.

Terry nodded glumly.

"We gave Huntoon to Max because you could talk Max out of actually going after him with a tommy gun. Now we know that we're dealing with a different, new Max, a Max with his brain in the red zone. So everything's quite different."

Terry nodded again, crossed his Florsheims on top of his leather-rimmed desk blotter. "But the idea is still the same. Once Huntoon gets out of town, gets back to Washington, the pot comes off the boil."

"Suppose—just suppose—Max figures out you can get to Washington from New York, what then?"

"I say out of sight, out of mind. Maybe Bryce is gone already. I've had Olive ringing him all morning. No answer." He fell silent.

"He'd be safer in England," Cassidy said. "Do you think Ike could use him? I'll bet Bryce would have lots of good ideas about invading Europe . . . or maybe combat in the South Pacific. He'd be better off taking his chances with the Japs—"

"Relax, Lew. It's gonna be okay. Maybe Max'll die—hey, you never thought of that. One of those half-assed out-of-his-head rages, breaks a couple of billiard cues over Bennie's metal head and, wham, apoplexy . . . he drops dead. Don't give up hope. Could happen."

They were still sitting in morbid silence pinning their hopes on an apoplectic stroke when Otto Birdall, the building maintenance super, showed up. He was white as the driven slush and his mouth was dry. He kept licking his lips and it didn't do any good. He said he had something he wanted them to see. He'd come to them first because they were detectives. He said it was the goldarnedest thing he'd ever seen and he'd seen plenty in his day. He said they couldn't take the elevator down. He'd had to shut it off. So they walked down, not so easy for Cassidy with his stick.

They followed Otto down the stairway to the lobby, then through another metal door and down the utility stairs to the basement. The boilers made the concrete room an inferno. They all began sweating right away. They went through another metal door and down a final flight of steel stairs to the subbasement. "Over here," Birdall puffed, pointing through an ancient brick keystone arch caked black with coal dust. The air contained particles of dust and the whole place shook with the rumble of subway trains. He flipped a switch. "In there. You go look. Once is enough for me."

They stepped into a narrow kind of pit which housed the base of the elevator shaft. The steel frame bounding the shaft at ankle level was sunk into concrete. Just above their heads were the protrusions from the frame that marked the farthest point of the cage's descent. At that level the door would open into the basement. All of which was well and good but who cared? What mattered lay at their feet, tied with heavy, greasy rope to the bottom frame of the elevator's skeleton.

The rope was tied tightly both to the frame and a man's ankles. It had rubbed through his socks and bitten into the flesh all the way to the bone. The crosspiece of the frame was bowed slightly as if pulled out of shape by Charles Atlas. The rest of the body was wearing an army officer's uniform, one of about a million wandering around New York.

Then came the bad part. The smell of blood was everywhere. The uniform was soaked with all the indignities of his death, the blood and urine and feces. Cassidy couldn't imagine what had happened to the top of the guy. There wasn't any head. The body lay crumpled and at the shoulders just a terrible, spongy, bloody mess, like nothing he'd ever seen in his worst nightmares. It was like a battlefield casualty. There were sharp collarbones jabbed up through his coat, splintered to the width of chopsticks and ripping the woolen fabric. Something which might

273

have been part of his spine stuck up out of the pulp which had once been a throat. He turned away but not before that one indescribable horror had impressed itself on his mind. He knew it would be there forever.

"Now, lookee here," Otto Birdall said from behind them. He pulled a lever which reactivated the elevator. The motor clanged on and it began its slow descent from far above. When it reached the level of the first floor, Cassidy thought he saw something moving, swinging like a hanging fern, from the bottom of the cage. It kept coming closer until the cage reached the brakes and stopped with a jolt a couple of feet above their heads. There was something hanging there, all right.

Terry gagged reflexively and Cassidy heard him exercising his will, grinding his teeth. Cassidy tasted bile. His mouth was about to turn inside out. The blackthorn stick slipped from his hand and clattered on the frame. Otto Birdall retrieved it, handed it to him. Terry gave in and puked on the gritty floor, stood gagging.

A head dangled from a rope tied to the undercarriage of the elevator cage. A head which looked like a ghoul's handiwork, distorted almost beyond recognition. A head and some stuff hanging from it, bloody, shredded stuff. The eyes had come loose, burst from their sockets, hung like wet marbles on the cheeks. The sockets were dark and clotted. The face was empurled with exploded veins. Teeth had bitten through the lips, through the rags which had been jammed into the mouth. The skull gleamed through the rips in the pink, lacerated flesh. Still, even with the distortion of the death agony, Cassidy recognized the face.

Colonel Bryce Huntoon's war was all over. It had indeed been hell.

•　　•　　•

It took awhile to piece it together.

Birdall called the police and they came and saw and turned the Dalmane Building into a stockade for the rest of the day. Cassidy stayed out of it altogether and Terry acknowledged that he knew the deceased but had no idea

why he'd been killed or why he'd met his end in the
Dalmane Building. The cops wasted lots of time questioning everybody in the place.

The story came clear and, in the privacy of their office,
Cassidy and Terry made their own additions and specula-
tions. Pops Dunleavy, the night super, reported that
Huntoon had come in late, around midnight, and said he
was leaving a message for one of the tenants. He wanted to
slip it under the door and Pops figured he was a bird
colonel or a brigadier, somebody he sure as the devil
wasn't going to argue with.

Pops went on making some pin money cleaning up a
couple of offices and about an hour later he heard several
men, four he thought, leaving the building. He hadn't been
around for their arrival so he figured they'd come from
one of the offices where they'd worked late. He hadn't seen
the colonel again, assuming he'd left.

Elmo Andretti had been up at Heliotrope waiting for
Max and his praetorian guard to show up but they hadn't.
Elmo had debated dropping by the office but it was one
o'clock in the morning and he'd had a brutal day. So he
went home, thus avoiding pressing the up button which
would have torn Huntoon's head from his body.

Terry and Cassidy had stopped at Muldoon's for a beer
and a cheeseburger after reading Dr. Epstein's file on Max
Bauman. They, too, had gone home. Cassidy had lain in
bed thinking about Cindy, wanting to call her, wanting to
hear her voice, knowing he mustn't . . . while Bryce
Huntoon had struggled helplessly, hopelessly, through the
watches of the night, waiting for someone to push that
button, knowing what would happen . . . waiting, waiting, waiting for the inevitable. Waiting to die.

Waiting for sweet little Olive, who came to work so
early.

•   •   •

Terry sat smoking one of the Havanas, savoring each
puff, looking fondly at it like he might at a particularly
toothsome chorus girl.

"You know, Lew," he said, "I'd never have believed Max could do such a thing. A killing is one thing. But what he did to Bryce . . ." He shuddered under the neat gray pinstripe. "Why?"

"Love. And that thing eating up his brain. He's gone over, all the way over."

"Like Irish Billy Worley, six, seven years ago? Ate all those folks out on Staten Island?"

Cassidy nodded. "He's just a killing machine now, that's all. He killed Huntoon not to get rid of Cindy's boyfriend. He killed him the worst way he could because he was punishing him." He blinked at Terry. "Punishment is scary."

"Punishment is crazy." He looked up and frowned. "You know what this means, of course—"

Cassidy frowned back at him. All he could think of was the dangling head, the stuff hanging out of it, and what Max might do to Cindy. But she was safe. There was no way Max could know where she was.

"It means," Terry went on, "that Max is not long for this world, one way or the other. And you know what that means? That means I'm gonna run out of these cigars. Lew, the man has treated me like a son. Do you realize what he's done for me, Lew? He's fixed it with the guys in the humidor room at Dunhill for me to go in and make withdrawals from his private stock. No greater love hath Max. But what happens when Max croaks? He's got an inventory of four, five thousand of these babies in the humidor room . . . who'll get 'em? Are they in his will? What if I'm cut off? Shit!" He stood up and began pacing.

"Frankly, Terry, I don't give a damn."

"You have no sense of proportion."

"Beyond the matter of Max's cigars, what do you think we should do? What do you do with a killing machine?"

"What a question!" He paced to the window and stood looking down on Vanderbilt Avenue and Grand Central.

"Don't jump," Cassidy said. "You might land on some innocent."

"As you say, my old friend, there are no innocents—"

Olive appeared in the doorway.

"Mr. Leary, there's a call for you—"

"Tell 'em they're five minutes too late, he just jumped out the goddamn window—"

"It's Mr. Bauman," she whispered intently, pointing at the phone.

"Oh, Lord," he said, "why me?" He turned to the window, tapped the pane of glass, spoke to it: "Don't go away, I'll be right back."

Cassidy carefully lifted his own telephone, listened.

"Max," Terry said. "Top o' the mornin'. Or afternoon, I guess—"

"Terry, I wanted to thank you again for your help last night. I'm afraid I wasn't myself, not feeling too well." He sounded fine now.

"I hope you're better today—"

"Oh, yes, I recover very quickly. I can't pretend that I found our conversation anything but deeply upsetting. But that, as the man said, is life." It was hard to remember that he was dying, that he'd cracked last night, that he'd done what he did to Huntoon.

"Have you heard, by the way," Terry said, "about Bryce Huntoon's misfortune last evening? He just went to pieces, you might say, right here in our building. Awful mess. They're still wiping him up. Got tangled in the undercarriage of our elevator."

"Yes, I know about that." Cassidy heard him breathing at the other end of the line.

"Let's not bullshit each other, Max. You shouldn't have done that, it was a bad thing to do. You're gonna get Bennie all worried about getting into Heaven again."

"I wasn't aware you were so concerned about the Colonel's well-being. Or Bennie's chances in the Great Hereafter—"

"I wasn't," Terry said. "But you had me set up for the killing. I resent that. It makes me feel like a heel."

"You are something of a heel, Terry." Max chuckled softly. "I've always liked that about you. What did you think? I was going to give the man a mention in dispatches? Nonsense, I say. It was a battlefield execution. A traitor. One thing a man learns, you have a problem, it's always best to attend to it and move on." His voice had begun to grow shrill. It was like hearing a banshee. "It was necessary to make an example of Colonel Huntoon. I don't enjoy being betrayed, I've never minced words about that. The man paid the price for his traitorous nature. As will anyone else who betrays me . . . Is that clear?" He was almost screaming, then stopped abruptly. He was panting.

Terry bored in. "I hear you were there in person for the festivities. Nice touch."

"Why would you find it wise to provoke me, son?" Max's voice had dropped to a normal, conversational tone. "Ask yourself, is it a wise stratagem?" There was a long pause. Cassidy looked at Terry. His knuckles were white, grinding at the telephone. "I want you to understand what happened last night. Look at it from my point of view. I was there to make sure the man knew why he'd come to such grief. He needed to see that he was paying the piper. Do you see that, Terry? Of course, he was in perfectly good health when I last saw him—"

"Yeah. He had plenty of time to think things over—"

"That was the point, wasn't it, Terry?"

"I suppose it was."

"You see, I knew you'd understand. Now, I also wanted to tell you I'd be coming by personally to deliver the check. Little enough for a job well done. Wait for me, please. Then I'm going up to Boston to find Cindy. I'll surprise her—"

"Why not just leave her alone?"

"Think about it, son, you'll see it just doesn't make any sense. What I've done, I've done for her. She must realize the painful consequences of her acts. It's a part of growing up, isn't it? I'm going to have a nice talk with her. Perhaps I'll meet her brother, take a walk through the Yard. Yes, I'm looking forward to it, now that we've cleared up our little problem." He sounded avuncular now, benevolent. "Give my best to Lew. Wait for me in the office, will you?

I'm looking forward to paying you off. A cashier's check, how does that sound?" He chuckled again.

"See you," Terry said, and hung up.

• • •

Terry wasn't smiling or laughing and his cigar was dead in his mouth.

"Boston," Cassidy said. "He's not going to like what he finds in Boston. Nothing."

Terry nodded.

"He's bound to come looking for her. We're the ones who've been watching her. He's going to come 'round asking us questions . . . You know what he's going to think?"

"I'll bite," Terry said. "Tell me."

"He's going to feel betrayed."

"I was afraid you were going to say that."

"I want to be with Cindy until this is over," Cassidy said.

"Look, there's no way he can find her—"

"Where there's a will there's a way. I'd feel bad if he did and I wasn't there—"

"You might feel worse if you are there. Take your gun."

"That house is full of guns."

"Don't argue, okay? Take the gun."

"What about you?"

"I'm not sure," he said, shook his head. "I'll wait for Max and see what happens. No point in running away from good old Max and his two grand." He slapped Cassidy on the back. "Don't worry, amigo. I'll be okay. If I can't outthink Max and the Three Stooges, I'm done, anyway. Go on, get going, Lew. Go keep the maiden safe. I'll see you later."

It began snowing while he walked to the parking lot. Big soft flakes, wet, heavy. The sky was dark, the way it looks in the summer when a storm is about to hit. The wind was bitter, killing.

It wasn't easy sorting out his feelings about Cindy. Even if he wanted no part of her anymore, he still had to think of what to do with her. She was like a ticking bomb waiting to make a mess of everyone near her . . . but, hell, he couldn't let Max have her . . .

Max hadn't killed Huntoon, he'd butchered him. He was trying to scare everyone, give a warning, cleanse himself of the stench of betrayal. Maybe he was trying to settle accounts so he could die. He'd slipped so far into madness and evil that there was no pulling him back. He was in a killing frame of mind. He could kill and then chat on the telephone as if he'd just given a recalcitrant associate a stern dressing down. When he learned that Cindy wasn't in Boston, what kind of fit might overtake him?

It would be ugly.

CHAPTER SIXTEEN

Waiting for the car, he called Cindy to tell her he was on his way out. She sounded happy and excited and relieved and told him she'd had a wonderful day. She'd poked through the bookcases and found *Emma* by Jane Austen. She'd been curled up by the fire reading all day. She'd put on some fresh logs for his arrival. "Are you all right, darling? You sound sort of funny—are you okay?"

"Fine, I'm just fine. Everything's just fine."

She didn't believe him: He heard the doubt in her voice. But she whispered him a kiss and told him to hurry because she missed him with all her heart.

He beat the rush hour out of Manhattan but the storm's intensity was growing by the minute. The highway was slick. He knew he'd be fighting to keep the little convertible from slipping off the shoulder. The wind was howling at the fabric top, finding every seam, every fit that was less than perfect. The heater was fighting its usual losing battle. The Ford was a summer car and it wasn't summer. He couldn't even imagine summer. He turned the radio on.

It was scratchy and dim. But it was a lifeline out of the storm. The army, navy, and marines had established a beachhead on an island called Eniwetok in the Marshalls. And the Germans were putting up a hell of a fight south of Rome at Anzio. But the Allies were holding fast. And General MacArthur had announced that an entire convoy of fifteen Japanese ships had been sunk en route from Truk to the Bismarck Archipelago. The air attack had lasted three days.

Three days . . . Three days ago he'd been happy, in love with Cindy Squires. Trusting her . . .

The snow held the countryside in a kind of wet death grip. Darkness came prematurely. According to the radio he was out in the middle of the worst storm of the winter. Pennsylvania and New Jersey and Ohio, all the way back to Chicago and the plains beyond, were closing down. Upstate Buffalo had already gotten two feet. Drifts were piling up at the sides of the road. He cruised slowly past a huge truck which had gone off the road. It lay on its side like a dying monster. The driver was standing by a couple of red flares waiting for help. Soon the truck would be just the biggest drift among many.

In the slow, nerve-racking going, he could clear Cindy from his thoughts. Everything he thought and felt was so ambivalent it made his head hurt. She had touched him so deeply in all the inexplicable ways you had to wrestle with when somebody came on strong, wanting you, loving you. Being loved was almost irresistible, particularly when you'd been so long alone, particularly when your emotions had been savaged by the loss of someone you'd loved more than you'd dreamed you ever could. When your pain was great, when your defenses were up all around the perimeters of your emotions, and someone still managed to reach you . . . well, then you had to take her seriously. She'd earned that much.

Cindy's sleeping with Bryce Huntoon seemed trivial when weighed in the scale with Max's madness and Huntoon's hideous death . . . What difference did it all make? All over the world people were under more pressure than they'd been designed to withstand and they were sleeping with anyone who might give them comfort. So she'd lied to him . . . The world was full of lies. She'd been honest about the other things, desperately honest about herself, honest about her feeling for him . . .

That all sounded great. He was a noble chap, a swell guy, he could forgive and forget because he was such a fine fella . . .

But had she been honest with him? Maybe she'd just wanted to get away from Max and he'd been a convenient means. But that was ridiculous, he was anything but convenient, he hadn't even been a panting, willing lover. She could just as easily, more easily, have left the club that night with some money, gotten on a train and run far and fast. But she had stayed within Max's reach and she said it was because of him. But maybe it was because there was no train that could go where Max couldn't follow . . .

He felt like a man running in a maze of snow and ice and wind, not knowing how to interpret what his eyes could see, half blind. Was it a dead end? Or was it the way out, the way to salvation and purification? Who was going to survive? The Beauty or the Beast? Who deserved to survive? Did any of them?

In the end he was moving through time and space in a capsule of wind and cold, as if he were the next to the last man on the next to the last day. The last man on the last day was looking more and more like Max Bauman. A hallucination pursuing him through the storm. But, of course, that was crazy . . . Max couldn't find them. He couldn't be everywhere, Boston and New York and somewhere lost in the storm. He couldn't be.

The roads were deserted. He couldn't even see the edges of the highway. The headlamps couldn't handle the solid, opaque snowfall anymore. The wind blew the glare back into his face, into his eyes like a searchlight. The wipers tried to keep their arcs of vision open but it was a lost battle. He managed not to miss the proper turnoff by crawling along at five miles an hour, then got fouled up in a snowbank and had to get out and put the chains under the rear wheels to get free.

He took the best run he could at the narrow path leading to the house and for a moment he thought he might make it. Then, with a groan from the clutch and gearbox, the plucky little Ford sloughed sideways, slipped into the shallow embankment which was deep with snow, and came to rest with its rear end flush against the poplar trees. The Ford was done for, for the duration of the storm, until a tow truck could get to it.

The wind rammed the door back on his ankle and bent it over the running board while he tried to get out. He wasn't wearing overshoes because he didn't own any. He stood with the snow heavy as cement, reaching halfway to his knees. He was half a mile from the house and the night was seething, whipping brutal lashings of ice and sleet. He couldn't see the house. He had to make sure he didn't stray off the path to the left, into the vast sloping meadow where he might easily wander aimlessly until he dropped. He had a sense of the poplars to the right. The wind beat at them, thrashing the bare branches. He had to keep that sound to his right, never lose it.

It was a slow process. The wind sucked his breath away and the snow sandblasted his face. He pulled the woolen muffler up over his mouth and nose. The snow clung to his eyelashes, weighed them down, began to harden. He brushed at the snow and it broke, brittle, like frosting on a cheap cake. He kept lifting one leg up out of the stuff as best he could but the bad one wasn't meant for anything like snow hiking. He pushed off on the stick, using it also to probe for the blacktop underfoot. Swinging the stiff leg against the weight of the snow was the hardest work he'd done since the Giants put an end to playing football. The sweat was pouring off him, soaking his clothing, while the world around him tried to freeze him to death. He'd have sold his granny for a beer.

In time he became a barely ambulatory snowman, shapeless, frozen, white, unreal. He wanted to lie down and die but he kept struggling onward. He wasn't really thinking anymore. He just kept on slogging. Each step was going to be his last but never was. And then the lights of the house blurred before him, grew clearer as he panted forward. His heart was doing a polka against his rib cage. Finally he made it. He was leaning like a snowdrift against the door, weakly hammering, until the door wasn't there anymore and he was falling into the bottomless void, just like Dick Powell playing Marlowe in *Murder, My Sweet.*

•   •   •

He came to on the kitchen floor. She'd shut the door and dragged him in and was gently toweling the frozen snow and slabs of ice from his forehead and eyes and nose. She pulled the scarf slowly, slowly away from the crusted face and unbuttoned the coat, dropping chunks of snow on the linoleum. She was whispering, telling him it was all right now, not to worry, and then she was digging the snow from his shoes so she could get the laces untied. It took a long time but he was finally propped against the cupboard under the sink. He liked watching her take care of him.

She got him a drink of cold water and helped him to stand and took him in before the fire. He was still shivering, teeth chattering, and she was all over him with dry towels and then a few square yards of Indian blanket. She was gentle, efficient, determined. All the feeling was coming back and it hurt like hell. She brought brandy and sat down, held him, kissed him, whispered that everything was fine, that she was there and she was going to make him feel better, all better, that she loved him . . .

•   •   •

She lay in his arms and he told her he knew about her affair with Bryce Huntoon. He told her she didn't have to lie anymore. She listened with her head cocked, the blond veil drifting across one eye. She looked as if maybe she hadn't recovered from the fright of his impersonation of Scott and Amundsen reaching the pole. She leaned up on an elbow.

"But I did tell you about Huntoon, Lew, my love. I didn't lie. I told you I tried to seduce the poor guy."

"No, no, you can relax, it's too late now to keep up the act. You told me he turned you down. God knows why I believed that. I know you had an affair with him." He was staring into the fire, feeling the heat. The logs crackled and sparks flew up the chimney. The wind whistled in the eaves. The house creaked like an old ship riding out stormy seas.

"Listen to me, Lew." She took his hand, tugging at his attention. "I did not have an affair with him. I told you exactly what happened, all of it. Why would I lie? I told you I'd have done it. I didn't lie to make myself look better—you're not making any sense. What do you mean you *know*?"

"I was in his flat. I *know*, Cindy. I saw the place."

She grabbed him, hard, and her voice was steely, full of anger he'd never heard before. "Look at me, you! Listen to me. I'm telling you that I've never been near his flat. I have no idea where it is. Do you hear me?"

"Cindy, for God's sake, I saw your things! Your lipstick, I know that color. Your perfume in the fancy bottle with the silver filigree. I know! So let's drop it—"

"No, damn it! I won't drop it! I'm a lot of things that aren't so pretty but I'm not a liar. I've never lied to you. And I won't have you thinking I did. I repeat, I've never been to his apartment or a hotel room or anywhere else! Get it? I once had a perfume bottle like that, a long time ago, but I haven't seen it in years—*years!* I have no idea where it is or what happened to it."

"I've seen that bottle before, Cindy, I know I've seen it before, you must have used it—"

"I told you, I haven't had it in years. What can I do to make you believe me, Lew? Why do you look at me like we're strangers? Anybody can buy that lipstick, ditto the perfume, it's French, it's called Diabolique . . . you've got to believe me, you must. I've never slept with Bryce Huntoon and never been to his place and there's no reason for me to lie about it . . . Tell me, why would I lie?"

His head was swimming. His eyes burned and he felt like somebody had put a mickey in his Pepsi-Cola.

"I don't know," he said. "I don't know anything, not anymore. I don't know why you'd lie . . ."

"Look, why don't you just ask Huntoon? He's honest as a rock, no lies in him—"

"I can't—"

"Don't be proud, Lew." She smiled, dazzled him, enchanted him with her little-girl mouth, her solemnity. "Go ahead, ask him!"

"He's dead, Cindy. Huntoon's dead."

She squinted up at him, as if he were a mirage. "What did you say? He's what?" She shook her head. "I don't understand—"

"Max killed him. Last night." There was no point in telling her about it. The details didn't matter and there had to be an end to the confusion. Somehow they all had to know the same story at the same time for a change.

"How? Why? Tell me."

"Because Max decided you had to be having an affair and Huntoon was the culprit. Max couldn't deal with it so he struck out, vengeance, punishment, whatever you want to call it. You don't want to know how he did it, believe me."

"But why would Max decide on him?" Her eyes were wide, silently pleading that it wasn't true. "Why Huntoon?"

"Because we told him—"

"You?"

"Terry said he could talk Max out of hurting him and since Max was positive you had a lover, he wanted a name. That's why he hired us to tail you in the first place . . . and we gave him Huntoon. Terry said he thought you were probably sleeping with the guy, anyway—"

"Terry! Damn him!"

"He told me I was too gullible, believing you when you told me Huntoon had turned you down flat. So Terry took Bryce to lunch and I searched his place and found your things—"

"Not my things, Lew. Please . . ." She wiped her eyes.

"Your lipstick, your perfume—"

"Oh, my God, I see now, I see it all . . . Terry, he salted the room! Oh, no . . ."

"What do you know about that? Salting?"

"It's something he used to tell me about, long time ago, before he ever introduced me to Max . . ." She bit at the thumbnail, brow furrowed. "Back when he was a cop. He told me how sometimes the cops would salt a guy's car or his office or his home, plant evidence, I mean, and then they'd discover the stuff during a search. He said they did it when they knew a guy was a crook but they couldn't get the goods on him. It's obvious—that's what he did with Huntoon and he left it for you to find while he took Huntoon to lunch. You found the stuff, you drew your own conclusions—that way he knew you'd go along with telling Max it was Huntoon."

"But the perfume bottle. It was right there—"

"Yes, of course. Terry's had it all this time. Sort of a souvenir of . . . of the old days."

"What are you saying?"

"Oh, Lew! Terry and I had a thing for a while, so long ago. I'd just come over from England and I was just a lonely kid. I met him at a party and he was nice and funny and seemed so worldly. I fell for him, I needed some- one . . . tell me you understand, Lew—"

"So he's had you, too. You're full of surprises." His stomach was groping downward, feeling for China. It was always the same when a woman told you something you didn't want to hear. Maybe it was the way you looked at them in the first place, but there wasn't anything you could do about that. Once you cared about them, they had you and you never knew when the pain would start. But it would, it was bound to, just as you were bound to die one day.

"Lew, it was years ago. I was close to him—and why shouldn't I have been? You know him better than anyone, you know what a charmer he is! You love him, Lew!"

"Funny, the way Terry never told me, once he knew a little about you and me. Jesus . . . so first Terry had you, then he handed you over to Max, who could really take care of you, give you a job . . . and along came the football hero—and Terry never told me the story—"

"But why would he? What difference would it make? You might have gotten angry with him and what would have been the point of that? Can't you see what's important? Max killed the wrong man . . . an innocent man! If you want to be angry with Terry, do it for the right reasons! Why can't you get free of worrying about yourself and your precious little ego?"

"Sure, sure, you're right." He tried to believe that: He knew she was right. "I'm the one Max should have killed." He was trying to make sense of it. "Terry knew that, so he saved me by throwing Huntoon to the lions . . . and then he couldn't protect him. Christ." He was drowning in the moral complexity, the sea of betrayal. Of course, the essence of the morality lay with Max: Killing people was wrong.

She slumped against him, worn out, the flames reflected in the sapphire eyes. "Terry did what he had to do. He's a realist, always the realist. He looks at the situation and sees what he has to do . . . He's like Harry Madrid. Maybe all cops are like that . . . They simplify. They don't dwell on the consequences. It's always simple for Terry in the end. One set of actions is always preferable to the others." She sighed, rubbed her face against his shoulder.

"I know where I've seen the perfume bottle," Cassidy sighed. "In his bedroom, on the bureau among his cuff links and rings and collar pins." He took a drink of the brandy she'd brought them in a single snifter. It burned all the way down. "I can't help thinking about it, Cindy. He used me. My God, how he used me to set up Huntoon! And he made me believe you'd lied to me, that you'd been with Huntoon—he had to know what that would do to me!"

"He *had* to, Lew, or you wouldn't have gone along with giving Huntoon to Max—"

"So?"

"So Max would have kept digging and finally he'd have found out about you and me and he'd come after you . . . us. He cares about me, too. He did it to save you, Lew. Us."

"Maybe, maybe not. I guess we'll never know. But Terry and I could have handled Max."

"No, no, you and Terry and Patton's army couldn't handle Max—this is their game, my love, their rules. I think it was all decided a million years ago, some of us had to die and poor Bryce came first. Better him than you, it comes down to that."

Later, with the house groaning and buckling and the wind banging at the windows, he felt her fingertips on his cheek, tracing cheekbones, eyebrows.

"Come on, kiss me, Lew. Make love to me, please."

He held her and kissed her hair and smelled the same perfume and she curled against him under the blankets and for a time he was sure she had the power to make everything okay. Max had been right in his demented way. She was the Daughter of Time, she was the light and the dark. Cassidy had the feeling she was eternal, that she would survive them all. She was way beyond the rest of them but he couldn't explain it even to himself. So he concentrated on holding her, smelling her, stroking her.

"Don't you see," she whispered, "it makes no difference who we've been with before . . . you loved Karin, I understand something of that. And you've had your share of women, I've had men. We're only human. But now we've found each other. Lew, I think it's real. I do, I truly do. It's like an opera, blood and passion and jealousy and madness and revenge and true love." She nibbled at his chest.

"I hope it's over."

"Oh, my poor Lew, it's not over. Not enough bodies for any self-respecting opera . . ."

"If there's a God, you're wrong. You know that."

"You mustn't forget Max because Max won't forget me. I told you, Max and I both can't get out of this alive. It's a given, darling. I've known that all along . . . that's why I went to Harry Madrid that time. Even then I knew one of us had to die . . . But don't think about it now, just go to sleep and I'll watch over you . . ."

He was tired, slipping away. But something clicked. "You went to Harry Madrid which time? When? Why did you go to Harry Madrid?"

"Back in '42. The mess that night in Jersey, when we saw the fireworks. I thought Max was coming, I knew he was meeting a bunch of gangsters . . . I . . . went to Harry Madrid. Made a deal with him. I told him about the meeting, I asked him to take Max for me, and he knew what I meant. I didn't care if he arrested him for whatever he was doing with Rocco, I didn't know—and if he killed him, well, I'd be free completely . . . Harry was going to kill him . . . and then Max didn't go . . ."

"Jesus. It was you . . . you set Max up to get killed —and the poor bastard loved you, Cindy!"

"So he's a poor bastard now, dear old Max! Lew, I was a prisoner. There was no other way out. And Harry Madrid was the right man. He'd have done it."

"You and Harry Madrid. He said he had somebody close to Max. Terry thought it was Bennie . . . Max thought maybe Terry had betrayed him. That's how deep it bit."

"And now it's all gone wrong again. Max is never going to die, Lew. He'll see me in my grave, all of us, Lew, unless, unless . . ."

"But you don't know about Max," he said. "You're gonna be all right. Max—he's already dying . . ."

"What are you talking about?"

"Max has a malignant brain tumor. His time's just about up. Don't ask me how I know, I just know."

The silence went on for a long time. All he could hear was the storm.

"Did you know that?" he said.

"No, I didn't." She seemed to be speaking from far away. "How can you be sure?"

"I'm sure."

"That's bad. If he's running out of time, don't you see?

He's got to get me right. He'll do anything to get me. Oh, hold me, Lew."

She was trembling uncontrollably. He gathered her to him. "I love you, Cindy. None of it makes any difference . . . it should but it doesn't. I love you."

She clung to him for dear life and later said, "Does anyone know where we are? Exactly?"

"Terry," he said.

•　　•　　•

He woke later, sensing that she was no longer beside him. He was stiff and ached from head to toe. The wind was rattling the windows again. The fire had burned low. He coughed, called her name.

"I'm here." Her voice came from the shadows.

"Come back to me."

"I heard something outside." She sounded about six years old. "I was frightened." His eyes adjusted, brought her into focus. She was standing beside a window. "I went to look. I thought I heard voices on the wind."

"Impossible," Cassidy said.

"No, it's not impossible, Lew, my love. I saw them. They're out there. They're here. They've come for me . . ."

CHAPTER SEVENTEEN

No matter how dark the night, there is light in it somewhere. And when there is snow in the night, that light is reflected in each flake. Standing beside her, he saw the shapes of the men, the shadows they cast, darker than the night, like ghosts or premonitions, flickering. They stood under a huge, leafless oak tree in the front yard. The tree's shadow clawed its way toward the house. They paced in and out of the shadows. Max had his hands thrust deep in his overcoat pockets. They had had to pass Cassidy's car, rammed down into the snowbank. Max's big Chrysler would have made short work of the snow, the chains grinding toward the house. And now . . . Cassidy took a deep breath. It would all be over soon.

He watched them for several minutes while Cindy got into slacks and a heavy sweater, which belonged to her unsuspecting hostess. She brought him his clothes. They'd dried out before the fire.

Bennie was out there, kicking snow as he walked. He

was wearing a bowler hat and it made the top of his head look like a planetarium rising from the crown of a mountain. Then there was Bob Erickson, who looked less like a banker in the middle of the night with a tommy gun cradled through one arm. There was a fourth man, tall and thin, a lanky black shadow Cassidy took to be a longtime favorite iceman of Max's, Cookie Candioli, strictly muscle with a sense of humor you could have found with Madame Curie's microscope. Of course, he hadn't come to laugh.

Cassidy went to the gun rack hung on the knotty-pine wall and took down two Purdeys, both with chased stock and metalwork. Bobby Vanderlipp had had them made in London after the Great War. Bobby was rich and therefore somebody was going to die at the business end of the best goddamn shotgun money could buy. The first was a side-by-side double barrel, the other an over-and-under. They were probably worth five grand apiece. In the top drawer of the chest beneath the rack he found neatly stacked boxes of shells. He loaded both shotguns and dropped some extra shells into his shirt pocket. He handed the side-by-side to Cindy.

"Can you use this if you have to?"

She hefted the gun, which looked absurdly large and brutal in her delicate hands.

"Don't worry about me," she said. "Stiff upper lip, there'll always be an England. Greer Garson. I can do whatever needs doing . . . to get out of here alive. Damn, it is heavy, isn't it?"

He went back to the window. They were coming across the deep snow, sinking in almost to their knees, closing in on the house. They stopped before the porch and conferred among themselves. They weren't worried. They had two sitting ducks in a country house, unwarned and helpless.

"How could they find out?" she whispered.

"Terry's the only one . . . They must have torn it out of him with pliers. You can bet he's dead, Cindy. Old Terry's dead."

Adiós, amigo . . .

"Max wouldn't, never. Not Terry. He thought of Terry as a son."

"That's the old Max," he reminded her. "Not this character. I'd say they tortured him until he talked. That would have been the only way to stop the pain. Tell them so they'd end it with a bullet . . . Max'd end it with a bullet if he loved Terry so much."

"I want to kill them," she whispered tonelessly.

He smiled at her in the darkness. "Speaking for myself, I'm sure as hell gonna enjoy it."

There were footsteps—only one man—on the porch. The snow squeaked as he walked slowly toward the door. There was no point in taking chances even if your prey was helpless, asleep.

"Cindy. Go to the light switch and flick it on just for an instant once he comes into the room. He'll be blinded, frozen in his tracks. I'll take him out."

She navigated in the darkness while he knelt and rested the bottom barrel on the back of the couch, pointed directly at the doorway. He saw his watch glowing in the dark. It was four o'clock.

The first guy through the door was going to pay one hell of a price.

The footsteps stopped.

The storm door was pulled back, wheezing on its hinges. The doorknob began to turn, rattling ever so slightly. The door was easing open, inch by inch by inch . . .

Cassidy heard the footfalls in the darkness, one, two steps into the room, the shape black on black, too hard for him to center the barrels on. Snow blew noisily along the porch.

Now, now, he willed her to do it . . .

She hit the wall switch and all the lamps in the room came on in a blinding flash.

The man stopped dead, threw an arm across his eyes.

Just as suddenly the darkness engulfed them again, like the hood dropped over a parrot's cage, but the afterimage of the man hung suspended before him as he adjusted the barrels.

The man with the long pistol in one hand, wearing a black-and-red-plaid parka, a matching hat with the ear-flaps turned down . . .

Cassidy centered on the memory of the man imprinted on his eyeballs and squeezed off both barrels and took the kick.

The shell casings ejected onto the floor and he slid two more into the chambers while the man was being sprayed back out into the night. Wood splintered, glass exploded, and he heard the corpse smack heavily onto the porch, slide across the slippery snow dusting, and crash off the edge, through the thick crust. The door had been blown off the hinges. It banged noisily, clattered off a wooden pillar, and pitched off into the snow. A blast of cold air poured in and the sound of the blast echoed and slammed off the walls and then after a while it was silent again.

She came and knelt beside him.

"They've got to come inside to get us," he said. "It'll be a war. We've got to dig in."

They pushed the couch over to the stairwell and got in behind it, hunkered down in the nook below the stairs. They sat with their backs to the wall and she shivered against him. He kissed her hair and wondered if he'd ever see her face again.

He looked around the room, trying to get a clear picture of where they could get in. There was the front door from the porch. Four windows in the room they were in, God only knew how many other windows on the ground floor. They'd have to break them, however, which was noisy. They were bound to be frozen shut even if not locked. Also, the back door into the kitchen. They were going to have to make noise and the misfortunes of Candioli had impressed upon them that they were in a fight. The night's prey wasn't going to die quietly in bed.

"Since we can pick them off, they'll create a diversion while they come in somewhere else." He felt around for the blackthorn stick, picked up the Purdey. He got up and hit his head on the bottom of the staircase and pulled the couch closer. The wind from the blasted doorway scoured the room, left it cold and trembling.

The tommy gun began its unmistakable burping and suddenly there was flying glass everywhere. Bullets chewing at the wall, slivers of wood spraying like tiny swords, splintering the knotty pine. He could see the flash of muzzle fire, like live electricity darting out, in the darkness beyond the holes in the wall where the windows had been. Slugs were thudding into the couch. He pulled her down on the floor. Slugs were ricocheting off the stone fireplace. It sounded like a Panzer division rolling through the house. They hunkered down, trying to pull the world over their heads. The gun kept chattering. Cindy was grabbing at his hand, her fingers ice cold, frantic. The blasting just kept on. The Fighting 69th could have marched past them up the stairs without fear of detection but in fact nobody charged through the doorway where Cookie had made his final exit.

Suddenly silence, nearly as oppressive as the noise, broke out. He thought he'd heard some extra creaking and glass breaking upstairs and maybe he had, but now it was quiet. An occasional bit of plaster or wood made a noise as it dropped to the floor, an afterthought.

They waited and nothing happened.

The chattering of the tommy gun came again, spraying the room from the doorway. He tried to get himself in front of Cindy and caught his bad leg on the sharp corner of something. He went sprawling into the darkness from behind the couch, the tongues of flame skittering across the room as the gun kept firing. As he hit the floor, bits of broken glass ground into his palms.

He felt the rush and thump of heavy shoes brushing past. He'd lost the shotgun, lost the sense of where he was in the room. It was like floating in an ocean.

He couldn't find Cindy but he heard the heavy snorting of the man who'd just come in, rushed past him. Bennie wouldn't leave Max for anything, so it had to be Bob

Erickson, who had definitely laid to rest all ideas that he was a banker. Cassidy lay still, trying to hold his breath.

Cindy sneezed from all the plaster dust in the air. She was behind him. He heard Erickson shift his weight as he turned. He pulled the trigger and stitched the wall with another long burst.

Cindy yelled something and hit the floor. Cassidy made a dive across an armchair, reaching for those jabbing orange and red tongues where the gun had gone off.

Cindy was yelling a blue streak, throwing ashtrays and vases and picture frames. Everything was breaking and smashing in the dark while he came down hard on Erickson. He went over bellowing with surprise.

A good deal of the air in his lungs whooshed out past Cassidy's ear. He smelled Erickson's Yardley. He rammed his head into the middle of the Yardley smell. Erickson grunted hard and fell back against something hard and howled with his finger jammed in the trigger guard. Half the ceiling fell down, plaster everywhere. The tommy gun was jumping between them. Cassidy stuck a finger in his eye. Erickson tried to twist the gun away but his arm didn't want to bend that way. Another burst of fire went bouncing around the room and then, whack, it jammed.

He was a resourceful son of a bitch. He turned the gun into a club and was swinging at Cassidy like Mel Ott going for the short fence at the Polo Grounds. The butt bounced off his forehead a couple of times, long foul balls, two strikes, and he rolled away with plaster chips in his eye, fumbling with the blackthorn stick, reaching for the little button. He found it and felt the heavy knob pop into his palm, working the bits of glass deeper into the flesh. Erickson was struggling trying to get some leverage to have another swing but Cassidy knew where he was, had his sleeve in his left hand, and had a pretty fair idea of where the center of his body might be.

He drove the sword home, felt it enter something solid. Erickson sucked in a terrible gasp compounded of surprise and pain and Cassidy yanked it out as he grabbed the blade, closed his hand around it. Cassidy pushed hard again and Erickson grunted. Cassidy tried to get it back out but the dying man toppled sideways and the sword went with him, twisting out of Cassidy's hand.

Bob Erickson of Saint Louis was making gagging noises and his heels beat a sad little tattoo on the floor as he fought a lonely, losing battle with the blade hacksawing its way through the contents of his chest. The flapping lessened and his breathing got wetter and sibilant as he blew bubbles, his life expanding like a membrane and bursting on his lips, and then Bob Erickson was still.

Cassidy lay there trying to get his breath back, trying to wipe the plaster out of his eyes, trying to figure out which end was up. He couldn't get the sword back. Erickson had somehow rolled over on it, like a man ritualistically embracing his killer. He curled around it, then flattened out on top of it. Cassidy felt around and found the point. It had gone all the way through him and was sticking up out of his back like a steeple.

The tommy gun was useless. The shotgun he'd used on Candioli was somewhere in the wreckage, among the broken glass and flaked chunks of walls and ceiling and the smears of blood and the chewed-up furniture. Where the hell was Cindy?

He straightened his bad leg and began to realize just how much it hurt. He pulled himself up to his knees, fighting the illusion that they were somehow out of the woods. He felt like he'd bagged his limit, two bad guys per night. But he was only half the way home.

He realized Cindy wouldn't know which one of them was alive. He had to say something. He couldn't have her using that Purdey on him by mistake. She'd never forgive herself.

"Cindy?" he whispered. "It's me. I'm okay."

Something moved. He crawled toward it, smelled her perfume. She was shaking. He felt the tremors across the space between them. "Are you okay?"

"Why not? I haven't done anything yet but scream like a dumb girl." She was trying to be tough.

He found the gun he'd dropped and picked it up.

"They're upstairs," she said. "I heard them clumping around like a comedy team. There must have been an outside stairway . . . I don't know. What'll we do?"

"Beats hell outa me. I'm not in much of a mood to go get them. They'll have to come downstairs to get us. Let's just wait. We got 'em right where we want 'em."

They sat down in the rubble.

The house made so much noise as it withstood the wind and blowing snow, it was impossible to tell what was going on above. An hour must have passed, maybe more, and his heart went back to beating like God had intended. He tried to figure it out. Bennie and Max were upstairs. They'd outfoxed themselves. Now they were trapped. They'd have to make a move.

As usual he hadn't considered all the possibilities.

Cindy was leaning against the couch which was losing its stuffing, dribbling it out through the bullet holes. They kept calm by touching hands. He kissed her and held her head to his chest and told her it would be all right. Not for Terry, not for everyone . . . *Terry*. He shook the thought out of his mind and faced the stairway and the balcony. The darkness of night began to fade almost imperceptibly and the grayness tinged with pink began to seep across the void. Snow blew past the window holes. The room had gotten colder with the door gone and the windows blown out. The fire was dead.

"Drop the hardware, Lew."

The voice came from behind him. He hadn't thought of everything. He never did.

Bennie the Brute was standing where there had once been a door. Now, as he swiveled to look, Cassidy saw his huge shape in the long black overcoat with the bowler on top. The polka-dot bow tie peeked out from behind the scarf. He was holding a Luger.

"Oh, shit, Bennie," he said.

"Ain't it the nuts, Lew?" A ghost of a smile played across his face. It was the same face Cassidy had seen out there on the corner selling funny toys to the kids. A big sweet psychopath and you could get Ed Murrow on the plate in his head. "I don't like this any more than you do, Lew. Let's face it. It's an imp-p-perfect world."

In the old days when Bennie was at his best he might have had some kind of chance. It would have been closer, anyway.

As it was, he was talking to Cassidy with this kind of sad, nostalgic look on his face, when Cindy turned toward him and fired the Purdey.

He never even noticed it. The twin explosions came almost simultaneously and the recoil blew Cindy backward against the wall.

Bennie left this imperfect world in a blur of black wool courtesy of Brooks Brothers, his bowler hat sailing away like youth and memory and hope getting out just in time. Both shells caught him waist-high. The top half of Bennie spun sideways and backward, following a trajectory not unlike that of Cookie Candioli's final flight. The bottom half of Bennie stood there for a while like a doubtful guest, then tipped over.

Cassidy got up and stood looking at him, part of him, amazed at what had just happened. He felt as if Bennie had been interrupted to death. Poor Bennie had made the same mistake twice. Twice when he had Cassidy down he'd have been better off just killing him. But he was a sentimental galoot, a softie at heart, and he hadn't taken the situation seriously enough. Maybe he didn't think a nice girl like Miss Squires would actually kill him. Cassidy could hear him saying it. *Hell of a thing, Lew, hell of a thing.* He wondered if Bennie would make it through the Gates of Heaven, if he'd meet him one day walking the Streets of Glory. Maybe they needed a guard up there.

The next thing he knew he was lying facedown in somebody else's blood and yet another pool of pain, brand-new shining pain. It felt like a sledgehammer had hit him in the back. He heard Cindy screaming. He heard the crack of the shot that hit him. He squirmed sideways like a crab and came up against Bennie's legs, his face in the wet snow on Bennie's galoshes.

When he'd rolled over onto his back and hitched up against the wall, he looked up and saw Max Bauman coming down the stairs one at a time. He had a .45 in his hand and he was crying, tears streaming down his sallow, sunken cheeks. He was wiping his nose on his sleeve.

"Bennie," he sobbed. "Jesus, Ben . . ."

He'd shot Cassidy in the back but high and to one side. He figured his shoulder was crushed. The pain was making him sweat in the cold. He had no feeling in his right arm. His fingers wouldn't move. He felt like a burning blade had been plunged into his back. He was seeing lots of little bright stars and everything was fuzzy.

Max came down the stairs slowly, a tired old man. He was still wearing his tux under his long formal evening coat, a homburg, black gloves, none the worse for wear following his hike through the drifts. All the snow had long since melted from his trousers and coat and he looked much as he always did. Except that now he was a ruin, old and sick and tired and shambling as he came down. Cassidy had seen him cry once before, a million years ago when he'd sat before the fire at the end of a long party and told the story of his son Irvie dying a hero. Going down with his ship.

Now Max was coming down the stairs to a room that looked like a battlefield, the men who'd been doing his bidding strewn dead at his feet. It was Max's kind of war and it had been going on a long time. Everybody was tired or dead. As if he were reading Cassidy's mind, he said, "Are they all dead now, Lew?"

"I sure as hell hope so."

He looked over at Cindy, smiled wearily. "Cindy. I've missed you, baby."

She tried to smile back, brushed her hair away from her face. "Well, we're all in quite a mess, aren't we, Max?"

"Funny the way things turn out, Cin. Who'da thunk it?" He shook his head, chuckled. "I'll be dead soon, you didn't know that, did you? Why did you always lie to me, Cin? Was I so awful?"

"Oh, Max, you were good to me. And I didn't always lie to you. I hardly ever lied to you."

"Only about the big things, I guess," he said. "Love, death . . . sure, death, baby. Harry Madrid and I had a little talk the other night, Cin. All about that shoot-out in Jersey that time. I couldn't believe it, Cin, couldn't believe you'd do that, set me up . . . ah, hell, it's all over now, anyway, isn't it? Put down the gun, Cin. It's empty. You used both barrels on Ben. You shouldn't have killed Ben—"

"But why not?" she asked. "Isn't that what this is all about? Who lives and who dies? You've already decided to kill me—"

"I'm not so sure of that now I see you. That's what I hoped for, that I'd see you and remember the good times and then I couldn't kill you. Oh, hell, Cin . . . if you'd have humored me another couple months I'd have died and you'd have come out safe and sound and rich. Instead"—he pointed with the gun at the carnage in the gray light of dawn—"it's the last act of *Hamlet*. And you killed Ben . . . But, then, how long can I miss him? Coupla months? Big deal." He wiped sweat from his forehead, looked over at Cassidy "And you, Lew. Whattaya got to say for yourself? I hear tell you've been fucking my little girl here while you were supposed to be looking for her boyfriend. Hey, the joke's on Max! God damn you, how I hate that kind of double-dealing crap! It's not worthy of you, Lew. Your father'd be disappointed in you . . . say, you shot up bad, Lew?"

"I'll live," he said.

Max laughed, coughed into his fist. It was cold. His breath hung like smoke between them. "Well, now you mention it, I don't really think you will." He pulled a pigskin cigar case from his pocket, bit the end from a cigar, and lit it with the flame from his gold lighter. The gun never wavered. He coughed again, a man coming down with a cold that didn't matter anymore. "Come over here, baby. Sit on the steps by me." She went and they both sat down. "Are you sorry, Cin?"

She shook her head. "Maybe. I don't know, I wish it hadn't ended this way . . . but I couldn't spend the rest of my life with you . . . a prisoner—"

"I was only asking for the rest of *mine*—"

"It could have been a long time, Max. And I'd fallen in love with Lew . . ."

Max laughed harshly, blew smoke at Cassidy. "A crippled, used-up, useless football player leeching off his buddy. You're telling me you love this piece of garbage?"

She looked at him as if she'd turned to ice as he spoke. She was so far away now he'd never reach her. Their eyes locked. He looked away first.

"This guy, he's nothing, Cin," he said, trying to soften his words, too late, "not good enough for you. What the hell is it with women, Lew? Is it just because you're younger? A better fuck?"

"I don't know, Max. I don't know what it is with women." His strength was ebbing. The pain in his back was growing dull, as if it had won and was now losing interest in the uneven contest. "Just lucky, I guess—"

"Well, your luck's run out, Lew."

"Tell me, Max, how did you find us?" The words sounded slow and clumsy, half formed.

"Oh, I had a talk with Terry. He's always been a good boy. Like a son to me."

"You kill him once he told you?"

"Oh, I don't think so. Mr. Erickson thought we should, being a very practical kind of fella. He said back in Saint Louie that's the way they'd do it. But I couldn't let him kill Terry any more than I could kill Irvie. No, Terry was just prompted to see the greater loyalty. You might say I drew on the reserves of loyalty." He shrugged, his neck scrawny behind the scarf. "I think he was a little under the weather by the time we left . . ." Max put his free arm around Cindy, pulled her close. She shrank back but he insisted.

"I'm in a helluva fix," Max mused.

"Look, Max," she said, "let's call all this off. I'll go back with you. I'll do whatever you want—"

"All these guys died for nothing? Get serious, Cin. Anyway, don't you see, there's no happy ending for me."

"I can give you a couple of pretty good months, Max. I'll stay with you until the end, until it's over . . . just don't kill anybody else."

"Dearest, Cin, I haven't killed anybody. You and Lew have been doing all the killing. I'm just a sick old man with a hell of a headache. And I'm fresh out of illusions. You can't replenish my supply, Cin. Think about it. What would I do with you for a month or two? They tell me I'll be blind in a month and then I couldn't even see you . . . blind old Jew and nobody left to trust . . ." He puffed blue smoke. He was beginning to cry again. He rubbed his red eyes and knocked the ash off onto his coat. He squeezed his forehead. But the .45 was pointed at her right breast, almost touching her. A .45 would make a hole in her the size of a baseball. Anyway, there was nothing Cassidy could do. He couldn't move and he was losing blood.

"Max, Max, Max. What the hell's going on here?"

None of them had seen the man coming up from the road, coming across the snow. For a moment Cassidy thought he was dreaming, searching out a final comforting fantasy.

Max looked up at the sound of his voice.

"How's it going, amigo? Long night, looks like. Doesn't look to me like you'll ever throw the high hard one again. You're running outa limbs, amigo."

"Terry," he said.

Terry wasn't alone. He'd come with his big old gun. It had a barrel like a broom handle and it looked like it had won the West all by itself. It was pointed at Max. Terry was standing in the doorway, not your lucky spot. He looked around slowly.

Then there was another movement on the porch. So slowly, like a liner docking, Harry Madrid came into view.

"What a mess," Terry said. "Lew's pal gets back from Palm Beach, he won't recognize the old homestead . . . somebody's gonna have a lot of explaining to do."

"Terry," Cassidy said. His vision was fading in and out, going to black, then coming back when he willed it. There wasn't much will left. Terry's face looked like Fat Hermann Göring had used it for a dance floor. One eye was purple and swollen shut. There were deep cuts across his cheekbones. They had split and needed stitches. Blood had dried and caked around his mouth and nose. His lips looked like they'd gone fifteen with Tony Janiro. He managed a broken, cracked smile. There was a black space where one of his front teeth had been. Harry Madrid was close now. He moved to steady Terry but Terry shook him off. Somehow they were allies for the last act . . .

"Max, your army's dying off. Looks like old Bob Erickson over there. Swordplay, Lew—I'm proudaya." Terry tried to laugh and winced. Max stared up at him, slowly puffing. "Listen, Max, this is serious. I just tripped over something out there on the porch. Looked like about half of Bennie to me. Pieces of Cookie Candioli out there, too. I'd say the old Cooker man has boosted his last hubcap. Some party you guys been having."

"Harry," Max said. "Whose side you on, anyway?"

"Always on the side of the angels, Max. Had to get you one way or another. Matter of principle. This was the best way. You're gonna have to die now, Max."

The sun was coming up behind Harry Madrid, a bright pink glow stretching across the snow. It hurt Cassidy's eyes. Maybe nothing awful could happen on such a beautiful morning.

"Put the heater down, Max. Give us all a break." Terry winked at him, good-natured.

"No, I can't do that, son. I'm a very sad old man this

morning but I don't feel at all benevolent. I know you're supposed to get all soft and easy at the center when you get ready to cross over . . . but I just don't feel that way, Terry. Maybe I'm bitter about the deal I'm getting—you think? So I die now, I die in a coupla months, what's it to me?"

He pushed the gun's thick, blunt muzzle up under Cindy's chin. She looked into Cassidy's eyes. He could have lost himself in the sapphire ocean of her eyes. He saw her and he saw a memory of Karin . . . Cindy, Cindy . . . The muzzle pressed into her white flesh. She was eternal, all women, he knew it as Max had known it. The Daughter of Time. Her eyes were speaking to him. She wasn't afraid.

"So, we got a Mexican standoff," Terry said.

"No." Max shook his head. "I win."

Her eyes weren't blinking. Her patrician face was expressionless. Her eyes were speaking to Cassidy. She saw him, she saw past him, she saw the limitless future called forever.

Then he knew what she was saying.

She was saying good-bye.

Max pulled the trigger and blew her head off.

A long sigh escaped from Terry.

Then the noise began and Cassidy let it roll over him and there was no escape.

Terry was shooting Max, breaking him up into chunks with the slugs, and it was taking forever. The cigar, the hat, the toupee, the face. The explosions came one after another and Cassidy just didn't give a shit. Terry had come back from the dead and Cindy was gone . . . all gone . . .

Finally the trigger was going click, click, click, one empty chamber after another.

Terry was kneeling beside Cassidy, his arm around his good shoulder.

"Time to call it a day, amigo." His gun clattered to the

floor. Harry Madrid bent down and together they helped Cassidy to his feet.

They went outside.

The sun was glaring on the snow and then it was fading away and Cassidy was colder than he'd ever been.

Everybody was dead.

Everybody but Harry Madrid and Terry Leary and Lew Cassidy.

CASSIDY

Okay, okay, I've heard it all.

So we weren't Romeo and Juliet. And we weren't Héloïse and Abelard. And we weren't Tracy and Hepburn. I know all that. I'm a college man, after all.

But we weren't Abbott and Costello either.

You could argue pretty persuasively that I only spent a few days with her and what can you tell about somebody in a few days?

Well, the answer is, I don't know. I don't know how you explain love and I don't know what would have happened if Max hadn't pulled the trigger and she had lived. I don't have a clue, frankly.

But I know what I felt for her and I know how deeply she touched me and I remember making love with her and I remember how she stood up to the bad guys at the end.

I remember her solemn face and the veil of blond hair and the blue of her eyes. The eyes, the good-bye eyes.

Some days I'd give anything if I could just stop thinking about those eyes, never remember them again. I see them saying good-bye and I think of the life she might have had and the years of beauty that will never be, all the years we might have had together. There is an old belief that on some distant shore, far from despair and grief, old friends will meet once more. Maybe I'll find Cindy on that distant shore. I would like that.

But I'm not planning on it.

It can be argued that at bottom she was very bad news, that she was the kind of woman who brings everything raining down on herself and all the guys who care about her. There was a hell of a pile of stiffs to support that particular thesis.

Still, it didn't matter.

What was she really? I don't begin to know. Maybe such women always exist primarily in men's imaginations, in the foggy valleys of longing and romance.

She'd been dead a year and a half and I still woke up in the morning having dreamt of her, still wanting to see her and speak to her and touch her. And knowing, of course, that none of it could ever happen again. But I wasn't altogether sure she was gone because something still whispered to me that I would find her again because she was indeed eternal, the Daughter of Time, the light and the dark. Yeah, Max had it right all along but she was a spirit, quicksilver, and he couldn't hold her.

Every couple of weeks I drove out to the lovely cemetery in Westchester and visited her grave.

For a while, I admit, the journeys were a little grief-stricken, pretty morbid, but then the sorrow and the weeping began to subside in the face of time.

Through the rest of 1944, through the D-day landings in June, through Tom Dewey getting the Republican nomination for the presidency and then losing to Roosevelt, who looked like he was dying and won anyway, through the German breakout which came to be known as the Battle of the Bulge, I didn't trust myself to tell anyone I was visiting her, bringing flowers like a suitor. It was just between the two of us and I didn't know what shape I'd be in if someone came after me.

I had this tendency to sit there on a bench near the

marker and let my memory wander wherever it wished. I would remember that day in the Oak Bar at the Plaza when she'd swept nervously in and sat beside me, then I'd go through the whole day and it would end with my stick sinking into Bennie's head . . .

Or I'd remember the way she'd moved against me that night we'd stood in the cold and watched the U-boats sink the ships off the Jersey shore . . .

Or I'd think about *Cézanne's Greetings* at Christmas . . . I'd think about *I love you* . . . and I'd think about the last good-bye look in her eyes . . .

I was remembering a lot of those things still by the summer of 1945 but the sorrow wasn't so intense anymore. Time had worked its surgical miracle on me. In return for my heart, my love, my feelings, Time granted me the numbness to survive the memories with my sanity intact.

Karin and Cindy.

The only women I'd ever loved and they were both dead.

•   •   •

Well, everybody got buried, of course, all in a flurry there.

Bennie didn't seem to have any people so Terry and I saw to it he wound up at the cemetery in Westchester. Not far from Cindy. It was something to smile about but I'm not sure why.

Bob Erickson got shipped back to Saint Louis, to the bosom of his family, and Cookie Candioli's people did for him. They all got buried.

And Max, too, of course. A very nice Jewish cemetery, next to doctors and lawyers and financiers and writers and teachers, very good company, indeed. But then he was a Harvard man.

One day there was a reading of Max's will. It turned out that he hadn't been kidding about looking upon Terry like a son. Terry needn't have worried about the cigars, for instance. Max left him the entire supply of Havanas, five thousand and eleven of them, all safe and secure in the humidor room at Dunhill.

But that wasn't all.

He left Terry the Long Island mansion.

And one thing more.

The club. He left Terry the club. Heliotrope.

•   •   •

Sitting in the cemetery. August sunshine warm on my face. Flowers banked at the stone, beautiful as she deserved. Kids laughing, dancing around a gravestone not far away. I was sitting remembering Cindy as if we'd had lots of good times together instead of just our few days. Sometimes I got to thinking about her very hard and it seemed that those good times stretched out further and further until they became something like a lifetime, a lifetime of our own. At least in the dimensions of my mind, which was really all I had left of Cindy. And I always thought of the little girl sitting on the tombstone in the little English cemetery wondering what it all meant.

A couple of men were coming toward me from way down by the road where I'd parked the same little Ford convertible. I watched them through the shimmering heat haze. They looked like unreal messengers from another galaxy, shapes shifting in the heat.

It was August. The dog days.

•   •   •

The war was over and the good guys had won.

The Germans surrendered on the sixth of May in a little red schoolhouse which was General Eisenhower's HQ.

General Jodl, Chief of the German General Staff, came to the schoolhouse and signed the unconditional surrender. Eisenhower wasn't there at the time. When Jodl and the representatives of the Supreme Allied Command, the Russians, and the Frenchmen had all signed, Jodl went to meet Ike. He asked for mercy. Probably figured it couldn't hurt to ask.

The European war ended at 2:41 Monday morning, French time. It was still Sunday evening, 8:41 Wartime, in New York. Of course, we were still slugging it out with the Japanese on Okinawa where lots of men were dying. And the flags were still at half staff because Franklin Roosevelt, who had seen us through so much, was dead.

New York got swept away in a premature celebration stemming from the first radio reports Monday morning. Mayor La Guardia in his high-pitched voice told the celebrants to knock it off in an emotional midafternoon speech. He told them that the end wasn't official yet, that for all they knew men were still fighting and dying over there, and a hell of a lot of people in Times Square began feeling pretty sheepish. The bobby-soxers and the guys and gals looking for a day off and an excuse for getting loaded calmed down and the crowd broke up and the mounted police cleared the area. By five o'clock there wasn't much of anybody left to read the *Times* bulletin board announcing that V-E Day would come the next morning at nine o'clock. But later the celebration began all over again and old-timers said the city had never seen anything like it. The din was incessant. Every boat on the East River and the Hudson kept their sirens and whistles going and the cabbies laid on their horns and total strangers went to bed together.

Six weeks later Eisenhower came back to the city's greatest welcome, four million people along the parade route to see the general. It had been quite a war, after all. And the marines were still fighting on Okinawa. Two days later Okinawa was ours but the cost was high. Lots of Japanese leaped into the sea rather than surrender.

A month later the British swept Churchill out of office in a Labor landslide that made Clement Atlee the new prime minister.

A couple days after that, on a foggy Saturday morning, a twin-engine B-25 bomber crashed into the north side of the Empire State Building, almost a thousand feet above 34th Street. Seventy-ninth floor. Thirteen people got killed. The wings were sheared off and fell into the street.

The gas tanks exploded. One of the engines ripped all the way through the building, tore a hole in the south face, plummeted almost seventy stories, and demolished the penthouse of a famous architect who lived at 10 West 33rd. The other engine fell over a thousand feet down an elevator shaft to a subbasement. A propeller embedded itself in a concrete wall and burning gasoline was everywhere. The steel girders at the seventy-ninth floor were bent eighteen inches out of shape. The pilot was a recently decorated bomber commander who was trying to find Newark in the dense fog. If it wasn't one thing, it was another.

On August 7 we dropped the first atomic bomb and 60 percent of Hiroshima was gone. On August 9 we dropped the second on Nagasaki and that night President Harry Truman reported to the people. And then, on the 15th, everybody went crazy again because the Empire of the Sun surrendered unconditionally. This time it was really over over there. The *New York Post* said so in a typical two-word front page: JAPS QUIT! Well, as Terry said, you could hardly blame them.

•   •   •

A car radio was playing loudly on a nearby path. Someone was waiting for mourners to pay their respects to the dead, and the day was made for music. The tune caught on the soft, hot breeze. It was the song everybody was singing and whistling those days. It was the official anthem of the end of the war, that summer of '45.

> *Kiss me once*
> *Then kiss me twice*
> *Then kiss me once again*
> *It's been a long, long time . . .*

It had certainly been a long time but the world was trying to get back to normal. The boys and girls were coming home to take up life again, if only they could remember how. They were in for a lot of surprises.

KISS ME ONCE

Haven't felt like this, my dear
Since can't remember when
It's been a long, long time . . .

The two men had emerged from the dark green shadows of a couple of mournful, dipping weeping willows and were trapped in the bright sunshine again.

I recognized them.

My father was still in uniform but it wouldn't be much longer now before he was back in civvies, back in the movie business. He'd had a good war, as people said. He'd finished out the war, after making a much-praised documentary about the fighting in the hedgerows, serving on the military intelligence staff of the Allied Command in Europe. I hadn't known he was back stateside but there he was, looking fit as a fiddle.

Terry Leary was with him, wearing a seersucker jacket and gray slacks and penny loafers.

"Lew," my father said.

"Dad." I stood up and hugged him tight.

"Terry said you'd be here. We looked everywhere else so he said this had to be the place. You all right, Lew?"

"Fine," I said. "I'm just fine."

We all three sat down on the bench.

"She's here, then?" my father said.

"In a manner of speaking, I guess she is. Mainly she's up here." I tapped my temple.

"I'm sorry about her, son. Sorry about the whole damn thing, sorriest about her. She was one beautiful kid."

"Well, she got a raw deal," I said.

"Right." He nodded. "I know what you mean. Can't get her out of your mind, I suppose."

"Never even tried," I said. "Just one of those things."

"But it's been a long time, Lew," he said softly, looking at the marker.

I smiled at my father. He was the last person I really loved. Oh, I loved Terry, too, but that was different. Loving Terry was a complicated proposition. Loving my father was like loving Karin and Cindy. It was simple. Like the love I'd feel if I ever fathered a child.

Terry was smoking one of the Havanas, legs stretched out, eyes closed, face to the sun.

"It's been a long, long time," I said.

We sat quietly, three chaps in a graveyard taking the sun. Thinking about a dead lady or two.

Finally Terry said, "Better get to it, Paul."

"I suppose so," he said.

"Get to what?" I felt a chill along the base of my spine, up my back, palpable tension like I hadn't felt in a long time.

"Well, I'm glad you're sitting down, Lew. I've got some pretty surprising news—"

He was pausing when Terry took the cigar out of his mouth, said, "Come on, Paul, get to it."

"Well. Yes, there's this news. I've just flown back from Germany. I was working on the art collection team, running all over hell's half acre interviewing people, checking out guys in internment camps, looking for paintings and vases and crosses and—well, you get the idea . . . damnedest thing you've ever seen, really . . ."

"Come on, Dad," I said.

"Well, we turned up all sorts of people and—oh, hell, I'm doing this so badly. Here's the point . . . ah, what I'm trying to say is this . . . Karin's coming home, Lew."

He brushed a fly away from his face and glanced heavenward, hopefully, impatiently.

"Karin," I said.

"We found Karin, Lew. She's alive and she's coming back."

A lot of things should have crossed my mind but nothing really did. He might as well have told me that they'd just discovered that the world is flat. Think about it. Somebody you hadn't seen in almost six years, your wife, someone you'd thought was dead ever since the bombing of Cologne in '42, someone was coming back. I didn't quite get it. I had to adjust everything within myself and it was a disconcerting job.

"Karin . . ." I blinked at my father, looked at Terry. "Karin's all right?"

"Oh, she's had some tough times. You can't imagine how beat-up that country is . . . but you know Karin, she's okay."

"Jesus, it's been a long time," I said. "When can I see her?"

"Soon. She'll be back soon. A few days."

I tried to swallow, discovered I couldn't.

"There's one thing, though," my father said. "One thing I've got to tell you . . ."

"You said she's all right—"

"She is, she is. But she's not coming home alone, that's the thing."

"Her father? He survived, too? But the paper said—"

"No, not her father. That's what I'm trying so clumsily to tell you, son."

"I don't get it. Who's coming back with my wife?"

My poor father sighed.

"Her husband. Karin's bringing back her husband."

After a silence that paralyzed us all, Terry said, "As Bennie used to say, it's an imperfect world, Lew."

Terry was smiling. He stood up.

"Come on, amigo. You need a drink."

He went off whistling.

Kiss me once then kiss me twice then
Kiss me once again
It's been a long, long time . . .

My father and I followed him through the glories of the August sunshine.

Something funny was going on.

But that's another story.